Our MAN From EARTH

TOMÁS Ó CUIRC

I0822744

A catalogue record for this book is available from the National Library of Australia

Copyright © 2024 by Tomás Ó Cuirc

All rights reserved, including the right to reproduce this book or portions thereof in any form whatsoever.

This book is, of course, fiction.

Publisher:
Inspiring Publishers
P.O. Box 159, Calwell, ACT Australia 2905
Email: inspiringpublisher.com
http://www.inspiringpublishers.com

National Library of Australia Cataloguing-in-Publication entry

Author: Tomás Ó Cuirc

Title: **OUR MAN FROM EARTH**

ISBN: 978-1-923087-52-1 (print)
ISBN: 978-1-923087-51-4 (ePub2)

Foreword

The old Gaelic song, "Molly na gCuach Ni Chuilleanáin" which our hero, Tom Glennon, sings in the Derry pub, is sung to more than one melody. The one I prefer, and which Tom actually sings, is the version sung by Muireann Nic Amhlaoibh of the group Danu. It can be heard on Youtube.

Aberystwyth University in Wales exists. The Welsh Institute of Astrophysics does not. The Australian National University In Canberra exists but the Australian Institute for Space and Remote Sensing Science does not.

Everything in this story could happen

Some of them did

BOOK 1

Chapter 1

Tom Glennon's childhood *on the family sheep farm in Connemara on the far West coast of Ireland. He is told that the family are emigrating to England.*

In Connemara in the far West of Ireland, Micheál MacLeannáin, tall, weatherbeaten - a sheep farmer in his thirties, called to his 10-year old son, Tomás - "Come along, Tommy – you and I will bring the sheep down from the mountain one last time".

"Why is it the last time, Daddy?"

"I told you. You and me and your mammy and your sisters are off to England next week. We are going to live over there. I have a job in the building trade with my cousin, Peadar Ó Ceallaigh".

"Will we have sheep there Daddy?"

"We will not. We won't be living in the country at all. We will live in the town where the building work is going on".

"What about the dogs?" said Tómas.

"They will have to stay here. Your uncle Séamus will need them. He will be managing the farm now. He is getting married and so the new wife will help him with the sheep until they have children of their own".

Micheál and Tomás were speaking to each other in Gaelic, the MacLeannáin farm being in a remote Gaeltacht area of Ireland where the Irish language was still spoken.

CHAPTER 1

"Get the dogs, Tommy".

Tomás went to the pen and released the three Border collies, starting a chorus of excited yapping as they realized they were going to do what they loved best - working the sheep.

"Come behind" called Micheál, bringing the dogs to him.

"Now - Hup!" he said pointing up Sliabh na Ceobhráin, Mountain of the Mist, the steep brown hill, covered with moor grass and heather, rising several hundred metres above them. The dogs needed no further instruction. They knew what they had to do, which was to round up the sheep and bring them down the mountain. Up the steep slope they ran.

Tomás gazed up at the distant white specks which were the sheep grazing high on the mountain. The darker shapes of the dogs could be seen racing above and around the sides of the widely dispersed flock. As they did so the sheep instinctively began to cluster together. When all the stragglers had been rounded up, the sheep - now in a compact flock - in response to pressure from the dogs running to and fro above them, began slowly to move down the slope. When the sheep reached the bottom of the slope Micheál, with the help of Tomás, drove them into the yards.

"Now Tommy. I want you to catch little boy lambs, one at a time, and bring them to me. Do you think you can do that?"

"I can of course" said Tomás who was a sturdy boy, well used to sheep. He approached the flock looking closely at the lambs. As soon as he recognised a male lamb, he leapt upon it, lifted it up and carried it to his father. Micheál was applying the tight rubber ring which would ensure that the lamb developed into into an infertile wether sheep rather than a fertile ram. After dealing with each lamb Micheál placed it over the rail into the next bay of the sheep yard.

Meanwhile, an elderly man who had been walking with his stick along the adjoining roadway stopped to watch Micheál and Tomás marking the male lambs. Eventually he spoke – "God bless the work".

"And you too, sir" said Micheál, giving the traditional response to this ancient greeting.

"I'm Seán MacGabhann, the brother of Tadhg MacGabhann, down the road. I am staying with him for a few days. No doubt you know him."

"I do indeed" said Micheál. "I know him well. We've had many a pint or two together"

"And you must be Micheál MacLeannáin" said the man.

"I am" said Micheál. "And welcome, Seán. I often heard Tadhg mention you. And how are you?"

"Ah sure not too bad, considering my age" replied MacGabhann. "Except th'oul arthritis has me kilt. This country would give arthritis to a frog."

"I believe you are a sheep farmer yourself" said Micheál.

"Indeed I am" said MacGabhann. "All my life. I see you are still marking the ram lambs. These days the Department is encouraging us to leave them entire. They put on weight more quickly and end up leaner than the wether lambs, and it is lean meat the customers are looking for nowadays".

"I am sure that's right" said Micheál. "But you sometimes get a ram taint in the meat when the male lambs have been running with the ewes. So I am still reluctant to make the change. But we are thinking about it".

"Would these be the Mayo/Connemara Blackface breed?" asked MacGabhann.

"They are indeed" said Micheál. "Of course, as you would know, all the Blackface sheep in Connemara are descended from those Scottish Blackface sheep which were brought in back in the 1800s, but these are the locally selected race, well suited to our hills".

"The little lad must be your son, Tomás" said MacGabhann. "I can see he is a helpful boy".

"He is" said Micheál "and he loves working with the sheep. But this might be for the last time".

"Oh, and why's that?" said MacGabhann.

"Because we're all off to England before the end of the week. I'll be bricklaying. My cousin Peadar Ó Ceallaigh is in the building business over in Manchester and I'll be working with him".

"You know the bricklaying, then?" said MacGabhann.

"I do" said Micheál. "After I left school, my father, God rest him, sent me in to Galway to learn. He said it might be useful to me one day to have a trade. And he was right. I have been over to England a few times already. There is good money to be made laying bricks over there".

"But won't you be sorry to leave all this behind?" said MacGabhann. "The mountains, the fresh breezes from the Atlantic, the flowing streams?"

"I will. I will indeed" said Micheál sadly. "I love it here. But this farm only makes enough to support one family. Séamus, my brother, is getting married and he'll be raising his own family soon. I'm the one with a trade. I can earn a good living and so I decided that I should be the one to go. We can always come back to visit. England is not very far away".

"Who's the girl your brother is marrying?" said MacGabhann.

"Aoife Ó Cuinn" said Micheal. "She is off a farm a little way over to the West. We know the family well".

"Now tell me" said MacGabhann "Did she bring any bit of land to the match?"

"Indeed she did" said Micheál. "Her father has given her a 15-acre field of good green grass at the bottom of the mountain".

"Did he, Begod" said MacGabhann. "She'd be worth marrying for that alone".

"Ah, No" said Micheál, laughing. "Séamus loves her anyway, she's a very nice girl and will be a good wife to him".

"Sounds like he's a lucky man, then. Ah well. I'll go on with my walk. Good luck over in England" said MacGabhann, setting off down the road.

"Thanks" said Micheál. "Now back to work, Tomás, and when we have the job done we'll let the sheep go back up the mountain".

Another hour proved sufficient. Tomás opened the sheepyard gates. The bleating lambs sought out their mothers, and the flock dispersed again up the hillside.

"We'll go back to the house now, Tomás" said Micheál "We'll wash our hands and then see what Mammy has cooked for dinner. What would you like it to be?"

"Bacon and cabbage, with potatoes and soda bread and lots of butter" said Tomás.

"Ah, boiled bacon and cabbage is it" said Micheál. "Well you're a traditional Irishman and no mistake. Do you know what? That's my favourite, too. We'd better make the most of it because we won't be able to kill a pig to cure our own bacon over in England".

▲

Chapter 2

Planetary Council meeting. *Planet Osmos of star Alpha Centauri, 4.37 light years from Earth. Voyager space probe from Earth has been detected, its visual and audio messages received. Council decides to investigate further.*

Forty trillion kilometres away from Connemara, the Planetary Council of the planet, Omnos, in orbit around the star Alpha Centauri A, was in session. The President of the Council spoke.

"Fellow members of the Planetary Council - I bring you today the most important news ever presented to this body."

He looked around to make sure that he had everybody's attention. He did.

"I am here to tell you that we now know that there is other intelligent life in this universe."

A rustle went round the room. "What..." "Are you sure..." "What kind of evidence..."

"Enough. Enough" said the President of the Council. "Science Councillor - you have the floor. Tell us what you have found".

The Science Councillor, a tall man with a commanding presence, rose to his feet. "You will be aware councillors that many years ago we began sending probes – we call them Explorer probes - out to space to see if we could detect the existence of other civilizations. You will no doubt also remember that while we have found planetary systems around stars to be common - indeed almost invariably present - planets with an environment suitable to support life are very rare. Nevertheless, after more than two centuries searching, we have succeeded. We have found not merely life, but intelligent life. We have absolutely incontrovertible evidence in the form of an actual artefact. It is a spaceborne object clearly constructed by quite an advanced civilization."

"How did this object get in to space?"

"It got in to space because it was put there. It is in fact itself a space probe. On your screens I will now show you a series of images sent back by our own space craft. This alien probe is equipped with a wide range of instruments and is clearly part of a scientific exploration of, we assume, the space environment around its planet of origin. The large parabolic structure we may assume is an antenna for sending information to, and receiving instructions from, the home planet. It is in fact still emitting a very faint signal, and this is how we came to detect it. Our own Explorer probes are all equipped to carry out a detailed three-dimensional scan, physical and chemical, down to the sub-micron level, of any object of interest that they encounter. Using the scan data we have been able to identify the instruments. In addition to cameras for sending back visual information they include, for example, ultraviolet and infrared spectrometers, cosmic ray and low-energy particle detectors, and plasma detectors. The instruments, while somewhat limited and unsophisticated by our standards, are all fully capable of measuring what they are supposed to measure. So, this spacecraft came from a civilization which is not only capable of hurling objects into space, but which is scientifically very advanced."

"Does your inspection of this space probe tell you anything else about the civilization that sent it up? What they are like

– you know – as people?" This from the Social and Emotional Affairs Councillor, a striking looking woman of late middle age with streaks of grey in her long black hair, one of the female members of the Council.

"Well as a matter of fact, Councillor, from this space probe we hope to learn a great deal about the inhabitants of the civilization from which it originated."

"Wait a minute" said the President. "How can you get that sort of information just from inspection of what is essentially just a flying package of scientific instruments?"

"Because, members of the Council, whoever launched this spacecraft has tried to make it easy for us. They actually sent us a message."

"How can they send a message to us?" said the President. They don't know we exist."

"True" replied the Science Councillor. "But the message is not strictly speaking to us. It is to any civilization that this probe might one day encounter. And, as it happens, it came to our civilization, and, I think we can safely say, to no other."

"So what does the message say?" demanded the President.

"We are still deciphering it" said the Science Councillor. "Surprisingly, it is encoded not in binary form but using a rather archaic analogue system. The message is contained in a gold-plated copper disc attached to the side of the spacecraft. You can now see it on your screens. From the detailed 3D analysis of the disc, sent by our Explorer spacecraft, we have been able to construct an exact replica and this is what we are currently analysing. On one side of the disc there is a spiral composed of a very thin continuous groove incised into the metal. The groove is not smooth but has tiny three-dimensional irregularities along its length. It is the manner of variation of these irregularities along the length of the groove that we believe encodes the information.

"How very odd" said the President.

"How do you propose to decipher it?"

"Well, as a matter of fact" said the Science Councillor

"on the other side of the disc the aliens have attempted to show us how. There is a drawing of the disc with a picture of what we take to be some kind of stylus at the outer edge. Below this there is a side image of the disc with the tip of the stylus sitting, we assume, in a groove. The disc must rotate on a turntable. As it rotates the tiny irregularities in the groove transmit vibrations to the stylus. With a suitable piezoelectric or magnetic transducer these vibrations can be converted to electrical signals which can be read out as sounds and/or visual images."

"But how do you know at what speed to rotate the disc?" asked the Engineering and Construction Councillor.

"Good question" said the Science Councillor. "Our alien friends have provided us with a way to calculate this. There is a simple picture, you can see here on your screens, of what we believe to be the spin-flip transition of a hydrogen atom. This has a time period of 0.704 billionths of a second. Just below the hydrogen atom symbol there is a small vertical line. We interpret this as representing the binary digit – one. So the spin-flip transition time, is to be used as the unit of time: very small, but fundamental.

Now let me draw your attention to the periphery of this simple drawing of the disc. You will see a series of ones and dashes. This, as I am sure you are all aware, is how numbers are represented in binary arithmetic. This particular sequence represents a very large number. But, when we multiply our unit of time by this large number we end up with 3.6 seconds and this is a very plausible time, mechanically speaking, for one rotation of the disc.

CHAPTER 2

So as not to keep you on tenterhooks any longer, fellow Councillors, I am happy to tell you that in the workshop of the Science Institute we have fabricated a stylus with a very small diamond tip, constructed a turntable with the appropriate rotation speed, and connected the whole thing through appropriate electronics to an audiovisual system. Our aliens obligingly made the first picture on the disc a simple circle, and this, after some false starts, enabled us to confirm that our readout setup actually works.

There is a great deal of information, of various kinds – some audio, some visual, some scientific - on this disc. I propose now to show you a representative sample. The first audio section consists of a series of short spoken messages, fifty-five in total, each with a different speaker, and each in what sounds like a different language. Plausibly, this is a set of welcome messages from our aliens to us, each from a different part of the alien population, with its own language. Quite apart from anything else this tells us that there are many different language groups on the planet, which in turn strongly suggests the existence of substantial genetic, or if you prefer it, ethnic, variation in their population. This is borne out by visual evidence, as we shall shortly see. I play for you now a short selection of these, presumptive, welcome messages."

The Councillors listened intently as the sounds of greetings in Portuguese, Cantonese, Arabic, English, Zulu, Hindi and Japanese came from the loudspeaker.

"Now, Councillors, we come to the big question – what do these alien people – and we must now call them people – actually look like? Well here, at least some of them, are."

On their screens there appeared, one after the other, images of human beings: Europeans, Africans, East Asians, Indonesians, Amerindians. Around the table a communal uptake of breath and expressions of surprise.

"But" said the President, "they look just like us. How can this be?"

"What were we expecting?" said the Science Councillor.

"Little green men? Let me say that I was not entirely surprised when these images appeared as we decoded the disc. Indeed I was rather pleased because it provides support for a certain view within evolutionary theory that I have always liked. First of all let me say that from some of the scientific images they sent it is clear that the basis of their genetics is the same as ours: double stranded DNA. This means that at the most fundamental chemical level they are on the same evolutionary path as we are.

"Well, yes" said the Engineering and Construction Councillor "but that doesn't mean that they necessarily arrive at the same endpoint as us."

"Not necessarily" replied the Science Councillor "but perhaps probably.

The view within evolutionary theory that I referred to holds that there are certain biological structures that have an inherently high probability of coming into existence if there is sufficient time. In mathematical terms you can think of such a structure as being an attractor in phase space. An attractor is a set of numerical values toward which a system tends to evolve, for a wide variety of starting conditions of the system. System values that get close enough to the attractor values remain close even if slightly disturbed."

"All right, all right." Said the President testily. "Don't blind us with science. In effect what you are implying, if I understand you, is that on two different worlds, spatially separated but with the same underlying biochemistry, it is not surprising that evolution could give rise to some very similar creatures."

"Well, yes" said the Science Councillor. "That is essentially it."

CHAPTER 2

"Anyway, before we go any further there are some sounds that you absolutely must hear. They have sent us numerous samples of their music, music which from its great variety we must assume originates in different cultures on their planet. You will now hear a few of the samples on the disc."

From the loudspeaker there came in sequence the sounds of Bach's Brandenburg Concerto No. 2, Chuck Berry singing "Johnny be good", an aria from Mozart's *The Magic Flute*, a traditional Georgian song, a Chinese folk melody and Beethoven's String Quartet No. 13. This was followed by a stunned silence broken eventually by the Arts Councillor.

"Councillors I am impressed. No, very impressed. Perhaps even astounded. These aliens are clearly very musical. It may be that we are technically more advanced than they are but musically? In my judgement they have nothing to learn from us."

"Where is the planet of origin of these people?" asked the Engineering Councillor. "Do you have any information on that, yet?"

'Well, as a matter of fact" replied Science Councillor "we do, and I am confident we will soon be able to confirm it. First of all I should point out that any information we have is already about four years old when we receive it. Our various Explorer probes were all launched a long time ago and by now are very far away from us. This particular probe is at a distance of about four light years and so it takes four years for its signals to reach us. In terms of controlling the probe this is not quite as big a problem as you might think. Every one of these spacecrafts is programmed to respond to, to investigate, any out-of-the-way phenomenon in just the same way as if one of us was on board telling it what to do. So already the probe has accurately determined the trajectory of the alien spacecraft. It has in this way already identified the star from one of whose planets the spacecraft came. It is in fact a star we know well because, at 4.37 light years distance it is the nearest star to us, and is also one of the brightest stars in our night sky.

"So, now we know where the planet of origin is "said the President "what is the next step?"

"The next step is already under way" said the Science Councillor. "Our probe is programmed to proceed to the planet in question, to take up orbit around the planet and to learn as much as possible about it and its inhabitants and transmit the information back to us. In particular, our probe will eavesdrop on all electronic information in the airwaves and from this we should be able to learn a great deal about the civilizations on the planet. Anyway, on the basis of the estimated distance, and the speed of our own spacecraft we know that it took up station in orbit some time ago and the first information has in fact just started arriving. No, I can't yet tell you anything it says. Interpreting it is going to be very difficult."

"Thank you, Science Councillor, for your presentation." said the President. "Yes, you were right. This was by far the most important news ever to be presented to this Council. Making sense of the electronic information harvested from the aliens' planet will indeed present great difficulty and no effort must be spared. With the Planetary Council's agreement" – a murmur of agreement around the room – "you are authorized to put together any resources you may need, teams of people with specialized expertise, or whatever, to address this task. When you think you have amassed a useful body of information about our aliens, their history, culture, scientific and technological sophistication, put it all together and provide this to all members of Council. We will then meet again to consider the implications."

Chapter 3

The music session *at the Kilcarra pub, Connemara. Micheál Glennon. Tom's father, plays the fiddle and says Goodbye to his friends.*

"Have you had enough, Tomás?" said his mother, Róisín Uí Leannáin, Micheál's wife, as the meal drew to a close.

"I have thanks, Mammy" said Tomás.

"Do you know what, Róisín" said Micheál. "I think I'll take my fiddle down to Hogan's pub in the village and play a few tunes with the lads there. It'll be the last time before we go to England".

"All right so" said Róisín "As long as you are only going to stay for a short time, you could take Tomás with you. You know he loves to hear the traditional music".

"I will indeed" said Micheál. "But we won't stay long".

With his fiddle in its case over his shoulder and Tomás at his side, Micheál walked the couple of kilometres down the road which brought them to the nearby village of Kilcarra. As they neared the pub, with the family name, Ó hÓgáin displayed above the doorway, they could hear the musical session already under way. They entered just as the last tune drew to its close.

"God save all here" said Micheál. He was enthusiastically welcomed in and invited to join the group of musicians seated together in a corner of the large saloon bar. Other locals and a handful of tourists were at the bar or sitting at tables

"Will you have a drink, Micheál?" said Tadhg MacDonnchadha, a big man with his uilleann pipes on his lap.

"I will" said Micheál, "but I will buy a round for the lot of us. As I think you know, myself and the family are off to England and God only knows when I will be able to stand a round of drinks in this pub again, so this is a bit of a farewell. Pints is it?" There was an appreciative murmur of assent.

"Good man yourself, Micheál" said one. "Begod, you were never slow to stand your round".

"Five pints of Guinness please Cáitlín, and an orange juice for the boy" said Micheál to the woman behind the bar. He took his fiddle out of its case, tightened up the bow hairs and rubbed them down with a piece of rosin.

"Why do you do that, Daddy?" asked Tomás.

"It gives the bow a better grip on the strings" said Micheál. "Otherwise, the bow would simply slide over the strings without making them sing".

"Give me an A, will you Seán" he said to the button accordion player. When the note was sounded he tuned the fiddle. The session then recommenced, with succeeding brackets of tunes, three in each. Reels, jigs, slip jigs, hornpipes, polkas and slides followed, different musicians starting different brackets as the inspiration took them.

"Will you ever get to play music in England?" said Seán. " I'm sure I will" said Micheál. "There are pubs over there now where they hold Irish music sessions. And it's not just the Irish who are playing. All kinds of people have taken a fancy to the Irish traditional music. The last time I was there I had an Italian, and a German playing alongside me. Even a couple of English!"

CHAPTER 3

"I'll have to be off soon, lads" said Micheál, putting down his fiddle. "There is still much to be done at home before we go, and it is well past Tomás's bedtime".

"Give us a song before you go" said Tadhg.

"Oh, I don't know" said Michael, showing the reluctance traditionally shown by people asked to sing. In fact he enjoyed singing in the pub and was glad to be asked but to put himself forward too much would not be well received.

"Arrah, go on" said one of the other musicians. "Give us Fáinne Geal an Lae".

"All right so" said Micheál and stood up to sing. As he did so a murmur went round the pub – "there's going to be a song" – and the conversation went quiet. In his strong tenor voice Micheál sang the old Gaelic song and then sat down again amidst the clamour of enthusiastic applause.

"Excuse me" said one of the bar customers, an American tourist. "Isn't the tune you just sang the same tune as On Raglan Road?"

"It is" said Micheál. "But what I sang is the original. It is an old song – Fáinne Geal an Lae means 'The Dawning of the Day'. 'On Raglan Road' is a poem which the poet, Patrick Kavanagh some years ago managed to fit into the same tune.

"What story does it tell?" asked the American.

"Young man walking along the shore of Lough Leine. Sees a beautiful young woman. Is instantly smitten. Seeks to make himself known to the girl. But she doesn't respond as he might wish but just asks him to leave her. So – sad ending" said Micheál. "Not so very different from the story of On Raglan Road".

"No. Guess so" said the American. "Thanks".

"Well. Time to go" said Micheál, slackening the bow hairs and stowing it and the fiddle in the violin case. "Come on now, Tomás.

We'll be on our way. Good Bye, lads. I hope to find you all playing here again when I come over on a visit ".

"We will, please God" said Tadhg.

"I hope all goes well with you in England". And followed by a chorus of good wishes, Micheál and Tomás went out of the pub to start their journey home.

"Now Tomás" said Micheál as they walked along the road "When we get to England you'll be going to school and nobody there will speak Irish. You can speak English well enough, can't you?"

"I can of course" said Tomás. "English is easy".

"Indeed it is" thought Micheál to himself. "And that is why so many of our young people are speaking it instead of their own native tongue. And that is what they hear all the time in pop music and on the TV".

"At home" he said "we will talk Irish amongst ourselves. We don't want to lose our own language".

Chapter 4

Osmos Planetary Council meeting. *What they have now learned about Earth. They are impressed with artistic achievements of Earth people. Decision to send an embassy.*

"Council members" said the President. " At a previous meeting you were told of the discovery, by one of our Explorer space probes, of the existence of an intelligent species on another planet not very far away in this galaxy. To find that we are not alone in the Universe is of extraordinary significance. The business of today's Council meeting is to consider the implications of this for our species, and what form our response to this revelation should take. Science Councillor - please bring us up to date"

The Science Councillor stood up and surveyed the room. "As you will have become aware, fellow Councillors, we now know a great deal about what I might call - our sister planet - and in particular, about the peoples who inhabit it. The reason we know so much is that our Explorer space probe was already programmed to eavesdrop on any intelligent radio communications it might encounter, to upload them and to transmit them back to us. So from the moment it established itself in planetary orbit, it started sending us information. A great wealth of this has now been received, and indeed continues to arrive, and using the substantial group of experts which the Council empowered me to set up, it has been analysed in great detail. Some of this information is in the form of spoken versions of one or other of the various languages which these people speak. Some is in the form of written information in the same languages, both recently created and archived. Some is music. Some consists of images. Some is merely numerical data."

"To make sense of this mass of information' said the President "we had to be able to translate these languages. How was that achieved?"

"I am happy to tell you" replied the Science Councillor "that we know how to do this. Using our powerful computer network, the analysis by our information technology and linguistic teams has now proceeded to the point that they have not only identified several of the most commonly spoken languages but have been able to create dictionaries and grammars. With this newly acquired grasp of the languages we can now actually understand much of the written and spoken information that has been received. This has enabled us not only to understand much of what is happening on that planet in these present times, but also, by accessing historical accounts, to understand how the various national and political situations that currently prevail in different parts of the planet came to be.

What we have learned so far has been digested, put together and organised by our editorial team and has been printed out in the volumes with which all Council members were supplied a few days ago. And no doubt you have all had a look at this already."

"Yes, yes. We've taken a look" from some members of the Council.

"In that case, what you will have learnt is that while all the sentient beings on this planet are the same species - which, by the way, using an ancient language, Latin, they no longer speak, they refer to – as "*Homo sapiens*", they are very diverse: to some extent physically in relation to size, general build, facial aspect and pigmentation, but much more so in terms of language, culture and religion. And while there seem to be no major wars going on at the moment, this species undoubtedly has a very violent history. Quite apart from innumerable local scale armed conflicts over the centuries, they have had two global wars, involving many nations, in the comparatively recent past."

"A propensity to violence does indeed seem to be a human characteristic" said the Social and Demographic Councillor, a man in his middle years.

"They are technically quite advanced "continued the Science Councillor "as we of course realised when we found their space craft, but they are well behind us in many respects. They still have, for example, problems with cancer and bacterial resistance to antibiotics. Mental disorders are common. Some hereditary diseases are still prevalent. There is much industrial pollution of the environment. They do not yet have fusion power. Although they are well aware of the problem presented by limited planetary resources, they are inefficient at recycling."

"A thing that struck me, when I read these documents" said the Engineering and Construction Councillor, "is the great importance in some, but by no means all, human societies of alcoholic beverages. "

"Indeed" said the Science Councillor. "We have our own, of course, but we have not developed such a culture around them as have some of their peoples. They create these beverages from a variety of sources. There is, for example, a woody perennial plant which they call "*the grapevine*", which bears bunches of berries which can contain 10-16% sugar when ripe. These they crush and ferment to produce what they call "*wine*" which can be quite alcoholic. They also use the seeds of certain grasses as starting material. The seeds are partially germinated to produce the enzymes which break down the starch in the seed to give sugars. These are then fermented. To create very high alcohol drinks, wine, or the fermented product from seeds are distilled. While alcoholic beverages are highly regarded in these societies, it is also apparent that over-indulgence causes serious health and social problems.

In other appendices you will find summaries of what, from their own published accounts, we have been able to ascertain of the historical origins of the various societies that prevail in different parts of their globe.

Oh, one other thing. We now know what is their name for their planet. They call it *"Earth"*, so we might as well use the same name."

"Thank you, Science Councillor" said the President. "I now open this matter for discussion. Social and Demographic Councillor - your thoughts please."

"I have now examined the, well let's call it the 'Earth' dossier, in some detail," said the Social and Demographic Councillor. "I have paid particular attention to the different kind of societies that exist on that planet, norms of behaviour, systems of morality, interactions between different societies, human interactions within particular societies, and so on. I have also explored a great deal of their fiction, both in printed and in acted performance forms, as a guide to the stories they tell, and how they see their fellow human beings. And the thing that strikes me most forcibly is how much more complex, and dare I say, interesting, human life on that planet is than what now prevails here on our own planet."

"Perhaps we weren't always so dull" suggested one of the councillors.

CHAPTER 4

"Perhaps not" said the Social and Demographic Councillor. "Perhaps in the very distant past, life on our planet might also have been turbulent and complex, if not quite at the intensity which prevails on Earth, but as we all know, for many years now our society has been stable and peaceful. And, it must be said it verges on the boring. Our gene pool does not seem to be throwing up the peculiar, often bizarre, frequently creative, people that apparently show up so often in the Earth population. Of course, some of these – the violent or antisocial ones, with whom Earth is also burdened – we would not want in our society. But nevertheless, the Earth human population as a whole is particularly variable and interesting."

"Arts Councillor" said the President. "I believe you also have been taking a close look at Earth society. What do you have to tell us?"

"Well, Mr President" said the Arts Councillor, an older man who, in his intense and preoccupied manner differed somewhat from the generally composed and equable demeanour of the other Council members. "I have indeed looked closely at all their forms of art - visual, musical, literary – and to say that I am impressed would be an understatement. .

The people of Earth are highly creative, not only in music but also in literature. As appendices in your printed volumes you will find a selection of some of their fictional writing, translated for your benefit into our own language, Omnic. There are many more you can access online as well as a variety of videos in which various fictional stories are performed by actors. These, of course, we have supplied with Omnic subtitles."

"How about the Performing Arts?" asked the Social and Demograhic Councillor.

"As far as the performing arts are concerned, within any given art form the levels of proficiency vary enormously. A lack of technical skill does not always discourage human beings from trying to express themselves artistically. But in the musical and visual arts extremely high levels of proficiency can be achieved by the best performers. These all undergo some years of professional training to develop their skills. In the case of literature, whether printed fiction or writing for live or televisual performance, training plays a lesser role. It seems that people either have the ability or do not. But what makes the greatest impression on me is the extraordinary level of creativity that is evident in all their art forms.

They have an enormous accumulated body of artistic achievement from earlier times but continue to produce more today. Wouldn't it be good if we had some of them here on our planet to enliven our own somewhat moribund arts scene" he added wistfully.

"Thank you, Arts Councillor" said the President. "And now, Council members, we have a very important decision to take. Are we going to make our own existence known to the people of Earth. Should we, in fact, send an embassy of some kind to that planet. Spaceflight Councillor, please give us your thoughts on the technical feasibility of launching an enterprise of such a nature."

"Well, Mr President" said the Councillor, a grizzled grey-haired man, of mature years but with the demeanour of an enthusiast "I have to tell you that as soon as I heard of the existence of this planet I immediately started thinking about how we might actually get there. Interplanetary space travel we have, of course, been doing for many centuries, but manned interstellar travel is another matter altogether. Can it be done? I believe that it can. None of our existing space ships would be suitable for such a long journey, but I am confident that one could be designed."

CHAPTER 4

"All right" said the President. "Let us assume it can be done. We must now decide if it shall be done. Councillors – please each of you give me your opinion on this very important proposal."

As he went round the table, the Councillors were all enthusiastically of the same opinion: that this momentous history-making embassy to Planet Earth should proceed.

"Thank you" said the President. "That is just what I expected. So, we shall go ahead. But there is, of course, a great deal of detailed planning to be carried out first. Spaceflight Councillor – put together whatever team you need to design and build an interstellar spaceship. To establish a good relationship with the people of Earth we should arrive with gifts. On the basis of what we already know of their state of development, I am confident that there are all kinds of useful scientific and technological information that we can offer them. Science Councillor – you can look into that. But we must also give thought to social and artistic matters. They will want to know about our society and we, of course, are very interested in theirs, especially their music and literature. Arts Councillor, I would like you to give thought to our interaction with Earth people in those areas. So, we have much to do. We shall meet again soon."

Chapter 5

***Glennon family arrive** in England. Micheál has a job bricklaying in the building business of his cousin, Peadar O Ceallaigh, in Stockport in the North of England. The family move in to a house that Peadar has found for them. They adapt well to life in Stockport.*

"Now Tomás" said Micheál, as they drove off the Dublin-Liverpool car ferry, "I want you to look for the M62 road, because that's the quickest route to Stockport, which is where Cousin Peadar will meet us and where we will be living."

The M62 was soon found and in no more than hour's driving they arrived in Stockport, once a separate town in the county of Cheshire but now swallowed up in the Greater Manchester conurbation. Micheál found his way without difficulty, as he had been there on previous bricklaying visits, to Peadar's house in the suburb of Heaton Moor. When they pulled up in the driveway Peadar emerged from his house.

"Fáilte romhaibh a Sasana!" (Welcome to England) he said, greeting the family. "How was the crossing? Was it rough?"

"Not at all" said Micheál. "The children enjoyed it."

"Good" said Peadar. "Let ye all come in now. You're just in time for dinner."

CHAPTER 5

"Now Micheál" continued Peadar as they sat down at the dinner table. "As I told you on the phone, tonight you can all stay with us. We have plenty of room. But I have some accommodation lined up for you that you might like to move into tomorrow if you think it might suit in the short term. One of the things I have been doing in the business recently is to buy up one or two of the old Victorian terraced houses, of which there are quite a few in Stockport, and we refurbish them. We fix any structural problems and then put in new bathrooms and modernize the kitchens. Usually we then put them back on the housing market and sell them and this gives us a useful margin. However, I have kept a couple back which I then rent to provide an ongoing income. There is one which has just got to the end of the previous tenant's lease. Quite large, with three bedrooms. And this one has a car space available from a laneway at the back, which you would find very useful."

"Sounds promising" said Micheál.

"Good" said Peadar. "I'll show it to you tomorrow. Oh, and it's within walking distance of a Catholic primary school. I'm guessing that's the kind of school you might prefer for the children."

"It is indeed" said Micheál's wife, Róisín, who had strong views on the matter.

"All right so" said Peadar. "Now Micheál, assuming the house will do, to begin with at least, how about you settle in tomorrow, Tuesday, and then if you are agreeable you can start work on Wednesday morning. We have bricks waiting to be laid in a new house we are building in Heaton Mersey. I'll pick you up first thing."

"Suits me" said Micheál. "I'm keen to get started".

The following morning, in their station wagon they followed Peadar's car to the house that was to be their first home in their new life in England. They pulled up outside the end house in a terrace of two-storey, weathered red-brown brick Victorian houses. Peadar unlocked the front door and they followed him in and explored the house. As he had promised, there were three bedrooms, these together with the bathroom were on the upper floor. Downstairs there was a sitting room and a kitchen/dining room at the back of the house. All newly decorated in light colours and modernised kitchen and bathroom. The furnishings were worn but serviceable.

"This terrace dates from the 1840s" said Peadar. "Double brick, solidly built – they built well in those days. What do you think? Will it suit?"

Micheál and Róisín looked at each other, both mentally comparing it with the much more cramped accommodation in the small stone cottage they had occupied on the family farm.

"I think it will do very well" said Róisín. "What do you think, Micheál?"

"Yes" said Micheál. "It should suit us just fine."

"Good" said Peadar. "Well, here are the door keys. I've left you some milk in the fridge and some biscuits and teabags and sugar to get you going but you'll be wanting to stock up the kitchen. There's a big supermarket in the town centre and a couple of small ones not far away. I'll see you tomorrow at seven. *Slán agaibh."* (Goodby to you all)

"*Slán go fóill*" (Goodby for now)responded Micheál.

"Now" said Róisín after Peadar had left, "Let's get the luggage and the bed linen out of the car. We'll make the beds and then have a cup of tea and a biscuit before we set off to the supermarket."

"Such a wide range of goods here" said Róisín to Micheál as they wandered round the aisles of the big Tesco supermarket.

"There are plenty of supermarkets as big as this in Ireland" said Micheál. "In Dublin, Limerick, Cork."

CHAPTER 5

"Oh, indeed" said Róisín. "I was just comparing it with the small SPAR supermarket back in Kilcarra. Mind you, that had all the essentials.

Now I have no sour milk at the moment to make soda bread so we must get a carton of buttermilk as well as plenty of ordinary milk. And wholemeal and plain flour and Baking powder. We'll need vegetables - potatoes, cabbage, onions, carrots - for dinner and I think we'll have sausages tonight. The English make some nice sausages. We'll get a sliced loaf for toast, Kerrygold butter and a jar of strawberry jam. Oh, and eggs, bacon and tomatoes and a bottle of vegetable oil, together with some salt and pepper. And Cornflakes and a pack of Quaker Rolled Oats for breakfasts.

We must have some fruit. I like the Cox's Orange Pippin apples, but they must be the English-grown ones. Imported ones don't have the same flavour. Get some oranges as well. If we get all that it'll get us off to a good start. We won't starve anyway.

Now Tomás, you heard me say all the things we want. You see if you can find where they are in the supermarket."

Tomás enjoyed helping his mother locate the groceries while Micheál followed along behind with one small girl holding on to each hand. After loading up the car with the food they strolled along to the Merseyway Shopping Centre to look at the shops. Róisín enjoyed shopping so she was looking forward to coming here again when they had accumulated some spare money.

That night as they were sitting up in bed, before turning the light off, Micheál said "Róisín my love, you know we have visited England for short times before, but this time, unless you think you won't be able to stand it, I believe we are here to stay. As you know there isn't enough income for two families back on the farm. I could probably pick up some bricklaying work in Ireland if we moved to Dublin or maybe Cork, but there is plenty of work for me here, with Peadar, and the money's good. How do you feel about settling down here? How do you feel about living in England instead of Ireland?"

"Well, I will miss Ireland" said Róisín. "Or at least I will miss the West, and Connemara in particular. But if we can't live in the West, then the idea of living in Dublin doesn't attract me. You must remember that I know this part of England well. I did my nurse training over here in Salford Royal Hospital, and I worked for a while in Stepping Hill Hospital, right here in Stockport before I went back to Ireland. I get on alright with the English, or at least the Northerners. And there are good schools here for the children.

Yes, I think I could settle down here, but if it doesn't work out, I suppose we shall have to think again."

"So we'll give it a go then shall we?" said Micheál.

"We will" said Róisín.

The following Sunday Micheál took his family for a drive in the Cheshire countryside to the South of Stockport.

"There's good land here, Tom" said Micheál as they looked out on the well tended fields of pasture and crops on either side of the road.

"Do we have land as good as this in Ireland?" asked Tom

"Oh indeed and we do and plenty of it. In Tipperary now and County Limerick or down in Cork, and in other counties as well there is grand land. The equal of this or better."

"But not in Connemara" he added, a little sadly.

Chapter 6

Osmos Planetary Council meeting. *The space ship for the journey to Earth is now ready and is described. Its crew, and the diplomatic and scientific members have been chosen.*

"Councillors" said the President, "The main item of business today is to have an update on the preparations, technical and otherwise, for our proposed embassy to Planet Earth.

First of all - our preparedness. Spaceflight Councillor - is the interstellar space ship ready?"

"It is" replied the Councillor. "My team has designed and constructed a suitable spacecraft, as requested. We are confident that we can achieve a velocity of 18% of the speed of light, so the journey of about 4.4 light years will take about 25 years to complete."

"Doesn't it take a great deal of energy to get up to such a high speed?" said the President.

"Yes it does. But with our fusion engines we are, in effect turning matter into energy and using that energy to project particles at enormous velocity out into space at the rear of the craft. This creates a corresponding thrust on the spaceship in the forward direction. But of course once we have achieved the desired speed, no more thrust is required as the spaceship will continue indefinitely at that speed in whatever is the preset direction through empty space. However, amounts of energy equivalent to those used for acceleration will be required to bring the spaceship to a halt when it arrives at its destination. As usual the ship has small gas-powered thrusters on the sides to adjust the direction of its trajectory and the orientation of the vessel to that trajectory."

"And the interior of the ship?" asked the President.

"Internally, the ship has extensive living quarters. My understanding is that we are sending a substantial team of our people on this embassy to Earth. I am assuming that because of the great length of the voyage, the crew will spend most of it unconscious, in stasis. The technology for this is well established, safe and reliable. Our current stasis machines are set up to, at regular intervals, electrically stimulate the muscles to keep them in working order. When the crew are awake, to keep fit they can make use of our large diameter centrifugal exercise ring where they will experience what will seem like a downward force equivalent to normal planetary gravity.

Also, I should mention that incorporated into the centrifugal ring there will be an illuminated hydroponic greenhouse in which small amounts of fresh green vegetables will be grown. While ample supplies of food, both frozen and processed will be carried on board, for psychological reasons we have considered it desirable to provide the crew with some plant food which will be absolutely fresh. The greenhouse has to be in the centrifugal ring because plants don't take kindly to growing in zero gravity."

"What about the cosmic ray problem?" asked the Science Councillor.

"The inhabited parts of the ship will be surrounded by substantial shielding to protect the crew from the damaging effects of galactic cosmic rays. These are highly energetic particles, mainly protons but including some heavier nuclei, travelling through interstellar space at near-light speed, which are very damaging to human tissue. Without protection, no one would survive a space journey of this duration. The shielding is of mixed chemical composition. Hydrogenated boron nitride, which does a good job of intercepting the high-energy protons, is a major component."

"I have a suggestion" said the Science Councillor.

"All right" said the President. "Let's hear it."

"If possible, the spacecraft should be surrounded by an outermost shell, composed of rock, or something that looks like rock. The reason is that when the ship arrives at planet Earth, it might be better not to announce its arrival straight away. This should be possible if our vessel looks like a stray asteroid rather than a spaceship. I think it would be highly desirable for the delegation to station themselves somewhere in Earth orbit and study Earth society at close hand for some time before making our presence known. We would be much better placed then to know with which Governments, organizations or whatever, we should first initiate communication."

"Yes, that's a very good point" said the President. "Would that be technically feasible?"

"Well, yes. I think so" said Spaceflight Councillor. "I believe we could make our spaceship look like an asteroid. It will be something of a challenge for the design team, but we can do it."

"Good" said the President. "Anything else, Councillor?"

"Only that, of course, the ship will have a captain whose responsibility it will be to get the vessel safely and speedily to and from planet Earth, and he or she will have a full complement of engineering and maintenance staff, as you would expect for a vessel of this size and complexity. There will be food production and serving staff - cooks and waiters, if you like, as well.

There was, as you might expect, enormous interest amongst the spaceflight community when this voyage was announced. However, enthusiasm to join the crew was greatly dampened as it was realised that this is going to require a fifty year absence with inevitable serious implications for family back here on Omnos. Nevertheless we were able to arrive at a core group of well qualified specialists, a mixture of older people whose family relationships had reached maturity and younger persons whose family responsibilities have not yet begun. We are in the final stages of selecting amongst these - psychological characteristics, particularly emotional stability, being the key criteria - for the actual crew."

"Thank you, Councillor" said the President. "And now Social and Demographic Councillor, how far have you got in selecting the members of the diplomatic part of the mission?"

"The task is pretty well complete, Council President. Just as the Spaceflight Councillor found, there was enormous initial interest in being part of this mission, much of which then evaporated when it was realised how very long its duration would be. Nevertheless we ended up with a very large pool of people amongst whom to make our selection. We have a strong scientific team. We have biologists, ecologists and geophysicists all intensely interested in the workings of a different planet. We have a couple of theoretical physicists whose role will be to communicate to their Earth confreres such understanding of the nature of physical reality that we believe we have arrived at here on Omnos. And of course we have engineers and applied scientists - medical, microbiological, agricultural - whose job it will be to transmit to the people of Earth the great mass of useful information - energy sources, antibiotic design, genetic engineering techniques, robotics etc. that we will be bringing with us."

CHAPTER 6

"But these technical people aren't leading the mission, are they?"

"No indeed. In addition we have what might be called the diplomatic core of the mission. The Head of Mission will be what we might refer to as our Ambassador to Earth. It will be the role of the diplomat members of the team to make contact with the various national governments of Planet Earth. I should mention that everyone on board, technical as well as diplomatic, will be fluent in English. We have chosen this out of all the Earth languages because it is clear from our study of all the Earth information already in our possession that English is the nearest thing to a common language, or "*Lingua Franca*" as they call it, on that planet. It is certainly the universal language of science and technology."

"Thank you, Councillors" said the President. "It is clear that our preparations for this historic mission are well advanced. We shall meet again soon."

Chapter 7

***Tom goes to school** for his last year of primary education. The fight and its aftermath. Tom performs well in the entrance examination for the prestigious St Thomas Aquinas Academy. Some years after their arrival in England, Micheál is taken on as a partner in his cousin's building business.*

"Tomás will start school tomorrow, Micheál" said Róisín. "He is just turning eleven so he will have one year of primary school and then continue on to secondary school. We've enrolled him at Our Lady Catholic Primary, not very far from here."

"Will you take him there yourself?" asked Micheál.

"I will tomorrow" said Róisín "but it is within walking distance so he can get there himself after that."

"Are you looking forward to it, Tomás?" said Micheál.

"I don't know, Daddy. But I suppose I have to go."

"You do indeed. But it will be very different from the small National school you were attending in Kilcarra. Much bigger and there will be plenty of children there from other countries as well. There are a lot of Asian and Middle Eastern migrants in this area. Now behave yourself there and work hard. We want you to get a good education."

"Are we migrants, Daddy?" asked Tom.

"Well, we are and we aren't" replied Micheál.

CHAPTER 7

"Ireland and England are next door to each other, as you know, and Irish people have been coming to England and English people going over to Ireland for hundreds of years. Indeed, for quite a long time we were all one country. That ended back in 1921, but England and Ireland still have what you might call a special relationship with each other."

Tom pondered on what his father was saying without entirely understanding it.

Next morning, having arrived at the school, Tomás was taken along to the Year 6 classroom, just as it was filling with children, and handed over to the teacher, a tall, forbidding woman with grey hair tied in a bun.

"And who might you be?" she said, looking down at him.

"Please missus, my name is Tom Glennon and this is my first day here."

"First of all, don't call me 'missus'. I am Miss Helen Gallagher. You will address me as Miss Gallagher or just as Miss. You must be the Irish boy I was told was joining the class."

"I suppose I must be, Miss."

"Indeed you are. Well Tom Glennon, you can sit here." And she led Tomás to a desk in the middle row. Tom sat down, put his school bag under the desk and then lifted the lid to find that he had already been provided with an exercise book, two pencils, a rubber and a ballpoint pen. He looked around him to see a mixture of boys and girls, the majority white, like himself, but with a sprinkling of brown and occasional black, faces. As the chatter and hubbub subsided, Miss Gallagher called the class to order.

"Quiet everyone, please. Now today, girls and boys, we have a new pupil at our school. Tom Glennon, who has come here from Ireland. Stand up, Tom, so that everyone can see you."

Tom stood up, feeling ill at ease as the other children turned and stared at him.

"All right, Tom, sit down. Now children, get out your exercise books. We are going to start today with Arithmetic."

"Oh, Good" thought Tom. "Arithmetic is easy."

At the lunch break, after eating his sandwiches, Tom went out into the playground with the other children. He did not yet know anyone, so stayed at the side, watching. As had also been the case at Kilcarra school, the boys and girls played separately. There was a group of boys near him, throwing a ball to each other. Tom noticed one of them, the biggest boy, eyeing him. The boy detached himself from the group and came over towards Tom, walking with something of a swagger.

"It would be good to say Hello to someone" thought Tom.

"Are you the Irish kid?" said the boy in a truculent tone.

"I am" said Tom.

"I don't like Irish kids" said the boy. He then pushed Tom very hard in the chest, making him fall over, kicked him in the ribs as he lay on the ground and then walked away.

Tom lay there for a moment, bewildered, hurt, and in tears. He was familiar with occasional playground rough and tumble with other boys, but this kind of wholly unprovoked, nasty, senseless aggression was a new and shocking phenomenon. He got to his feet and stood there for a while not knowing what to do and for the rest of the school day his mind was in turmoil.

When Tom arrived home Róisín could see that he was very upset about something.

"Tom, my dear, you look very unhappy. Come here to me now and tell me why." She sat Tom down next to her on the sofa and put her arm around him.

Tom burst into tears and then, through his sobs told his story.

"I was in the playground at lunchtime today, Mammy, and a boy came up to me and he said he didn't like Irish kids and then he knocked me over and kicked me."

CHAPTER 7

"And are you hurt?" she said. "Where did he kick you? Let me see."

"Just here, Mammy" said Tom, pulling up his shirt and singlet and showing Róisín a bruised area on his side. She felt it carefully.

"Does it hurt if I press it a bit, like this?

"Not much"

"Well, I don't think much damage has been done. No broken ribs. I shall have to have a talk with your Daddy about this when he comes home."

When Micheál came home an hour or so later, Róisín made tea and they sat down at the table together.

"Micheál, there was a problem with Tom at the school today."

"What kind of a problem?" said Micheál with quick concern. "Is it to do with his schoolwork?"

"Oh, No. Nothing like that" said Róisín, and she related Tom's story to him.

"What will we do? Should we say something to the school?"

Micheál thought for a moment. "No, I don't think that would be a good idea. We don't want Tom to get the reputation of looking for the protection of the teachers every time he gets into strife with some other boy. No, I think this is a problem Tom is going to have face up to himself. I must have a talk with him. Where is he?"

"Kicking a ball around in the back garden" said Róisín. "I will call him in."

When Tom came in from the garden, Micheál called him over. "Sit down at the table with me, Tom. I want to have a word with you about what happened at school today. Mammy told me the story. Now tell me, Tom, did you try to defend yourself against this other boy?"

"I never got the chance, Daddy" said Tom, indignantly. I didn't know he was suddenly going to push me over. I had no idea he was going to attack me."

"And if you had known, would you have stood up to him?"

"I would!" said Tom.

"Is this boy bigger than you?"

"He is"

"Is he a lot bigger?"

"No. Not a lot."

"So, do you think you could reach his nose with your fist?"

"Indeed I could" said Tom.

"Well, Tom. I don't want you to actually pick a fight with him, but if he starts to knock you about again, then punch him as hard as you can on the nose. And if that doesn't stop him, hit him some more."

"Now, Micheál" said Róisín, anxiously. "I don't want Tom getting into fights."

"Neither do I" said Micheál "but he must be prepared to stand up for himself."

The next day at school, Tom again went out to the playground after lunch. He did not yet know any of the other children and being hesitant to join in with any of the games that were going on, stayed by himself and watched. He then noticed his assailant from the day before coming towards him, this time with a couple of hangers on. Tom braced himself for what he feared was to come and formed his right hand into a firm fist.

"You still here, Irish kid?" said the boy and made as if to push Tom over again. Tom fended the attempt off and then stepped forward and punched the boy as hard as he could on the nose. Since Tom was a strong boy for his age, already used to physical work on the family farm, his punch was very effective, and to Tom's surprise the boy's nose started bleeding.

"Ow!" said the boy. "Ow! That hurt. I'll show you!" and he threw a wild punch which hit Tom in the face. This enraged Tom and now filled with righteous anger he began to pummel the other boy with both fists. The boy in turn hit back.

"Fight. Fight. Fight." went up the chant from a ring of boys who had gathered around to watch.

Suddenly they heard "What's going on here?" in a loud man's voice.

A large male teacher, Ignatius Donoghue, appeared, pushed through the ring of boys, grabbed hold of Tom and his opponent and pulled them apart.

"We will not have fighting in the playground! You!" he said, glaring down first at Tom. "Who are you and why are you fighting?"

To which Tom, still fully fired up, replied in loud indignant tones "My name is Tom Glennon Sir and we came over from Ireland for my Daddy to help my Uncle Peadar with the building business and I came to school for the first time yesterday and this boy came up and said he didn't like Irish kids and he pushed me over and kicked me and I was very upset and when I got home I told my Mammy and she told my Daddy and he asked if this boy was bigger than me and I said a bit and he said could I reach his nose with my fist and I said I could and he said not to start a fight because Mammy doesn't want me to be fighting but if this boy attacked me again to punch him hard on the nose and just now Sir this boy came up and tried to knock me down again so I punched him on the nose and then he hit me back and then we started fighting and then you came Sir."

When Tom finished there was a hushed silence. The other boys were looking at him open-mouthed. The teacher looked down at him with some interest.

"Well, Tom Glennon. That was certainly a very long sentence."

He turned to Tom's opponent. "Is that true? Did you push Tom Glennon over yesterday and kick him? Tell the truth!"

"Aw well. I suppose I might have" said the boy in a surly voice.

"So. You thought you could bully the new boy did you? Well, it looks as if this time you bit off more than you could chew. What's your name, boy?"

"Riley, Sir. Jim Riley."

"Riley, is it. Now tell me Riley – with a name like that, from what country do you think your ancestors came?"

"Dunno, Sir."

"Well I'll tell you. 'Riley' is an Irish name, so your ancestors came from Ireland. So you are an 'Irish kid' too."

"Like at least half the kids in this school" thought the teacher to himself.

"Think about that, Riley. And also – stop the bullying. We won't have that at this school. Don't grow up to be a bully. No-one likes bullies"

"Now, back to your classes both of you. Except you had better go to the boys' toilet and clean yourself up first, Riley."

The following day, Tom went out to the playground again in the lunch break. After a few minutes, while he watched the other children, wishing he could join in, two boys approached him. Tom felt a bit apprehensive. Were these friends of Riley? Was he going to have to fight again? When they arrived, after looking at him for a moment, one of them, a tall bespectacled boy, said

"Are you Tom Glennon?"

"I am" Tom replied.

"And did you fight Jim Riley yesterday?"

"I did."

"And did you really make his nose bleed?" said the other, a slightly tubby cheerful-looking boy.

"I did" said Tom.

"Gosh. Can we join your gang?" said the tubby boy.

"I haven't got a gang" said Tom, nonplussed.

CHAPTER 7

"But we could start one!" said the first boy, enthusiastically.

"We could call it – the Glennon Gang. And if we stick together, Riley will leave us alone"

"Does he bully you?" asked Tom.

"Yes he does" they both said.

"But if there are three of us he will leave us alone. You know – like the Three Musketeers." Said the second boy.

"All for one and one for all" he declaimed, striking a martial pose.

Tom began to feel that the situation was beginning to get ahead of him.

"Well, I don't know about all that" he said. "But I tell you what. The three of us could go up to Riley and tell him that if he tries anything with any of us, he will have the three of us to deal with."

"Yes. Let's do that" said the bespectacled boy.

"Oh, by the way, I am Pat Byrne. Pat is short for Patrick."

"And I'm Tim Daley" said the other boy.

"Well, Hi Pat and Hi Tim. You already know who I am. Anyway, Let's go and see Riley now" said Tom, who was still feeling fired up after acquitting himself so well on the previous day.

"Where is he?"

"He's over there" said Tim. "Bouncing a ball against the brick wall."

They walked purposefully over to Riley.

"Hey Riley, we want to speak to you" said Pat, who seemed to have become the spokesman for the group. Riley looked at them, not knowing quite what to make of this sudden confrontation.

"What do you lot want?" he asked in an aggressive tone.

"We have a message for you" said Pat.

"Oh Yeah. What?"

"We are the Glennon Gang. Any attack on one of us is an attack on all of us. All for One and One for all is our motto. So watch out!"

"Hmph" snorted Riley. "We'll see" he said, somewhat uncertainly, and turned away.

"How was school today, Tom?" Micheál asked him as the family sat down to dinner.

"School was good today."

"And did you have any trouble with that boy that pushed you about yesterday?"

"I did. He tried to knock me over again so I hit him hard on the nose as you told me. And I made his nose bleed."

"Oh the poor boy" said soft-hearted Róisín, always sensitive to any account of human suffering.

"For the love o'God, Róisín" said Micheál in affectionate exasperation. "This lad was attacking our son."

"Well, yes, I suppose that's right" said Róisín. "So what happened next, Tom?"

"Well he hit me back and then I hit him back and we were fighting until a teacher came and stopped us. And he asked us why we were fighting and I told him this boy had knocked me over and kicked me the day before and you had told me to stand up for myself and so when he tried to do it again I hit him. He then asked the boy if this was true and he admitted it was. And he asked the boy his name and he said he is Jim Riley"

"And are you in any trouble now?" anxiously asked Róisín.

"No. I don't think so" said Tom. "He told Jim Riley off and then said we mustn't be fighting as the school doesn't allow it."

"Anyway" said Tom, proudly. "There will be no more problems with Riley now. I've got a gang."

"What!" said both parents together.

CHAPTER 7

"Now Tom, we don't want you mixing with rough boys" said Róisín.

"Ah No, Mammy. These aren't rough boys at all."

"Well I suppose that's alright if you're sure" said Róisín.

"Anyway, you have some friends now" said Micheál, who was more amused than alarmed by Tom's revelation.

"Yes, Daddy, I do." Said Tom.

About half way through the third, and last, term of the school year, one day at the end of the last class as the children gathered their belongings to go home, Miss Gallagher called Tom over to her.

"Tom, I have a letter here for you to take home to your parents. Make sure you give it to them."

"I will, Miss Gallagher."

"Miss Gallagher gave me this letter to give to you, Mammy" said Tom on arriving home. After reading it, Róisín looked concerned.

"She says she would like Daddy and myself to come in to the school to see her. You are not in trouble are you, Tom?"

"Not at all, Mammy. I behave myself."

"All right. I'll talk to Daddy about this."

The following day, having made an appointment, Róisín and Micheál arrived at the school, shortly after classes had finished, to see Tom's teacher.

"We got your letter Miss Gallagher. Tom's not in any trouble is he?" asked Róisín.

"Not at all, Mrs Glennon. Quite the contrary. As you can imagine, I keep a close eye on all the children in my class to see how they are developing, and I have to tell you that Tom is coming along exceptionally well. He is particularly good at maths and seems to have a keen interest in Science. Now here in England, in addition to the usual locally controlled secondary schools, we have what are referred to as 'Academies'.

These are funded directly by the Department for Education in London. While they have to teach the core subjects, especially English and Mathematics, they are free to specialize in certain areas – it could be performing arts, or business or foreign languages. Now as it happens there is one of these Academies not very far from here – St Thomas, named after St Thomas Aquinas. It was started by the De La Salle Brothers, but now the staff is nearly all lay. It's speciality is what we call the STEM subjects – Science, Technology, Engineering and Mathematics. It is also, as it happens, a boys-only school.

St Thomas Academy has a very good reputation. Places are very much in demand, so they have a competitive entrance examination. Now I don't know whether you would be interested in Tom attending a school like that but if you are, I think Tom would do well enough in the entrance examination to be accepted. The exam is designed to assess intelligence rather than book knowledge"

Róisín and Micheál looked at each other.

"What do you think, Micheál?"

"Yes. I think he should go for it" said Micheál without hesitation. "This could set him on the pathway to becoming a scientist or an engineer. I would have studied Engineering myself if my parents could have afforded to send me to university."

"I agree" said Róisín. "This sounds like an opportunity not to be missed. Thank you, Miss Gallagher, for telling us about this. Will you be able to put Tom's name down to take the exam?"

"Yes I will" said Miss Gallagher. "The exam will be a fortnight from today. There will be some other children from this school also taking it."

A couple of weeks later, Tom with other boys from Our Lady Catholic Primary School, was taken along to a large Examination

Hall made available for the purpose by the local Government secondary school. He was pleased to see that his friends, Pat and Tim, were also taking the exam. While most of the children were from Catholic primary schools a significant proportion were from government or Anglican schools. Although St Thomas Academy was Catholic, part of its deal with the Government was that it accepted a quota of non-Catholic boys.

Tom found the questions challenging but by the end he felt he had done pretty well.

"So how was the exam?" asked his mother when he arrived home.

"It was quite hard, Mammy. But I think it went pretty well. There were very few questions I couldn't answer."

"Good" said Róisín. "Let's hope you gave the right answers. Well, we'll know soon enough. I believe the results are out in a couple of weeks."

A week before the end of term Tom was again given an envelope to take home to his parents. Róisín opened it to find a letter headed 'St Thomas Aquinas Academy'.

"Dear Mr and Mrs Glennon

On the basis of his excellent performance in the entrance examination, we are pleased to offer a place at St Thomas Aquinas Academy for your son Thomas, for the coming academic year beginning on 1 September.

If you wish to accept this offer please indicate this on the enclosed form which should be returned to his teacher at Our Lady Catholic Primary School. ....

"Tom. You got in to the St Thomas Academy. Well done!"

"Oh" said Tom, not at all sure what the implications of this were. "I suppose that's good."

"It's not just good. It's very good. Now what would you like as a special treat?"

"Can we have apple pie for pudding, Mammy?" apple pie being a special favourite.

"You certainly can. Apple pie it is."

"What do you think, Micheál?" said Róisín to her husband when he arrived home from work. "Tom has got into the St Thomas Academy."

"Has he Begod" said Micheál. "Good man, Tom. More power to you!"

In the staff room, on the last day of the school year, the teachers were chatting about how the year had gone.

"I see we got several more boys into St Thomas this year, Helen" said Ignatius Donoghue – the teacher who had stopped Tom's fight with Jim Riley at the beginning of the year - to Helen Gallagher, Tom's teacher.

"Yes, we did" said Helen. "Including three from my class. We have had the individual scores back now of all the children that did the exam, and one of them – Tom Glennon – actually came top."

"Tom Glennon? Oh, I know him" said Ignatius. "He got into a fight with another boy on his second day at school and I had to pull them apart."

"I'm surprised" said Helen. "Tom doesn't strike me as being an aggressive boy."

"He isn't. The other boy – Jim Riley – you may know him, a troubled boy from an unhappy home, was the aggressor. But in Tom Glennon he got more than he bargained for."

The Glennon family settled down well in Stockport. On Sundays they went to Mass at the large Gothic Revival Catholic church, Our Lady and the Apostles, and Róisín soon made friends in the large Catholic community. Micheál was making good money at bricklaying and with their frugal lifestyle they managed before long to accumulate enough to think about buying their own house rather than renting. The three-bedroom terrace they rented from Peadar suited them well so eventually Micheál made an offer to buy it. Peadar was happy to sell. Having accumulated enough already for a substantial deposit, they had no difficulty getting a mortgage and the purchase was completed.

"Perhaps when we get rich we will buy ourselves a fancy detached house out in Cheshire" said Micheál to Róisín.

"Hmm, maybe" said Róisín, who was beginning to like living in their inner city urban environment with its nearness to shops, schools, church and her friends.

Every year they would spend part of their summer holiday back in Connemara, staying in the old house that they used to live in on the family farm. Here they would reconnect with friends and relations, speak nothing but Irish, drive to the coast and swim in the cool Atlantic waters. On some evenings Micheál would play the fiddle and sing in Hogan's pub in the village. Tom enjoyed giving his uncle Séamus an occasional hand managing the sheep.

One afternoon, after they had been living in Stockport for four years, when Micheál arrived home he told Róisín that he had important news.

"What is it?" said Róisín, apprehensively. "I hope it is good news"

"It is indeed" said Michael. "Wait 'til I tell you. As you know, Peadar and I get on well together in the work. Now Peadar has never enjoyed the business side of the job. He knows I'm good with figures. And over the last few years I have become well acquainted with parts of the building trade other than just bricklaying. And I get on well with the men. Earlier today Peadar said he would like me to come and see him in his office after we finished work. So I did. And he asked if I would be interested in coming into a partnership with him and take over some of the tasks which he finds onerous. He said we could try it out for a year and then, if it was working, make it permanent."

"So what did you tell him?"

"Well, I told him I was interested but I should think about it first. Especially, I said I should talk it over with you, but I would let him know tomorrow."

"What kind of things would you be doing?"

"Oh, talking to the clients – the people we are building for, interacting with suppliers, keeping the men up to the mark, talking to the accountant. Things like that. But I would still do some bricklaying. If only to keep my hand in."

"So what do you think? Are you interested?"

"Yes, I must admit that I am. It would be a big change. Laying bricks all day can get a bit boring. Going more into the management side would give me more variety. And if after a year I find that I don't like it after all I can just go back to bricklaying. If it works out, Peadar says he would change the name of the business. It would become *O'Kelly & Glennon, Builders*. How would you like to see that in big letters on the side of a truck?"

"I would like it just fine, I suppose. But what do you think? Would you like to take this on? Will you enjoy it?"

"Yes, after thinking about it I would like to accept Peadar's offer. It will be a challenge but I think I can handle it. But what do you think?"

"Well, if you think it's the job for you, and I can see that you do, you should accept. Will you get paid more?"

"Oh, yes" said Micheal.

"Well that's a good reason in itself" said Róisín.

Chapter 8

Osmos Planetary Council meeting. *They decide to ask the governments of Earth to provide an ambassador to come with their embassy on its return to Omnos.*

"Today, Council Members" said the President "we are once again convened to discuss the forthcoming diplomatic mission to Planet Earth. You will recall that it is the Social and Demographic Councillor's team which is responsible for putting together the diplomatic part of the mission. They have come up with an interesting suggestion that the Councillor will now put before you. Councillor?"

"Thank you, President" said the Social and Demographic Councillor. "Let me say straight away that our suggestion may well prove not to be feasible but we think it is worth a try. What we propose is that once we are well established in Earth orbit and once we have made clear our good intentions and entirely positive attitude to the people of Earth, and in particular once we have already transferred useful new technology to them so that they feel somewhat in our debt, we should invite them to send an Earth representative back with us when we return to Omnos. He would be, if you like, the Earth Ambassador to Omnos. He would come to us in the spaceship with our returning team."

His announcement was met with mixed rumblings and mutterings of surprise, disquiet and scepticism from the Council members.

"Order Please" said the President. "We will now have your initial responses, and questions. Science Councillor?"

"My initial response" said the Science Councillor "is that will be very difficult to find a suitable person. It will pretty certainly be a one-way visit. Any Earth human taking on this task would need to be highly motivated. So I have two questions. First, what particular qualities would we like to see in an Earth ambassador, and Second, what kind of person is in fact most likely to volunteer."

"The ideal Earth ambassador" responded the Social and Demographic Councillor "would be someone who can interpret and explain the nature of Earth society - the people, the history, the politics, the culture - to us. This would mean a person who is not only intelligent and highly cultured, but also with broad, rather than narrow, interests. Unfortunately, I suspect that the kind of person most likely to volunteer for this assignment would be a scientist, driven as so many scientists are, by insatiable curiosity, curiosity in this case to explore a new planet. While there are no doubt highly cultured scientists, I can't help feeling that our chances of getting the broad combination of qualities we want are lower if the selection is made only within the Scientific community of Earth."

The Science Councillor was not happy about this generalization about the scientific community, but had to concede that, statistically at least, there was something in it.

"So" he said "we'll probably get a scientist, if we get anyone at all, and we'll be looking for a scientist with broad cultural interests. Not impossible by any means."

CHAPTER 8

"I suppose" said the Arts Councillor "that once we have indicated our desire to have an ambassador from Earth, and once we have specified the kind of person we are looking for, it will be up to Earth governments to see if they can find a suitable candidate."

"Well, Councillors" said the President. "Do any of you see any problem with having an actual ambassador from Earth come out to Omnos?"

"I don't see that we would have a problem" said the Spaceflight Councillor. "He can't do us any harm, and it would certainly be very interesting and valuable for us to have an actual Earth person to talk to, to give us a more hands-on feel for their society and culture. If Earth can find a suitable candidate, I am all in favour." There was general agreement from the other members of the Council.

"So be it" said the President. "The diplomatic section of our mission will convey to the Earth governments, or to that body they call the 'United Nations' which seems to be the nearest thing they have to an actual Earth Government, our interest in having an Earth ambassador come to Omnos. Given the difficulty in finding any suitable candidate at all, we obviously can't be too specific in our requirements, but it would not be inappropriate for us to make some suggestions as to the qualities we are looking for. Arts Councillor – any suggestions?"

"Yes, I do" responded the Arts Councillor.

"We already know that the people of Earth have a very rich and diverse musical culture. Furthermore it is apparently not uncommon for people who are not themselves full-time musicians to nevertheless have significant musical talent. I don't think we are looking for a professional musician but we can ask the Earth government to find us an ambassador who, in addition to other appropriate personal qualities, has a useful level of competence on one, or more, of their musical instruments. We also, of course, want a generally cultured person who is at least familiar with literature and the visual arts."

"Thank you, Arts Councillor. Further comments? Social and Emotional Affairs Councillor?"

"What the Arts Councillor proposes as qualities to look for in whoever Earth sends us are of course highly desirable" responded the Social and Emotional Affairs Councillor. "But we would also want someone who is psychologically stable. And it would also be good for it to be someone who is actually pleasant. Someone we might actually enjoy interacting with."

"True" said the President. "Please send us someone nice. That might be a bit hard to specify. Let's hope they appreciate the desirability of that without our having to spell it out."

"Well, yes" said the Social and Demographic Councillor. "What about the ambassador's metaphysical views? Most of the people of Earth adhere to one or other of their four or so major religions. Do we want an ambassador who, as a believer himself, can give us some insight into religious belief on Earth? Or do we want an atheist?"

"Not much point in requesting an atheist" said the Spaceflight Councillor. "We have atheists of our own. I can't see that an Earth atheist would have anything new to tell us."

"So" said the President. The list grows. I don't give much for our chances. We can but ask."

"It occurs to me" said the Science Councillor "that once our mission arrives in Earth orbit they may be able to initiate the selection process themselves. They can search what on Earth is called, the 'Internet'. All kinds of information – professional and personal - about individual people, is accessible there."

"Worth a try" said the President. "Social and Demographic Councillor, ask your diplomatic team to give some thought to how they might implement the Science Councillor's suggestion.

Well, that's about it for today. Until our next meeting - Thank you all."

Chapter 9

***Tom thrives at St Thomas** Aquinas Academy. He hopes for a career as a research physicist. In his final year he takes the Cambridge University entrance examination. He is awarded a scholarship to Saviour College. His musical tastes and abilities, especially in jazz piano, develop. The family receive disturbing news about the health of Róisín, Micheál's wife.*

At Tom's new school, St Thomas Aquinas Academy, all the boys in Year 7 were, like himself, newly arrived so he was not the odd one out any more. Pat and Tim from Our Lady Primary School had also passed the entrance examination so he was starting off already with two friends. In the playground at lunchtime he had no problems mixing in with the other boys, kicking a ball around or playing games such as Tig or Relievio. Surrounded as he was all day by boys from the North of England, Tom, without conscious intent, and without even noticing that it was happening, began to speak less and less with an Irish accent. In time, he came to speak English with something of a Lancashire intonation but never ungrammatically as some of the other boys did.

The 'official' school games, that is to say those games in which the school established teams to play other schools, were Rugby in the Winter and Cricket in the warmer months. Every week, for every class there was a Sports afternoon where the boys in each class would play one or other of the official games. Tom enjoyed cricket but disliked rugby. While he was prepared to tackle, and be tackled on the field, as occasion required, he privately thought it a thuggish game. He, like most of the boys, much preferred Soccer, a spontaneous game of which could be started at any time on any surface with any ball.

While Tom settled well in his new school, the same could not be said for the Glennon Gang. While he himself would have been happy to let it go, his friends Pat and Tim were enthusiastic that it should continue from Our Lady Primary into St Thomas Academy. Undoubtedly, membership of a gang, even a very small one, conferred some prestige in the playground and they acquired some new members. But of course there were other "gangs", impromptu assemblages of boys in the playground, and sometimes fights erupted between the Glennon Gang and other gangs. Tom generally acquitted himself well in these conflicts, fighting boys his own age and size. One day, however, he found himself in a fight with another boy, Christy, of about his own height but older and stronger, and Tom came off the worst. This was bad news for the rest of the gang. One of them, who had not been present came up to Tom and asked – "Did Christy really beat you in a fight?" Tom acknowledged that he did.

This setback increased Tom's doubts about being part of the more rough and tumble aspects of playground culture and he resolved to withdraw and concentrate instead on things he was good at. One of these was music. He played the fiddle. His father, Micheál, had bought him a second-hand instrument and showed him the rudiments. He would play Irish traditional music – jigs, reels, hornpipes – along with his father either at home and occasionally when he was taken along to Irish music sessions in a local pub. But his real passion was the piano. One day a week he had a one-hour lesson from a piano teacher who came into the school and then did his daily practice on an old piano which his parents had bought. He was happy to play the standard student Mozart, Beethoven, Bach classical pieces but once he was exposed to jazz piano, especially blues and boogie, this became his main musical interest. He sought out recordings of the great black American pianists - Jimmy Yancey, Albert Ammons, Pete Johnson, Pinetop Smith, Champion Jack Dupree, Meade Lux Lewis, James Crutchfield, Memphis Slim - and did his best to reproduce their sounds on the piano at home. With repeated practice Tom began to develop the strong left hand essential for piano boogie. His ability to perform passable boogie went down well with the other boys at school. There was a piano in the Music Room and whenever opportunity arose he would often be urged to play. His tastes developed with time, and while he never lost his love for blues and boogie, he experimented with block chord jazz piano playing in the style of George Shearing and greatly admired, without ever expecting to achieve, the piano pyrotechnics of Oscar Peterson and Art Tatum.

Each form had a teacher responsible for it. But unlike at the primary school where one teacher taught the class everything, at the secondary school the boys were taught by specialist subject teachers who came in to their classroom when that particular subject was to be taught. Tom was a good student and had no particular difficulty with any subject but what he liked best, what he developed a strong interest in, was Science. Very early in his school career he decided that what he wanted to be was a research scientist. Because of its reputation, St Thomas Academy was able to attract good teachers but some of Tom's teachers made a stronger impression on him than others. Tom had a natural aptitude for mathematics, which naturally led him towards the physical end of the scientific spectrum, Physics and Physical Chemistry. And in the Senior School he had the good fortune to be taught by a Physics teacher with a genuine and infectious enthusiasm for his subject. Tom's career focus now sharpened and while he remained interested in all aspects of Science, his aim now was to become a physicist.

Towards the end of each term there were written examinations and the boys in each class were graded on the basis of their performance, all the way from coming first to coming last. In Tom's class there developed, somewhat to the teachers' amusement, strong competition amongst the cleverest boys to see who could come top in the term exam. This was usually Tom. Every year, the school sought to identify the most promising boys in Year 12 and encouraged them to take the Oxford and Cambridge entrance examinations. Cambridge, because of its stellar scientific reputation, was where Tom wanted to go. In the winter, some time after the end of their last school term, he and a few other boys from his class went up to Cambridge to take the examination. On the basis of his performance, Tom was offered a Scholarship to Saviour College, one of the oldest of the colleges that make up Cambridge University. He was thrilled with his success and of course accepted.

The Cambridge academic year did not begin until the following September, so Tom had eight months to fill in. He spent the first three months earning money as a labourer in his father's building firm, occasionally being allowed to do some bricklaying under Micheál's supervision. When April came he decided that he had accumulated enough cash and set off to travel around Europe by hitchhiking and by train.

Tom had something of a flair for languages. French had been one of his favourite subjects at school and he had made himself fluent. He taught himself Spanish, which he found to be a straightforward language and could make himself understood in Italian. German, however, he found more problematic. He spent an enjoyable and satisfying four months travelling around the Continent, conversing freely with the people and enjoying the local cuisine in, listening to the local music, and interacting with other young people of divers nationalities in youth hostels. He revelled especially in the richness of European architecture, from the great Gothic cathedrals of France to the glories of the Italian Renaissance in Italy. He swam in the Mediterranean, experiencing, for the first time, seawater which was actually warm. Tom returned home with a strong sense, despite his origin on the farthest Western fringe, the Atlantic edge, of the continent, of being himself a European, an heir to, a member of, one of the great cultures (Tom himself considered it to be the greatest) of the world. It had been for him a transformative experience.

He returned home impatient to set off to Cambridge to begin his training as a scientist. He was welcomed warmly by his parents and sisters and they listened eagerly around the dinner table as he regaled them with an account of his adventures on the Continent. The following day, however, he could not help noticing that Micheál and Róisín were somewhat subdued.

"Is everything alright, Da? Mammy and yourself seem a bit low."

Micheál looked across at Róisín who after a few moments gave an almost imperceptible nod.

"Call the girls, will you Tom. There is something we want to tell you."

They sat round the dining room table, with Micheál holding Róisín's hand. He looked round at his assembled children, Tomás, Aoife and Gráinne.

"We have some not-very-good news for you. Mammy is not quite as well as she usually is. She has been diagnosed with cancer of the liver She is to have an operation next week. Please God it will be in time."

CHAPTER 9

There were small involuntary gasps and cries from the girls. Tom felt as if a massive hand had gripped his heart. He loved his mother dearly and was shocked to the core by the thought that he might suddenly lose her. Although they were a loving family, they were not normally very demonstrative, but Tom rose to his feet, walked round to Róisín and gave her a warm hug and a kiss. His sisters did the same.

The following week, as Tom went up to Cambridge on the train, he was still eager to commence his university journey but his enthusiasm was tempered by the lurking anxiety about his mother at the back of his mind.

BOOK 2

Chapter 10

Osmos Planetary Council meeting. *The Council is informed that, because of the very high regard in which Earth artistic abilities are held, a proposal has been made to use genetic engineering to create populations on Osmos with Earth genetics. The feasibility of this proposal is discussed. The decision as to whether to proceed with it is left for further consideration.*

"Once again, fellow members of the Council" said the President "we are here to discuss the forthcoming mission to Planet Earth. The specific matter to consider today is what I can only describe as an extraordinary proposal from the Science Councillor. A proposal so extraordinary in fact that when he first brought it to me I could not believe that it could even be within the realm of the possible. But he assures me that it is. He will now give an account of it and you can judge for yourselves."

"Thank you, President" said the Science Councillor, rising to his feet. "First of all, I should explain that I did not originate this – yes, I must say, revolutionary – proposal myself. It came from two of the younger scientists on my team and in a moment I will ask them to explain it to you themselves. First of all let me say how it came about.

I was giving members of the Science Directorate my report on the Council discussions on the Planet Earth project. I gave them an account of what we have already been able to find out about the people of Earth, and amongst other things I told them that we have already concluded that in all forms of the arts - music, literature, sculpture, painting - they are highly creative. I mentioned in passing the Arts Councillor's casual remark that, in view of what he considers to be the rather moribund state of our own Arts scene, what a pity it is that we can't bring some of them here. He, and the rest of us, just assumed that such a proposal could never be realistic and so as you recall we did not discuss the matter."

No indeed" commented the President. "Short of landing on the planet and kidnapping some of their Arts community, which of course is unthinkable, it was not feasible."

"A couple of days later" continued the Science Councillor "I received a call from a young member of the team saying that he would like to come and see me on a matter in relation to the Planet Earth Project. And what he brought me was no less than a proposal, a mechanism, by means of which the creative abilities of Earth people might in fact be brought to our planet. I will let him rather than myself give an account of it because it involves genetic engineering of a highly sophisticated nature. He is a genetic engineer, whereas I, as you know, am a physicist. So, with your permission, President, I will ask Dr Anla Phocos to address the Council."

A young man, who had been seated at the side of the Council Chamber stood up and walked to a lectern at the end of the room.

"President. Members of the Council. The proposal I am about to outline to you may well seem bizarre, perhaps even something of a fantasy. I have, however, discussed it intensively with a number of my genetic engineering colleagues and the consensus is that what I am here proposing can indeed be done."

He spoke with confidence, with no sign of being abashed by, or even particularly impressed with, the august group he was addressing. He had the air not only of a man on top of his brief, but also with a hint of intellectual arrogance.

"Hm. Another clever dick scientist" thought the President to himself. "Not my favourite kind of person. He is going to have to make a good case to persuade me. Still, we'd better hear him just in case he really is on to something."

"As you all know" continued Dr Phocos "genetic information is stored in long strands of DNA in the nuclei of cells. There is also DNA in the mitochondria in the cytoplasm but that DNA is concerned only with the energy-generating mechanisms of the cell and so is of no interest in the present context, that context being the inheritance of artistic ability and of creativity. The information in DNA is coded, i.e. is written, in terms of the sequence of the four bases - adenine, thymine, guanine, cytosine - or A,T, G, and C, as they are commonly abbreviated. Any given gene will be a certain length of DNA strand with a certain quite specific sequence of A, T, G and C. As I trust you also already know..."

"Alright. Don't be condescending" thought the President.

"...the cell first makes an RNA copy of the DNA sequence, in which as it happens the thymine is replaced by uracil, a similar pyrimidine base, and then uses the RNA to synthesize a protein with the sequence of amino acids along its polypeptide chain ultimately determined by the original sequence of A, T, G and C in the DNA gene. And it is the protein which finally does the work, which carries out some particular biological function.

So, Council members" he said, warming to his theme "As it happens we have the ability to synthesize, to create, DNA strands of any given sequence of the four bases, A, T, G and C. That is to say, supply us with a sequence and we can make a copy. Or, in other words, if we know the base sequence of any particular gene, we can copy that gene. And, not only are we able to make genes, we also have the ability to insert those newly made gene copies into the DNA of the chromosomes in the nuclei of living cells. Equally we have the ability to excise particular DNA sequences, i.e. particular genes, from chromosomes and replace them with other sequences. This has, as perhaps you may already know, been standard practice for some time in the treatment of genetic disorders."

"Thank you for the Biochemistry lesson, Dr Phocos" said the President impatiently "but what is it that you actually have in mind?"

"Well, having outlined for you what we are currently capable of, I come to what we actually propose in relation to the Planet Earth project. It is that once we have established good relations with the people of Earth we should ask the governments of certain specific countries, countries chosen on the basis of historical artistic achievement, to supply us with cell samples of a selection of their population. Not just of their known artistic achievers, although some of these should be included, but from the population at large, because it is likely that the genes for artistic ability are widely distributed. Cell samples could typically be harvested with a small swab from the inside of the mouth or could be a drop of blood from a pinprick. These samples will be analysed in a purpose-built laboratory in our spaceship. We now have the technology to carry out a complete analysis of every chromosome within the cells. This means not only determining the DNA base sequence in every gene, but also in what order the genes are arranged along each chromosome. The people of Earth have 23 pairs of chromosomes in their cells, just as we do and in the way I have outlined we arrive at a complete record of all the nuclear genetic information, and how it is distributed amongst their chromosomes, for every human from whom we have received a cell sample. Needless to say, all these enormously detailed analyses are entirely automated. Our technicians on the ship simply have to feed each suitably prepared sample into the machine."

"What about the chromosome proteins?" asked the Science Councillor. "Don't you have to analyse those as well?"

"The chromosome proteins present no problem" replied Dr Phocos. "For the benefit of Council members, I should explain that the DNA strand is negatively charged and it is held in the chromosome by binding with histone proteins which are positively charged. There are essentially just four kinds of histone protein and they are the same in every chromosome and so determination of their structures is a very minor part of the total analysis."

"So" continued Dr Phocos, "when our analyses are complete we will have the complete genetic information of some thousands of Earth people. And this information will, of course, be in digital form. What we then do is send this information, in some suitable radio waveband, back to our own planet, Omnos.

Now, Councillors, not only do we have the ability to completely determine the nuclear genetic information in any individual, but once we are provided with that information we have the technology to use it to construct a new nucleus. For each gene, once we receive the DNA base sequence, we then synthesize a DNA copy of that gene. The DNA strands are then wrapped around histone proteins to make what are called nucleosomes. A number of these, like beads on a string, a DNA strand being the string, constitute the reconstructed gene which we can then attach to the appropriate point on the chromosome protein core."

"Are you going to have to construct Earth histone proteins as well?" asked the Science Councillor.

CHAPTER 10

"No. We can use our own Omnian histone proteins. They are very similar to the Earth ones and will work just as well. And when we have done this for all the genes belonging on that chromosome we now have a complete new chromosome. As each chromosome is completed it is inserted inside a nuclear membrane. We obtain this by simply taking one of our own cells and removing the chromosomes from within the nucleus. We then have an empty nuclear membrane sac into which we can insert the new chromosomes as, one by one, we construct them. And then finally we have a fully functional, genetically complete nucleus already containing the biochemical machinery for transcribing the DNA into RNA which, in the manner I referred to earlier, is then used for making the proteins of the living cell. This Earth human nucleus is now inside one of our own Omnian cells which can then go to grow, divide and differentiate in a normal manner. All this very complicated process is, of course, entirely automated."

"That's enough detail, Dr Phocos" said the President, irritably. "Just give us the essentials"

"Oh, all right" replied Phocos. "I'll keep it simple."

"More condescension!" thought the President.

"In summary" said Phocos "the sequence is as follows. Nuclei are collected from human individuals on Earth. These are completely analysed on our ship. The resulting information in digital form is sent to Omnos. Here we use this information to reconstruct fully functional human nuclei. Each of those nuclei thus contains all the genetic information of that specific human person who provided it in the first place."

"But what about the human mitochondria?" asked the Spaceflight Councillor. "They contain their own DNA. Don't you have to analyse that as well?"

"No" replied Phocos. "We are confident that the mitochondria do not contain any of the genes determining creativity. Their only function is to provide energy for the cell. When we reconstitute human cells the mitochondria from our own cells will do perfectly well. Any more questions on this first stage of the project? If not, then I will continue to Stage Two.

What I have described to you so far has all been essentially straightforward, although very advanced – I might say, state of the art - genetic engineering. This, we are confident we can carry out. We already do this kind of thing with domestic animals. The second stage of the project, although it includes a scientific component, has major psychological and social implications which go well beyond the laboratory sciences. My colleague, Dr Janno Allti" he said, turning to a young woman sitting next to him "will explain this to you."

"The stage magician introduces his pretty assistant" thought the President sourly to himself. "Hmm, she is actually quite pretty" noticing her luxuriant curly brown hair, regular features and well-formed figure as she rose to her feet and walked to the lectern. She looked directly at him and allowed a faint but unmistakable smile to flicker across her face.

"Not above using a bit of feminine charm, either" he thought.

"Well ... er ... Dr Allti. Please tell the Council about the second stage of the project"

"Ooh, I had a narrow escape there!" he thought. "I nearly addressed her as 'My dear'. That wouldn't do. These young women don't like that sort of thing at all."

"Council members" she began, speaking confidently, but without any of the arrogance exhibited by her male colleague. "By the time the first stage of this project is completed we will have, here on Omnos, living cells genetically derived from thousands of selected Earth Planet humans. What we want to do is to use these cells to create a corresponding number of Omnian people each of whom will carry the genes from one of the chosen Earth individuals. In each case we will select one healthy cell from the cells we have in tissue culture and use an appropriate hormone treatment to convert that cell into an embryonic cell. In effect we can make it equivalent to a fertilized egg cell. After about 30 hours, suspended in a suitable medium, this cell will divide into two. Division will continue and by the end of three days this proto-embryo will be made up of 16 cells. At this stage it can be transplanted into the lining of a uterus and if all goes well it will there continue dividing and differentiating until by 9 months it is a fully developed baby, ready to be born."

"But into whose uterus?" asked a female member of the Council.

"Yes. That is indeed a difficult question. How do we find the thousands of uteruses, which of course means thousands of willing women, in which to implant these little Earth humans? Furthermore, assuming that problem is solved and that the appropriate number of births take place, then we will have brought into existence thousands of new Omnian citizens, each carrying a unique genetic inheritance from a member of a specific ethnic and cultural Earth community. How then are these children best to be reared in order to elicit the particular creative potential of the Earth genetic and cultural populations from which they originate? In addressing these questions we leave the world of Genetic Engineering and enter the world of Social Engineering."

After a short period of silence, the President of the Council spoke.

"These are indeed very difficult, but not necessarily unanswerable questions. I think it would be unwise to try and come up with answers now without a great deal of further reflection. When we have done that we will reconvene and address these matters in depth. I will ask each member of the Council in the meantime to discuss the proposals we have heard today with their own teams, consulting widely with outside experts if necessary. At our next meeting we can have an informed discussion and decide how we are to proceed. Thank you Dr Phocos and Dr Allti. You have given us a great deal to think about. We may well call on your expertise again."

"Well, Janno. That seemed to go quite well" said Phocos to his colleague as they left the room. "I saw you making eyes at the President. That probably helped."

"I did no such thing" she responded indignantly.

"Oh, I think you did" he said, laughing. "But never mind. It did us no harm."

Chapter 11

***Tom's first year at Cambridge**. Rich social life, college rowing club, joins jazz band. Meets Australian friend, Mick Hennessy. Tom performs poorly in first year exams. Nearly loses the option of being allowed to do Physics Part II, a necessary gateway to a Physics Ph D. Narrow escape teaches him a lesson. Resolves to work hard from now on.*

On a day at the beginning of October Tom took the train to Cambridge to begin his first year at the University. Arriving at Saviour College with his cases, he presented himself at the College Porters Lodge within the College Gatehouse. The Head Porter and one other porter were in attendance, both wearing black bowler hats.

"And who might you be, Sir?" said the Head Porter, addressing Tom in somewhat severe tones.

"My name is Tom Glennon. I am coming up to the University for the first time and I have a place at Saviour College."

"Indeed, Sir. Let me see." He glanced through a list on the desk in front of him.

"So you do, Sir. So you do" he said looking up at Tom again. "Welcome to Saviour College. I am the Head Porter, Mr Bates, and this is one of my assistants, Mr Crowther."

"Hi" said Tom. Mr Crowther grunted in acknowledgement.

"I see that you are a Scholar, Sir" continued the Head Porter "and so as such you will have the good fortune to be able to stay in College for your full three years. Your rooms are Number 2 in the Dirac building - one of our more recently constructed student accommodation - in Chapel Court. If you go through the archway on the other side of this court, which we call First Court" – Tom looked around at the mixture of 16th and 17th century pleasing reddish-brown brick buildings which made up the rectangular court, with green lawns in the centre, to which the Gatehouse gave entrance and saw an archway on the far side – "you will see the Dirac building on your right."

On the wall behind the Head Porter's desk there was a board covered with numbered hooks, each with a key. He removed one of these and handed it to Tom.

"Here is the key to your rooms Mr Glennon. As you cross the Court, please do not walk on the lawn. That is a privilege reserved for Fellows of the College"

"Thank you" said Tom and set off with his luggage on the path around the lawn. That the building he was going to be living in was named after Paul Dirac, one of the great 20th century theoretical physicists seemed to him, given his own interest in Physics, to be a good omen. Emerging through the far archway he saw that he was now in a court of similar size to the first, enclosed within three-storey buildings of student accommodation. Having an amateur interest in the architecture of earlier centuries Tom noted that on three sides the buildings were a pleasing mix of 18th-century and mid-19th Victorian Gothic. The right-hand side of the court, however, was of mid-20th century construction. He would have preferred Georgian but conceded that the design was pleasing enough. The open entrance gave access to a wide hallway leading to a corridor extending to the right and to the left. Number 2 was at the end of the left-hand arm.

CHAPTER 11

On opening the door, Tom found a generously sized study with a desk facing the window which looked out onto the Master's garden. There was also an old settee which some previous inhabitant had left behind. There was a small attached kitchenette with a washbasin and a fridge, kettle, toaster, microwave, and electric hob. There was a small adjoining bedroom with a single bed already made up. "This" said Tom to himself "will do me very well."

He remembered that undergraduates had to wear gowns at Dinner in Hall and when out in the town in the evening. Having stowed his luggage he set off for the town to find a shop where they sold second-hand student gowns. That evening he sat down to his first dinner as a Cambridge undergraduate in the Saviour College Hall with its high vaulted ceiling and wood-panelled walls hung with portraits of previous Masters of the College. The Hall was not full as only the new undergraduates, the freshmen, had arrived so far. The second and third year students were due to come on the following day. Seated on his left Tom saw a tall, rangy, youth with a shock of unruly dark hair, a fair but weather-beaten countenance and an open, cheerful demeanour.

"Hi" said Tom. "I'm Tom Glennon"

"G'Dye" said his neighbour, loudly and cheerfully. "Air yer gowin'. I'm Mick. Mick Hennessy."

Tom was momentarily thrown by this address but then realised that what he was hearing was, not just an Australian accent, but a particularly strong one, and what his neighbour had actually said was "Good Day. How are you going?". He noticed some of the other undergraduates within earshot glancing at each other with faintly supercilious smiles. As something of an outsider himself in English society he immediately felt solidarity with the tall Australian boy.

"I'm going fine, Mick. And yourself?"

"Good, myte. Real good".

You're Australian I assume?"

"Yes, I suppose that's fairly obvious" replied Mick with a cheerful grin.

"Whereabouts in Australia are you from?"

"Some distance inland from Coonabarabran in New South Wales. My parents have a farm."

As a farm boy himself, Tom was immediately interested.

"What kind of a farm?"

"Grazing. Mainly sheep. Some cattle. We occasionally sow a wheat or canola crop if the rainfall has been good."

"How big is your farm?"

"Oh, not very" said Mick, apologetically. "Only about three thousand hectares."

"Three thousand hectares. That's seven and a half thousand acres!" exclaimed Tom, mentally comparing it with the small family farms amongst which he grew up in the West of Ireland. "Sounds very big to me."

"It's nothing special in our part of Australia" said Mick. "But of course it is much lower density farming than you have out here. Much lower rainfall for a start."

"What are you here to study, or to 'read' as they say here?" asked Tom.

"Science" said Mick. "Physics mainly. I want to become a physicist."

"Same here" said Tom. "We'll probably be going to some of the same lectures."

The following day Tom had an appointment to see the Dean of the Chapel, the Reverend Dr Peregrine Corbyn-Heathcote. Turning up at the Dean's office at the appointed time he knocked on the door.

"Come in."

CHAPTER 11

He entered to be confronted with a tall, austere man, in clerical garb, seated behind a desk. The man looked down at a list on his desk and then up at Tom for a moment or two with a severe and penetrating gaze.

"You must be Mr Glennon."

"Yes" said Tom.

"Sit down, please, Mr Glennon."

Tom sat down in one of the upright wooden chairs in front of the desk.

"You are one of this year's Scholarship winners, I see, Mr Glennon."

"Er... Yes. I suppose I am"

"And you will be reading Science."

"Yes."

"Now, tell me Mr Glennon. Will we be seeing you at our services in the College Chapel?"

"Well...No" said Tom.

"Are you not a believer, then?"

"Indeed I am a believer" said Tom, stoutly, "but I am a Catholic, not an Anglican."

"Ah. I see. Which school?" asked the Dean. "Downside, Stonyhurst, Ampleforth?" naming the three best-known Catholic 'public' (i.e. private, fee-paying) schools.

"None of those" said Tom. "I was at St Thomas Aquinas Academy, in Manchester. It is a Catholic selective school."

"Indeed" said the Dean. "I can't say I have heard of it, but for you to get a College Scholarship they must have given you a good education. Perhaps we'll be getting some more boys from there in the future" he added thoughtfully.

"Well, Tom Glennon" said the Dean, now speaking in more friendly tones "while I am sorry we won't be seeing you in the College Chapel, no doubt you will make your arrival known at the Catholic Chaplaincy in Fisher House. It remains only for me to say – Welcome to Saviour College – and while we are in different branches of the Christian Communion, remember that I am here for all students to talk about any aspects of religion or spirituality at any time."

He rose to his feet, came out from behind the desk and shook Tom firmly by the hand before ushering him to the door.

At Saviour, as in the other Cambridge colleges, every undergraduate was provided with a Tutor. This would be one of the College Fellows whose role was to provide all-round pastoral support, information, advice and guidance to the student. In short, to generally keep an eye on him. More often than not the Tutor would be an academic in some discipline other than the one the student himself was studying. Tom's Tutor was a Mr Rossborough, a Senior Lecturer in the English Department. Tom was summoned to make himself known to Mr Rossborough on his first day in College.

"So, you are Tom Glennon" said Mr Rossborough. "Have a seat, Tom."

Tom was relieved to observe that Mr Rossborough had, like himself, something of a North of England accent. In a friendly way he asked Tom about himself, his family, his schooling, his interests.

"Well Tom" he said, finally. "You have an excellent academic track record so far. We expect great things of you. You and I will be having occasional chats on how you are getting on here at the university."

Other College fellows were Tom's supervisors in Physics, Chemistry and Mathematics, the three Major subjects he had chosen for Part I of the Natural Sciences Tripos. With these he had direct person-to-person tutorials, sometimes with one or two other students, sometimes on his own. His Physics supervisor, Dr

CHAPTER 11

David Walkinshaw, still quite young but already with an established reputation, was Tom's favourite: he never bothered to set assignments but always had interesting Physics topics to talk about.

In the first weeks of term, Tom and the other 'freshers' were bombarded with invitations to join a wide variety of clubs and societies or to take part in this or that activity. In addition to becoming a physicist, Tom hoped to actually enjoy his time at Cambridge and so was open to engaging in a variety of non-academic pursuits. Saviour was one of the more prominent rowing colleges, with its own boathouse on the River Cam. Tom liked anything to do with boats and so joined the College Boat Club. He was a strongly built young man and was assigned to the Saviour Second boat, out of the five boats that the Club operated. This meant training on the river every afternoon but Tom did not mind that and it helped to keep him fit.

He also joined the University Jazz Club. He found a group which had formed a band and - even better - had persuaded one of the city pubs to let them perform there one night a week. The leader and organiser, Clive Deergold, was the clarinettist of the band. Tom offered his services as a pianist.

"It would be good to have a pianist" said Clive. "A piano is just the thing for laying down the chord sequences, but of course we'll have to audition you."

They found a piano not currently in use in a college Common Room. Clive had brought Reg, the band's trumpet player, along for the audition. Tom sat down and began with his version of the well-known 'Pine Top's Boogie', as performed by Pine Top Smith. He continued, imperfectly but vigorously, with Albert Ammons' 'Boogie Woogie Stomp' and then concluded with a couple of slower and reflective Jimmy Yancey tunes, 'East St Louis Blues' and 'State Street Special'.

"Sounds good" said Clive. "Let's see how you go with a chord sequence." He opened an exercise book he had brought with him and placed it on the piano music shelf. Tom saw that on each page there were three tunes, well-known traditional jazz standards. Under the name of each tune there were, set out like a table, three or four lines of capital letters - G, D, A etc., sometimes accompanied by a number, as in G7, or a subscript lower case m, as in Dm. He realised that each letter indicated the chord to be played for each bar of the music, such as a major chord or a seventh chord, or a minor chord based on the note indicated. He started playing one of the chord sequences, four beats to the bar, alternating left and right hands.

"Something like that?" he said.

"Yes. That would do" said Clive. "I'll be leading the band, so for each tune I will indicate the tempo at which it is to be played. I will first tap my foot twice, just to get your attention so to speak, and then I will tap four times at the required tempo and we immediately start."

"I see you've brought your clarinet" said Tom. "How about we have a go at a couple of tunes."

"OK" said Clive. "Let's do that. We'll do 'St Louis Blues' followed by 'When the Saints go marching in'. The chord sequences are on the pages in front of you."

He opened his instrument case, fitted the clarinet sections together and played a few experimental notes.

"Are you ready?"

"I am."

They played the tunes, the first one slowly, the second at a rapid pace.

"That went pretty well" said Clive. "What do you think, Reg?"

"Yes it did" said Reg. "Tom's got the hang of it already."

CHAPTER 11

"Well Tom" said Clive. "We'd be happy to have you as a member of our band. What do you say?"

"Glad to join" said Tom. "But I don't want to play only the chord sequences. As we play each tune I would like to have the occasional solo."

"Of course" said Clive. "We call ourselves 'The Uni Stompers'. We play every Tuesday night at the Touchstone pub in Marketplace Passage and we rehearse once a week on Monday afternoon in the Music practice room at my college where there is a piano. We'll start next Monday and you'll meet the rest of the band."

"OK" said Tom. "I'll see you there."

Tom hugely enjoyed his time with The Uni Stompers. He got on well with the other musicians and he enjoyed the atmosphere of the old pub where they played where there was always an audience of appreciative undergraduates. The Stompers also got the occasional gig playing for dances and Tom liked the interaction he could feel between the band and the dancers.

His relationship with the College Rowing Club was more problematic. The senior members of the club put on a special evening for all the new members at which these older undergraduates deliberately sought to make the new boys drunk by plying them with beer. Tom, who up to that point had rarely drunk alcohol, had no idea of his capacity and soon went over his limit. He weaved his way unsteadily back to his rooms in College feeling increasingly unwell and was catastrophically sick almost as soon as he stepped in the door. He collapsed onto his bed and lay there with his eyes closed and the whole room apparently going round and round. He woke up the next morning feeling very ill and found to his shame and embarrassment that his 'bedder', the woman who came each day to make beds and clean up in the college rooms, was dealing with his vomit of the night before.

He mumbled an apology to her before collapsing back onto the bed again.

Although this experience did not make him turn teetotal, it was a few years before Tom could bring himself to drink beer. The first taste brought back disagreeable memories. In time, however, the memories faded and he could drink beer again.

The rowing itself he enjoyed. Being out in the fresh air and on the water, pulling hard on an oar in unison with the rest of the crew and skimming along the river at a steady rate was very satisfying. In the first week in December, just after the end of the Michaelmas term the first race of the rowing season, the Fairbairn Cup, was held. This involved the time taken to row over a specified length of course. More interesting were the 'bump' races, which have evolved to take account of the fact that the River Cam is too narrow for boats to row abreast.

The boats all start in a line with a space of one and a half boat lengths between each boat. When the starter gun is fired all the boats begin rowing, and the aim is to catch up with the boat in front and bump it, i.e. make contact at any point, with it. When this happens the bumped boat is out of the race and has to pull over to the side so that the other boat can row through and start chasing the next boat, or try to keep ahead of a pursuer, as the case may be. Thus at the end of the day the order of boats along the river will have changed. The following day (the races take place over a few days) the boats begin in the order in which they ended up the day before. The boat which ends up at the front on the last day is 'head of the river'. In the following year the boats start in the same order as that in which they ended up the year before. The Lent bumps are held at the end of February/beginning of March. The Easter bumps are held in June.

Tom was rowing, 3 position, in the Saviour College 2nd boat. In that year the Lent Bumps were held in the last week in February.

CHAPTER 11

The weather was very cold, and there was snow everywhere on the ground. His boat had gone quite some distance when the boat behind caught up and bumped them. They were therefore out of the race and accordingly pulled in to the river bank to let the following boats through. So as to leave as much room for these boats, the four rowers on the river (as opposed to the bank) side of the boat drew their oars in as far as they could, and the Saviour oarsmen remained in their seats watching the boats go past. Unfortunately, as the oars on one side of the boat were drawn in, by pulling them up, but not out of the water, the boat rose on that side and went down on the other side. Engrossed as they were in the race they did not notice that the side of the boat adjoining the bank had actually gone below the river level. Water quietly started pouring in and suddenly they found the boat was sinking. All the oarsmen ended up in the water. Tom sank nearly to the bottom and looked up through green water towards the surface. The boys all quickly swam to the side and clambered out. Given the low water temperature, an air temperature at or below freezing, and the fact that their clothes were soaking wet, they were in some danger of hypothermia, but all they could do was to pull the boat out, empty it, set it up for rowing again, and as soon as the river was clear, set off back to the Saviour College boathouse.

Towards the end of the third, and last term of the university year, the Saviour College Boat Club held its annual dinner in the college hall. After the food and drinks there were speeches by the Captain of the Club and other officials. These were followed by songs of quite surprising and confronting vulgarity which to Tom's taste were unpleasant rather than amusing. A large Greetings card was circulated around the table for members to sign their names, possibly with jocular or other comments as they saw fit. When it came to Tom he duly signed his name, "Tom

Glennon", and passed it on. The card kept circulating and eventually came to Tom again. He had nothing to add but glancing at it before passing it on he saw that someone had scrawled, next to his name, "Who are you Glennon?" He was momentarily taken aback. What did they mean? And then the penny dropped. He was being put in his place. He was not one of the Public school boys who made up most of the Rowing Club membership. He was being reminded that he was not 'one of them'.

"No, indeed I'm not" thought Tom to himself. "And Thanks be to God for that."

As well as playing jazz with the Uni Stompers Tom had not forgotten his musical roots. He found a pub where there was an Irish music session every Friday night and took to going along there with his fiddle and joining in.

Despite all his extracurricular activities Tom had not forgotten why he had wanted to come to Cambridge in the first place. He still wanted to become a physicist. He attended his lectures, taking notes as appropriate, and his laboratory Practical classes in Physics and Chemistry. In the third term, however, when the time for the end of academic year examinations arrived, he realized with dismay that with the time he had spent on music, and on rowing and on generally socializing with his friends, he had not allowed enough time to prepare for them thoroughly. He knew, after the exams, that he had not performed as well as he should.

On his return to College after Christmas, in the third week in January, Tom received a message to see his Tutor, Mr Rossborough.

"Come in, Tom. Sit down. You have received your first year exam results now so perhaps you have some idea about why I want to talk to you."

"Well...yes. I suppose I do" said Tom, somewhat hesitantly.

CHAPTER 11

"Overall, you got a very low 2.2. In fact you came within a hair's breadth of getting a Third. When we discussed your courses when you first arrived, it was your stated intention to complete Part I of the Natural Sciences Tripos in two years and then proceed to a Part II in Physics, with the hope of doing well enough to go on to do a Ph. D. On the basis of your performance in the first-year exam I am afraid it does not look as if you would be able to achieve this. I am of the view that it would be better if you reconcile yourself to taking the full three years to do Part I of the Tripos. If you do, and achieve a reasonable class in the Final, third-year exam, say a good 2.2 or even a 2.1, then you will leave here with a good general Science degree. This would qualify you for all kinds of scientific careers - Science school teaching, the scientific civil service, or in industry or whatever.

I am sorry to have to say this, Tom, but your poor performance in the exam leaves me little option. Now go away and think about it and by all means come back and talk to me again if you think that would help.

All right?"

"Yes" said Tom, rising unsteadily to his feet. "Thank you." He left Mr Rossborough's study and wandered back to his rooms. He felt that he had received a hammer blow. If he couldn't take the Physics Part II Natural Sciences Tripos he could not do a Ph. D. Without a Ph. D., the first step on the scientific research ladder, he would never become the physicist that since his teen years he had so passionately wanted to be. His hopes were in ruins. And it was his own fault. He had freely and enthusiastically chosen to play in a jazz band. He had chosen to take up rowing and spend his afternoons on the river. He had chosen to spend so many of his evenings hanging out with friends. To have not allowed enough time to prepare for the exams was due to his own carelessness.

On his way back to his rooms he encountered his Australian friend, Mick Hennessy.

"Jeez mate what's the matter? You look real crook."

Tom told his story.

"That's seriously bad news" said Mick, who, having fewer distractions had done well in the First-Year exam and was on course to continue smoothly on his chosen academic trajectory.

"I was hoping you and I would be doing Part II Physics together."

Tom's life up to this time had had its ups and downs but nothing of this magnitude had ever hit him before. Although he was previously unaware of it he had an inbuilt propensity for depression and this event tipped him over into a significant episode. He was still in the grip of this when he went to his next Physics supervision with Dr Walkinshaw. Because of his lively mind and enthusiasm for the subject, Tom was one of Dr Walkinshaw's favourite students and he was concerned about this change in demeanour. There were no other students present so he took the liberty of asking .

"You don't seem to be your usual self today, Tom Glennon. Is there a problem?"

"I am afraid there is" said Tom. "I performed badly in the end-of-year exam and Mr Rossborough, my Tutor, thinks I am not good enough to complete the Part I in two years and then go on to the Part II. He thinks I should just settle for doing a three-year Part I. That would mean the end of my hope of doing a Ph. D. and going on to a research career in Physics."

"Why do you think you did so badly in the exam? Given your track record up to now you shouldn't have found the exam such a problem."

"Just too many other activities" said Tom despondently. "I rowed, I played in a jazz band, spent too much time chatting with my friends, and I just didn't allow enough time to prepare for the exam."

"I see" said Dr Walkinshaw, thoughtfully. He had already assessed Tom as being of exceptional promise and thought it would be a great pity if as a result of youthful misjudgements he was prevented from going on to do research in Physics.

"Look. I'll have a word with Mr Rossborough. I'll see if anything can be done. OK?"

"Oh yes. Thank you" said Tom fervently.

The next day Tom was again summoned to his Tutor's office.

"Sit down, Tom. I have been talking with your Physics supervisor, Dr Walkinshaw. He thinks that despite your lamentable performance in the first exam in your university career, you are in fact capable of going on to a research career in Physics. Are you?"

"Yes, Mr Rossborough. I believe I am."

"Hmm" said Rossborough, looking searchingly at Tom.

"I understand that you have been spending a lot of your time in extracurricular activities. You will really have to cut back on those if you are to be allowed to go on to a Physics Part II."

"I will" said Tom, fervently. "I will." resisting the temptation to say "Cross my heart and hope to die" as he might have said in his childhood days.

"Hmm" and then, after a prolonged pause "All right. You can set your sights on doing a Part II."

"Oh, thank you" said Tom.

"It's Dr Walkinshaw you should thank. He thinks you are capable of significant achievement in Physics. Don't disappoint him."

Tom left his Tutor's office buoyed up with an enormous sense of relief. So far as his scientific career was concerned he had been on the edge of falling over a cliff but had been saved at the last moment. He was now filled with grim determination. He was going to buckle down, work hard and get the Physics degree that would start him off on his longed for career as a research physicist. The next time he met Mick Hennessy he told him the good news.

"Well good on yer, Tom" said Mick, visibly delighted.

"We'll be doing Physics together after all."

Chapter 12

Tom's third, and final, *undergraduate year. The health of Róisín, his mother, takes a turn for the worse. Amongst his more arts-oriented circle of friends Tom meets Glenys. He falls painfully in love but she tells him she already has a boyfriend.*

Tom said a sad farewell to his fellow musicians in the Uni Stompers. They were sorry to lose him but as students themselves they well understood his reasons for leaving. On the other hand he had no regrets about leaving the Saviour College Rowing Club. For exercise he chose instead to go for long runs along the river towpath. These helped him to think about whatever aspect of Science he was dealing with at the moment. Every Sunday Tom went to mass as he had throughout his childhood. Quite apart from his religious beliefs it had not escaped him that in his present situation he needed all the help he could get. By preference he went to Our Lady and the English Martyrs, the large Catholic church on Hills Road, rather than to the University Catholic chaplaincy. He liked its Victorian Gothic architecture.

Tom continued to go to the pub Irish music sessions: these were a welcome break from his intense concentration on Physics, Chemistry and Mathematics during the day. Tom was now working very hard. In the second year exam he was awarded a 2.1, just a little short of a First. To his great relief this was good enough for him to proceed on to Part II of the Natural Sciences Tripos in Physics and he looked forward to his third academic year at Cambridge with keen anticipation.

Tom spent much of the Summer Vacation back in Connemara, enjoying being immersed once again in the farm activities. He also cycled and hiked around his beloved native countryside, and occasionally swam again in the cold but bracing Atlantic waters. It was good to be speaking nothing but Irish.

Back in Stockport before heading off to university at the beginning of October, he could not help noticing that Róisín, although still running the household, seemed to be less energetic than usual and to be thinner. As he travelled on the train back to Cambridge to begin his final year, his enthusiasm at the prospect of finally being able to concentrate on Physics was overlain by worry about his mother.

When Tom came home in March for the Easter vacation he was concerned to find that Róisín had just gone in to hospital.

"Things have taken a turn for the worse with your Mam, Tom" said Micheál. "It looks as if the cancer has got away from us. She is having chemotherapy now, but the doctors are not optimistic. We are visiting her every day. Let you now go in to see her yourself. She will love to see you."

Tom went in to his mother's ward in Stepping Hill Hospital and was shocked by her shrunken and wasted appearance.

"How are you, Mammy?"

"Not so good at the moment, Tom *a stór*. But Please God I'll get better soon."

"Well, let's hope so, Mammy. Let's hope so" said Tom without in his heart having any expectation that she would indeed get better.

"Are you in any pain?"

CHAPTER 12

"Oh no. Hardly at all now. They have grand pain-killers here in the hospital."

"Well that's good" said Tom. And they talked for a while about family matters, and he described to her how well he had seen things were looking back on the farm in Connemara during his holidays.

He kissed his mother and said goodbye, and left the hospital filled with foreboding.

In Cambridge, Tom got on well with his fellow science students. These for the most part were, like himself, clever boys from the provinces, with regional accents. It puzzled him sometimes that, despite their evident intelligence they did not seem very articulate and most of them appeared to have a limited range of interests. Tom, by contrast, in addition to having a wide knowledge of classical music as well as jazz, took a great interest in literature, including the moderns, and loved to talk about them with fellow enthusiasts. In another circle of acquaintance, however, he found more kindred spirits. Through his jazz band friends, none of whom happened to be scientists, he found himself mixing with Arts students, doing degrees in a variety of non-science subjects - Classics, Languages, History of Art, Architecture, Music, Philosophy. His free time in the evenings, when he was giving himself a break from study, was mainly spent in their company. Here he encountered more girls than amongst his Science friends. Also unlike the science girls, who generally wore 'sensible' clothes, some of the female members of his new circle of acquaintance chose to wear striking, even glamorous, apparel.

So far as girls were concerned Tom was inexperienced and naïve. He had not yet had a girlfriend. The only members of the opposite sex that he knew well were family members - his mother, his sisters, various female relations. Although highly articulate with, on a variety of subjects, well-formed opinions which he was not reluctant to express, when talking to girls at close quarters he felt ill at ease and never knew quite what to say. In an event which brought his deficiencies home to him, and which he sometimes remembered ruefully in later years, a young woman in the group, of striking appearance, very well and expensively dressed, and with a confident manner, having heard Tom hold forth in the group conversations, suddenly took a close interest in him. She sought him out and introduced herself. Tom, however, when confronted with this glamorous apparition at close quarters did not know how to cope, and stumbled in his responses. When she saw that the conversation was going nowhere she took pity on him and withdrew. He sometimes later thought to himself "If only I had been more confident with women, who knows where that might have led!"

There was another girl in the group with whom Tom felt more at ease. Glenys Bohm was of a little less than medium height, dark-haired, with a pale flawless complexion. Pleasantly attractive rather than being merely pretty, she was Jewish, her father a psychiatrist. She herself was studying psychology. Tom found her very easy and pleasant to talk to and tended to seek out her company when she was present in the group. As his final year progressed he found that she was occupying more and more of his thoughts, to such an extent eventually that he realized, to his dismay, that he had actually fallen in love. He believed that Glenys enjoyed his company but had no idea whether she felt anything more than that. Thoughts of her now occupied so much of his mind that he was finding it difficult to think clearly about Physics. He decided that the only thing for it was to make his feelings known and to ask if she would let him be her boyfriend.

Tom was by now so emotionally fraught that he could not trust himself to express what he felt for her coherently in spoken words. What he could do, however, was write, something for which he had a natural facility. Accordingly he sat down and composed a letter in which he described how his feelings for her had grown during the months of their acquaintanceship. That they had now reached an intensity such that he must declare himself to be desperately in love with her. And could she offer him any hope that his feelings might to any extent be reciprocated. He did not post this letter, but taking his courage in both hands he sought Glenys out, gave her the letter saying

"Glenys, could you please read this."

She took the letter, looking at him with some concern, as though to say – "Tom what is this?"

She read it carefully. Paused for a while and then read it again. She sat now for several moments with the letter in her hand and her eyes downcast. She then looked up at Tom, her expression being one of sympathy touched with sadness.

"Tom, Tom you know I like you. I really enjoy your company. I do. I am very flattered that your feelings for me have become so strong. But I have to tell you that I don't reciprocate them in the way that you would like. I don't want to hurt you but I must tell you the truth. And also I should tell you that I already have a boyfriend, of whom I am very fond. Ben and I have now been going out together for some time."

Tom knew Ben, one of the members of the social group, but had not been aware that he and Glenys were in a close relationship. He knew there was nothing more to be said. In a voice as steady as he could manage he said

"Thank you, Glenys. You were very kind" and turned and left without saying anything else.

▲

Chapter 13

***Tom is called urgently** back to Stockport where Róisín is in her last moments in hospital. Back in Cambridge, his mother's death combined with Glenys's rejection tip him over into deep depression. The final examination looms but Tom finds that he is not getting through his preparation fast enough. He prays in utter desperation. His prayer is answered. His mind starts working again. Final exam success.*

Walking back to his rooms feeling crushed after what was undoubtedly a rejection, he tried to come to terms with his situation. It was clear to him that so far as Glenys was concerned he must abandon all hope, and that he should indeed strive not to think about her at all. For a start he would cease associating with any social groups where he might meet her. In fact, given the imminency of his Final exam, he thought perhaps he had better stop socializing altogether and concentrate on preparing for it. He knew nevertheless that he had just suffered a major emotional body blow from which he would take some time to recover.

The Physics Part II final examinations were at the end of the Easter term, some weeks ahead. Tom had worked hard during his third year. He had attended his lectures, laboratory experiments and tutorials, consulted the prescribed textbooks, read certain key scientific papers and on the basis of all this had systematically constructed a set of revision notes covering his course, which he proposed to go through intensively in the four weeks preceding the exams. On the basis of his previous experience of preparing for examinations he was confident that his estimate of the length of time required for this final revision and memorization was just about right.

Although he knew that his revision material was well prepared and suited for his purpose, his rejection by Glenys had left him feeling damaged and disheartened and he did not feel up to starting his final exam preparation yet. Another blow then followed. He received a message from the College office saying that his father had phoned and that he was to go home straight away.

Tom immediately caught the next train North from Cambridge station. When he arrived home he found one of his sisters, Aoife, waiting for him.

"We must go straight to the hospital, Tom. Mam is nearing the end."

They took a taxi to Stepping Hill hospital and went up to the single room to which their mother had now been transferred. There they found Micheál and Gráinne sitting on either side of the bed where Róisín lay, apparently asleep but with her eyes occasionally flickering open.

"Thank God you're here just in time, Tom" said Micheál. "Mam will very soon be gone from us. The priest came earlier and gave her the last rites." His voice was unsteady and it was clear that he had been weeping.

"What I would like now is that each of us on our own spends a short time with Mam to say our goodbyes while the others wait outside. We'll then come back in here and be all together." And so one by one, Micheál, Tom, Gráinne, Aoife, spent a few minutes with Róisín holding her hand and telling her they loved her. They reassembled and sat down around the bed and Micheál held his beloved wife's hand.

The family did not have long to wait. Róisín appeared to sink into a deep sleep. Her breathing became slower and fainter until, suddenly, it stopped. After a few moments of stillness and silence, Micheál spoke.

"She's gone. She's gone. Your Mam, my Róisín, has now left us." His voice broke and great sobs burst forth. The girls, also weeping, went to put their arms around their father. Tom, despite his best efforts to not give way, found himself weeping as well.

After a few minutes the first intense emotions subsided to the extent that Micheál was able to speak.

"Well now children, we must get a grip on ourselves. There are things to be done, arrangements to make. We will tell the nurse that Róisín has died. I will phone the undertaker and they will come and take her away and prepare her for the funeral. I've already forewarned the parish priest that we would like to have a Requiem Mass for your Mam when the time came and he was happy to say one for her."

Róisín's Requiem Mass in the parish church was well attended. In addition to members of the Irish community there were other friends she had made in the parish. At the cemetery, however, attendance was limited to family members, some of whom came over from Ireland, and a few close friends. As the coffin was lowered into the grave Tom thought what a pity it was that his mother was not being buried in the company of her ancestors in the graveyard of Kilcarra church back in Connemara. But it was not to be.

"Oh well" thought Tom to himself. "We have thrown in our lot with this country now so we must expect to be buried here."

After the funeral Tom went straight back to Cambridge to complete his final, and crucially important, university term. But, arriving back at his rooms he felt very low in spirit. His mother's death combined with his rejection by Glenys had tipped him over once more into depression. He got out his carefully prepared revision notes and realized that he now had just about enough time left to get through them before the Final set of examinations. He set to work but found to his dismay that his mind, normally so clear on anything to do with Physics, was just not functioning with anything like its normal intensity and the revision was proceeding very slowly. After two days it became obvious that at his present rate of working he simply could not complete his revision before the Part II Final exams. While it was unlikely that he would fail altogether, there was no way he would get the First class, or good 2.1 degree, that he would need to be accepted for the Part III Physics year and then on to do a Ph. D. and realise his passionate vocation to be a research physicist.

This prospect was devastating. Tom knew that he had it in him to be certainly a good, perhaps even a very good, scientist. But it seemed that despite his abilities, despite his all his hard work and thorough preparation, he was going to falter at the last hurdle. It would all be taken from him. Like other Catholic children, Tom had been brought up to say his prayers every night before going to bed, and this was a practice he had maintained. That night, on his knees at his bedside, he prayed as he had never prayed before. He prayed in utter desperation, from a depth of desolation he had not previously experienced. He knew that help from God was now his only hope.

"God – I can't do this alone. Please help me" was his final desperate prayer.

Despite his turmoil he slept well. After breakfast he sat down at the table where his revision notes were laid out and once again started the process of reading, understanding and memorizing their content, beginning from the point he had reached the day before. But now something had changed. He found that he was no longer having to force himself to think, to push through a fog of depression. His mind was clear, as clear as it had ever been. He found himself proceeding through his revision material steadily and efficiently. The following day was the same, and the day after. It became clear to him that at the rate he was now working he would have comprehensively completed his revision by the time the exams commenced. He would be ready for the challenge.

How had this come about? This overnight transformation. Was it God's response to the utter desperation of his prayer? To his recognition, his acknowledgement, that nothing else could save him? To his *De profundis clamavi ad te, Domine* (Out of the depths I have cried to thee O Lord)? No other plausible explanation suggested itself. Yes, this was a gift. Undeserved, but - Oh he was grateful. The phrase "Thanks be to God" is of frequent occurrence in Irish speech. When Tom used it now, he meant it.

His Part II Physics examinations began towards the end of May – eight separate 2-hour exams over a 10 day period. Despite all his preparation Tom did not find the exams easy, but none of it was beyond his capabilities. The standard questions consisted of bookwork material followed by a problem to be solved. These he coped with entirely competently, although there were a few problems which he realized he had not got quite right. But in addition there were Essay questions each of which required a full length treatment of some specified topic. Fortunately some of these happened to be on areas of Physics in which Tom had already taken a particular interest and he was able to indulge himself, writing in a lively manner about some of the scientific bees in his bonnet. Where he thought it appropriate, he did not hesitate politely to disagree with some of the accepted interpretations. One of the Essay questions in particular – "Discuss to what extent hidden-variable theories are a legitimate counter to the fundamentally indeterminist view of physical reality currently accepted in Quantum Mechanics" – was right up Tom's street and he responded enthusiastically and at length.

When the exam ordeal was finally over Tom felt that overall he had acquitted himself well. That night when he went in to the Saviour College Hall for Dinner on his last night before going home for the Summer vacation, he sat down next to his Australian friend, Mick Hennessy.

"G'Dye Tom. Air d'yer gow?" which Tom understood as "Good Day, Tom. How did you go?", the question referring to the Physics Part II Final exams which they had both now completed. Some of Mick's exam papers had differed from Tom's since in choosing his units for the year, he had opted for more Experimental Physics than Tom.

"I think on the whole I did OK" said Tom. I may have fluffed a couple of the problems, but generally OK. How about you?"

"Yair. Much the syme, myte" said Mick, on whose Australian accent three years in Cambridge had had no effect.

"I reckon we'll both be back next year for Part III. Whadaya think?"

"I'd say we are in with a chance" more cautiously responded Tom. Of Mick's success he had no doubt. He knew his friend, despite his, perhaps deliberately rough-hewn manner, to be both well organized and of exceptionally high intelligence.

Back home in Stockport, Tom spent a few weeks earning money labouring in the family building business to generate the funds for a short holiday in France before heading off for his usual Summer sojourn on the farm in Connemara. Just before he was due to set off to the Continent a letter arrived addressed to him, from the University of Cambridge.

"This must be my exam results."

With trepidation he slit open the envelope and drew out the letter. Yes! He had been awarded a First! Now he could safely proceed to a year of Part III Physics, and provided he performed well, could then go on to a Ph. D. and begin at last his hoped-for career as a research physicist.

Chapter 14

***Omnos Planetary Council** reconvenes to discuss the Earth population recreation project. To maximise the probability of capturing Earth artistic abilities it is proposed to create three distinct populations, corresponding to the East Asian, African and Caucasian peoples of that planet. It is decided that the project will proceed.*

The President looked around at the Planetary Council, reconvened a hundred days after its previous meeting.

"You will recall, Council members, that at our last meeting we identified two major problems to be addressed if the genetic transplantation part of our Planet Earth Project is to succeed, and indeed if it is to go ahead at all. The first is to find the large number of Omnian women who would be willing to bear all the babies carrying Earth peoples' genetics. The second problem is how to rear these children in such a way that each of them incorporates, and thus becomes eventually able to express, their specific cultural inheritance. So far as this Council is concerned, the primary responsibility for addressing these questions falls to the Social and Demographic Councillor and his team, but I asked all of you to give these matters your best consideration and pass your contributions on to the Social and Demographic people. This I understand you have now done and on the basis of your various contributions, and their own detailed consideration of these matters, the team has now put together concrete proposals which they believe could satisfactorily address these problems and which the Councillor will now outline for us. Councillor?"

The Social and Demographic Councillor rose to his feet.

"Fellow Councillors. You will now have access on your screens to a detailed account of what we propose. I would like, nevertheless, to summarize the essentials for you now so that we may discuss it. The first problem, how to find the mothers we need, we believe is soluble. Since we made the existence of Planet Earth, and its variety of populations and cultures, known to our own people, there has been enormous interest. The Omnians just can't get enough of Planet Earth, especially its music, literature, television series, paintings, sculpture, whatever. Once we announce we are looking for mothers to bear and bring up Earth babies we are confident our program will in fact be oversubscribed. Merely wanting to bear an Earth baby will of course not in itself be a sufficient qualification for a woman to enter our program. We have requirements which must be met. To begin with, since children do better when reared by a father as well as a mother, the woman must already be in a stable relationship with a man. This means that we will be selecting not so much individual women, but couples. And obviously the man as well as the woman must be enthusiastic about rearing an Earth baby. We will be looking for young couples who have not yet had children. To be rearing an Earth child at the same time as rearing their own Omnian children we think would be too complicated.

The second problem, how to rear these children in such a way that they effortlessly express their specific Earth cultural inheritance, is much more difficult. Before we start designing what we might call the child-rearing programs, we have to decide from which ethnic/cultural groups on Earth we will choose to obtain the requisite genetic material. You will no doubt all by now have acquired some understanding of the racial complexity of the earth population. We cannot possibly cover all the groups and subgroups. To keep our whole project manageable we are of the view that we should restrict our selection to just three of the major genetically and culturally distinguishable Earth populations. The three we have chosen are Caucasian/European, African and East Asians. Each of these major groups is comprised of a large number of subgroups. So it was necessary in each case in each case to identify a subgroup which is culturally active and of reasonable genetic homogeneity.

Selection of suitable Earth source populations for the genetic transplantation part of the Planet Earth Project has now been carried out. You will find an account of the specific genetic subgroups chosen, and the reasons for their selection, in the document headed, "Selection of Earth Populations for Genetic Transplantation" with copies of which you have all been provided.

Selection of Earth Populations for Genetic Transplantation

East Asia

The East Asian subgroup chosen are the people of Japan. For our purposes they have a number of things to recommend them. The first is that Japan itself is geographically isolated, consisting as it does of one major island with three smaller, closely contiguous islands. In addition, for a long period, ending only in the mid 19th Earth century, the reigning government chose also to remain politically isolated and prohibited contact with peoples of other nations. For these two reasons the Japanese population is ethnically and culturally highly homogeneous, more so than other East Asian subgroups. Their main qualification, however, is their very high standard of visual aesthetics, widely admired by cultured Earth people of other nations. Over the centuries this has been expressed in paintings on hanging scrolls, folded screens and sliding doors as well as in wood-block prints. Also in patterns on textiles and in flower arrangement. Their pottery is also known for its combination of simplicity and elegance and the same is true for Japanese garden design.

The Japanese also have a rich musical tradition played on a variety of indigenous instruments: wind – different kinds of flutes, stringed – predominantly plucked rather than bowed, percussion – drums of all sizes and wooden clappers. However, it must be said that Japanese traditional music is almost entirely for home consumption. It has not proved particularly popular outside Japan.

Japan also has an ancient literary tradition, dating back to the 7th century of what on Earth is called the Common Era. There is a highly prestigious international literary prize, referred to as the Nobel Prize for Literature which was established in Earth year 1901. It is awarded, not for an individual work but for a lifetime contribution to Literature. Three Japanese authors have won it, which tells us that, notwithstanding its ancient origins, Japanese literature is alive and well and of a high standard today.

Africa

Choosing a suitable subgroup to represent Africa was particularly problematic. This is because of the enormous variability of the subgroups within the very large African continent. As is well known to plant breeders, if the maximum genetic variability in any species is sought it will be found in that region where the species originated. And this is true of the people of Earth as well. *Homo sapiens* originated in Africa and the peoples of that continent exhibit much more variability than the human populations in other regions of the planet. Most of the African subgroups have an orally transmitted, but not a written, literature. Everywhere, however, there are rich musical traditions so it was decided to make music the main criterion for choice. The subgroup chosen is the people of Mali. The Republic of Mali is a large but sparsely populated country in the Western part of the African continent. It is ethnically diverse with numerous different tribes, but the Mande people make up about 50% of the population and so to limit heterogeneity it is proposed to seek our genetic source material from them. They have a rich store of traditional music, consisting mainly of songs, and they have developed their own native instruments – plucked strings, xylophones and drums. Interestingly, Malian music is quite well known and popular outside the African continent.

Mali's literary tradition is largely oral rather than written and is mediated by singers known as *jalis* who recite or sing histories and stories from memory. Nevertheless, in the present day there are Malian novelists whose works are printed in the conventional manner. They commonly write in the French language. Mali was for a time a colony of the European country France and their educated classes have French as a second language.

Caucasian/European

In all European subgroups music is important and indeed is considered to be a central element of European culture. The musical profession is highly respected although not always well remunerated. Professional musicians perform predominantly the works of highly respected orchestral composers, mainly from the past. There are also many musicians, of varying levels of competence, who perform the current popular music. What we are looking for, however, is a subgroup in which there is a substantial body of traditional indigenous music which is still actively performed. To help us in this search we investigated what kinds of music are performed in public houses and taverns, that is to say places where alcoholic liquor is sold and consumed and people congregate. Current popular music is frequently performed as you might expect but in various places around the planet, particularly in the major cities, here and there we found what are referred to as "Irish pub sessions".

Ireland is an island on the north western fringe of the European continent. Its total population is about 7 million, 5 million in what is known as the Irish Republic, constituting about 80% of the landmass, and 2 million in what is known as Northern Ireland, politically part of the larger island of Britain, situated to the east of Ireland. The land is organised into 32 counties, 26 in the Republic, 6 in Northern Ireland.

The Irish are one of the Celtic peoples of Europe. The Celts as they are called used to be found over much of northern Europe but now, in what we might call their purest form, are to be found in Ireland, in Wales - an area in the West of Britain, and in Brittany, a peninsula on the north-west coast of France, one of the major countries of the European continent. Celtic peoples generally have a reputation for musicality and each of the three kinds of Celt that I have referred to has their own native music. What distinguishes Irish music is that it has been taken up with enthusiasm by musicians in other European countries. Irish music takes two forms. There are the songs, or 'airs' as they are sometimes called, frequently sad, many of great beauty. Then there are the dance tunes, which in their origin are meant to be danced to. There are very many of these, perhaps thousands. They have a variety of time signatures, each corresponding to a different kind of dance. Jigs for example are in 6/8 time. Reels are in 4/4 time. Although this is what you might call functional music, intended for dancing, it includes a very large number of very pleasing melodies which musicians - let us say on the violin, flute, accordion etc. - greatly enjoy playing, especially in an ensemble with other musicians. And this it seems is what has given rise to the Irish pub sessions. Musicians who like to play this kind of music simply come together informally in any pub that is happy to have them and they just play whatever Irish tunes take their fancy on that particular evening. The supply of tunes is effectively unlimited and so what tunes actually get played are simply those which happen to emerge in the musicians' memories at the time. They do not normally play from printed music.

Most of the musicians playing in Irish pub sessions in the various European cities and also cities in other continents - North America, Australia, Japan - are not themselves of Irish nationality although some may be of Irish descent. It seems that this music has a universal appeal to many musicians regardless of their ethnic origins.

Back in its country of origin, Ireland, this music, under the general name of "Irish Traditional Music" is taken very seriously and is actively performed. To maintain standards there are regular national and local festivals, under the name *fleá cheoil* (music festival) at which individual musicians, and also groups of musicians compete, as well as performing for the general public. There are also international summer schools in Irish traditional music to which musicians come from all over the world. And there are numerous Irish traditional music groups which take the music to perform on concert stages in other countries.

In addition to music, Ireland also has a substantial literary tradition.

The very earliest literature can be traced back to about the sixth century of the Earth Common Era. Literature in the native Gaelic language, and to some extent in Latin, the European lingua franca, flourished up to about the 17th century CE. There was in fact a professional class of poets, known as *filí*. But in that same century traditional Gaelic society was finally destroyed by invading armies from Britain and from that time on Irish literature was mainly written in English. Even in English, however, it continued to flourish and in modern times the Nobel prize for literature has been awarded to Irish writers no less than four times.

And finally, another promising feature of this subgroup is that we can identify areas within their country which are ethnically homogeneous, or nearly so. Associated with invasion and military conquest there has been, as you might expect, over the centuries a substantial movement of people from Britain to Ireland and as the result of intermarriage many people in that country are of mixed origin. But genetic studies have shown that has you move West across the island the British contribution becomes less and less. So much so that in the Western regions of the country the people are predominantly of native Irish, Celtic, origin. Interestingly, while the traditional music is played in all parts of the country it is in the Western counties of Donegal, Sligo, Mayo, Galway, Clare and Kerry that it is strongest. So, on the grounds of ethnic homogeneity, it is from these Western regions that our human genetic material would be sourced.

CHAPTER 14

So councillors. On the grounds outlined in this document, our final selection for the three Earth subgroups on which to base our genetic transplant project are Japan, Mali and Ireland. In the case of the Mali genetic transplantation, the Omnian parental couples will be selected from amongst our own tropical equatorial population because they have dark skins as do the people of Mali on Earth."

"Thank you Social and Demographic Councillor" said the President. "You and your team have performed the task we assigned to you in a very thorough and professional manner. But before this Council finally accepts your recommendations we should discuss it a bit further. Councillors?"

"Yes, I have a question" said the Science Councillor. "Did you at any point consider the Jews as has one of your subgroups. My reading around the background documentation tells me that they have made major contributions to Music, both as performers and composers. There are also highly regarded Jewish writers."

"We did indeed consider the Jews" said the Social and Demographic Councillor. "Particularly because of their contribution to Music. But we had to rule them out on the basis of ethnic heterogeneity. There are many different ethnic groups all identifying as Jews. Even when we try to zero in on one of these groups we find further heterogeneity. The original Jews were Iron age Semitic people originating in what is known as the Middle East. But DNA analysis has shown that 65 to 81% of the mitochondrial DNA of the Ashkenazi Jews of Europe - culturally the most important subset of these people - is of European origin. And it is no use going back to the modern state of Israel, which identifies itself as the Jewish state, and which is located in that part of the Middle East where the Jews originated, because there the population is genetically more mixed than ever.

"It seems to me" said the Social and Emotional Affairs Councillor "that once we arrive on Earth and make our plans known, there will be disappointment amongst some of the other nations that they were not chosen for our project of recreating certain Earth populations on Omnos. Particularly in Europe, where every nation has a high regard for its own culture, will there be ill will towards Ireland because we have chosen it and not them?"

"This problem has occurred to us" said the Social and Demographic Councillor. "But there is no way of avoiding it. We believe that three Earth cultures is the maximum feasible for transplantation to our planet. Fortunately the Irish are generally popular within Europe with the possible exception of some people within Britain."

"Why is that?" said the President." Surely it should be the other way round. The British should be unpopular within Ireland because of their history of grievous oppression in that country. Given that the Irish have never oppressed Britain, why should they be unpopular within Britain?"

"Perhaps because it is always hard to forgive those you have wronged" said the Social and Demographic Councillor, sententiously.

The President looked at him suspiciously.

"Is that a piece of ancient wisdom, Councillor - or did you just make it up?"

"Oh, ancient wisdom I think" said the Social and Demographic Councillor, while thinking to himself "Perhaps I did just make it up. Sounds good, anyway."

"Hmm" said the President. "Well, regardless of that it does not seem as if the choice of Ireland as the European/Caucasian representative will cause much trouble. So we will stay with that choice. Any more questions?

No? Well in that case we will proceed to the second major problem, namely how to rear these children in such a way that each of them incorporates, and thus becomes eventually able to express, their specific cultural inheritance. Social and Demographic Councillor. You have the floor again."

"In addressing this problem" said the Social and Demographic Councillor we have sought the help of the Social and Emotional affairs Councillor and the Arts Councillor, and their teams of experts. The approach we have arrived at is summarised in the second document with which you have been supplied, "Inculturation of the Genetically Transplanted Earth Populations."

Inculturation of the Genetically Transplanted Earth Populations.

Language

In order for the children in the three genetic transplant populations to acquire their cultural inheritance they will need to be exposed to their language and culture from the moment they are born. As is well known, our neuropsychologists and language experts many years ago developed foolproof methods of teaching languages. This involves achieving direct access to the language centres of the brain while a person is under sedation and in effect programming those language centres with a new language complete with correct pronunciation. All our would-be parents will in this way be provided with mastery of the language appropriate to the culture in question. They will speak to their children only in that language. In addition, from an early age the children will be exposed to recorded sound and video material from their cultures of origin, including as they get older appropriate works of fiction in both printed and video form.

We will invite the governments of each of the three nations we have chosen to provide us with recorded educational material suitable for children of different ages. We have no doubt that they will be very happy to assist us in this way. Our own language, Omnic, will be taught to the children as a second language. English will be taught as a third language.

Music

Since music is an important part of each of these three cultures, each of these three groups of children need to be taught the music specific to their origins.. In addition we will need to provide the specific musical instruments used in the three different nations."

These are formidable problems, but we believe they are soluble. As it happens Earth music is already being taken up enthusiastically by our own musical community. Earth musical notation presented no problem. And it turns out that there is plenty of instructional material for different instruments available online on the 'Internet' as it is called. And there is also a wealth of printed instructional material which is also available online. Many of our dedicated musicians have already taken the trouble to master the relevant Earth languages so that they can read these manuals. Constructing the requisite musical instruments is a challenging project but is already underway. Information on shapes, dimensions and materials of construction can also be found online. Also of course, some of these instruments are similar to our own. We should mention that none of all this work that has been carried out so far to create Earth musical instruments is anything to do with our Planet Earth Project. It is entirely to do with the enthusiasm amongst Omnian musicians to reproduce Earth music in an authentic manner.

CHAPTER 14

Reproducing those Earth instruments constructed out of metal, normally an alloy of copper and tin which they refer to as "brass" is comparatively straightforward. The wooden instruments, such as those which they referred to as the 'violin family', are more problematic. We have to identify woods on Omnos with similar acoustic properties. And apparently the precise gradients of thickness of the belly and the back of one of these instruments is of great importance for quality. This will present challenges for our musical instrument makers. Nevertheless we am confident that by the time we are bringing these children into the world we will have musical teachers competent to instruct them how to play the music of their origins and the appropriate instruments on which to do it.

"Thank you Councillor" said the President. "It sounds as if on the basis of the work you have all done, the technical and administrative problems of this great project can be solved. But that does not mean that the project should necessarily go ahead. What we have in mind here is something that will have enormous, and I must say unforeseeable, consequences for our planet, for our society. What we now have to decide is whether in fact we should proceed. I propose now to halt council proceedings for the space of two hours in which time I would like you all to have discussions amongst yourselves. We will then reconvene and make our final decision. I ask the Social and Demographic Councillor to talk generally among you and to arrive, if he can, at some assessment of the broad feeling of the Council."

After the specified time the Planetary Council reassembled in the Council chamber.

"Well Councillor" said the President to the Social and Demographic Councillor "what is the result of the Council's deliberations? Is there a consensus emerging?"

"Unfortunately not" replied the Councillor. "The Council appears to be evenly divided. Five of our 10 members believe that this is an exciting project which not only could be carried through successfully but which would have positive transformative effects on Omnian society in the long run. The other members while freely conceding the exciting and even creative nature of the project, feel that the long-term consequences for Omnos of this change in our population structure are not only unforeseeable, but could be problematic. So it is left to you as the President of the Council, with your casting vote, to make the final decision. All members have, however, made it clear that, regardless of their present views they will support that decision."

"So" thought the President "it's going to be up to me. The long-term implications are indeed problematic. This proposal if it goes ahead will be of historic significance for our planet. Yes, it will be transformative. But in a good way? Or not? My instinct, such as it is, inclines me to the view that overall the effects will be positive. I think it could put new life and variety into our somewhat bland, perhaps even moribund, society. Also of course, although I won't still be President when it finally comes into being, it will be my legacy. I will be remembered for this if for nothing else."

He brooded for a little longer. Then -

"Well Council members, I have arrived at my decision. The genetic transplantation part of our Planet Earth Project, the recreation of three Earth peoples and cultures on Omnos will proceed."

Chapter 15

***Tom returns to Cambridge** for an Honours year in which he will seek to obtain the Master of Natural Sciences degree which will then be the gateway to embark on a PhD. The M. Sci. involves a research project as well as course work. Tom does well at both.*

Tom went up to Cambridge to begin his fourth year as an undergraduate to take Part III, a necessary stepping stone on the way to his hoped-for career as a research physicist. Having completed three years he was already entitled if he wished to graduate with a B.A. degree. The fourth year, if he was successful, would give him the honours degree of Master of Natural Sciences, M.Sci., on the basis of which he could expect to begin his research for a Ph.D. Two thirds of the marks for Part III Physics were allotted for course work, and the third for a research project. The students were provided with a list of suitable research projects from which they could choose. Tom saw one which took his fancy. It was in Astrophysics, an area of science in which Tom was already very interested. The title was "Stellar heating of planetary atmospheres by radiative transfer". Tom put his name down for it and his choice was accepted. His supervisor for the project was an Associate Professor in the Department, Dr Jim Metcalfe, a Yorkshireman. Tom went along to Dr Metcalfe's office to find out about the project. Dr

Metcalfe was a cheerful-looking, slightly chubby man in his forties.

"So you are Tom Glennon and you're here to hear about the research project you have chosen. Come in Tom and sit down and I'll tell you about it. One of my research interests is exoplanets, thousands of which as you know have now been discovered. Many of these are gas giants like Jupiter and Saturn in our solar system. But where some of them differ from Jupiter and Saturn is that they are located quite close to the star around which they are travelling. Which means that they are subjected to intense radiative heating. And I am interested in the penetration of heat into the gaseous atmospheres and what might be the consequences for the future evolution of these planets. Now you know what radiative transfer is don't you?"

"Yes" said Tom. "It is the transfer of energy in the form of electromagnetic radiation."

"Exactly. And it is in the form of electromagnetic radiation that heat from the associated star penetrates into the atmospheres of these gaseous exoplanets. Now in this research project what I want you to do is to construct a user-friendly numerical modelling procedure by means of which we could calculate for any given exoplanet at a particular distance from its star, the penetration of heat into, and the consequent vertical temperature distribution of the atmosphere of the planet. You can assume that the atmosphere consists predominantly of molecular hydrogen, as seems pretty well invariably to be the case. Absorption of photons within the atmosphere we can attribute mainly to trace quantities of other gases such as methane, ammonia, water vapour and your procedure should allow the user to specify the concentrations of these. Scattering of the photons, which is also of course a major part of the vertical attenuation process, you can attribute to interaction between the photons and the hydrogen molecules. You can assume Rayleigh scattering from which you will be able to obtain the wavelength dependence and the scattering phase function.

Well Tom. Do you think you'll be able to handle this?"

"I think so" said Tom. "Yes I think I can see what kind of calculation procedure would be required."

"Indeed" said Dr Metcalfe, looking closely at Tom. "Well, that's encouraging. Tell you what. If you find you have some time left over after constructing the modelling procedure, give some thought to the structure of the steady-state radiation field which is set up within the planetary atmosphere. See if you come across any interesting relationships."

"Okay" said Tom. "If I have the time, I'll do that."

"Good" said Dr Metcalfe. "From your accent I'd say you are from the North."

"Yes" said Tom, but choosing not to mention that he had started life not in the North of England but on the far Western edge of Ireland.

"Aye, Ah thought so" said Dr Metcalfe suddenly relapsing into broad Yorkshire.

"Ah'm a Northerner meself. Good. We'll be in touch again to see how you are getting on."

"This lad looks promising" he said to himself as the Tom left his office.

Tom diligently addressed all his coursework. He was taking no chances this time and was determined to perform well enough to be allowed to proceed to a Ph.D., but his main interest was his research project. For his numerical modelling of the light field he chose to use the somewhat laborious but conceptually simple Monte Carlo procedure. This involved following the stellar photons into the gaseous atmosphere one at a time and on a random basis subjecting them to absorption and scattering events, with appropriate selection of scattering angles. In this way, after processing millions of photons, the computer arrived at a picture of the steady-state light field. From this it was possible to calculate the localised rate of energy absorption and the consequent temperature distribution of the gaseous atmosphere as a function of depth. Tom incorporated this into a software package by means of which someone could enter the physical parameters of the system - atmosphere depth, chemical composition, distance from the star, stellar characteristics, and end up with the temperature depth profile of the exoplanet atmosphere. He tried his program out with various sets of input data and the results seemed plausible, so he concluded that his main research objective had been achieved.

Tom still had some spare time before his thesis had to be submitted and so he decided that, as suggested by Dr Metcalfe, he would give some thought to the characteristics of the light field established within the planetary atmosphere. He knew that the radiant intensity would diminish in an approximately exponential manner with increasing depth from the surface. There were a number of differently defined "vertical attenuation coefficients" in terms of which this diminution with depth could be characterised. He applied his mathematical skills to investigating ways in which these might be related to other properties of the atmospheric light field. He wrote his analysis and conclusions up together with his software program in his thesis for the M.Sci. degree.

In the final days of the academic year, just before leaving Cambridge for his vacation, Tom was called in to see his supervisor, Dr Metcalfe.

"Well Tom, I wanted a word or two with you about your thesis."

"Uh Oh" thought Tom. "Maybe my thesis isn't as good as I thought."

CHAPTER 15

"Is there a problem with it?" he said hesitantly.

"Not at all, not at all" said Dr Metcalfe reassuringly.

"So far as your thesis itself is concerned, I have what you might call good news, then a bit of bad news, and finally some more good news.

"First, the good news. Your thesis is just fine. Certainly of the standard required for the degree. In itself, of course it won't be sufficient. You also have to have done well in your exams on the coursework. And there we will just have to wait until the results come out."

"Thanks for the good news" said Tom. "And the bad news?"

"Your theoretical work on the light field within the exoplanet's gaseous atmosphere. First, I am pleased that you followed my suggestion to explore this. But your proof that one of the definable vertical attenuation coefficients - you know, the irradiance-weighted one - is precisely equal to the reciprocal of the average photon depth."

"But the derivation is correct isn't it?" said Tom in some alarm. He had gone over his maths carefully and had been confident that there were no errors.

"Yes, yes. Your derivation is just fine" said Dr Metcalfe. "But your conclusion, unfortunately, is not original."

This was a blow. In deriving his result - something which had given Tom a great deal of satisfaction and pleasure - had he been simply following in someone's footsteps?

"But I couldn't find anything like this in the astrophysical literature" said Tom. I looked at everything I could find on the radiation field within planetary atmospheres."

"I am sure you did" said Dr Metcalfe "but this finding was not published in an astrophysical journal, but in an oceanographic one. This relationship was shown by an Australian scientist some years ago to apply to the light field within the ocean."

"The ocean?"

"Oh yes. Just like a planetary atmosphere the ocean is a fluid medium within which absorption and scattering processes take place and on which there is a stream of incident radiation from a nearby star. So similar relationships apply."

"I see" said Tom, somewhat disconsolately. "Yes, I suppose that must be right. I never thought of looking in the oceanographic journals."

"That's alright Tom. Very understandable. But I told you I also had a bit of good news after the bad news."

"Yes" said Tom, perking up a bit. "What is it?"

"Your proof is much shorter, neater and mathematically more satisfying than the oceanographer's proof. I think it might be worth a short note in one of the astrophysical journals."

"Gosh" thought Tom suddenly feeling more cheerful. "Maybe I am going to get an actual publication. Already!"

"Well, thank you Dr Metcalfe. That is a bit of good news."

Chapter 16

***Tom goes back to Ireland** for his annual holiday. After visiting the family farm he decides to tour around. While staying in Derry in Northern Ireland he visits a pub where he hears Irish music being played. He joins the session, playing his fiddle, and gets to know an attractive young woman playing the flute. Introduces himself. She does likewise - Molly Cullinan, in training as a nurse. He invites her for a dinner date.*

Leaving Cambridge for the vacation, Tom first went home to Stockport where he spent a few weeks earning money labouring in the family building business. He then set off to Connemara for his annual summer visit but this time after only a week on the farm he went into Galway city to rent a car. He had often thought that he did not know his native land as well as he should. The time had now come to remedy that. He first set off South through Clare and Kerry and then headed across County Cork, exploring the long peninsulas extending out into the Atlantic Ocean which form the south-western corner of Ireland. He stayed in bed and breakfasts and in the cheaper hotels. He had brought his fiddle with him and sought out pub music sessions wherever he could. He then turned North and drove up the East coast, stopping for a few days in Dublin where he attended a couple of sessions at the well-known Cobblestone pub. Continuing on

North through counties Meath and Louth he then crossed the border into County Armagh in Northern Ireland. As a Catholic from the Republic he realised that he would now have to pay some attention to just where he was going. He did not want to accidentally stray into one of the more extreme Orange Unionist neighbourhoods. In Belfast, capital of the province, Tom managed to find a B and B in the Western, more Catholic, part of the city, from which he cautiously explored the City centre. Although Belfast had its charms, Tom thought that he might feel more at home in the predominantly Catholic city of Derry (known to the Unionists as Londonderry) in County Derry on the western border of the province and so that is where he headed next. He found a B&B in the almost entirely Catholic Bogside area of the city. Here he felt entirely at ease roaming the streets.

Walking past one pub, Maguire's, in the evening he heard the unmistakable sounds of an Irish music session in progress. He immediately hastened home to the B&B, which was not far away, to collect his fiddle and then returned to Maguire's. The music was being performed by half a dozen musicians seated around a table at one end of the room. Tom went up to the crowded bar, ordered a Guinness and then sat down near the musicians to listen. He noticed that the flute player was an attractive young woman with dark curly hair. After a while at the end of a bracket the musician next to her stood up, put his fiddle away in a case and then said goodbye to the remaining musicians before leaving. Tom saw this as an opportunity to join in the music and perhaps to get to know the young woman. He picked up his instrument, went over to the group and said "Is it okay if I join you? I do play in sessions back in England."

"Certainly you can. You're welcome" came the response. When the music restarted - a bracket of fast reels - it became obvious to the rest of the musicians that Tom was well up to their standard and they looked on him now with visible approval. After a few more brackets, jigs and hornpipes, the musicians took a short break. Tom saw his opportunity to get to know the girl he was sitting next to.

"Hi. This is a good session. I'm enjoying it. Is this a regular event in this pub?"

"It is indeed" she replied. "Every Wednesday. And some other musicians play here on other nights."

"Your flute has a very nice tone" said Tom. "I think the wooden Irish concert flutes have a more appropriate sound for traditional music than the metal Boehm system flutes, and your playing does it full justice. Is your instrument locally made?"

"It is" she said. "It was made by a flute maker down in Liscannor in County Clare."

"I play the flute myself a bit" said Tom "but nowhere near as well as you. I just have a simple six hole wooden flute. I am saving up for a concert flute with all the keys."

"Well" said the girl with a smile. "I am not going to tell you I also play the fiddle because I don't, but like every other Irish musician I sometimes play the whistle. And occasionally I have a go on the concertina."

"You know, there is something of a tradition of women concertina players and Irish music. It began with Mrs Elizabeth Crotty in West Clare back in the 1950s" said Tom. "Anyway, I think I should introduce myself. I'm Tom Glennon. I was born in Ireland, on a farm in Connemara, but the family emigrated to England when I was 10. My dad's in the building trade. I'm a graduate student in Cambridge and I'm just about to start my Ph.D. I hope to be a research physicist."

"Do you indeed?" said the girl, observing Tom with increased interest. "That's quite an ambition."

"Yes it is" replied Tom "but, please God, I'll get there eventually."

"Well by the cut of you I'd say you will" said the girl, looking at Tom appraisingly.

"I'm Molly Cullinan. I'm from Kerry. My family have a farm on the Dingle Peninsula. I am a student too. I'm studying nursing in the hospital system up here, in Derry and in Belfast."

"My Mam was a nurse in her younger days, before she got married and started to rear a family" said Tom.

"And did she go back to nursing when the family were grown up?" asked Molly.

"Ah, No" said Tom, sadly. "She died a couple of years back. Cancer."

"I am sorry to hear that" said Molly with quick sympathy, momentarily putting her hand on Tom's. "I'd say you miss her."

"I do indeed" said Tom. "I do indeed. But sure family bereavements must happen to all of us. It's no use staying gloomy. Now listen, I am just about ready for another Guinness. Can I get you something?"

"I suppose you can. Thank you. I'll have an orange juice."

Tom looked over to the bar, preparatory to rising to his feet and noticed that a young man standing there appeared to be glaring at him in a hostile manner.

"Will you look at that fellah over there giving me the evil eye. What's the matter with him?"

"Oh him" said Molly, dismissively. "It's because he sees you talking to me."

"Why" said Tom. "Is he your boyfriend?"

"Indeed he is not" said she with a touch of anger. "He'd like to be but I won't have anything to do with him."

"All right" said Tom, rising to his feet. "I'll get the drinks."

He walked over to the bar, to a space next to the hostile young man.

CHAPTER 16

"A Guinness and an orange juice please." Tom spoke in what was his normal everyday voice these days - standard English with a slight Lancashire intonation.

"Are you an Englishman?" said the young man in an aggressive voice.

"Indeed I am not" said Tom. "I'm Irish."

"Well, you sound like an Englishman."

"That's because I went to school in England" replied Tom. "I was born in Ireland and then we went over to England."

"I don't believe you're Irish at all" said the young man in rising tones. "You're just pretending."

"Kevin, just give it a rest." This from an older man further down the bar who had started taking an interest in what was going on.

"No I won't give it a rest" said the young man angrily. "He's a Sassenach, here to spy on us."

"Kevin, I said give it a rest. Stop it now." said the older man, more loudly and in tones of undoubted menace. Kevin said nothing. He seemed taken aback, with a touch of fear. The older man turned and looked at a heavily built man at the end of the bar. Having caught his gaze he looked back at Kevin and then flicked his head towards the doorway. The heavily built man nodded, walked over to Kevin, took him by the arm and marched him out through the doorway.

The older man came up to Tom.

"Sorry about that" he said. "Kevin's had a bit too much to drink tonight. So despite the accent, you are an Irishman? *An bhfuil Gaeilge agat?* (Do you speak Irish?)

Tom realised he was being put to the test.

"I'll show him" he thought.

"Cinnte tá gaeilge agam. Tá mé liofa. Rugadh agus togadh i gConamara mé. Tomás MacLeannáin is ainm dom, 'Tom Glennon' as Béarla "

(Indeed I speak Irish. I am fluent. I was born and raised in Connemara. Tomás MacLeannáin is my name,' Tom Glennon' in English.)

Tom went on to give a brief account, all in deliberately rapid Irish, of his family history and how it was that he had gone to school in England.

"Well" said the man. "There's no doubt you are the real deal, a true born Irishman. But you can pass for an Englishman, that's for sure."

"I suppose so" said Tom, uncertainly, not sure where this was heading.

"That could be useful" said the man.

"Allow me to introduce myself. I'm Seán McAteer. I am in business here in Derry. Tell me, just as a matter of interest, what are your views on the Republican issue? Would you like to see the six counties of Northern Ireland be united with the Irish Republic?"

"I suppose so" said Tom. "Eventually."

"Let me give you my card" said McAteer, handing Tom a business card inscribed with 'McAteer Building and Construction Supplies' with a Derry address and phone numbers. "In case you'd like to discuss these matters further."

"Okay" said Tom, "but now I must take these drinks back" and with a feeling of some relief he carried his Guinness and Molly's orange juice back to where the musicians were sitting.

"Do you know who's that you were talking to?" said Molly looking at him with some concern.

"I've got a pretty fair idea" said Tom. "I think he was trying to recruit me."

"And do you want to be recruited?" she said.

"Indeed I do not" said Tom.

CHAPTER 16

"I'm glad to hear it" said Molly.

The music recommenced with slip jigs - Coleman's, Elizabeth Kelly's delight, Maire Rua - all well known to Tom. He then decided to lead off the next bracket himself with a set of reels – Rakish Paddy, Sporting Paddy and The Dunmore Lasses. During the next momentary break in the music, a sudden thought occurred to Tom and he turned to Molly.

"Now your surname is Cullinan isn't it?"

"It is. And so?"

"And so your name in Irish is Molly Ni Chuilleanáin."

"Of course. That is the name by which I am known back in Kerry. I was brought up speaking Irish before I ever spoke English."

"As I was too, in Connemara" said Tom.

"But did you know there is a song about you?"

"Ah, go away out of that" said Molly, laughing. "There is not."

"There is too" said Tom. "It's called *Molly na gCuach Ni Chuilleanáin,* 'Curly-haired Molly Ni Chuilleanáin." It's an old Gaelic song.

"Do you know what" said Pat, one of the other musicians, sitting next to Molly on the other side, overhearing this conversation. "I think he's right. There is such a song. Do you know it, Tom? Could you sing it?"

"Well I suppose I could" said Tom. "If I can remember it."

"Sing it then" said Pat. And turning around to the others "Tom's going to sing us a song."

The message went around the pub. "Shush, someone is going to sing." And the hubbub ceased as people waited expectantly for the song.

Tom rose to his feet, cleared his throat and launched into the song.

Verse
Ar meisce cha dtéim níos mó
Braon leanna go deo ní bhlaisfidh mé
Ó chaill mé mo chailín beag óg
A chuireadh i mo phócaí an t-airgead
Chorus
Is fada liom uaim í, uaim í
Is fada liom uaim í ó d'imigh sí
Is fada liom thíos agus thuas í
Molly na gcuach Ní Chuilleanáin

Verse
Dhéanfaidh mé tigh ar an ard
Is beidh ceithre ba bainne breaca agam
Ní ligfidh mé 'n duine dá gcomhair
Go dtiocfadh Moll óg Ní Chuilleanáin

Verse
Drunkeness for life I forego
Strong ale I will taste never more
Since I lost my young little girl
Who used to put money in my pockets

Chorus
I miss her, I miss her
I miss her since she left me
I long for her above and below me
Curly-haired Molly Ni Chuilleanáin

CHAPTER 16

Verse
I'll build a house on the hill
And four speckled cows I'll own
I'll allow no other person near them
Until young Molly Ni Chuilleanáin comes

And continued to the end of the song. When he finished and sat down there was loud and enthusiastic applause from the pub audience, with shouts of "Good man yourself!" and "More power to you!" from around the room.

"There" he said to Molly. "I told you there was a song about you. You are Curly-haired Molly Ni Chuilleanáin"

"Oh go on with you" she said. But he could see that she was pleased if a little flustered.

"Well done Tom" said Pat, the violinist. "Begod you can sing as well as play."

The music continued for about another hour and then the musicians began to pack up their instruments preparatory to leaving. Tom was already beginning to feel interested in Molly and did not want to lose contact with her.

"Molly, I was proposing to stay around Derry for another day or so. Any chance you'd like to come out to dinner with me tomorrow?"

"Well" said Molly, somewhat hesitantly. "I suppose I wouldn't mind. But nothing too fancy."

"Good" said Tom. "Could you suggest a restaurant? I am sure you know the Derry restaurants better than I do."

"I know a nice Vietnamese one just near here" said Molly. "Not too expensive. I'll be free at about seven."

"Just the thing" said Tom. "If you tell me where it is I'll meet you there at seven tomorrow."

After spending the following day getting to know Derry town and the surrounding countryside, Tom parked his car and set off on foot to the restaurant Molly had suggested. He arrived there at five minutes to seven and waited outside. By 10 minutes after the hour he began to feel a little anxious. Was he being stood up? But at a quarter past seven Molly arrived. He could see that she had taken some care with her appearance, unlike her casual apparel of the day before. Perhaps this was a good sign.

As the meal progressed they talked together and soon found that they were chatting very freely. They exchanged their family origins and found them to be very similar: small farms in the West of Ireland. They had much in common and by the end of the meal they were entirely at ease with each other.

"Tell me Molly - when do you finish your nursing course and where will you go then?"

"I finish next year" said she "and I have already been offered a job in Salford Royal Hospital over in England."

"Oh I know Salford" said Tom. "It's not very far from where my family live in Stockport. Perhaps I can come and visit you when I am home on holidays."

"Do" said Molly. "I would like that."

"Tell you what" said Tom. "We must exchange email addresses and mobile telephone numbers so that we can keep in touch."

"Yes, let's do that" said Molly.

Chapter 17

Leaving Ireland, Tom *returns to the family home in Stockport. His father, Micheál, tells him that he is thinking of getting married again. Micheál's intended, a widow, Barbara Hanrahan, comes to dinner to meet the family.*

At the end of his motoring holiday in Ireland Tom returned to Stockport to get his belongings together before going back to Cambridge.

"Tom" said his father one evening when they were alone, the two girls being out. "Have you got a moment? I have something to tell you."

"Of course, Dad" said Tom. "What is it?"

"I am thinking of getting married again" said Micheál.

"Oh, are you? Who to? Someone we know?"

"Indeed you do" replied Micheál. "You remember Mrs Hanrahan, Brigid Hanrahan. She was a good friend of your mother and is a long time parishioner at our church. She lost her own husband to cancer, lung cancer, a few years ago. Her children are now grown up and have left home. Aoife and Gráinne, your two sisters, are now into their teens and I think would benefit from having an adult woman in the house. As a man, I don't think I am well equipped to guide their final upbringing myself. Brigid and I have always got on very well, we are both rather lonely so I suggested to her that we get married. I'm happy to say she agreed."

Tom remembered Mrs Hanrahan as a pleasant, cheerful motherly woman. As a friend of their mother she had often visited their home especially during Róisín's final illness, when she needed company. He also thought that their father would benefit from having a companion. He had seemed low in spirits in the couple of years since his wife died.

"Well that's just fine, Dad" said Tom. "I remember Mrs Hanrahan. She was always friendly and always took an interest in how myself and the girls were getting on. Good. She'll be great company for you."

"Well thank you Tom" said Micheál. "I am pleased you are happy about it. I'll tell the girls when they get home."

Tom suspected that his sisters might be a bit less positive. To have another female come into the house was inavoidably somewhat problematic. Nevertheless, he was sure that they would realise that one day they would be leaving home and that it was better for their father not to be left alone.

"Tell you what" said Tom. "How about you invite her round and we'll all have dinner together. That will help the girls and myself to start getting to know her better."

"That's a good idea" said Micheál enthusiastically. But then, in some dismay "but who will cook it? I'm not much of a cook and since your Mam died we have been relying a lot on takeaway. That won't be good enough."

"Just leave it to me" said Tom. "Living in a share house this last year in Cambridge we all have to take it in turn to do the cooking. I believe I can now do a very respectable beef and vegetable casserole."

"Are you sure?" said Micheál, somewhat doubtfully.

"Absolutely" said Tom. "I will surprise you."

CHAPTER 17

"All right" said Micheál. "I'll leave it to you. I'll give Brigid a ring and see if she can come tomorrow."

The following day Tom purchased a kilogram of chuck steak and set to work, with potatoes, carrots, onion, minced garlic, dried herbs, salt, beef stock and red wine all ending up in the same big casserole pot as the steak, and simmering gently for some hours to be ready just in time for dinner. Brigid arrived punctually at six and seemed a little nervous, understandably as this was her first meeting with the whole family together in her role as a prospective stepmother. But all went well. The girls were soon chatting freely with Brigid. Tom's casserole was greeted with somewhat surprised acclaim and the apple pie which Brigid had brought with her satisfactorily completed a meal which they would later look back on as a significant family event. When Tom set off for Cambridge the following week he did so feeling that he was leaving his father and his sisters in safe hands.

Chapter 18

***Tom goes back** to Cambridge to begin his PhD. Chooses Astrophysics as his preferred area of research. His research supervisor, Jim Metcalfe, suggests he studies the atmospheres of exoplanets. Tom embarks on the creation of an all-purpose General Circulation Model applicable to any kind of exoplanet.*

To support himself for the three years of his Ph.D. Tom had applied for, and been awarded, a studentship from the UK Research Council. As this was not in itself enough for living expenses as well as University fees, his father, whose building business was doing well, was happy to provide Tom with an allowance to cover the gap. In fact Micheál was more than happy to support his clever son, the first in their family ever to go to university and of whom he was very proud. Tom was very pleased to hear from his Australian friend, Mick Hennessy, that he too had been awarded a scholarship and would be doing his Physics Ph.D. at Cambridge at the same time as Tom. They agreed to live in the same shared house accommodation as before.

On his return to Cambridge to begin his Ph.D., Tom went in to the Cavendish Laboratory off Madingley Road to see the Head of Astrophysics, Professor Jeremy Dowsett, to discuss possible research topics for his degree.

CHAPTER 18

"Come in, Tom" said the professor, a friendly looking middle-aged grey-haired man with a neatly trimmed beard. "Take a seat. Did you manage to have a good holiday? Are you fully recovered from your very intense final year?"

"Yes thanks. I'm fully recovered from the stress of the Honours year and I had a good holiday. I hired a car and spent a few weeks touring around Ireland" said Tom.

"Ireland, Eh" said Professor Dowsett, with a searching look at Tom. "A beautiful country indeed. I know it well. The country of your ancestors I surmise?"

"Yes it is" replied Tom, hoping that this would not prove to be a problem.

"I see that for your Honours degree research you did a nice bit of work under the supervision of Dr Metcalfe on radiative transfer in an exoplanet atmosphere. We are discovering all kinds of new exoplanets around other stars these days and they are a hot topic. Jim Metcalfe has a strong research interest in exoplanetary atmospheres. How about you go and have a talk with him and see if there is some particular research project that might take your fancy."

"All right" said Tom. "I'll do that."

Tom already knew that he got on well with Jim Metcalfe, an important consideration if Dr Metcalfe was going to be his Ph.D. supervisor. The professor's suggestion sounded promising so Tom continued on to Dr Metcalfe's office.

"Hi Tom. Here you are, back again. What can I do for you?"

"Hello Dr Metcalfe. I've just been to see Professor Dowsett to discuss possible research topics for my Ph.D. He said that since I've already done some research on exoplanetary atmospheres, and since you have an interest in this area, you might be able to suggest some project which I would find interesting."

"Well, yes" said Dr Metcalfe. "I suppose I might. In fact, there is one I have been thinking about over the last couple of weeks which you might find interesting. One of the unexpected findings that has emerged from our observations of exoplanets in recent years is that so many of them orbit surprisingly close to their star. We don't know for sure how they get to be so close. It seems unlikely that they actually formed there, but that they originally came into existence in the protoplanetary disk further out and then somehow migrated inward. There are hypotheses, but as yet no generally agreed mechanism, as to how this could occur. So we have the interesting question - what happens to an exoplanet when it gets close to its sun? In particular, what happens to its atmosphere when it is exposed to the increased stellar radiation? Does it boil off so to speak, i.e. evaporate away into space, and if so how quickly? This is not something we can actually measure but it seems to me we might be able to carry out some quite realistic modelling to give us some kind of a feeling for the likely fate of these planets.

Now in your Honours year research you have already established a useful picture of the stellar radiation field that will be established in a planetary atmosphere, and this is where the heat will come from, and so that could be a good starting point.

So that is one possible Ph.D. research project in the exoplanetary field, but there are plenty of others" and he went on to outline some of these.

"Anyway Tom, if you think exoplanets might at least be a useful starting point for a career in astrophysics, but of course not one you have to be committed to forever, have a think about it. Do some literature reading, and perhaps let me know in a couple of days time."

"All right" said Tom. "I will." "

CHAPTER 18

Tom read widely in the astronomical literature over the next few days reading papers on exoplanets. There was plenty of material there to attract his interest. It was clear that exoplanets were by no means well understood so there was a great deal still to be found out about them. In particular of course, there was always the particularly interesting question of whether any of these planets could support life. Tom eventually decided that this area would indeed be, as Dr Metcalfe had suggested, a useful starting point for what he hoped would be a research career in astrophysics. He went to see Dr Metcalfe and told him that for his Ph.D. he would be happy to tackle a research topic on exoplanets.

"Good" said Metcalfe. "Well I am the local guru on exoplanets so I would be the natural choice as your supervisor. How would you feel about that? If you are at all unhappy about that prospect, feel free to say so and we will try and find someone else."

"No, that suits me fine" said Tom, who already knew from his honours year that he could get on well with Dr Metcalfe.

"All right" said Metcalfe. "Let's begin. First of all let's dispense with the formalities. We are going to be working closely together for the next three years and so now forget 'Dr Metcalfe' and just call me 'Jim'. So far as the research goes, how about you kick off with the problem I mentioned earlier - namely, what happens to an exoplanet atmosphere when it finds that it is getting close to its star. I think that by making some plausible assumptions based on radiative and general thermal physics, together with observations on planetary atmospheres in our own Solar System, we might by using numerical modelling arrive at some realistic scenarios describing the likely behaviour of such atmospheres. If you think that is interesting have a preliminary go at it and then get back to me and we will discuss whether it is worth persevering with."

"Okay" said Tom. "I will."

"Right" said Jim. "First I'll find you a place to work." He took Tom down the corridor where there were a number of offices, and opened the door of one of them. There were three desks, each with its own computer.

"You'll be sharing this office with two other graduate students. "You might as well stake your claim to one of these desks now. We will have your name, and the names of the other students, put up on the door.".

The following day Tom chose one of the desks and set himself up for work. He began by considering the simplest possible case, a planet with a completely still atmosphere exposed to stellar radiation. He was easily able to show that in such a case a density gradient would become established, with the warmest, least dense, gas at the top transitioning to cooler, more dense layers lower down. The rate of change of the gradient with depth depended upon the specific light absorption and scattering properties of the atmospheric mixture in understandable ways. He realised of course that this was a very improbable situation, unlikely ever to occur on a real planet, but thought that he should get it out of the way as a limiting case. The accepted view was that planetary atmospheres were invariably turbulent due to the interacting effects of heat from the planetary core, planetary rotation and radiation from the nearby star. So Tom now immersed himself in the published literature of the field of atmospheric fluid dynamics, familiarising himself with the variety of tools and concepts – Navier-Stokes equations, turbulent energy transfer, potential vorticity, stochastic structural stability, eddy diffusivity, baroclinic turbulence etc. - to be found in this complex, and in his view rather messy, area of science.

For the main body of his thesis research he decided to concentrate on those smaller kinds of exoplanet orbiting close to their star, which had recently been observed. His aim was to carry out numerical computer modelling, using those fluid dynamical and radiative energy transfer equations which seemed best suited to the purpose, to arrive at a plausible, and hopefully realistic, picture of the state of the atmosphere on such an exoplanet and its development with time - in particular, how long it might take for such a planet to lose its atmosphere altogether. He realised that developing a comprehensive computer model of the kind he had in mind was going to be a substantial undertaking. First he had to understand the physics of all the processes simultaneously going on in the atmosphere and then for each process create an appropriate differential equation which he could then implement in his computer model. A challenging task which he relished. He knew, of course, that some numerical models of planetary atmospheres – known as General Circulation Models – had already been developed. He would need to familiarise himself with these so that he did not waste time reinventing the wheel.

Chapter 19

Tom begins to think *how nice it would be to have a girlfriend, perhaps even get married one day. Not many Catholic girls in Cambridge. He thinks of Molly in Derry. Where is she now? He remembers that she was to come to Salford Royal Hospital. He gets in touch by email. They start going out together whenever he visits his family in the North of England. She becomes his girlfriend*

Although he had every intention of working hard at his research Tom felt that, unlike in the last two intensive years of his undergraduate degree, he could now allow himself time in the evenings and at the weekends to socialise and pursue his other interests. Tom began by deciding to restart his musical career. He was still a member of the Jazz club and by asking around managed to find a drummer and a double bass player who would be happy to form a jazz trio with him. As he was the lead musician it was naturally called the Tom Glennon Trio. By offering their services free, which at this early stage they were happy to do, they managed to find some gigs in pubs and clubs around town.

He would often go out with Mick Hennessy and his other housemates but increasingly thought how nice it would be to have a girlfriend. Perhaps even, some way down the track, to get married and have a family. As a Catholic, Tom thought it would be best if he married a Catholic girl, perhaps an Irish Catholic if he could find one. Cambridge, however, being in one of the least Catholic parts of England was not a promising place in which to start looking. He would occasionally take the train up to London on a Saturday and attend dances which were held at one of the big Catholic parishes but found that he had little in common with most of the girls he met there.

It was while he was thinking gloomily about how difficult it was proving to find a girlfriend that Tom remembered Molly Cullinan, the girl he had met in Derry and with whom he had got on very well. He would love to meet up with her again but Derry was a long way away.

"Hang on!" he suddenly said to himself aloud. "Didn't she tell me that she had a job in Salford Royal Hospital waiting for her when she finished her nursing course. I wonder if she's there now. How can I find out?"

He remembered that they had in fact exchanged email addresses and mobile phone numbers. He had jotted hers down on a scrap of paper but where was it? After several minutes of fruitlessly racking his brain, it suddenly came to him. He had stuffed it into the spare string compartment of his fiddle case. Was it still there? Yes it was! So, what to do now?

"If I ring her directly she might find it all a bit sudden and respond negatively" he thought. "Whereas with an email she has time to think about it." So, now to construct an email with a positive tone but not too demanding.

Hi Molly

I expect you remember me. I played together with you and the other musicians in the pub session in Derry earlier this year. And we had dinner together the following evening. You told me that when you had finished your nursing course you were coming over to a job in Salford Royal Hospital. Are you over here yet? As you know I am down here in Cambridge doing my Ph.D. However, my family home is up in Stockport, which is not very far from Salford, and I often go up there on the weekend or during holidays. I was wondering if we could perhaps get together some time, maybe for a meal or a film.

If you think that might be a good idea, let me know and we will work something out.

Slán agus beannacht.

Tom Glennon

There was no reply the following day. Or the day after. Or the day after that. But just when he had given up hope, when he had sadly come to the conclusion that Molly had no interest in him, an email arrived.

Hi Tom

Yes, I have started my job in Salford Royal now. Let me know when you are expecting to be in Stockport again, and we will see if something can be arranged.

Slán go fóill

Molly Cullinan

This was a cautious response. But it left possibilities open. Tom intended not to let this opportunity slip by.

A few weeks later Tom decided that it was time he visited his family. He emailed Molly.

Hi Molly

I am coming up to Stockport this weekend. Are you free on Saturday night? How would you like to come with me to a film in Manchester? We could have a meal first. I think my Dad would lend me his car so I could pick you up.

Slán

Tom

The reply came the next day.

Hi Tom

CHAPTER 19

Yes, I am free this Saturday night and would be happy to go to a film with you. If you have a car you can pick me up outside the nurses' hostel, where I am staying, at about 5:45.

Slán

Molly

Late that Friday Tom took the train up to Stockport. As always, his family were very glad to see him. As the evening meal came to its close, Tom asked Micheál - "Dad, is there any chance I could borrow your car tomorrow evening?"

"You can of course" said Micheál. "Any particular reason?"

"Well yes" said Tom. "There's a girl I met in Ireland earlier this year. She's a nurse and is now over here in Salford Royal Hospital. We got on very well and I'd like to see more of her, so I asked her out to come to a film with me tomorrow night."

"That's fine, Tom. By all means take the car."

Molly had told Tom the address of the nurses hostel. He arrived there at 20 minutes to 5, parked the car and stood outside waiting for Molly. As promised she emerged at 5.45. Tom waved and called out.

"Hi Molly. Over here."

"Hi Tom" she said and smiled as she came over.

"I assume you haven't eaten" he said.

"No" said Molly.

"Do you fancy Indian" he said. "There are plenty of Indian restaurants in Manchester."

"Indian would be fine. I like Indian food."

After parking the car they found an Indian restaurant in Deansgate, not far from the Odeon cinema where they intended to go later. As before, on their previous date in Derry, Tom and Molly got on very well together. He enjoyed her company and had the impression that she enjoyed his. The conversation flowed freely. He left the choice of film to Molly. She opted for a romantic comedy which happened to be on the Odeon at the moment. Tom enjoyed it well enough although, like a lot of scientists his cinematic tastes leaned more towards science fiction.

Tom drove back to the nurses hostel and they got out of the car together.

"Well Molly, I really enjoyed our evening together."

"So did I, Tom and thank you."

"Would you like to come out with me again, perhaps on my next visit to Stockport?" said Tom.

"Yes I would" said Molly.

"Alright so, I'll be in touch" said Tom. He wondered "should I now give her a kiss?" but hesitated, not wanting to risk rejection.

"Is he going to give me a kiss?" thought Molly. "I wish he would." She sensed his hesitancy and decided that he needed a bit of gentle encouragement. It certainly would not do for her to just ask him to give her a kiss. On the other hand there might be a roundabout way of getting the message across.

"Tell me Tom. Have you read *Great Expectations*, you know, by Dickens?"

"I certainly have" said Tom. "I've read all of Dickens."

"Well Tom. Before we go out again, have a look at it and see if there is anything that Estella says to Pip, that might be relevant."

She smiled at him and then turned and went up the steps into the nurses hostel.

"What on earth did she mean by that?" thought Tom to himself as he drove away. As soon as he got home he sought out *Great Expectations* amongst his Dickens collection. He remembered that Pip had been summoned to Miss Havisham's house and ordered to play with her ward, the rude and haughty Estella. He leafed through the relevant chapters looking for anything that Estella said to Pip. Some of it was not very promising. At one point, she asks Pip - "Am I pretty?" to which in the case of

Molly, Tom would be very happy to respond "Yes." But a moment or two later Estella slaps him across the face and says

"You little coarse monster, what do you think of me now?" He hoped this was not the quotation that Molly had in mind. But at the end of chapter 11 he found what he was looking for.

"Come here! You may kiss me if you like."

Tom laughed aloud.

"Yes Molly, I would like. And next time I will."

A few weeks later Tom decided once again to go home for the weekend. And again he arranged a date with Molly for the Saturday night. Coming back from the film he parked the car and walked with Molly to the nurses hostel. When they stopped he saw that she was looking at him in an expectant manner.

"Now Molly" he said, with a serious face. "I did actually follow your suggestion and I looked at what Estella said to Pip in *Great Expectations.* And I must say I was rather taken aback, perhaps even alarmed. Are you really going to call me a little coarse monster and slap me across the face?"

"Of course not, you big eejit!" she said.

"Oh well, in that case I shall assume it was the other thing she said - 'You may kiss me if you like' " and Tom took Molly in his arms and kissed her full on the lips. It was clear from her response that this was what she wanted him to do.

"So, Molly na gCuach Ni Chuilleannáin, am I now your boyfriend?"

"If you want to be" she said with a smile.

"I do. And are you my girlfriend?"

"Yes, I suppose I am" said Molly. Tom kissed her again and then walked back to the car feeling on top of the world.

Chapter 20

***Tom finds he is becoming** very fond of Molly. Invites her to come and have dinner with his family in Stockport. They like her. He decides to ask her to marry him. Molly does not say No but says that she is not quite ready for such a big decision. Suggests that Tom come and visit her family in Ireland.*

Every time Tom went home to Stockport for the weekend he would go out on a date with Molly. He was pleased to find that they had much in common in addition to their similar family backgrounds. They both had a passion for Irish traditional music. She was an avid reader and, rather to his surprise, shared his liking for the 19th century English novelists – Jane Austen, Dickens, George Eliot and Trollope. In the 20th century while they both liked the novels of Graham Greene, Evelyn Waugh and Anthony Burgess, he could not persuade her to like James Joyce's *Ulysses*. She always had interesting, often of course sad, stories from the hospital. His own experience in the Cambridge Physics department did not provide as much conversational fodder, but he contributed the little there was. Sometimes when the opportunity offered, instead of going to a film they went to a play or a classical music concert.

Now that Tom was 'officially' her boyfriend, Molly wanted to show him off to her friends. After their next date, when they returned she said – "Tom, come in to the hostel with me for a moment and meet some of the other nurses. I have mentioned you to them and they want to have a look at you."

"OK" said Tom, thinking "Oh dear, is this going to be some kind of ordeal." However, it was not an ordeal. Most of the nurses in the hostel common room were country girls from Ireland and Molly individually introduced him to all of them. They took a keen, cheerful, and openly inquisitive interest in him, wanting to know his background and origins, and he soon felt entirely at home. After that Molly often brought him in to the hostel for a chat with the girls after their outings.

Tom enjoyed Molly's company and had the strong impression that she enjoyed his. It soon became clear to him that he was getting very fond of her. He decided that the time had come for her to meet his family. In his next email he suggested to her that for a change, instead of going out to a restaurant followed by a film, she come back to Stockport with him and have dinner with the Glennon family. She readily agreed.

His family were by now well aware that he was 'going steady' with a girl and so were very interested to meet her. The dinner went very well. Molly could see that these were people much like her own family and soon felt entirely at ease, chatting away freely to Tom's sisters Gráinne and Aoife, and to Brigid. After dinner Tom took her back to the nurses hostel and returned home.

"Well, what did you think of Molly?" he said to his assembled family in the sitting room.

"We liked her" said his sisters. "Yes" said Brigid. "She comes across as cheerful and intelligent."

"And sensible as well" added Micheál. "But then of course nurses have to be sensible."

When they were alone together later Micheál put the question directly to Tom.

"Well Tom, how serious are you? Do you have it in mind to ask Molly to marry you?"

"I might do. I might do" said Tom. "I am not quite sure I am ready to take the plunge just yet."

"Well it is a bit early in your career" said Micheál. "After all, you are still a student and have not yet got a job. But if you become convinced that she is the right girl for you, don't be too slow about asking her. A nice girl like that might get snapped up by someone else."

"Yes she might" replied Tom, to whom this worrying thought had already occurred.

On the train back to Cambridge Tom brooded some more about what his father had said to him. Molly might indeed get snapped up by someone else. Some young doctor at the hospital with glittering career prospects might take a fancy to her. He realised with something of a shock that if he lost Molly he would be devastated. Having her company, having her as part of his life had, without his fully realising it, become very important to him. Did he want to marry her? Did he want to share the rest of his life with her? As he thought about it, the answer became clear. Yes he did! And the time had come to do something about it.

On his next visit Tom met Molly as usual outside the nurses hostel. It was a mild June evening.

"Molly, since the weather's so nice, how about we take a stroll over to Buile Hill park before we head off to a meal" he said in untypically serious tones.

"Yes, that would be pleasant" said Molly, mildly surprised at this departure from their usual plan and wondering if Tom had more in mind than simply a walk in the park. And if so, what?

When they came across an unoccupied park bench in amongst the trees of the park, Tom said "can we sit here for a while? There's something I want to say. Something important."

CHAPTER 20

"Uh Oh" thought Molly. "This sounds serious."

"Is it about - you know - us?" she said hesitantly.

"Yes" said Tom.

"Oh dear" thought Molly in some alarm. She had become very attached to Tom and very much enjoyed their outings. "I hope he's not going to say he wants to end it. Or that he has to go away or something."

"All right Tom. What is it you want to say to me?"

"Well Molly. We have been going out together for quite a few months now. I think we have got to know each other pretty well. We have a lot in common and get on very well together. In this time I have become very fond of you and there is nothing I like better than being in your company."

"Is this the good news before the bad news?" thought Molly.

He turned to face her and took hold of her hand. Looking directly into her eyes he said "Molly my love, I would like to have you with me for the rest of my life. Will you marry me?"

Molly did not have an answer ready. It had certainly crossed her mind that one day Tom might become serious and she was not entirely sure what her response should be when that happened, but she just had not expected that the need for such an important decision would arrive so soon. While she was not quite ready to say 'Yes', she nevertheless thought that Tom might in fact be a very nice husband and she did not want to lose him by simply saying 'No' right now.

"Now Tom, Tom. I am very fond of you - I am sure you know that. But I don't know that I am quite ready yet to make such a big decision. Can we leave it for a little while? I think, as I am sure you do, that marriage is for life and so we must be certain in our own minds that this decision is the right one for us."

Tom was downcast by her response but at the same time he thought that not all was lost.

"So you are not saying No?"

"Indeed I'm not" said Molly. "But I would like more time. I'll tell you what. The summer holidays are coming up. How about we leave it until we come back? Will you be going over to spend some time in Connemara as usual? I'll be over in Kerry at about the same time. Perhaps you could come down and say Hello to my family."

"Aha!" thought Tom. "I expect she'd liked to see what her family make of me. I suppose that's fair enough. After all I took her to see my family."

"Good idea" said Tom. "I should be able to manage that. I'd like to get to know your family."

BOOK 3

Chapter 21

***Tom holidays as usual** in Ireland. Visits Molly's family in Dingle, Co. Kerry. Makes a good impression.*

At the beginning of July Tom went over to Connemara as usual to spend a couple of weeks on the family farm. At the beginning of the second week he went into Galway, hired a car and set off on his journey southward into Kerry. In the afternoon he arrived in Dingle where he had booked a room in a small hotel. He knew Molly was already in residence at the farm of her own family and he phoned her.

"Hi Molly my love. I've arrived and am staying in Dingle. I'll be spending the morning doing a bit of touring around the Dingle peninsula, so how about I come over and say Hello to your family in the afternoon?"

"Yes do that" said Molly. "We'll expect you sometime after lunch."

Tom spent the morning driving around the Dingle peninsula, had lunch, and then following the directions given him by Molly, he arrived at Gortnakilla, the Cullinan farm, at about 4 o'clock in the afternoon. He saw an extensive single storey stone house with the usual farm outbuildings. Rising up behind the house he saw steep brown hills not unlike those of his native Connemara, with sheep dotted here and there up the slopes. In the fields at the foot of the hill there were cattle. He noted with interest that these were not of the commonly seen breeds such as Shorthorn, Angus or Hereford. They were horned cattle, predominantly white in colour, their hides dappled with black patches and spots. He suddenly recognised what they were: they were Droimeann cattle, one of the few ancient Irish native breeds still in existence.

"That's interesting" thought Tom. "I must ask Molly's dad about them."

He drove up the driveway, got out of the car and knocked on the door of the house. It was opened by a late middle-aged, grey-haired, friendly looking woman who he guessed was Molly's mother. To establish beyond doubt his native Irish credentials he chose to speak in Gaelic.

"Dia duit a bhean an tí. Tomás MacLeannáin is ainm dom. Is cara le Molly mé." ("God be with you woman of the house. Tomás MacLeannáin is my name. I am a friend of Molly's.")

"Dia is Muire duit, a Thomáis. Fáilte romhat. Tar isteach. Is mise Niamh Uí Cuilleannáin, mathair le Molly" ("God and Mary be with you, Tomás. Welcome. Come in. I am Niamh Uí Chuilleannáin, Molly's mother") she replied.

She led Tom down through the hallway into a sitting room where the rest of the family except for Molly's father, were assembled, no doubt awaiting his arrival. She introduced him first to Molly's younger sister, Sinéad, and then to the older brother, Colm, and younger brother, Seán. Tom shook hands with each of them.

"An mbeidh cupán tae agat, a Thomáis?" ("Will you have a cup of tea, Tomás" asked Mrs Cullinan.)

"Ba mhaith liom cupán tae, go raibh maith agat" ("I would like a cup of tea, thank you" replied Tom.

Tea and a cake were brought and conversation ensued. Tom learnt that Colm was at agricultural College, no doubt with a view to one day taking over the farm from his father. Seán was at

Trinity, studying science and was quite excited to meet a real-life research scientist. Sinéad was just about to go up to University College Dublin to do an Arts degree with a view to becoming a teacher. Tom found that he was getting on well with Molly's family and was impressed by the high value which they clearly put on education.

At about 5 o'clock Molly's father, Pádraig, came in from the farm. He divested himself of his boots and oilskin, washed his hands, and came into the sitting room where Tom was introduced to him. Pádraig was tall, weatherbeaten, and with what seemed to Tom a somewhat grim demeanour. He sat down to have tea and cake with the rest of the family.

"So you're Molly's boy friend?" he said, giving Tom a penetrating look.

"As the man who's trying to steal his lovely daughter I suppose he naturally looks at me with some suspicion" thought Tom. "I'd better do my best to make a good impression."

"Yes I am" replied Tom. .

"Well Tomás. Tell us something about yourself. Your family are farming people I understand."

"Yes we are" said Tom, and he told Pádraig about his early years on the family farm in Connemara and how his father had left to go into the building trade in England because the farm could not support two families, and that his father now had a thriving building business in England.."

"And yourself? Are you going into the building business?"

"No" said Tom. "I am a scientist with a degree in Physics. I am currently doing research towards getting a doctorate."

"And do you think you'll get your doctorate?"

"I do" replied Tom confidently.

"And assuming you do, what kind of a job do you eventually hope to get?"

CHAPTER 21

"Eventually I hope to have a post in a university, teaching and doing research."

"And if you don't get that, what will you do instead?"

"I don't expect to remain unemployed for long. There is always a demand for people with mathematical skills" said Tom.

"Hmm" said Pádraig, not sounding entirely convinced.

Molly's younger brother, Seán, winked at Tom. From the grin on his face it seemed that he was enjoying observing this interrogation.

"Still, I suppose" thought Tom. "You can't blame a girl's father for grilling a prospective suitor about his employment prospects."

To Tom's relief, after a silent pause general conversation now recommenced. Molly gave him an encouraging smile.

"I see you are running suckler cows as well as sheep" said Tom to Pádraig.

"We are indeed" said Pádraig. "It's another string to our bow."

"We do the same on the farm in Connemara" said Tom. "But only half a dozen or so. We don't have much area of the better land at the bottom of the mountain. We mainly use Angus cattle. We tried the Charolais but they did not do as well. Would those be the Droimeann breed you have out there?"

"Yes they are" said Pádraig, looking at Tom with new interest. "You know about the Droimeann then?"

"Just a bit. They are one of the ancient breeds aren't they?" said Tom, who suspected that this was a subject dear to Pádraig's's heart.

"Like the Kerry cattle, and the Dexters and the Irish Moiled?"

"They certainly are" said Pádraig. "They originated right here in Kerry, on the Iveragh Peninsula on the other side of the bay. Would you like to come out and have a look at them?"

"I would love to." Tom's interest in the cattle was genuine but at the same time he realised that showing his interest might incline Pádraig to take a more favourable view of his daughter's suitor.

Pádraig took Tom out to the field where the cattle were. They were quite tame so Tom could get close enough to have a good look at them. He was able to carry on an interesting and knowledgeable conversation with Pádraig about the practicalities of rearing the calves from the suckler cows to a saleable weight, and the advantages and disadvantages of various breeds. When they went into the house again Tom had the clear impression that Pádraig was taking a more favourable view of him.

Tom was invited to stay for dinner - roast lamb from one of their own sheep, together with homegrown potatoes and vegetables. Clearly, he thought, a family which strives to be self-sufficient. He liked that. After the meal when the dinner things had been cleared away, once again there was conversation in the sitting room. He sat on the sofa next to Seán and chatted to him about research.

"Molly tells us that you're a musician" said Pádraig. "I believe you play the fiddle."

"I do" said Tom "but also the piano."

"We can't offer you a piano" said Pádraig "but we do have a fiddle. How would you like to play us a tune or two?"

"Uh Oh" thought Tom. "Looks like I am to be put to the test again. Well, I think I'm up to that challenge so here goes."

"I'd be happy to play you a tune or two" he said.

"Grand" said Pádraig. "Seán. Take the fiddle and the bow down from where they are hanging on the wall and give them to Tom."

Seán did as he was bid and handed the instrument to Tom together with a tuning fork which he got from a drawer of a desk at the side of the room. The violin was already approximately in tune, suggesting that it was in regular use, but Tom tuned it accurately nevertheless. He saw Molly give him an anxious look. She must be afraid I might not be up to the task he thought. But I will be. Just wait.

To warm up he began with a few well-known jigs – The Blarney Pilgrim, Jimmy Ward's, Kesh, followed by the five- part slip jig, Kid on the Mountain. He then proceeded to play two hornpipes, The Humours of Tullycrine and Mickey Callaghan's Fancy, after which he increased the tempo with a high-speed rendition of three reels, The Dunmore Lasses, Rakish Paddy and The Star of Munster. Finally he slowed right down and played two slow airs – Limerick's Lamentation and Eanach Dhúin with as much soul and cosmic sadness as he could muster.

When he finished playing there was a respectful silence. Then Colm, the older son spoke.

"That was good, Tom. Very good. Begod you had me nearly in tears with the slow airs."

Molly gave Tom a triumphant smile. He knew he had passed the musical test with flying colours. Having just made what he was sure was a good impression he judged that the time had come for him to take his leave. He rose to his feet and handed the violin and bow back to Seán.

"Well, I must be off back to Dingle to my hotel now. I'll be wanting to make an early start tomorrow on my long drive to Connemara so I'll say goodbye. Thank you for the hospitality, and especially the lovely dinner. There were 'Goodbye Tom' murmurs around the room.

"Please God we'll see you again some time, Tom" said Molly's mother.

"Please God you will" he responded, and he meant it.

"I'll see you out" said Molly, and came out of the house with him to the car.

"Well, how did I do?" asked Tom.

"I think you did very well" said Molly. "You even, eventually, made a good impression on my father, and he's hard to please. Taking an interest in his cattle certainly helped and he liked your fiddle playing. He's a very good fiddler himself."

"So my visit was a success. Good" said Tom. "Well, now I really must be off. Any chance of a kiss?"

Molly glanced back at the house to see if anyone was watching and then gave Tom a brief but enthusiastic kiss. As he drove away Tom wondered – will she now say 'Yes' when I ask her again? Perhaps she'll want to see what her family thought of me.

Going back into the house Molly went into the sitting room where the family was still assembled.

"Well. What did you think of Tom Glennon" she asked. The response was generally favourable.

"He seemed a very pleasant, well brought up young man" said her mother.

"I liked him" said Seán. "We had a great chat about Science."

"I took quite a fancy to him" said Sinéad with a broad grin. "I'll have him if you don't want him."

"Hands off!" said Molly.

"Grand fiddle player" said Colm.

They looked expectantly towards the head of the household, Pádraig, to see if he had an opinion to contribute.

"He knows a thing or two about livestock, I'll say that for him" said Pádraig eventually. "I'd say he's an Irish countryman at heart, despite the English education." The family looked at each other: from him this was praise indeed.

Chapter 22

Tom returns to Cambridge *and throws himself into his research. It goes well. Continues going out with Molly. Decides to take the plunge and once again ask her to marry him. This time she says Yes.*

Tom returned to Cambridge after his holiday feeling cautiously optimistic about his relationship with Molly. He would have to give some thought about how long to leave it before asking her once again to marry him. Perhaps not on their next date but not too long. Certainly before the memory of her family's warm response to him had chance to fade. In the meantime, now in his second Ph.D. year, he threw himself enthusiastically back into his research.

His aim was to create a user-friendly numerical model of an exoplanet atmosphere into which any set of data - planet size, proximity to host star, radiative characteristics of star, atmosphere depth, gaseous chemical composition etc. - could be entered, and which would then arrive at a realistic picture of the state of that atmosphere. His particular interest was to make it possible to calculate the survival time of the atmosphere of such a planet when it found itself dangerously close to its star. To achieve this he designed his model to determine what proportion of the gas molecules at the outer periphery of the atmosphere, assuming a Maxwell-Boltzmann distribution of kinetic energies, would acquire escape velocity in a given period of time. Since this would vary with the molecular species it also provided a mechanism by which the atmospheric composition would change with time. His supervisor, Jim Metcalfe, was pleased with Tom's progress and made useful suggestions towards fine-tuning the detail. Like all graduate students, Tom was required to give an occasional seminar and his, to the Astrophysics group, was well received.

A few weeks after coming back from Ireland Tom got in touch with Molly and arranged another date. While this, as always, went well he chose not to say anything about marriage this time. She gave him one or two quizzical looks and he suspected that she was expecting him to ask her again. On their next outing, a month later, Tom decided that it was now or never. He would ask her once more to marry him. If she said No then it would be a great blow. He would be very sad. But he would not ask again.

In fact, since Tom's first proposal, Molly's views had undergone a significant positive change, influenced in no small part by her family's favourable response to him. She had come to realise that she was very fond of Tom and that she would in fact very much like to be married to him. Indeed his failure to repeat his proposal on their previous date was something of a worry to her. Was she actually going to lose him?

How could she get him to ask her again? Give him a bit of a nudge? Say something like – "Tom, was there something you wanted to say to me?" No. That's too obvious. The initiative must come from him.

At the end of the meal Molly looked a little anxiously at Tom across the restaurant table. He had been unusually quiet. And then –

CHAPTER 22

"Molly you remember when we took a stroll in Buile Hill park, back In June?"

"I do, Tom. I do"

"And I asked you to marry me."

"You did."

"Well now, Molly. I'm asking again. Molly Ni Chuilleanáin - will you marry me?"

"Yes, Tomás MacLeannáin. I will."

"What! You will? You really will?"

"I just said I will and I meant it."

"Well thanks be to God for that! Oh Molly, Molly. I am so happy now."

"And so am I, Tom. So am I."

"Let's not bother with a film tonight, Molly. You and I have so much to talk about."

Outside the restaurant they kissed passionately, and then walked back to the car, hand in hand.

Chapter 23

***They choose an engagement** ring and tell the good news to Molly's friends at Salford Royal Hospital. In anticipation of living together after getting married, Molly moves to Addenbrooke's Hospital in Cambridge.*

On his next visit Tom came early so that they could go in to a jeweller in Manchester to choose an engagement ring for Molly.

"Now Tom" said Molly. "I'd like a nice ring, of course, but you must not spend a lot of money. You are only a student and when we are married we won't be rich. We'll be living on your student stipend and my nurse's salary and while we won't exactly be poor, money will be tight."

"All right" said Tom. "I won't be extravagant." He was privately pleased that Molly apparently shared his own instinct for frugality, derived no doubt, like his own, from growing up on a small farm. They eventually settled on a ring with a prominent blue zircon surrounded by small diamonds, which Tom could just about afford. There would be no mistaking its presence on Molly's ring finger.

That evening, when they returned to the nurses hostel, Molly brought Tom into the common room again, happy to show him off to her friends not just as a boyfriend any more but now as her actual fiancé. Tom said Hello to the girls, who by now he knew well –

CHAPTER 23

"Hi ...Bernadette...Maeve...Mary...Siobhán...Teresa..."

There was great interest in the news that now they were engaged to be married and Molly's ring was much admired.

"Tell us Molly. How did he propose? What did he say?" they demanded, happy to cause the maximum embarrassment to Tom.

"Oh, never you mind" said Molly.

"I'll tell you what" said Tom. "Will I tell you the way of it?"

"Ah do! Do!" they chorused.

"Well, as you know both Molly and myself are off the land, as indeed are the rest of you."

"Yes" they said.

"This being the case" said Tom "you will appreciate that when a match is being made, there are certain important matters which need to be sorted out first."

"There are, of course" agreed the girls.

"So" continued Tom. "When the day came for me to pop the question, I called my darling over to me. "Molly my love" says I 'Will you come over here and sit on my knee for a moment. I have something to say.'"

"Ooh" said the girls.

"'Tom *a ghrá'* says she 'I will of course'" and she came and sat on my knee. And she put her arm around me. And gave me a kiss."

"Ah pay no attention to all this" said Molly. "He's just making it up."

"No, don't stop. Go on, Tom, go on " said the girls.

"I will" said Tom. "I will. So then I says to her – 'Molly *a stor*, tell me. Do you have any bit of land?'"

An intake of breath from the audience.

"Oh Tommy my lovely Tommy", says she, "sure 'tis divil the bit of land I have at all." After a shocked silence, "*Is mór an trua sin*"

(That's a great pity) says I. Then a long pause. And finally – "Oh well, never mind Molly, I love you almost as much as if you did. Will you marry me?" And that's how the match was made."

"Not a word of truth in any of it" said Molly. "Of course not" said the girls, laughing, "but it makes a good story."

"Actually, in his story" said Molly. "He never says whether I said 'Yes'. Perhaps I didn't. So there."

"Well, thanks be to God you did - eventually" said Tom.

Since Tom was only in the middle of his PhD research they realised that when they were married they would be living in Cambridge. In anticipation of this, Molly sought and obtained a position in Addenbrooke's Hospital in Cambridge. This meant that from now on they could spend the much more time together.

Chapter 24

After a 6 month engagement *Tom and Molly are married, with a full nuptial mass, in the Catholic church in Dingle. They honeymoon in Mallorca.*

The news of their engagement came as no surprise to the Glennon and Cullinan families and was welcomed by both. So now decisions had to be made as to the date and location of the wedding. Tom and Molly had agreed to have a 6 month engagement so there was plenty of time for the planning. It was, of course, up to the family of the bride to organise the wedding ceremony. Amongst the churches on the Dingle Peninsula they chose St Mary's, a large Victorian Gothic church in Dingle town. Like so many Irish Catholic families, the Cullinans had relatives who had entered the church and one of these, Father Timothy O'Regan, a parish priest in the North of England, said he would be more than happy to officiate. A day in May was finally chosen. Many of the Cullinan relatives lived within easy driving distance, but hotel rooms had to be booked for members of the Glennon extended family from Connemara and other distant parts. Suspecting that the Cullinan family finances might be somewhat more straitened than his own, Micheál managed, with some difficulty, to persuade Pádraig to accept a substantial contribution towards the significant cost of the wedding reception to be held in a local hotel following the ceremony.

The great day finally came. Since, somewhat to Tom's private regret, it wasn't the custom in the West of Ireland for the groom to wear the full morning suit and top hat regalia, he wore a smart dark suit, especially bought for the occasion. Tom had asked Mick Hennessy to be his best man. He was happy to oblige and indeed looked forward to visiting Ireland, the land of his ancestors. The night before the wedding, Mick together with Molly's brothers Colm and Seán, took Tom out to the Dingle pubs where Irish music was to be heard, for his last drink as a bachelor.

As believing, practising Catholics Tom and Molly had chosen to have the full nuptial mass for their wedding. A friend of Molly's from the nurses training College was to be maid of honour. Her sister Sinéad and two cousins made up the three bridesmaids. Molly's brothers, Colm and Seán, had volunteered to be two of the groomsmen and a Connemara cousin of Tom's, Ciarán, made up the third. As the congregation arrived at St Mary's Church the bride's family and friends were placed on the left and the groom's on the right. The priest stood at the front facing the congregation. Tom and his best man came into the church through a side entrance and proceeded to the front of the church where they waited.

The organist started playing, signifying that the ceremony was about to begin and the congregation rose to their feet. The three bridesmaids and three groomsmen entered from the back of the church, escorted one another up the aisle and then lined up to the left and to the right, respectively, at the front. They were followed by the maid of honour who also placed herself on the left. Then finally the bride arrived, in a flowing white bridal gown with floral headdress and veil, walking on her father's arm to a triumphant organ accompaniment, slowly down the aisle. When she arrived at the front Tom stole a look and thought he had never seen her so beautiful. Molly and Tom, as bride and groom then proceeded to kneel side-by-side on a two person prie-dieu in the centre at the head of the aisle. The congregation then knelt or sat down again and the nuptial mass with Father Tim O'Regan as the celebrant, began.

The mass proceeded through its stages as far as the Gospel, after which there was a homily by Father O' Regan. The end of the homily marked that point in the nuptial mass at which the Rite of Marriage was to be carried out. The congregation and the couple all rose to their feet. The priest addressed the bride and groom.

"Tom and Molly, have you come here to enter into Marriage without coercion, really and wholeheartedly?"

Tom: "I have."

Molly: "I have."

Father O' Regan: "Are you prepared, as you follow the path of Marriage, to love and honour each other for as long as you both shall live?"

Tom: "I am."

Molly: "I am."

Father O' Regan: "Are you prepared to accept children lovingly from God and to bring them up according to the law of Christ and his church?"

Tom: "I am."

Molly: "I am."

Father O' Regan: "Since it is your intention to enter the covenant of Holy Matrimony, join your right hands and declare your consent before God and his church."

Tom and Molly turned to face each other and clasped their right hands.

Tom: "I, Thomas Daniel Glennon, take you, Molly Fionnuala Cullinan, for my lawful wife, to have and to hold, from this day forward, for better, for worse, for richer, for poorer, in sickness and in health until death do us part."

Molly: "I, Molly Fionnuala Cullinan, take you, Thomas Daniel Glennon, for my lawful husband, to have and to hold, from this day forward, for better, for worse, for richer, for poorer, in sickness and in health, until death do us part."

Father O' Regan: "May the Lord in his kindness strengthen the consent you have declared before the Church, and graciously bring to fulfilment his blessing within you.

What God has joined, let no one put asunder.

Let us bless the Lord."

Congregation: "Thanks be to God!"

There followed the blessing and the exchange of rings. Tom placed Molly's ring on her ring finger, saying "Molly, receive this ring as a sign of my love and fidelity. In the name of the Father, and of the Son, and of the Holy Spirit."

In similar manner, Molly placed Tom's ring on his ring finger, saying "Tom, receive this ring as a sign of my love and fidelity. In the name of the Father, and of the Son and of the Holy Spirit."

The nuptial mass then continued through its various stages to the finish. Tom and Molly retired to a table at the side where they signed the marriage register before witnesses, then returned to the church with beaming smiles, hand in hand, as man and wife, and standing side-by-side joined in the ancient Irish hymn – *Be Thou My Vision* - which brought the ceremony to an end.

The wedding reception was a cheerful and successful event, enjoyed by all with the possible exception of the married couple upon whom attention was focused. The maid of honour gave a speech in which she related some of the escapades of Molly and herself when they had been students together. As best man,

CHAPTER 24

Mick Hennessy gave a short speech the main thrust of which was to assure the bride's parents that their daughter had married a good bloke. The father of the bride said how sad they were to lose their daughter but expressed their confidence that she had found a good man. The cake was eventually cut and pieces distributed, after which the bride and groom retired to change into their travelling clothes and prepare for their departure. They waved goodbye to the assembled family members and then set off in their hire car for Limerick city where they had a hotel room booked for the night.

The following morning they flew from Shannon airport via London to Mallorca, where they were going to spend their honeymoon in Port De Soller, a small town and holiday resort on the North coast of this Mediterranean island. They spent the next two weeks bathing in the warm sea, kayaking, exploring the old streets of the town and of the capital, Palma, walking in the mountainous country behind Port de Soller, enjoying the local cuisine and, of course, enjoying the lovemaking which their marital status now made permissible.

Chapter 25

***Tom and Molly begin** their married life in married student accommodation in Saviour College. Tom completes his exo-planet atmospheric general circulation model. It is published and well received. He writes his PhD thesis, is examined, and accepted. He applies for, and gets, a postdoctoral fellowship in the Physics Department in Oxford.*

At the end of their honeymoon, Tom and Molly flew back to England and returned to Cambridge to begin their new married life together. In addition to its undergraduate accommodation, Saviour College had a small number of one or two bedroom apartments, with kitchen and shower room, available for married students. Tom and Molly had managed to secure one of these and into this they moved when they arrived back in Cambridge. They soon settled into a daily routine, Molly to her nursing at Addenbrooke's Hospital and Tom to his research in the Physics Department. Their shared income was adequate for their frugal lifestyle. Tom left the management of the family income to Molly, liberating him to concentrate all his mental energy on his PhD project. The cooking, however, they shared. Whilst Tom was entirely happy with Molly's plain, if unadventurous, cuisine he enjoyed cooking. After struggling all day with physical concepts, mathematical equations and computer code he liked to have something hands-on and practical to do.

By the beginning of his third year the structure of Tom's exoplanet atmospheric general circulation model was complete. The task now was to turn it into a form such that anyone could easily use it: that is to say, they could enter the numerical values of the various physical and chemical parameters of any real or hypothetical exoplanetary atmosphere and arrive at a realistic, if approximate, picture of the equilibrium state at which that atmosphere would arrive and its possible future development with time. In this final stage of his project, Tom put a great deal of effort into making his model as user-friendly as possible. His supervisor, Dr Jim Metcalfe, when Tom demonstrated the model to him, was impressed and assured Tom that in this aim he had succeeded.

Tom wrote a paper setting out the essential structure of the model and providing some numerical examples of its application. This, after some revision by Jim Metcalfe, was submitted to *The Astrophysical Journal*, under the names Glennon and Metcalfe, and was accepted for publication. The Physics Department was happy to have this software package made freely available to other scientists. Interested researchers from around the world soon became aware of its existence and asked for copies. Amongst exoplanet astronomers it became widely known as the Glennon Model.

Having written the paper was a great help to Tom when it came to writing his thesis, in so far as this had forced him to structure his thoughts on his complex research topic. The thesis was, of course, much longer than the paper. It comprised six chapters and Tom went to a great deal of trouble to make it readable for any physical scientist, not just exoplanet specialists. His effort paid off. When the time came for his viva voce examination, with one external (Oxford) and one internal examiner, the external examiner a distinguished Oxford astrophysicist complimented him on the clarity of his writing. It seemed that so far as Physics PhD theses go, Tom's was a welcome change. When the examiners report came back, Jim Metcalfe was pleased to tell Tom that he had passed with flying colours. So now, although the degree ceremony was still to come, he could think of himself as Dr Glennon. Molly and his family were of course delighted, but no one was surprised.

Even before his third year was over Tom had been giving serious thought as to where he might go next. The standard next step for young scientists wishing to continue in a research career was to apply for a post doctoral fellowship, preferably in some institution other than the one where they had obtained their PhD. In the general scientific journal, *Nature*, Tom had seen an advertisement inviting applications for a specific named fellowship - the Lindemann Fellowship - in the Physics Department, Oxford. Since astrophysics was one of the subject areas specified, Tom decided to throw his hat into the ring.

As part of his application he would have to put together a research proposal. He had already decided to continue with exoplanets, a field which was not only interesting, but in his view likely to be fruitful with plenty of discoveries waiting to be made. While continuing with atmospheric modelling, a field in which he already had something of a reputation, he was keen to apply his abilities to the problem of extracting atmospheric composition information from the astronomical spectroscopic measurements on the light which had passed through an exoplanet atmosphere. He was aware that very often these measurements were at the lower limits of what could be achieved by existing instrumentation and any improvements in the analysis of the data would be valuable. He also had some ideas, stimulated by discussions with his experimental physicist friend, Mick Hennessy, about possible improvements to the measuring equipment.

Jim Metcalfe put him in touch with exoplanet researchers in Oxford. They already knew of him because of the Glennon model, and were keen to have him join them. Having taken that step he prepared his application. While it included his CV and small, but relevant, publication list, it consisted mainly of his research proposal. The prestigious Lindemann Fellowship was heavily oversubscribed. Within the Physics Department a committee was charged with the task of reading all the proposals and winnowing them down to a shortlist of three. Tom's was one of the three and so with the other candidates he was invited to Oxford for an interview with an assessment panel consisting of three members of the selection committee, two of them full professors in the department.

After general questions, designed to assess Tom's background, and whether as a person he would be generally compatible with the Department's philosophy and atmosphere, they got down to specifics. Although he had not yet been through the degree ceremony they were courteous enough to address him as 'Dr Glennon'.

"Tell us please, Dr Glennon, what you might be seeking to detect in exoplanet atmospheres?"

"Well, the holy Grail" said Tom "would be to detect oxygen. This would be an unmistakable sign of the presence of life on that planet."

"And why is that?" asked his interlocutor.

"All exoplanets" said Tom "start off with anaerobic, highly reducing, atmospheres. Any oxygen present is in combined. form, such as CO, CO_2 and H_2O. While very small amounts of oxygen can be formed by abiotic mechanisms, we are confident that substantial concentrations, such as in our atmosphere, can only be generated by photosynthesis. In the case of our own planet there is evidence that oxygenic photosynthesis, by cyanobacteria, began about 3 billion years ago but it took about another billion years for the oxygen to mop up the reducing compounds and start appearing as molecular oxygen in the atmosphere. Making the plausible assumption that a similar sequence must occur on other planets, then we can take the presence of detectable oxygen in a planetary atmosphere as a sign that at least photosynthesising life forms of cyanobacterial type have evolved on that planet. The presence of ozone, nitrous oxide or methane would also be indicative of the presence of life.

The oxygen-producing photosynthesisers must have evolved from previously existing anaerobic photosynthesisers, such as the photosynthetic bacteria that we have in anaerobic environments on the Earth. So, an as yet unanswered question is, do those organisms make a detectable contribution to a planetary atmosphere, and if so what? If we knew the answer to that question we might be able to detect life even before oxygen has appeared. At the moment the ball is in the court of the microbial biochemists."

"And how is this transition from anaerobic photosynthesisers to oxygen-producing photosynthesisers believed to take place?" asked the chairman.

"It requires mutation to bring about replacement of the bacteriochlorophyll in the photosynthetic active centre with a chlorophyll *a* molecule. This chlorophyll-containing active centre, when it receives absorbed light energy, reaches an excited state with an energy level higher than the corresponding bacteriochlorophyll-containing one: energetic enough in fact to pull hydrogen atoms out of a water molecule, thus liberating oxygen."

CHAPTER 25

Tom went on to give an account of his proposed approach to extracting more information from these spectroscopic data together with some possible modifications to the astronomical spectroradiometers used to obtain these data. The assessment panel asked him some more questions, picking up on some of the specific points he had made and then finally the chairman said

"Thank you Dr Glennon. You have made some interesting points. The Physics Department will let you know its decision about the fellowship very shortly."

"Well gentlemen? Your impressions?" asked the chairman when Tom had left the room.

"Good" said one of the other two committee members. "Very bright. Articulate. Knows his stuff. On top of his brief."

"Yes, that's my impression too" said the other committee member.

"Wide-ranging in his interests. He seems to know his biophysics as well as his exoplanet atmospheric physics."

"He certainly presents very well" said the chairman.

Three weeks later, Tom received a letter from the Oxford Physics Department. He had been awarded the Lindemann postdoctoral Fellowship! As soon as Molly arrived home from her shift as a nurse at Addenbrooke's Hospital, he told her the good news.

"Molly, you know the postdoctoral fellowship I applied for in Oxford?"

"Yes Tom, what about it?"

"I got it! I just heard today."

"Oh Tom, that's tremendous! So, we'll soon be moving to Oxford."

"Yes we will. In a few weeks time."

"Well" said practical Molly. "We must start thinking ahead. We will have to find somewhere to live, so we had better start finding about the housing situation in Oxford. And I will be looking for a nursing post in an Oxford hospital."

"I don't think you will have any problem there" said Tom. "Oxford is a bigger city than Cambridge and I think they have three or four hospitals."

Chapter 26

They move to Oxford, *where they rent a small house, and Molly finds a nursing post in one of the Oxford hospitals. Tom's research prospers, publications follow, he begins to develop an international reputation. As his three-year fellowship draws to a close, Tom looks for a more permanent job. He applies for a lectureship at the Welsh Institute of Astrophysics attached to the University in the coastal town of Aberystwyth. Goes for an interview. Is offered the post.*

As soon as they received the good news about the Lindemann Fellowship, Tom and Molly set about preparing for the move to Oxford. At the top of their priorities was finding somewhere to live and they made several journeys from Cambridge to Oxford in search of housing which might be affordable, given their limited means. They investigated the urban area of Kidlington about 12 km north of Oxford city. This consisted of a small, attractive ancient English village surrounded by a large, somewhat nondescript, suburb and it was here they thought they might find something they could just about afford. Outright purchase proved impossible; even with their joint income the necessary mortgage could not be obtained. They managed nevertheless to find a small semi-detached house to rent, and this was their home for the next three years. They also bought a small second-hand car.

Tom got on well with his colleagues in the Physics Department. His research prospered and publications followed. In particular, on the basis of collaboration with microbial biochemists in North America and in Britain, he was able to arrive at promising proposals as to how the presence of anaerobic photosynthetic and non-photosynthetic bacteria on an exoplanet might be detected by their contribution to the planet's atmosphere. He now began to receive invitations, expenses paid, to attend, and present papers at, important international conferences in his field - a sign that he was now becoming known in the astrophysics world.

When his third year in Oxford began, Tom knew that the time had come to start looking for a new job to begin when his fellowship ended. He scoured the advertisements in the employment columns of *Nature*, *The Times* and *The Guardian* looking for suitable possibilities. They were plenty of jobs advertised for physicists in industry but he had his heart set on academia because of the freedom it would give him in his research. One advertisement in particular caught his attention. It was for a post as assistant lecturer/lecturer in the Welsh Institute of Astrophysics, attached to the Physics Department in Aberystwyth University. Aberystwyth being a coastal town on the Welsh coast, he thought it might be a pleasant environment in which to live. He discussed it with Molly and she liked the prospect of living by the seaside. He submitted his application together with CV, publication list and the names of some senior scientists, including his former supervisor, Jim Metcalfe, who knew his work and could give an informed opinion as to his abilities.

Some weeks later Tom received an invitation to come to Aberystwyth for an interview. He decided that Molly should come with him so that they could look at the town together. They booked themselves into a B&B and set off early for the three and a half hour drive to Aberystwyth to give themselves time to look at the town. When they arrived Tom phoned Gareth Morgan, director of the Astrophysics Institute and also a professor in the Physics Department to find the time and place of the interview. Professor Morgan welcomed him to Aberystwyth but had some somewhat discouraging news for him. It seemed that the Department of Welsh History was also seeking to appoint a new lecturer but the university has decided, because of budgetary constraints, that only one new lectureship, not two, could be created. So not only was Tom in competition with other candidates for the Physics lectureship but the Physics Department itself was in competition with the Department of Welsh History. Furthermore in the interests of fair play there was to be a humanities representative on his interview committee and a scientific representative on the Welsh History committee.

Tom turned up next day at 10 AM for his interview in the Physics building. The committee consisted of Professor Morgan, Dr Elizabeth Hopkins, a physical chemist, Dr Jack Barclay, a senior lecturer in the Biochemistry department and - as the humanities representative - Professor Arwyn ap Rhys from the Department of Celtic Languages. The scientific members interrogated Tom about his research and also his teaching experience. Professor ap Rhys remained silent, just listening to Tom's answers. Eventually the scientists had asked all the questions they needed to and turned to look expectantly at Professor ap Rhys. Giving Tom a penetrating glance from deep set eyes under bushy eyebrows, he said

"Tell me, Dr Glennon, do you happen to speak Welsh? I ask because this is a Welsh-speaking part of Wales and we like to do everything we can to keep our language alive."

"Uh Oh" thought Tom. "This is the part of the interview where I blow it."

"No, I am afraid not" he replied.

"Ah..." said Professor ap Rhys in a disappointed tone. But then Tom had an inspiration.

"But I do, however, speak another Celtic language, namely Irish."

"Indeed" said Professor ap Rhys, looking at Tom with new interest.

"*An bhfuil Gaeilge agat i ndáiríre?*" (Do you really speak Irish?)

"Ah Ha!" thought Tom. "As professor of Celtic languages, no doubt he can speak Irish himself and is putting me to the test. Well, this is one test I can certainly pass."

"*Cinnte tá Gaeilge agam. Is as* Éirinn *mé. Rugadh agus togadh sa Gaeltacht i gConmara. Tá mé liofa.* (Indeed I can speak Irish. I am from Ireland. I was born and raised in the Gaeltacht in Connemara. I am fluent.)

"*Mar sin feicim. Cinnte tá Gaeilge agat. Go raibh maith agat.*" (So I see. Indeed you can speak Irish. Thank you.)

replied Professor ap Rhys. Tom noticed the scientific members of the panel looking somewhat bemused while this exchange was going on. Since it seemed that Professor ap Rhys had no more questions to put, Professor Morgan brought the proceedings to a close after one final question.

"In the event of the University choosing you, would you accept an assistant lectureship?"

"No I would not" replied Tom, who had a realistic but positive view of his own worth as a scientist. "I would want the full lectureship."

"I see. Well that will be all. Thank you Dr Glennon."

Tom left the Physics department and went to rejoin Molly.

"Well Tom, how did it go?"

"A bit hard to say. More or less okay I think. But one odd thing happened" and Tom recounted his exchange with Professor ap Rhys.

CHAPTER 26

Just before lunchtime Tom received a phone call from Professor Morgan.

"Thanks for coming, Tom. Of course no decision has been made yet, and you are aware that there are a number of candidates for the lectureship. By the way I am not sure what kind of ethnicocultural rabbit you were pulling out of the hat back there but you did make quite a good impression on Arwyn ap Rhys. You'll be hearing from the University in a couple of weeks time."

"Do you know what, Molly my love. I have a feeling that I am in with a chance. Let's take a look at the town and see if we would like to live here."

They took a stroll around the town centre and along the seafront and then drove out to take a look at the housing estates on the periphery.

"Well Molly, what do you think?"

"I like it. I think this might be a pleasant place to live."

"So do I. So now we'll just have to wait and see if I get offered the job."

The following morning Tom and Molly drove back to Oxford.

Three weeks later a letter arrived from Aberystwyth University. It offered Tom the post in the Welsh Institute of Astrophysics combined with a lectureship in the Physics Department. Without delay Tom replied, accepting the offer.

Chapter 27

***They move to Aberystwyth**. Can now afford to buy a small semi-detached house. Tom finds his dual post as a researcher in the Astrophysics Institute and a lecturer in the Physics Department entirely congenial. Reputation grows. Invitations to international conferences. Is asked to write a book on exoplanets. Favourable reviews. Begins to take an interest in dark matter. Promotion to Senior Lecturer. Molly's longed for pregnancy finally happens but a miscarriage leaves Molly desolate.*

Although lectures did not begin until September, Tom's appointment began at the beginning of August. This allowed time for settling in, both academically and domestically. The university provided short-term rental accommodation for new staff to give them time to make their own long-term residential arrangements, so Tom and Molly had somewhere to stay when they began their life in Aberystwyth. Tom's salary as a full time lecturer was much better than his previous postdoctoral stipend. In addition Molly had no trouble finding a nursing position in the local Bronglais hospital. Their financial position was now such that they should have no difficulty obtaining a mortgage for a house, if they chose to buy one. Accordingly, without delay they started visiting estate agents, looking for a small to medium house, not too far from the University and the hospital. They soon found a modest three bedroomed semi detached house in the Waun Fawr suburb, on the Eastern side of the town which they thought would be suitable. There were other university people, particularly young couples, also living in the same area which made it more attractive. They made an offer and it was accepted. Tom's peripatetic life as a young scientist in temporary employment had now ended. At last they owned their own home and could start a family.

The week after Tom took up his post there was a conference of the members of the Astrophysics Institute and the Physics Department to arrange the distribution of the teaching duties for the term amongst the staff. As so often happens when a new member of staff is appointed, he finds that he has been lumbered with a lecture course that no one else wants to teach. Tom found that Quantum Mechanics was now his responsibility. In fact he did not find this to be a problem. He had long been fascinated by quantum theory, in particular for its implications for the nature of physical reality. Nevertheless, although he relished the challenge, he realised that to have these lectures ready in time he must immediately set to work.

Tom found his new career as a researcher in the Astrophysics Institute and a lecturer in the Physics Department, entirely congenial. Although research was his prime interest he enjoyed teaching and interacting with students. What he did not enjoy was sitting on university committees, of which there seemed to be a large number. Also, by keeping his head down he managed to keep his administrative duties to a minimum. In this he modelled himself on the famous physicist, Richard Feynman, whose standard policy in relation to university administration had been "let George do it."

Totally focussed and driven as he was, his research prospered. Exoplanets continued to be his main interest and he collaborated in his research with colleagues in America and Europe who had direct access to the data from the telescopes set up to study these planets. He also became very interested in dark matter, that strange invisible material which permeates the galaxy and which can only be detected by its gravitational effects on the stars in the galaxy. In this he collaborated with other theoreticians and with particle physicists to hypothesise various as yet undiscovered particles of which dark matter might be composed, and then to come up with ways in which they might be detected.

His reputation grew and with it there came invitations to present papers, often of a review nature covering exoplanet astronomy, to international conferences. After presenting one such paper at a conference in Boston in which he gave an overview of the current state of research in this area, he was approached by a woman, tall, with an authoritative manner who introduced herself as Dr Felicity Chandler, a commissioning editor for a prestigious university press.

"I enjoyed your presentation" she said. "Lucid and comprehensive, if I may say so.

"We think that this field has changed so much over the last few years, that it is time for an update. You know, an overall picture of the field, of how it presently stands and where it may be going. Having heard your talk I think you might be just the person to do it. Is there any possibility you might be interested?"

"I don't know" said Tom. "While I have more than once been asked to give some kind of general account of the exoplanet field, I hadn't been thinking of actually writing a book."

"I dare say not" said Dr Chandler. "But perhaps you could give the possibility some thought and if you are interested let me know." She gave Tom her email address.

"All right" said Tom. "I'll think about it."

CHAPTER 27

Back in Aberystwyth, after the conference Tom's thoughts turned to the possibility of writing the book suggested by Dr Chandler. It would be an extra burden but he was confident that he could write just such a book as she proposed. Furthermore he knew that he did always derive satisfaction from creating order out of disorder, of creating a coherent structure in what was a complex and messy area of science. Eventually he decided that this was a challenge he would accept. But first he thought he should run it past Professor Morgan, Director of the Institute.

"I think that would be an excellent idea, Tom. It would be a useful addition to the literature. But it will be no small task. Are you sure you can manage it?"

"I believe I can" said Tom.

He emailed his acceptance to Dr Chandler. She sent him a contract to sign and also indicated to him the approximate length of book that the university press had in mind. Tom set to work without delay. The first task was to get the broad structure of the book straight in his head and from this he proceeded to a series of chapter topics. A chapter to which he devoted particular attention was one with the title 'Conditions for the origin of life' in which he specified not only the physicochemical requirements - liquid water and a plentiful endowment of organic chemicals, but also gave an account of current hypotheses as to the nature of the earliest forms of living material. He did much of his writing at home in the evenings. After about a year of intensive effort he had a draft ready which he sent off to the University press. This was deemed acceptable and with relatively little editing his book was sent off to the printers and was published shortly thereafter as *Exoplanets: Origin and Evolution*. It was generally well received and was favourably reviewed in *Science* and *Nature*. In recognition of his growing reputation, the University promoted him to a senior lectureship.

Tom and Molly soon settled down to their new life together in Aberystwyth. They both had interesting jobs. Their seaside town with the hilly Welsh countryside close by provided a pleasant environment. They now for the first time had a garden and they both took to gardening with enthusiasm, Tom keen to grow his own vegetables, Molly preferring flowers and shrubs. In the warmer weather they occasionally went for a swim, but by preference from the sandy Borth Beach, 10 km north of the town rather than from Aberystwyth's own pebbly beach. They made friends among the other younger members of staff and often entertained. Molly, always an ardent reader, joined a book club. And Tom discovered to his delight that one of the local pubs actually hosted Irish music sessions and he, with his fiddle, became a regular attender. Separated as it was only by the breadth of the Irish Sea from Ireland, reception of Raidió Éireann in Aberystwyth was quite good so that Tom could not only listen to their traditional Irish music programs but also keep in touch with the news from what he still regarded as his native land.

They both felt that on the whole fate had treated them well. Over the next few years, however, something of a dark cloud began to develop over their life together. This was not a problem in their relationship. They remained fond and devoted to each other. It was rather that starting a family was turning out to be not as easy as they had thought. In the summer of their fourth year in Aberystwyth, however, it seemed that success was at hand. Molly became convinced that she was at last pregnant. She was overjoyed when her GP confirmed that this was indeed the case. She told Tom the good news as soon as he arrived home from the University. He was delighted: on his own account of course, but especially for Molly's sake as he knew how important it was to her to have children. Together they started planning their much anticipated future life as parents. Sadly, however, it was not to be. A few weeks later while Molly was doing her shift at the hospital she found that she was bleeding. This was accompanied first by cramps and then by severe belly pain. She had herself admitted to the emergency department and it soon became clear that she was in fact having a miscarriage. The hospital phoned Tom who came in haste. Molly had been put in a private room for an overnight stay to give her time to recover and Tom found her there, weeping inconsolably at the loss of her baby. He put his arms around her and held her close. Eventually the sobs subsided and she began to come to terms with what had happened.

"This is indeed a terrible blow my love" said Tom. "But we'll try again."

"Yes we will, we will" said Molly. "But you know I am already thirty three and the biological clock is ticking."

Chapter 28

The career of Mick Hennessy, *Tom's Australian friend at Cambridge, spent mainly in the United States, has also prospered. Tempted back to Australia to oversee the creation of a new scientific institution – the Australian Institute for Space and Remote Sensing Science, in Canberra the National capital. He phones Tom up and offers him a post, at the level of full professor. After discussion with Molly, Tom accepts.*

At the same time as Tom's scientific career had been developing in Britain, his Cambridge friend Mick Hennessy had also been making a name for himself as an experimental and instrumentation physicist in America. After his PhD he had been awarded a postdoctoral fellowship in the Harvard Physics Department from which he had continued on to a tenure track appointment as an associate professor at MIT, with every expectation of proceeding to a full professorship in the near future. His rising scientific reputation had not escaped the notice of the academic world in Australia and he had already been identified as one of those high performing expatriate scientists who it would be good to tempt back to their native land. Tom had kept in touch with Mick and they had followed each other's careers with interest.

Some months after Molly's miscarriage, when Tom and Molly were sitting down at home after their dinner, he received a phone call. It was Mick Hennessy, phoning from Canberra, the Australian national capital.

"G'day Tom. How's things?"

"Oh, pretty good, pretty good. And yourself?"

"Great, mate. Great. And has Molly recovered?" Tom had told Mick about the miscarriage.

"More or less, I guess. But she is still a bit down."

"Sorry to hear that. That must have been a real blow. Perhaps better luck next time. Anyway give her my love."

Although Mick's good wishes were sincere, Tom was a bit surprised that he had phoned all the way from what he assumed was America, to convey them. The reason for the phone call now became clear.

"Now Tom I have a proposition I'd like you to consider. To give serious consideration to. Don't make any decision now. Take your time and think about it. The situation is that I have now come back to Australia. The government here is establishing a new scientific institution, to be called the Australian Institute for Space and Remote Sensing Science. They asked me to head it up and I accepted. I am now looking for staff. We will be based in Canberra on the ANU (Australian National University) campus but will also have a lab at Jervis Bay on the South coast. I want to have a good theoretician for the mathematical side of the work and I think you're the man. Our Institute will have links with the Physics Department and the Research School of Physical Sciences at the ANU. You would be appointed as a full professor and of course there would be some teaching duties which go with the job.

Now, would you like to think about it and then get back to me. I'll send the full details to you by email. I think you will find the salary is quite a bit better than your present one."

"Gosh, this is a bit unexpected" said Tom. "I'm not in the remote sensing field."

"Well, maybe you are a bit more than you think" said Mick. "Studying exoplanets from Earth as you do, might be called very remote sensing. But more to the point, you are an expert on radiative transfer and radiative transfer is central to problems of studying our own planet from space. This is especially so when it comes to studying the ocean. Incoming solar radiation is transferred through the atmosphere down into the ocean where it undergoes a variety of complex absorption and scattering processes. Some of that radiation is scattered back up through the surface again and it is this emerging radiation which contains the information about what is happening down in the depths. We observe this from space and then try to extract the information. This is an active field already but I think we can do better with the new satellites and instrumentation that we will be developing in the Institute."

"Well I must say that does sound interesting" said Tom. "But I do have other interests as well, particularly dark matter, and I have collaborative research going on with other people particularly in the US."

"No problem. By all means continue your collaborations and of course you will find plenty of good physicists to interact with at the ANU, where astrophysics is something of a speciality. Well anyway Tom, think about it. And of course you will need to talk about it with Molly. And when you are ready let me know."

"OK. I will."

Tom had taken the call on the landline which was in the hallway of the house. He returned to their sitting room where Molly was curled up on the sofa reading a book. She had heard snatches of the conversation in the distance.

CHAPTER 28

"Who was that you were talking to?"

"It was Mick Hennessy."

"Oh, was it indeed. Where was he ringing from? I thought he was in America."

"Well, he's not even in America now. He's moved back to Australia. The government there are creating a new scientific institution, to be called the Institute for Space and Remote Sensing Science. It is to be in Canberra, which is the national capital. And they have asked him to be the head of it."

"That's nice. Sounds like he's doing well. Is that why he rang you up? To pass on the good news?"

"Actually no. He rang up to offer me a job there."

"What!" Suddenly Molly was all attention. "Oh. What kind of a job?"

"Much the same as I do here. Research with some teaching as well. It would be a full professorship. Quite a promotion from my job here."

"And would it be better paid?" asked Molly, who was always more interested in the domestic practicalities than the esoteric world of research.

"Oh yes. Australian academic salaries are somewhat higher than here and of course a professor gets paid more than a senior lecturer anyway.""

"Well that would be nice. But do we want to move to Australia?"

"I've never really thought about it before" said Tom. "But we do have a bit of a family connection. Two of my grandfather's, that is my mother's father, older brothers went off to Australia a long time ago. They both got married so we already may have some cousins over there. On my father's side in fact my great great grandfather went off to Australia and never came back."

"Hmph!" said Molly. "I don't like the sound of that."

"No indeed" said Tom. "Don't worry. There is no fear of me doing that!"

"Yes I know" she said. "But anyway, how do you feel about it? What's your first reaction?"

"Well, I have to say I feel tempted. To be offered this post amounts to recognition of me as a scientist. And I have always taken an interest in Australia because of the family connection. Moving to a new environment, to a different continent, would in itself be very interesting."

"Ye-es. But how do we know it's a nice environment?"

"Well, there's one way to find out" said Tom. "Let's go online and get the facts". Tom opened his laptop and started Googling the climatic data for Canberra and Aberystwyth. "We'll compare Canberra with Aberystwyth. First, summer temperatures. The average daily maximum here in July, our warmest month, is 19 C. The average daily maximum in Canberra in January, their warmest month, is 29 C!"

"Gosh, that sounds warm."

"Yes, it does. But the average minimum daily temperature in January is only 14 C, so it cools down at night. That's probably because of the altitude which is about 600 metres."

"What about the winter?"

"Our average high in January is 8 C. Their average maximum temperature in July, their coldest month, is 12 C."

"Well, that's quite cold so they do have a proper winter, but it is better than 8 C. How about rain?"

"Our annual rainfall here is about 1300 mm. Canberra's annual rainfall is less than half - about 600 mm."

"Do you know what?" said Molly. "That might be a distinct improvement. We get so many rainy days here. I find them quite burdensome, although coming as we both do, from the West of Ireland we should be used to rain."

CHAPTER 28

"True. But having lived for so long in cool wet climates perhaps you and I have by now earned the right to move somewhere warmer and drier."

"Perhaps we have."

"Well, this is certainly an interesting prospect which has suddenly opened up" said Tom. "But this would be a very big decision and we don't want to rush it. Let's think about it and in the meantime I will see if any of my colleagues know anything about the environment for science in Australia and especially if they know anything about Canberra."

In the mail a few days later there came the official job offer together with detailed information about the new Institute. In addition there was a brochure about the city of Canberra, its origin and environment.

The more he thought about the Australian post, the more inclined Tom became to accept it. This being so he thought it only fair that he should let the director of his institute know that he might be leaving. Accordingly he arranged to see Professor Morgan in his office.

"I thought I should let you know, Professor, that I have been offered a job in Australia. I haven't actually decided yet but there is a very real possibility that I may accept it."

"Well Tom, we will be very sorry to lose you. But of course you must feel free to pursue what you believe are your best career options. May I ask what is the job?"

Tom explained about the new institute being set up in Canberra, and about Mick Hennessy being its first director and how he had got directly in touch with Tom and offered him a professorship.

"A full professor, Eh? Well that would certainly be a real promotion for you. New full professorships are a bit thin on the ground over here at the moment. So it's in Canberra? I know Canberra. I did two years there as a post-doc."

"What's it like? The place, I mean?"

"Oh, I liked it. It is a planned city, being as it is the national capital. Geometrically laid out. And just about everywhere you look there are hills covered with the Australian bush. It is some way inland but it is only a two hour drive to the New South Wales South Coast with endless beaches and seawater much warmer than here."

"And what about Australia as a place to do science?"

"Pretty good on the whole. Australia doesn't have an economy big enough to support the very expensive science such as is carried out in the US or in Europe, but there is plenty of good research going on there anyway. They are particularly active in the Plant sciences, as you might expect given their very large agriculture industry, but they also have a good record in astronomy and astrophysics. The ANU, where you are thinking of going is particularly strong in this area."

"And what about the Australians themselves? How did you get on with them?"

"Oh, the Australians are all right. Some of them might seem a bit rough but they are friendly."

"Since you liked it, did you ever think of going back?"

"Oh yes. And I've had one or two job offers. And I liked the weather. Warmer and drier than here" he said looking at the rain streaming down the window.

"But I'm a local boy. Both my wife and myself have strong family connections in these parts and we can't quite tear ourselves away. Anyway, Tom. When you have decided, let me know because we will have to start thinking about filling your position here."

As he left the director's office Tom was wondering how easy Molly and himself would find it to tear themselves away from their native land and family connections.

CHAPTER 28

"But then" he thought to himself "moving from Ireland to England was a big break already so a further move to Australia doesn't seem so dramatic. Strange, isn't it. We Irish love Ireland but we always seem ready to leave it."

When he got home that evening Tom told Molly about his discussion with Professor Morgan. As it happened she had sought out two Australian nurses who were working at the Bronglais hospital and told them about the move that Tom and herself were considering. They both thought it was an excellent idea and were keen to return there themselves when their stays in Britain, undertaken to acquire further experience, were finished. One of them thought Canberra was a bit cold but then she came from subtropical Queensland.

"Well Tom, my love. What are your feelings about this Australian proposal now?"

"Well, I have to say I am beginning to feel quite positive about it now. Canberra sounds like a nice place. The weather will certainly be better. The ANU is by repute an excellent university. And there is no doubt it will be a substantial promotion. How about you?"

"Cautiously positive I suppose. The Australian girls told me that I would have no difficulty finding a nursing job over there. I like the prospect of warmer and drier weather. I think our standard of living will go up and that's always good. So I am very happy to go along with whatever you think is best. If you want to go, that is absolutely fine by me."

"I'll tell you what" said Tom. "Let's think about it overnight and see if we can arrive at a decision tomorrow."

During the next day Tom chatted about his new job possibility with some of his other colleagues in the institute. They generally regarded it favourably, some being openly envious.

By the time he returned home at the end of the day. His mind was made up.

"Well Molly, I have thought about it some more, and talked to some more people about it and my feeling now is that I should accept the job. We will go to Australia."

"All right, Tom. Australia it is."

Early next morning, at a time which he estimated would be late afternoon in Australia, Tom phoned Mick Hennessy.

"Hi Mick. Tom Glennon here."

"G'day Tom. I was hoping to hear from you. Well. Have you made the decision?"

"I have. And I have decided to accept your offer of the post in the new Institute. I'll put my acceptance in writing, in an email."

"Tremendous news, Tom! And how about Molly?"

"We talked it over at length together, and she's fine with it."

"Good. Good. Well, as soon as we get your email I'll set the machinery in motion over here. Our administration will be in touch with you with all the details. And they will arrange your flights – business class, of course. Also, they will arrange to have an apartment ready for you on the ANU campus. I'll meet you at Canberra airport when you arrive."

"OK" said Tom. I'll look forward to it."

Chapter 29

***Tom and Molly tidy** up their affairs in Aberystwyth, say goodbye to their families, and fly off to Australia. Mick Hennessy welcomes them to Canberra and shows them around. They like what they see.*

Tom and Molly began their preparations for the big move to Australia. They put their Waun Fawr house on the market and soon found a buyer - another young academic couple. More problematic was the task of breaking the news of their departure to their families, both of whom were dismayed at the news. But the realization that in these days of modern air travel, Australia was no longer so far away as it used to be, helped them to come to terms with it.

The Great Day of Departure finally came. It was late March. They had chosen to spend their last week in Ireland and so the first leg of their journey was the flight from Shannon Airport to London. Tom's family had come over from England to see them off and Molly's family came up from Kerry. While the tearful goodbyes were being said, Tom could not help contrasting in his mind their relatively pain free leave-taking with the travails of the Irish emigrants of old departing on sailing ships from Cobh in County Cork and commemorated in so many of the old emigration songs. Odd lines came to his mind.

"I'm bidding farewell to the land of my youth, to the home that I love so well..."

"So fare thee well sweet Ireland, my own dear native home..."

"Since I lately took the notion for to cross the briny ocean and I'm off to Philadelphia in the morning..."

"But those days are now all over and I must go away, so farewell unto ye bonny bonny Sliabh Gallion Braes..."

"It's far away I am today from scenes I roamed as a boy, and long ago the hour I know I first saw Illinois..."

But still, he said to himself, while it may not be so traumatic, it is no small enterprise that we ourselves embark on today.

At London Airport they transferred to a Qantas flight for their journey to the other side of the world. Looking out of the window as, after a long and tedious journey, the plane began its descent to Sydney Airport, Tom saw Sydney Harbour below him with its well-known icons, the Harbour Bridge and the Sydney Opera House, and the water glinting in the sun. Seeing this attractive scene as his first sight of Australia he took to be a good omen. As they flew from Sydney to Canberra, Tom looked down on the wide-ranging grazing lands of inland Australia, homesteads and farm dams with water in them dotted here and there, and ranges of hills covered with brown-green Eucalyptus forest. At Canberra airport, after collecting their luggage from the carousel they were met by Mick Hennessy.

"Tom. Molly. Welcome to Canberra! Its great to see you. I won't bother to ask you how was your flight. They are never much fun. But here you are at last."

"Hi Mick. Good to see you too."

"We have a nice apartment arranged for you on the ANU campus. I'll take you there now. You'll find it well set up for your immediate needs. Now, you're going to need time to recover from your journey so I propose to leave you to your own devices for the rest of today but tomorrow, if its alright by you, I will collect you at about six and bring you to dinner at my house."

"That'd be fine, Mick. We'll look forward to it."

"Good. I have left a street map of Canberra in the flat and I've marked on it a couple of supermarkets within easy walking distance so that you can stock up with the essentials."

"Thanks."

"Seems to be very pleasantly warm" said Molly. "We're near the end of March now, which is the same as the end of September back in Britain. Is it always as warm as this in the autumn?"

"Not always" replied Mick. "But the autumn is generally pleasant here. They are predicting a maximum of 23 degrees today. That's not unusual for this time of year."

"That would be considered a good midsummer temperature back in Aberystwyth." said Molly.

"Or in Connemara" added Tom.

"Well" said Mick. "Wait until you experience the height of the Canberra summer. There may be some days you will wish you were back in Aberystwyth. But only a few. OK, so here we are."

He drew up outside a small two-storey apartment building, helped them bring their luggage into a ground-floor flat, and gave them the keys.

"Today being Friday we'll leave your official arrival in the Institute until Monday. I'll be on my way and I'll be in touch about dinner tomorrow. Oh, one other thing. Jet lag tends to play havoc with your sleeping patterns. I have left some melatonin tablets in the bathroom. You may find it helpful to get you back on track if you take one of these at about your normal bedtime. I always do when I get back from overseas. So, until tomorrow."

The apartment, with a bedroom, bathroom, sitting/dining room and small kitchen, was well set up for their needs. The fridge was already stocked with milk and butter. There was coffee and also tea in the pantry. After unpacking their luggage, Tom and Molly decided to get better acquainted with their immediate environment. They walked around the spacious ANU campus and then continued on into the nearby Canberra city centre. They were pleased with what they saw. While it lacked the period charm found in old towns such as Aberystwyth, the general aspect was pleasant enough. As well as a substantial shopping mall and separate specialist shops, there were innumerable cafes and restaurants. As far as the practicalities of life were concerned, this was going to be an easy city to live in. On the way back to the ANU they stopped at one of the nearby supermarkets to buy meat, vegetables and fruit for their evening meal. Molly also bought plain and wholemeal flour and buttermilk so that she could make brown soda bread.

That night, with the help of melatonin, they managed to get a useful amount of sleep and during the day they continued their exploration of the city centre. Looking for somewhere to take lunch, they found a variety of cafes and restaurants in and around the Garema Place pedestrian plaza, eventually settling for the Irish-themed King O'Malley pub. After the meal they sat for a while, Tom with a pint of Guiness and Molly a glass of wine and observed the passing throng, men, women and children, predominantly of European stock like themselves, but with a substantial admixture of East Asians, South Asians and Middle Easterners. Looking around him at the trees, sculptures, a small water feature with water flowing over a pair of bronze figures, plentiful benches for people to sit, restaurants, small shops and the variety of humanity on display, Tom felt that as a central point within the city of Canberra, this was not at all bad. It was not Trafalgar Square or Times Square or La Place de la

Concorde but for a medium-sized, unpretentious city, 17,000 kilometres from the centres of European civilization, it would do very well.

He noticed that there was a blackboard outside the pub announcing live music performances on different nights during the week.

"Hey Molly. Look! They have Irish music sessions here on Sunday afternoons. We should bring our instruments and join in."

"But are you sure we'd be welcome?" said Molly.

"Oh, I think so. The normal rule in Irish music sessions all over the world is that anyone who can play an instrument and comes with an authentic repertoire is welcome."

They strolled back to their apartment on The ANU campus and shortly after five, Mick Hennessy arrived.

"I'm not taking you to dinner just yet. What I propose to do is to take you on a bit of a drive around Canberra, particularly around the lake." He was referring to Lake Burley Griffin, around which the city is distributed. He took them on a tour, not just of the lake and some of the adjoining bush covered hills but also of the significant buildings of this capital city, particularly the new and the old Parliament House, the National Gallery, the National Museum and others.

Tom was impressed.

"It is a very scenic city, being set as it is around a lake, with forest covered hills being part of the view wherever you look."

"Yes, that's why Canberra is often referred to as the bush capital."

"It's quite low density isn't it?"

"Yes it is" said Mick. "You need a car in Canberra. Although there is a public transport system."

They then arrived at the Hennessy household in the inner city suburb of O'Connor, not far from the ANU, where they met

Mick's wife, Rebecca, and their two young sons. Rebecca was American. Mick had married her during his long stay in America, and their children were born there.

"You've been here about two years now haven't you Rebecca? How are you finding Australia?" asked Molly who, being somewhat apprehensive herself about the move to a new country, was interested to hear the experience of another woman in a similar situation.

"Oh, I like it" said Rebecca.

"The summers are hot but not muggy as they are in the north-eastern USA. Australians think Canberra has cold winters but they are nothing to what I was used to back home. I was brought up in American suburbia and Australian suburbia is not very different. If you're looking for the big city experience Canberra might seem a bit quiet but you can always visit Sydney to find that. Crime rates, especially gun violence, are much lower here than back in the US. Canberra is something of a special case with its predominantly educated, law abiding, middle-class population but even in Sydney there is nowhere near the amount of violent crime that exists in cities such as New York. Of course there are lots of things I miss, particularly certain products I can't find in the shops and I miss my extended family back home, but on the whole, yes, I am settling down very well."

"Well that's encouraging" said Molly.

"And your boys. They are now going to grow up to be Australians."

"Oh that's all right" said Rebecca. "They are so young that they will soon forget they were ever American. Of course they can retain their American citizenship if they want to although they will soon be naturalized Australians as well. And yourself?"

CHAPTER 29

"We'd love to have children" said Molly, a little sadly. "And we've tried. But so far no luck. Just one miscarriage."

"Oh that's just too bad" said Rebecca with genuine sympathy. "I do hope you get there in the end."

"Thanks" replied Molly.

Chapter 30

***Tom and Molly settle down** in Australia. They like Canberra and its surrounds and buy their own house. After three years they pay a visit to their families in Ireland and England. Tom's father's building firm undergoes lucrative takeover. There is some concern about his health.*

"They've got a nice house" said Molly, when they got home. "With quite a good sized garden as well."

"Yes" said Tom. "And near to the uni as well. But houses in these inner city suburbs are likely to be much more expensive than those further out, so I don't know whether we will be able to afford one of those to begin with. Apparently we can stay in our university accommodation for up to 3 months. That should give us time to find something, but we'd better get onto it straight away."

On Monday morning Tom went into the Institute for Space Science and Remote Sensing (ISSRS) to take up his new post. Mick showed him his new office and then took him around to be introduced to his new colleagues. Following this he had a meeting with the head of the Physics Department to discuss what might be his best contribution, as a professor of Physics in his own right, to the teaching in that department.

Tom soon settled down in this new phase of his scientific career. He knew many of his colleagues already, having met them at astrophysics conferences around the world. As a theoretician rather than an experimental physicist, he did not have to set up a laboratory and so was able to go on with his research without a break. He continued his interaction with the observational astronomers who were using spaceborne telescopes to observe the exoplanets, new examples of which were being discovered. He also continued his cooperation with other theoreticians and particle physicists in their search for an explanation of the nature of dark matter.

Molly, with her qualifications and several years of experience in the British hospital system, had no difficulty finding employment in Canberra and was taken on as a Registered Nurse in the Calvary Hospital. As Mick had forewarned them, it soon became clear that they needed a car in Canberra and so they bought a small, second hand EV, and in this they spent their first few weekends driving around the Canberra suburbs looking for somewhere to live. They eventually decided that for the time being they would rent rather than buy and found an apartment in the suburb of Bruce which had the advantage that it was near to Calvary Hospital where Molly would be working and was also on a bus route to the centre of Canberra which passed close to the University.

Towards the end of their first year in Australia they decided that the time had now come to buy their own house. With their joint incomes they would be able to get a sizeable mortgage, which gave them a wide choice of houses in Canberra. Their preference was to stay in their present suburb and they in fact soon found a three-bedroom townhouse with a small garden, which took their fancy, and duly became Australian homeowners. They soon made friends, Tom at the university and Molly at Calvary, and now having a house of their own they were able to entertain. Tom played his fiddle regularly at the King O'Malley pub Irish music sessions on Sundays, and Molly sometimes also came, to play her flute.

Canberra as a place to live came up to their expectations. In the depth of winter it was indeed, as their Australian colleagues complained, a cold place but, used as they were to British winters, it presented no problem to them. Some days in the summer they found excessively hot, but the humidity was generally low making the heat bearable. In the summer holidays, and often at weekends they would take the 2-hour drive down to the New South Wales South coast around Batemans Bay, with its endless uncrowded beaches below the bush-covered hills of the Great Dividing Range, and rent a house for as long as they needed. On the other weekends they would often take a drive around the surrounding countryside of the New South Wales tablelands. It was clear that this was a much warmer and drier environment than that of the British Isles. In most summers the grass in the fields, or "paddocks" as they were called in Australia, dried off, changing from green to pale gold, greening up again with autumn rain.

"You know" said Tom to Molly "while this is not as productive per unit area as the land we are used to, it is still good sheep country. It is actually good for the sheep to have one dry period a year. It helps them to get rid of parasites."

And while they could never find this Australian countryside as attractive as the beautiful Irish countryside they were used to, they began after a while to find it quite pleasant especially when, interspersed with the paddocks, there were patches of native bush dominated by the dark, brownish green foliage of the eucalyptus trees.

CHAPTER 30

They kept in touch with their families by phone and by email but after three years in Canberra they decided to fly home for a visit. They stayed first with Molly's family in Kerry. While her father, Pádraig, was still active, the farm work now was increasingly being carried out by Colm, the oldest son. From Kerry they drove up to Connemara where they stayed for a few days in the cottage on the Glennon family farm. Tom enjoyed doing farm work again, giving his uncle Séamus a hand with the sheep flock, and thought wistfully how good it would be if he could be a farmer as well as a scientist. They then flew over to England to stay with Micheál, Tom's father and his wife, Barbara, in Stockport.

"How's the business going, Dad?"

"It's going very well" said Micheál. "We've expanded. We became a company - O'Kelly & Glennon Ltd., with Peadar and myself as the shareholders. We have a bigger workforce. It's a long time since I laid any bricks. I work from our own office building. Peadar wanted to lighten his load, so I became the CEO. And now, in confidence, I can tell you that we are about to be taken over by one of the big building firms. They will buy our shares for a very healthy sum."

"What do they get out of it?"

"They get the whole thing. Our workforce, our equipment, our order book, the goodwill, the reputation that we have built up over the years."

"Does that mean you will lose your job?"

"Not at all. They want me to stay on to run this part of their business. You might say I'm part of the package."

"That's all very impressive" said Tom. "But don't overdo it. You are getting older too."

"Oh, I'll be fine" said Micheál. "I can handle it."

Tom noticed a quick glance of concern from Barbara. Later he managed to catch her alone.

"How is Dad? How's his health?"

"I am a bit concerned" said Barbara. "As he said, the business is much bigger now. That is mainly his doing. But he works long hours. And his blood pressure is higher than it should be."

BOOK 4

▲

Chapter 31

They return to Australia. *Molly has a second miscarriage. Tom participates with international colleagues in an attempt to identify a dark matter particle. The result is negative. Disenchanted with the many failures to find a particulate basis for dark matter, Tom comes up with the hypothesis that it is in fact non particulate in nature.*

While they had enjoyed revisiting Ireland and England, Tom and Molly were glad to be back in Australia. They were now very settled in their new country and intended to become Australian citizens. They continued to hope for children and a year or so after their return Molly once again found herself pregnant. This time all went well through the first three months but half way through the second trimester, once again pain and bleeding were followed by a miscarriage. Once again, Molly was desolate. To Tom also it was a blow but his main concern was the effect this second loss might have on Molly's mental and emotional wellbeing. She remained low in spirits for some time but then, to Tom's great relief, slowly became her old, cheerful, self once again.

"Tom, *a stór*, I've been thinking. I don't think we are ever going to have children now and we must just become reconciled to that. Now in my late thirties my fertility must be down and my two miscarriages suggest that I have some problem bringing a baby to term anyway."

"It's not your fault, Molly. Don't be blaming yourself."

"Yes, I know, I know. I won't. But there's something I have been thinking about for some time now. While I may never have babies of my own, I think I can be of assistance to other women who do have babies but are having problems with them. Here in Canberra there is the Caroline Chisholm Home for Mothers and Babies. They provide support for women who are pregnant or have new babies but who, for whatever reason - perhaps domestic violence, or something like that - don't have the family support that most women have. I thought that I might offer to help in some of my spare time. I am sure they will be happy to have a nurse around and I would love to be handling babies even if they are not mine. What do you think?"

"Sounds like a good idea" said Tom, thinking that for Molly to immerse herself in other women's problems might be just the thing to stop her thinking about her own.

"But save some of your spare time for me!"

"Never fear. I will. I will. You won't be neglected."

The Caroline Chisholm Home was, as expected, very happy to have a Registered Nurse to assist and so Molly started spending some of her evenings and occasional parts of the weekend helping out. Tom missed not having her around as much as he would have liked but he could see that for her this voluntary work was fulfilling.

In his own work, he and his particle physics colleagues in the United States had come up with yet another hypothetical particle which they thought was a plausible candidate as the fundamental constituent of dark matter. And this time they had been able to propose an experimental procedure which should make it possible to detect it, if indeed it existed. The proposed experiment was, at great expense, carried out at a site deep underground below the Italian Alps. The results were negative. So they had not discovered the nature of dark matter. On the other hand, the experiment told them that no particle with the properties they proposed in fact existed. Which, in a negative way, was at least something.

Having invested quite a lot of time and effort without much to show for it, Tom was feeling disenchanted with the search for the elusive particle supposedly underlying dark matter.

"Maybe" he thought to himself one day "the reason why no one can find the dark matter particle is that it doesn't exist. Perhaps dark matter is not in fact particulate. But if it isn't, what else could it be?

Let me see. Perhaps we could think of it as some kind of structureless cloud permeating, extending through, the whole galaxy. It has density, mass per unit volume. It must, because it is gravitationally active. In fact this is the only way we can detect its existence. Does its density vary within the galaxy? Does it get higher as you approach the gravitational centre of the galaxy? Only if it is compressible. If it is not compressible, what happens as you approach the outer edge of the galaxy? Does the dark matter cloud have a sharply defined surface or does it peter out to nothing in the way a cloud of gas molecules would? If the dark matter of the galaxy has an outer surface perhaps we should think of it as not so much a cloud but as a gel."

Tom enjoyed himself for some time speculating about the possible nature and properties that a non-particulate dark matter might have. However he had already decided to leave the dark matter field and concentrate his energies on his first love, exoplanets, not least because exciting new observational data had been accumulating to which he was keen to apply his analytical skills. As his parting gift to dark matter astronomy he decided to organise his speculative musings into a coherent discussion paper. This he sent off to *Essays in Physics*, a journal which allowed physicists to air some of their more radical thoughts.

Chapter 32

***They receive a phone** call from England to tell them that his father has had a stroke. Tom flies to England. Micheál receives the last rites, dies and after the requiem mass is buried next to Róisín. Tom returns to Australia which he is increasingly thinking of as home.*

Late one evening, two years after his last visit, Tom received a phone call from England. It was his father's wife.

"Tom, it's Barbara here."

"Hello Barbara. We don't get many phone calls from England. What's going on? Is there some news?"

"Yes, but not good news I am afraid. Your father has just had a stroke. A serious one. The prospects may not be good. Do you think you could come over?"

This was a hammer blow to Tom, although such a possibility had been at the back of his mind since Barbara had told him about Micheál's high blood pressure.

"That is indeed bad news. I will of course come over. Straight away."

"What is it Tom?" asked Molly, her concern aroused by hearing the tail end of the conversation.

Tom told her what had happened.

"Oh dear. That is terrible. You must go as soon as you can."

CHAPTER 32

"Yes. I will go online and book the earliest possible flight."

Two days later Tom was in England and arrived at the family home in Stockport.

"Oh Tom. I'm so glad you're here" said Barbara.

"What happened?" said Tom.

"It was last Tuesday. I got a phone call in the afternoon from Micheál's secretary. She said he had collapsed in his office. They called an ambulance and he was taken to Stepping Hill Hospital. I went there straight away. He is paralysed down his left side and has trouble speaking. He is going in and out of consciousness. The doctor I spoke to is very concerned that there might be another stroke. Now that you have arrived we can go to the hospital and see him."

At Stepping Hill Hospital they found Micheál in a bed in a private room. Tom's sisters, Aoife and Gráinne, were already there at the bedside.

"Tom's arrived, Daddy" said Gráinne, leaning over to speak directly to her father, who appeared to be asleep. His eyes flickered open.

"Tom, Tom. Are you here?" said Micheál, speaking with difficulty, his voice slurred. He reached out his right hand.

"I am, Dad. I am" said Tom. He grasped his father's hand and squeezed it.

"Thanks be to God" said Micheál. "I have all my children here."

"You have, Daddy. You have" said Gráinne. "And, please God, you will have us with you for many years yet."

"I don't know...I don't know..." His voice faded and his eyes closed.

A middle aged man in a white coat entered the room.

"Hello" he said. "I'm Dr Cassidy. I am looking after Mr Glennon", his accent and surname revealing his Irish origin. Tom and his sisters introduced themselves.

"Let's step outside into the corridor" he said. "So that I can give you my assessment of the situation."

"I have to tell you that the outlook is not good. Your father has suffered a massive stroke. It came close to killing him. Unfortunately in cases like this there is very often a subsequent stroke, following soon after, from which the patient does die. Tell me – is Mr Glennon a religious man? If he is, then I assume he is a Catholic."

"He is" said Barbara.

"In that case" replied Dr Cassidy "you might want to call his parish priest, to administer the last rites."

It was these words, like an ice cold hand on his heart, that told Tom that his father was about to die.

"Thank you, doctor" said Barbara. "I'll ring the priest." She phoned the presbytery and asked to speak to the parish priest but he was not there. However, a retired priest, Father Hanley, who had stayed on to help out in the parish, was present and he, on hearing what had happened, undertook to come to the hospital as soon as he could.

The family returned to the room and looked at each other. Aoife and Gráinne were quietly weeping. Barbara's red-rimmed eyes and sad expression revealed that she had already wept. Tom found it difficult not to break into tears. He took a grip on himself.

"It looks like things are much worse than we thought. Dad might go at any minute. We don't want him to die alone, but we don't have to be all here all the time. How about we take it in turns?"

"Yes. Let's do that" said Aoife.

"Yes, let's" said Gráinne and Barbara.

"All right" said Tom. "We'll wait until the priest has been. And then Barbara and I can go back to the house and try and get some rest while Gráinne and Aoife stay here with Dad. Then we will arrive back at about midnight so that you two can go and have a bit of a sleep if you can, and come back here tomorrow morning. We can all be here for most of the day tomorrow and then in the evening do the same as today. How about we do that?"

A little later, Father Hanley – grey haired, elderly - arrived. He carried a small black leather case containing the sacred oil, holy water and crucifix, together with the violet stole that he would don while administering the sacrament.

"Hello Barbara, Aoife, Gráinne. And you must be Tom. Your father often speaks about you. This is a desperately sad business. And unexpected. Micheál seemed to be in excellent shape the last time we met. I pray that we are not going to lose him.

I have a little booklet here for each of you with the order of administration of the sacrament so that in the prayers you can say the appropriate responses. Now I don't know if Micheál will be able to make his confession, but just in case, to begin with it would be best if, just after I have wished peace upon this house you step outside so that I can ask him. You can then return for the rest of the ceremony."

They re-entered the sick room and stood around the bed.

"Peace be to this house" said Father Hanley.

"And to all that dwell in it" responded Barbara, Aoife, Gráinne and Tom, after which they went out to the corridor. After a few minutes Father Hanley beckoned them in and once again they stood around the bed and administration of the Sacrament continued, beginning with

Priest. Our help is in the Name of the Lord.

Response. Who hath made heaven and earth.

Priest. The Lord be with you.

Response. And with thy spirit.

The priest then continued with the traditional prayers, the family responding as appropriate. And Micheál was anointed and blessed in accordance with the ancient custom of the Catholic Church.

When the ceremony was finished they left the room again.

"Thank you for coming, Father" said Barbara.

"Ah, how could I not" said Father Hanley. "Let me know if there is any change in Micheál's condition."

"I will" said Barbara.

Back at the house, after a brief meal, Tom settled himself in an armchair in the hope of getting some sleep before spending the night at the hospital. Barbara did likewise. Tired as he was after his long air journey from Australia he did manage to doze off for a couple of hours. The alarm he had set woke him up. The time was about 11 pm which he estimated was about 9 am in Canberra. Knowing that Molly would be up and about he phoned his home number.

"Tom. What's the situation? How is your father?"

"The situation is very bad, I'm afraid. Dad's stroke was a very serious one. He is intermittently in and out of consciousness but the doctor has told us to be prepared for the worst."

"Oh dear. Oh dear. That is awful, terrible."

Tom could tell that Molly was very upset. She was fond of Micheál.

"Molly my love, if the worst does indeed happen I will need to stay on here for a while to help sort things out."

"You will of course, Tom. Do whatever is necessary. I will pray for Micheál but I fear it is late for that."

"Yes, I am afraid so. Now Molly I must go. Barbara and I have to go back to the hospital to relieve Aoife and Gráinne who have been watching over Dad since this afternoon. We will have the night shift. I'll keep you informed of any developments."

CHAPTER 32

"All right, Tom *a stór* . Good bye."

Tom and Barbara returned to Stepping Hill Hospital to take over from his sisters.

"Any change?"

"No. Nothing" they said.

The hospital had provided comfortable bedside chairs for them, but Tom did not want to fall asleep. Early next morning the doctor came in to examine Micheál again.

"Any sign of improvement, Doctor?" asked Tom.

"I'm afraid not. The contrary, if anything. I think you should be prepared."

"We'd better get the girls to come in now" said Tom to Barbara. She said

"Yes. I'll ring them."

Soon the whole family was assembled around the bedside again. Around mid morning, Micheál appeared to emerge into consciousness. His eyes flickered open and Tom could hear that he was trying to speak. Listening closely he realised that Micheál had reverted to speaking in Irish, the everyday tongue of his early life.

"An bhfuil tú istigh a Thomáis?" (Are you here, Tomás?)

"Tá mé istigh a Dhaid" (I am here, Dad)

"Agus Gráinne. Agus Aoife?" (And Gráinne. And Aoife?)

"Táimid istigh a Dhaidí" (We are here, Daddy) said Gráinne, grasping her father's hand.

"Tá Barbara istigh, fosta." (Barbara is here too)

Tom could see that Micheál was struggling to speak again.

"Sílim go bhfuil tá mé ag dul anois. B'fhéidir feicidh mé Róisín arís."

(I think I am going now. Perhaps I will see Róisín again)

Tom and his sisters saw no point now in trying to persuade their father that he was not going to die.

"Cinnte a Dhaidi, feicidh tú Mhaimí" (Indeed Daddy, you will see Mammy)

said Gráinne.

"He knows he is dying" said Tom to Barbara who, not being an Irish speaker would not have understood what Micheál was saying. "And he said that perhaps he will see Róisín again."

"I am sure he will" said Barbara, who did not at all mind that in his final hour Micheál's thoughts should turn to the first love of his life rather than herself.

Micheál spoke no more but relapsed again into unconsciousness. They remained by the bedside.

Later in the morning Micheál's breathing suddenly stopped. They immediately told the nurse who then called the doctor. He examined Micheál and then turned to them and shook his head.

"I am afraid that was the end" he said. "Pretty certainly another stroke. I am afraid there is nothing we can do."

He then left the family in the room to give them time to come to terms with what had happened. Emotionally exhausted, Tom sat there for some time with his head in his hands. His sisters and Barbara quietly wept. Eventually Tom pulled himself together.

"Well, Dad is gone now and we must now start making all the necessary arrangements" he said.

"Yes" said Barbara. "Tom. If you want - and if you and the girls don't mind, I can look after all that. It gives me the chance to do one last thing for Micheál."

"Well, thank you Barbara. I don't mind. Aoife, Gráinne?"

"No. We don't mind" they said.

Knowing Barbara to be a sensible, competent woman, Michael had every confidence in her ability to manage the funeral arrangements. They waited at the hospital until the undertaker came to take Micheál's body away and then returned to the house. Later that night, Tom phoned Molly and told her the sad news.

CHAPTER 32

"Oh Tom. I am so sorry to hear that. I was very fond of your father. I could not have asked for a nicer father-in-law. And you. How are you and your sisters coping?"

"Not too badly, I suppose" said Tom. "We could see the end was coming and so had time to be mentally prepared. We will be having a Requiem Mass for Dad before the funeral. He will be buried here, next to my mother. I will fly back home as soon as I can, after that."

The Requiem Mass for Micheál was held in Our Lady and the Apostles, his parish church. It was well attended, Micheál being well known and popular, not just in the Irish community but in the parish generally. At the beginning of the mass, Tom said a few words on behalf of the family. He briefly recounted Micheál's origin on a farm in the far West of Ireland, his move to England to work in his cousin's building firm, starting off as a bricklayer but eventually turning to management and becoming a successful businessman. His marriage to Róisín in Connemara, their happy relationship and his unfailing kindness as a father to their three children, his great distress at losing her to cancer and his final contentment with his second wife, Barbara. The mass ended with the congregation singing 'Be Thou My Vision', Micheál's favourite hymn. As the coffin was carried out on the shoulders of Tom, Micheál's brother Séamus, two cousins from Ireland and two of Micheál's friends, a solitary uilleann piper played the lament, *Eanach Dhúin*.

At the cemetery, Tom and his sisters, together with Barbara and family members over from Ireland, stood around the grave as his father's coffin was lowered down. Having had the foresight to purchase a double plot some years before, Micheál was being buried next to Róisín. The parish priest said the prayers for the deceased. All those present said the final prayer together –

"Eternal rest grant unto him, O Lord, and let perpetual light shine upon him. May his soul and the souls of all the faithful departed, through the mercy of God, rest in peace. Amen."

As soil from the gravediggers' shovels began to fall down upon the coffin, and it progressively disappeared from view, Tom thought to himself – "My mother and father both now gone. I suppose that marks the end of a chapter in my life."

He was keen to get back to Australia, a country which increasingly he now thought of as 'home'. He said Goodbye to his sisters, to Barbara, and to Séamus, his uncle, and flew from Manchester Airport down to London, where he caught the first available Qantas flight to Sydney.

Chapter 33

Mixed responses to Tom's *dark matter hypothesis. He becomes involved in remote sensing research and participates in an ocean remote sensing project in the sea at a location off the South coast.*

At Canberra Airport Tom's spirits lifted when he found Molly waiting for him. He kissed her and held her close.

"Well Tom, my love. How are you now?" she said, anxiously, concerned about the possible effects his father's death might have on him.

"Oh.... still feeling rather shattered, I suppose. It was a great blow to suddenly lose him like this. I know he was getting close to seventy but he was still physically vigorous and we thought he had many years of life left in him. But, I am coming to terms with it."

The following day Tom was back at work at the Institute. Mick Hennessy knew that Tom had rushed off to England because of concerns about his father. Tom now told him that Micheál had in fact died while he was there.

"Gee, that's very bad news, Tom" said Mick, who had met Micheál when he first became friends with Tom, during his time as a graduate student in Cambridge.

"Sorry to hear it. Are you sure you are OK to come back to work straight away?"

"Oh yes. I'll be fine" said Tom. "Work is just the thing."

His speculative paper in *Essays in Physics* had now appeared and, as he found when opening his emails, had aroused quite a range of responses, from cheerful encouragement to verging on the abusive.

"A non-particulate form of matter? Pretty weird, Tom. But stay with it. Who knows?"

"This is just stupid. Matter has to consist of particles. Anything else is inconceivable."

"Tom. How can I break it to you. This is a crazy idea. Crazy. But, but, but. Considering the present state of theoretical physics, with string theory proliferating in all directions but going nowhere, we must at least look at some crazy ideas. If you can stay out of the loony bin, then persevere but don't tell anyone I said so."

"I have to tell you, Professor Glennon, this kind of thing is not good for your reputation."

"Are you out of your f***ing mind?"

were a sample. Although Tom had not been quite 100% serious when he sent his highly speculative paper off to *Essays in Physics*, the responses he was getting, perhaps particularly the hostile ones, disposed him towards staying with this subject, at least for the time being. One email in particular he found interesting and encouraging.

"Dear Professor Glennon

I am a graduate in Physics of the Indian Institute of Technology – Bombay. I have just completed my PhD in theoretical Physics here at Cambridge, and am about to begin a postdoctoral fellowship in the Department of Applied Mathematics and Theoretical Physics. I found your paper in *Essays in Physics* very interesting. While I already have a research project for my Postdoctoral Fellowship I would very much like in addition to look closely into the possible existence of an additional state of matter such as you suggest. Would you have any problem with my exploring your proposal further?

Yours Sincerely
Priyam Seshadri"

Tom was pleased with the possibility that some bright young physicist would take an interest in his hypothesis but was slightly concerned that it might harm their career. It is OK, he thought, for me to take risks since I am established but for a young scientist just starting, it is another matter.

He replied –

"Dear Dr Seshadri

I have no problem at all with you pursuing your own investigation of my hypothesis. You may do so with all my encouragement. Given its highly speculative nature, however, I hope you won't let it distract you too much from your day job, i.e. your main postdoctoral project. Otherwise – go for it!

With best wishes
Tom Glennon"

Like many other Irish musicians, Tom wrote the occasional tune on the basis of any interesting musical phrase that might pop into his head. One such tune he jotted down one day seemed to him to end on a plaintive interrogative manner, reminiscent of the way he felt about the fruitless search for the nature of dark matter. Accordingly he decided to call the tune - The Unanswered Question.

The Unanswered Question

One of the research interests of the Institute for Space Science and Remote Sensing where Tom was based, was remote sensing of the ocean from space, with particular reference to the assessment of primary production - the photosynthetic conversion of carbon dioxide to biomass by oceanic phytoplankton - in different areas of the ocean, because of its central role in the global carbon cycle, and thus its relevance to global warming. The phytoplankton, consisting as it does of countless trillions of minute algal cells - cyanobacteria, diatoms, dinoflagellates - containing light-absorbing photosynthetic pigments - chlorophylls, carotenoids, biliproteins - changes the colour of the sea. By measuring the extent of the resulting subtle colour changes it is possible to determine the concentration of phytoplankton and estimate the associated primary production in different areas of the ocean.

Because of its global environmental significance, this was a subject which interested Tom. In addition he liked the idea of doing some science which was actually socially useful. Molly took an interest in his research so he decided to tell her about it.

"Molly, you know about remote sensing, don't you?"

"Of course I do. It's where you have satellites up in space with cameras and other things looking down at the Earth's surface."

"Yes, exactly. Well, you may be interested to know that I am about to start on a remote sensing project myself."

"Are you indeed? Good. That could be more useful than some of the other stuff you do."

Molly tended to be sceptical of the value of Tom's research on the atmospheres of exoplanets.

"It means you will be studying this planet, for a change. So how will it work?"

"Well, it isn't a camera that we have in this particular satellite. It's a spectrometer. It measures the amount of light at all the wavelengths, from blue to red, coming out of the ocean and we use this information to calculate just how much plant matter there is in different parts of the ocean."

"That sounds pretty straightforward" said Molly. "Why do they need a clever fellow like you?"

"But it's not straightforward! Although the spectrometer is looking straight down at the ocean, about 90% of the light it receives doesn't come from the ocean at all. It is light which has been scattered up out of the air below by gas molecules and dust particles. So all that atmospheric light must be corrected for before we can see the signal actually coming from the ocean."

"So. Is this where you come in?" said Molly.

"It is indeed. There are already atmospheric correction procedures out there which have been published. But I think I can make a better one. Now, you know I have done a lot of work on exoplanet atmospheres, work which you think was a bit of a waste of time?"

"You're right there" said Molly.

"Well. It just happens that one of the computer programs I developed for modelling the behaviour of radiation in various kinds of exoplanet atmosphere, I believe might be just the thing for calculating the atmospheric correction in remote sensing of the ocean on this planet. So there! Maybe my exoplanet research wasn't a waste of time after all."

"Hmm. And how are you going to know if it does the job?"

"We'll put it to the test. We're collaborating with some of our oceanographer colleagues on this. We will choose a day with clear skies, so that clouds don't interfere. The oceanographers have organised a boat. We head out anything up to several kilometres from shore, starting from Jervis Bay on the South coast. At a variety of locations they will carry out measurements within the water, including absorption and scattering coefficients, sunlight penetration etc. They will take samples back to the lab to determine the phytoplankton concentration, species composition and so on. We download data from the satellite covering the period of sampling. From the data we calculate, using various algorithms, including mine, phytoplankton levels, absorption coefficients, turbidity etc. and then see how they line up with the real values actually measured in the sea."

"And are you going to go out in the boat?"

"I certainly am! Looking forward to it."

Two months later, in the early summer, a suitable date was chosen for the field work. Tom left Canberra in the early hours for the 3-hr drive to Jervis Bay, arriving at 10 in the morning. The rendezvous, with two university oceanographers from Sydney, was at the jetty of the Royal Australian Naval College which was being made available courtesy of the Australian Navy's Hydrographic Service. The Hydrographic Service took a keen interest in remote sensing of the ocean because of its potential for mapping seawater depth in coastal regions. They also supplied the boat – a small fishing trawler, without fishing gear, about 15 m in length, with two crew. The oceanographers – Drs Jim Sutcliffe and Jessica Ryan – were loading their sampling and optical equipment on board when Tom arrived. He made himself known to them and they welcomed him aboard. By 10.30 everything was ready, they cast off, and proceeded first to a number of preselected sites within Jervis Bay and then out through the heads into the Pacific Ocean where several other, nearshore, sites had been chosen. They were fortunate not only in having clear skies but also calm waters, with only a moderate swell. Tom had taken seasickness pills before setting off and so had no problems with the motion of the boat. At every site, as well as taking water samples, the oceanographers lowered instruments into the water to measure the underwater light field at various depths. As the third scientist on the boat, Tom was given the job of measuring the absorption coefficient of the seawater at each location, which he did by lowering an instrument called a PSICAM (Point Source Integrating Cavity Absorption Meter) over the side and taking measurements at 2 m depth intervals down to 20 m.

"You know, the PSICAM was actually invented in Australia" said Jim as he instructed Tom in its use.

"That's good" said Tom. "Pity it wasn't made in this country too" he said, noticing the German manufacturer's name on the casing.

Late in the afternoon, the program of sample collection and in-water measurement at the preselected sites was complete and the boat returned to the Naval College jetty. The oceanographers departed for their Sydney laboratory where the samples would be analysed and Tom set off for the long drive back to

Canberra. He arrived home just after eight to be welcomed with a hug and a kiss by Molly.

"Home is the sailor home from the sea and the hunter home from the hill" she declaimed.

"That's a nice line" said Tom. "Did you make it up?"

"Not at all" she said. "It's a quotation. It is from a poem called 'Requiem' by Robert Louis Stevenson and it is also on his tombstone."

"Is it bedad?" said Tom. "And aren't you the well educated woman."

"Indeed and I am" said she. "And how was the great voyage? Did you get seasick?"

"I did not get seasick and I really enjoyed going out to sea. I must find an excuse to do it again." And as they sat down for a late dinner he told Molly about his day.

The following morning at the Institute Tom downloaded the data from the remote sensing satellite spectrometer covering the offshore locations they had visited the day before at the time the samples were taken. First he used the standard correction algorithm to remove the contribution of atmospheric light and in this way estimate the light actually coming from within the ocean. He then repeated the procedure using the correction algorithm which he had developed on the basis of his exoplanet atmosphere modelling research. He then compared these two values with the actual sea level values measured from the boat and was pleased to find that his atmospheric correction algorithm was providing slightly, but usefully, more accurate estimates. He emailed his findings to his oceanographic colleagues in Sydney who would use them in their calculations of oceanic phytoplankton levels as seen from space, to compare with the actual phytoplankton levels measured in the samples taken from the boat. It was clear from their reply that the oceanographers were pleased with what he had done.

Molly took an interest in Tom's work and so that evening he told her what he believed he had achieved.

"So what now?" she said. "Will you write a paper on it?"

"Oh no" he said. "It is too early for that. We must get my algorithm tested out by other remote sensing workers in other oceanic locations. I will email the algorithm and the results we have achieved here to overseas colleagues and suggest to them that they try it out themselves. If other people also find that it works better than the currently used system then we will have material for a joint paper to be published in the appropriate remote sensing journal."

Chapter 34

***Tom receives a letter** from a firm of solicitors in England informing him that he is to receive a substantial amount of money from his father's estate. He decides to use it to realise his ambition to be a part-time farmer as well as a scientist. He buys a block of grazing land in New South Wales North of Canberra.*

One day, about three months after his father's death, when Tom came home from work he found that a letter from England addressed to him had arrived in the post. It was from the firm of solicitors which Barbara had appointed to administer Micheál's estate after his death. He opened it when Molly and himself sat down to dinner. Its contents took him by surprise.

"Wow!"

"What is it?" asked Molly.

"It is from the solicitors who are administering my father's estate. Apparently he left quite a lot of money. You know he sold the O'Kelly and Glennon building firm to a large construction company a year or two before he died?"

"Yes, I remember" said Molly.

"Well apparently it was worth rather a lot. The capital is now to be distributed equally between Gráinne, Aoife and myself. The solicitors want to know my bank account so they can transfer the money. Barbara gets the house and also a superannuation income, so she is well looked after."

"Oh that's good" said Molly. "I am glad to hear that Barbara will be all right. So how much money will *you* be getting?"

"Well, the figure here is in pounds sterling. But converting it roughly I'd say it is equivalent to quite a few hundred thousand Australian dollars."

"That's nice. What will you do with it?"

"I don't really know" said Tom. "But there's no hurry. Just leave it in the bank for the time being."

But he was not being entirely frank. There was a project he'd had in mind for some time, which now with this sudden influx of cash suddenly became feasible. He was not, however, quite ready yet to share this with Molly.

What in fact Tom had in mind was to buy some land and become a part-time farmer. He had no intention of giving up or even reducing his scientific activities, but remembering with fondness his early years on the farm in Connemara he thought it would be both interesting and satisfying to have his own small farm here in Australia where he could occupy himself at the weekends. He realised that his only chance of finding some land would be in the State of New South Wales, North of the border of the Australian Capital Territory. To the south of Canberra city, the land, for quite some distance, all belonged to the Commonwealth government.

"How about we go for a drive in the countryside and maybe have lunch at Yass?" said Tom to Molly after breakfast on Saturday.

"Alright" said Molly. "I wouldn't mind doing that."

Mid-morning they drove out north from Canberra along the Barton Highway. When, after 35 minutes driving they came to the hamlet of Murrumbateman Tom chose to turn right off the highway down the Murrumbateman Road.

"Let's have a look down here" he said. They continued on for some distance, exploring down various country lanes to the left and the right of the road. They called in at one of the wineries for which this district was known and purchased a couple of bottles of Shiraz. And then, because time was running on, they turned around and went back to the highway, where they turned right and continued for another 20 km to Yass, a pleasant, and by Australian standards old (early 19th century), country town. After a pub lunch they returned to Canberra.

The following Saturday Tom once again proposed that they go for a drive in the countryside and once again Molly was happy with the suggestion.

"This time" said Tom "we could take the other road to the north, the Federal Highway, and aim to have lunch at Bungendore. How about you drive this time "

"Suits me" said Molly.

About 10 km along the highway they turned right along the Macs Reef Road and then again right when they came to the Bungendore Road and proceeded to Bungendore itself, another small country town. All the way along as they drove Tom was keenly appraising the surrounding countryside, as he had on their previous trip, making his own assessment of its agricultural potential. After another pub lunch they returned to Canberra.

Tom's clear impression, relying on what he hoped was farming intuition derived from his ancestors, was that the land in the Yass Murrumbateman area was superior. Some online research revealed that those parts of the countryside which he liked the look, of had deep soils derived by weathering of volcanic rock whereas the others had shallow soils derived from sedimentary rock. He knew now where to look. Armed with this knowledge he made himself known to a number of estate agents who dealt with rural blocks of land, and told them what he had in mind.

That evening at the dinner table as they finished their meal, Tom found that Molly was looking at him in a searching, even appraising, way.

"You are up to something, Tom Glennon" she said.

"Me? Not at all" said Tom, somewhat defensively.,

"Oh yes you are" she said. "And I have a pretty good idea what. You know - women understand men better than men understand women."

"Oh indeed" said Tom in a sceptical manner.

"Yes indeed" said Molly.

She may well be right, thought Tom to himself.

The following Saturday after breakfast, Molly turned to Tom and innocently enquired - "another countryside jaunt today, Tom?"

"Well actually" responded Tom enthusiastically "in fact I was thinking ...." and then came to a halt as he saw Molly looking at him with a triumphant smile.

"Don't I know well what you were thinking" said Molly.

"Now that you have a bit of money, you are looking to buy land. Inside that prominent, well respected, internationally known scientist there is a land-hungry Connemara farmer."

"Ah, sure I suppose you're right" said Tom, apologetically.

"It's just that I thought we might enjoy having some land of our own. Where we could run a few sheep or cattle. Grow vegetables. Maybe build a cottage. It would give us plenty to do on the weekends."

"Well Tom, my love" said Molly. "In fact I think that's not a bad idea at all. And you don't have to apologise for wanting to buy land. Amn't I of the same kind of farming stock as yourself? We can look for land together."

"We can indeed" said Tom, happily, very pleased with Molly's positive response.

He shared with Molly the results of his thoughts and investigations so far, and showed her on the map the general area within which he thought they might find a suitable block of land

"Somewhere between Yass and Murrumbateman is our best bet" he said.

Over the next few weeks most of the rural blocks that estate agents brought to their attention were not suitable. They generally had large, recently built, houses on them and as a consequence were too expensive. A few months later, however, they received a phone call from a Yass estate agent about a property which had just come on the market which seemed well suited to their requirements. It was down a lane off the Dog Trap Road north-west of Murrumbateman. They arranged to meet the agent there on a Saturday morning. He explained that this block, about 100 acres in extent, was to be split off from an adjoining larger property. The owner had received permission to subdivide. The agent drew to their attention some of its advantages. In particular, mains electricity was available on the owners adjoining block from which a standard overhead cable connection could be made to a suitably located electricity post on the new block. A shallow gully near the lower end of the property provided a good location for digging a dam. In addition, he assured them that this was good country for finding underground water in the rock. In sinking a bore they may well not need to go any deeper than about 50 m.

They both liked the look of the property. The pasture seemed good, not seriously weed infested. There was a patch of remnant Eucalyptus bush extending from the adjoining land, in an upper corner of the block which made a pleasing backdrop. They asked the agent to give them a moment for a private discussion.

"Well Molly, what do you think?"

"I like it. What about you?"

"Yes I like it too. The land is good. Availability of mains electricity is a real bonus. I like the trees. I think this would suit us very well."

"All right. Let's seize the moment. Tell the agent we are interested and are prepared to make an offer. But offer a bit less than the asking price"

"Okay. I'll do that."

Tom returned to the agent.

"Yes, we think on the whole this would suit us so we are prepared to make an offer."

Tom proposed a sum $100,000 below the asking price.

"Do you think the owner would accept that?"

"Hmm. I am not sure" said the agent.

"We can pay cash, straight up" said Tom.

"We don't have to arrange a mortgage. So there will be no delay."

"Well that could certainly help" said the agent. "I know the owner is in a bit of a hurry for the money. I will put your offer to him and get back to you straight away."

"Okay" said Tom. "I'll look forward to hearing from you."

The following afternoon Tom received a call from the agent.

"Look" said the agent. "I think we're nearly there but you will need to go up a bit."

"How about another $20,000?" said Tom.

"I'll get back to you" said the agent.

The following morning the agent called again.

"The owner will accept your increased offer" he said.

"Good" said Tom. "We have a deal. I will instruct my solicitors."

That evening when he came home he told Molly the good news.

"Well, Molly my love. I think it's in the bag. We are going to own our bit of land after all."

"Well done, Tommy!" she said, and gave him a hug and a kiss.

Chapter 35

***With Molly's enthusiastic** encouragement, Tom has a cottage built on their land, carrying out much of the work himself. It becomes their frequent weekend retreat. Tom by now is a regular fiddle player in Canberra Irish music sessions.*

Once contracts were exchanged and the property was securely theirs, Tom wasted no time in proceeding to the next stage of his project, which was to build a house. In consultation with Molly he drew up a plan for a simple, but roomy two bedroomed cottage with a veranda along the South side. He had this neatly drawn up by a draughtsman and then submitted it to the Yass Shire Council. After some weeks he received permission to build. He intended to do as much of the construction as possible himself. In this, his previous experience in his father's building firm stood him in good stead. But first he knew he would need power and water. The property owner from whom he had bought the land, was happy to let Tom have an electricity supply, connecting by overhead cable to the high voltage mains running across the adjoining property. Water, however, was more problematic. There is no guarantee that underground water will be found. Nevertheless, the estate agents optimistic prediction proved to be sound. Tom called in a bore driller, who walked around the block and with the help of divining rods chose what he thought was a suitable location. Sure enough, at 60 m depth in the cracks within the volcanic rock they struck a good water supply. Like all bore drilling, this had been a very expensive operation but was well worth it. The final stage was to have a trench dug from the electricity pole to the bore for the cable to power the submerged water pump. Construction could now begin.

"I propose to do as much of this building myself as possible" he said to Molly. "I will do the concrete footings and lay the bricks."

"Are you sure you are able to do that?" said Molly, a little anxiously.

"I am indeed" said Tom. "I laid plenty of bricks when I was working for my father. It will be a double brick house, rather than timber framed with a single outer brick wall like most Australian houses are."

Tom began by having a small electric cement mixer delivered to the site together with a self assemble garden shed to store his tools and bags of cement. With great care Tom measured and pegged the house site. He hired a backhoe operator to dig out the trenches for the footings, had a load of reinforcing rods and mesh delivered to the site and then set up the reinforcing in the trenches in the manner he has often helped his father to do. After a building inspector from the Shire Council had inspected his work and deemed it acceptable, he called in a concrete truck to fill the trenches and then roughly smoothed off the top of the concrete himself.

Molly and Tom had already spent some time at brick suppliers in Canberra and had finally chosen a brick they liked. Several pallets of this brick were then delivered to the site together with a load of 'brickies' sand and numerous bags of cement. Now Tom could start laying bricks, beginning with the very precisely located corners of the walls, as his father had taught him. From here on they spent much of their weekend time on their new farm, Tom laying bricks and Molly beginning the creation of a vegetable garden. After a plumber had laid the underground piping, Tom called in a concreter to install a concrete floor throughout the house. After he had completed the brickwork and installed the windows, Tom's contribution to the structure was finished. The roofer, plasterer, tiler, plumber, electrician and painter were then called in to finish the job. Finally, Tom had a 5000 gallon water tank installed to collect the roof rainwater, a precious resource in the Australian environment.

At last! Tom and Molly had a house on their land where they could stay whenever they wanted. And indeed, having furnished the house, mainly with second-hand furniture, this is what they did. Most of their weekends now were spent on the farm, which they had decided to name Gortnakilla, after Molly's family's farm back in Kerry. Tom had a small dam excavated in the gully at the lower end of the farm, for livestock watering. Also, using treated timber posts, he constructed a small cattle yard with a loading ramp. Rather than running a flock of sheep he decided to take the easier option of simply buying in a small herd of steer calves each year, fattening them up and selling them when they were ready.

Their life in Canberra now settled down to a pleasant routine. During the week they worked at their jobs, blessed as they both were with satisfying careers. Tom and Molly frequently interacted socially with the friends they had made amongst work colleagues. Occasionally they would dine out at a restaurant or go to the cinema or a theatre. They spent their weekends at Gortnakilla, gardening or doing farm jobs or simply enjoying the countryside. They went to the 9 o'clock morning mass at St Augustine's parish in Yass, this being the nearest Catholic church. And especially they enjoyed each other's company. Tom often reflected upon how fortunate he had been to find such a lovely wife. Having no children, they became emotionally very invested in each other.

As a physicist, Tom was well aware that Science had no explanation of why a universe, rather than nothing at all, should exist and in particular, why the properties of this universe were so very precisely tuned as to make possible the evolution of intelligent life. To believe that the universe just somehow made itself out of nothing, required just as much an act of faith as to believe that it was brought into being by something outside itself. He preferred the latter hypothesis, especially since it also offered an explanation of the existence of Consciousness, a phenomenon for which there was no explanation in the reductionist physicochemical view of reality. He was bemused by what he regarded as the simpleminded atheism adhered to by so many of his biological colleagues.

Tom had become a regular fiddle player in Irish music sessions in Canberra. Occasionally Molly would come as well, to play her flute. Observing the musicians who came, it pleased Tom to see that, as in other Irish music sessions he had attended around the world, being Irish or even of Irish ancestry was in no way a requirement for enjoying the playing of Irish music. The great corpus of Irish traditional music, he often thought to himself, is Ireland's gift to the world. And what a curious musical phenomenon it is, he thought. First we play one set of tunes, whatever has just happened to pop up in someone's memory. Then another set. And another. And another. Jigs, reels, hornpipes, slip jigs. All evening, with no tune ever being repeated. And although people certainly come to the pub to hear the music, we are in no way performing for them. We are just immersed in this universe of melodies. He decided to try and encapsulate the phenomenon in a short poem: four five-syllable verses.

CHAPTER 35

The Session

Aloof from the throng
musicians playing
intently weaving
endless melodies

It was three syllables too long to be classified as a haiku but he decided to send it off to the Canberra Times anyway. They published it in their weekend edition.

Chapter 36

***Tom and his colleagues** discover an exoplanet around the star Alpha Centauri A. Molly tells Tom that she may have a heart problem. They visit their families in Ireland. Back in Australia they enjoy spending weekends on their farm. Then, one Sunday in Spring ... tragedy strikes.*

Tom's research at the Institute continued to go well, with spectroscopic data on newly discovered exoplanets frequently being sent to him for analysis. However, the holy Grail of oxygen in a planetary atmosphere, which would be an infallible sign of the presence of life, had not so far been detected. Tom persuaded one of his astronomer colleagues to use a small amount of his precious time on one of the spaceborne telescopes to look very closely at the star Alpha Centauri A, a Sun-like star slightly larger than our Sun and about 50% brighter. To their delight they found an Earth-sized planet orbiting the star at a distance somewhat greater than that between the Earth and the Sun, but still within what was regarded as the habitable zone. They seized the opportunity to closely examine its atmosphere using transit spectroscopy. As it passed in front of its star it was possible to obtain a faint glimpse of the light passing through the planet's atmosphere. Additional atmospheric information was acquired by observing the planet as it disappeared and reappeared from behind the star. Detailed analysis of the spectroscopic data revealed a strong indication of the presence of oxygen: not conclusive, but undoubtedly suggestive. Although the result was not absolutely watertight, Tom and his co-workers decided to go ahead and publish their observations anyway because of the enormous potential importance. This discovery aroused great interest mainly because of the biological implications of the presence of oxygen, but also because of the relative nearness - 4.37 light years - of the planet's host star, Alpha Centauri, to our Solar System.

He continued to cooperate with the ocean remote sensing community, helping them to achieve the best possible atmospheric correction of the data from the spectrometer in the satellite. He gave two lecture courses in the Physics department: one on quantum mechanics, the other on his own speciality - radiative transfer in atmospheres and oceans. His highly speculative hypothesis, that dark matter is non-particulate in nature, continue to generate active correspondence and discussion. He was pleased to see that the young Indian physicist, Dr Seshadri, who had taken an early interest, had published a paper in *Essays in Physics* analysing the properties that a non-particulate form of dark matter might have. On the whole, however, Tom had to admit to himself that the response of the Physics community, while in no way dismissive, was on balance rather more negative than positive.

At one Physics conference which he attended in the United States, he was vigorously assailed by Professor Jacob Schreiber, an eminent, but frequently choleric, theoretical physicist.

"This non-particulate hypothesis of yours, Professor Glennon. It really won't do. It can't be experimentally tested."

"It's too early to say that" said Tom. "All the implications of the hypothesis are not yet entirely clear. As they become clearer it is entirely likely that someone will find a way to put it to the test. Anyway, it is arguable that it has already been tested. One of the predictions of the hypothesis is that all attempts to find a particulate basis for dark matter will fail. And so far this has proved to be the case."

"Oh really!" responded Professor Schreiber in disgusted tones and walked away.

Molly had advanced in her career at the Calvary hospital. While continuing to work as a nurse in the wards, she had trained to become, and had qualified as, a Perioperative Nurse Surgical Assistant (PNSA). This meant that she now spent some of her time directly assisting surgeons in the operating theatre. This, while often challenging, she found very rewarding. In addition, as a PNSA she earned professional fees in her own right.

While not blessed with the children they had hoped for, Tom felt that with the careers they had both achieved, their pleasant countryside weekends, their active social life, their comfortable standard of living, their good health and above all their love for each other, they were indeed fortunate people.

"Seven good years to look back on" he thought to himself as the seventh year of their sojourn in Australia drew to a close.

One evening as they sat down together at the dinner table, Tom had the impression that Molly was a bit subdued.

"You don't seem quite as lively as usual my love" he said. "Is there any problem?"

"Well, nothing dramatic" she said. "But something just a little bit worrying."

"What's worrying you?" asked Tom.

"You know that once a year every member of the nursing staff gets a thorough health checkup?" she said.

"Yes, I know" said Tom.

CHAPTER 36

"Well I had mine today and although I am generally in good shape, they told me I have a bit of a heart murmur."

"Is that serious?"

"Generally not" said Molly. "Most heart murmurs don't mean anything much at all. But occasionally they can be a symptom of something more serious."

"But you don't have any chest pain, or anything like that?"

"No, thanks be to God" said Molly. "But I'll have to keep an eye on myself anyway just in case anything does develop."

"How about this trip to Ireland we have planned for July?" said Tom. "Will you be all right for that?"

"Oh yes" said Molly. "I'm looking forward to it."

July duly came and Tom and Molly set off to once again to visit their native land. As usual half their time was spent with Molly's family in Kerry and the rest on the Glennon farm in Connemara. His uncle, Séamus, was very interested to hear Tom's account of the agricultural environment in the Southern Tablelands of New South Wales and its differences from that to be found in the cool moist lands of the West of Ireland.

"You know, I wouldn't mind owning some of that myself" he said.

"I am sure you would do very well there" said Tom. "But the farms need to be big to be viable. A couple of thousand acres at least, to make a good living. But you never be able to tear yourself away from here would you?"

"I suppose not" acknowledged Séamus. "Because of all the family history here, this land has a grip on me."

On the way back to Australia they stayed for a couple of days in England with Barbara, Tom's stepmother who was still living in the family home in Stockport she had shared with Tom's father, Micheál. Just before they left, to fly from Manchester to London airport to catch the Qantas plane,

Barbara, who had spent a long career as a nurse, had a quiet word with Tom.

"How is Molly?" she enquired

"Oh, all right I think" said Tom. "Why do you ask?"

"Nothing much really" said Barbara. "It's just that she doesn't seem quite her normal self, that's all."

"Well, I hadn't really noticed" said Tom. "But thank you for mentioning it. I'll keep an eye on her."

The following day they flew back to Australia. When they got back to their Canberra home Tom sat together with Molly on the sofa and put his arm around her.

"Oh, Tom my love. I'm so glad we got to see Ireland again."

"Ah sure Molly *a stór* we can see Ireland anytime we want, as long as we can afford the plane fare."

"Yes, I know I know. But.... I just wanted to see it now."

"Well I suppose we did see it."

"Yes we did."

Tom had the impression that something was casting a shadow over Molly.

But given the even tenor of their lives and the good fortune of their situation, he could not imagine what that might be.

Back in Canberra they picked up the threads of their lives again, Tom engrossed in his research at the Institute, Molly continuing her nursing career at Calvary Hospital, frequently working as a surgical assistant in the operating theatre, and their weekends spent in their much-loved cottage and garden on the farm, Gortnakilla. July gave way to August, the wattle trees burst into golden bloom and the southern hemisphere winter drew to its close. In September, the first month of Spring, the weather became warmer. In preparation for the new growing season Tom thoroughly dug over and raked their vegetable garden and then planted seed potatoes. Molly sowed carrot and parsnip seeds in her vegetable patch but Tom had the impression that she was not quite as energetic in her gardening activities as usual. On the first weekend in October they chose to go to the 6 o'clock Saturday vigil Mass at St Augustine's in Yass after which they returned for a late dinner in their cottage.

"Tom, let's go to bed early tonight" said Molly. "I'm feeling a bit tired."

"Alright" said Tom. "Let's do that. I did quite a bit of hard labour in the garden today and wouldn't mind an early night."

After washing the dishes they watched ABC television for an hour or so and then got ready for bed. Tom switched off the light and then got into bed beside Molly.

"Tom" said Molly. "I am feeling a little bit down tonight, for some reason. Could you hold me close please."

"I will of course, *a stór*" said Tom.

Molly turned on her side. Tom moved up behind her, put his arm around her and held her close. She snuggled back up to him.

"Good night, Tommy."

"Good night, Molly my love."

Morning came. Tom was woken by the cheerful carolling of the magpies in the trees. He got out of bed and drew the curtains.

"Looks like another nice day out there" he said.

There was no reply. He went over to the bed.

"Do you want to have a bit of a lie-in in this morning? No reason why you shouldn't. We have nothing urgent on today."

Still no response.

"Molly? Are you okay?"

Now Tom began to feel concerned.

"Molly. What is it? Why don't you say something?"

He gently shook her shoulder. She did not respond.

Now concern turned to alarm.

"Molly, Molly. Please wake up!"

He felt for a pulse in her wrist. He could feel nothing. In increasing desperation he now tried to detect the carotid pulse in her neck.

Again nothing.

He put his hand against her face. It was quite cold.

The terrible truth began to dawn on him.

"Oh No.... Oh No.... Dear God No.... Molly, Molly, Molly... Oh No..."

BOOK 5

Chapter 37

The spaceship for the Embassy *to Earth has begun its journey from the planet Omnos. Twenty five years later NASA observe what appears to be a large asteroid heading for planet Earth. Despite early fears that it will collide, on the basis of later and more accurate measurements they conclude that it will in fact be gravitationally captured by Earth and will end up in geosynchronous orbit.*

The spaceship for the Planet Earth Mission was now ready to begin its long journey. It had been assembled in space from all the components which had been constructed on the planet's surface and ferried up to orbit. The crew and the large diplomatic and scientific team were already on board and preparing to go into stasis. The President of the Omnos Planetary Council was having his last meeting with the appointed Head of Mission, Dr Irban Limnos, a senior academic historian and linguist.

"Well Dr Limnos, you won't set foot on Omnos for at least 50 years so it is unlikely that you and I will ever meet again. On behalf of all the people of Omnos I thank you for taking on this arduous task, and of course with all my heart wish you good fortune."

"Thank you, President" said Dr Limnos. "It is a daunting, and will be an arduous, task but I am confident that with the team we have assembled it will be successfully carried out. Indeed if all goes well, by the time our expedition returns there will be three societies of Earth people established here on Omnos. That is something exciting for us to look forward to."

"Yes" said the President. "I am keenly looking forward to seeing at least the beginning of that myself. And now you must board your shuttle and begin this historic journey."

Twenty five years later the members of the Omnian team on board the great space ship slowly emerged into consciousness. When they were finally awake they commenced the program of exercise and dietary supplements designed to get them into full physiological and mental working order again. When he felt ready Dr Limnos had his first conference with the spaceship captain, Frin Ebbli.

"How far away we now, Captain?"

"As our present speed, about 30 days journey" replied Ebbli. "You can just about see planet Earth on our telescope, but it is very small. No detail is yet visible."

"What is our current speed?" asked Limnos.

"In the region of 5000 to 6000 kilometres per second" replied Ebbli.

"When we get to about 4 billion kilometres from Earth please slow us down to about 30 kilometres per second, but still aim at Earth. We will adjust the trajectory slightly a bit later."

"It shall be done" said the captain.

In the Oval Office, the President of the United States looked up from his papers as he heard a knock on the door. The Chief of Staff entered.

"Mr President, there are some NASA scientists here who want to speak to you."

"I don't have any NASA scientists on my schedule for this morning."

"I know, sir, but they say it is urgent and very important."

The President, a tall, grey-haired, man with old-fashioned round-lensed spectacles and a somewhat forbidding demeanour, thought for a moment.

"I have an awful lot on my plate at the moment, but if NASA say this is important then it probably is. I'd better see them."

"All right. Show them in. But we'll have to keep this short."

The NASA scientists were ushered into the room, all three with the same expression of grim concern.

"Well gentlemen. Take a seat. And tell me what this is about."

"Thank you for agreeing to see us Mr President" said the spokesman in urgent tones. "But what we have to tell you is so significant that we felt it couldn't wait. I am Dr Clement Atkinson, leader of the Comet and Asteroid monitoring team at NASA. These are two of my colleagues, Dr Emmet Riley and Dr Jane Chauvel. As you may know, at NASA we have for many years been carrying out observations in space on the lookout for any comets, asteroids or any kind of rocky debris that might be heading towards Earth. I have to tell you that in the last couple of days we have observed what appears to be an asteroid of significant size that is indeed travelling on a trajectory towards this planet. It is still some distance away and so we can't be absolutely certain, but on the basis of our preliminary observations it does seem to be coming towards us. Also, which is quite unusual, on the basis of its trajectory it is clear that it is coming, not from our own asteroid belt but from outer space, outside the Solar System. "

"How big is it?" said the President.

"Because of the distance it is hard to say" said Dr Riley "but our rough estimate is that it is about a kilometre in diameter. If it is solid rock it will weigh about a billion tonnes"

CHAPTER 37`

"How does that compare with previous asteroids that have hit Earth? Like the one that killed the dinosaurs" asked the President.

"That asteroid, the one that hit the Yucatan Peninsula 65 million years ago, is thought to have been about 10 km in diameter" replied Riley.

"So this one, if it hits us, won't do as much damage as the dinosaur one" said the President. "It won't - you know - wipe out most of the life on Earth, will it?"

"No. We don't think so" said Atkinson. "But it will do enormous damage. How many lives it destroys will depend on just where it gets. Impact in a major urban area is likely to cause the deaths of millions in addition to wide-ranging destruction of buildings and infrastructure. If it lands in the middle of the ocean, on the other hand, say the Atlantic or the Pacific, the results should be less catastrophic. There will still be a massive tidal wave or tsunami with major destructive consequences on coastal cities either side of that ocean."

"Will you be able to predict just where it will hit?" asked the President.

"Yes, but not until it gets much closer and we can accurately measure its trajectory" said Atkinson.

"And when will that be?"

"Probably in about two weeks."

"When it gets that close, can't we just blow it up? You know, send missiles with nuclear warheads." asked the President.

"That, Mr President, is a matter on which you will need to consult your Joint Chiefs of Staff, but on the basis of what we know we doubt if that is a viable solution. We may indeed be able to cause some fragmentation of the asteroid but the fragments will just keep on coming" said Atkinson.

"Can't we just vaporise it?"

"No one has nuclear explosives that powerful" said Atkinson. "Not us, not the Russians, not the Chinese. No one."

"So what can we do?" said the President. "Surely we can't just sit here and wait for the worst to happen. Isn't there something?"

"Dr Chauvel has a proposal" said the NASA team leader. "There is no guarantee it will work, but we think it's worth a try and if we do give it a go we must start making preparations now."

"Well Dr Chauvel?" said the President.

Dr Chauvel, a slim young woman with short dark hair and hornrimmed glasses, spoke up.

"What I propose is that we use our rockets, as many as possible, not to try and blow the asteroid up but to push it enough off course so that it doesn't hit the Earth. When the asteroid gets close and we have characterised its precise shape, size and trajectory, we can identify the best point on its surface at which to apply a lateral force to change its direction. This would involve rockets flying up to intercept the asteroid, and then crashing into the specified region of its surface at right angles to the asteroid trajectory at full speed. This will require some structural modification of our present rockets which would need to begin without delay. Also, the more rockets the better and so we would need to ask the Russians to come in and help.

There is however, it must be said, grave doubt about whether our rockets can actually fly fast enough to intercept the asteroid in the way I have described. The asteroid may well be travelling too fast for this to be possible. We will know better when it comes closer and we can measure its speed accurately."

"If indeed it turns out that the asteroid is travelling too fast for us to simply catch it up and push it aside, there is one variation on Dr Chauvel's proposal that might just do the trick" said Dr Riley, an African American man of medium height with thinning hair.

CHAPTER 37`

"On the basis of our most accurate measurements of its speed and trajectory, we calculate a point in space near to Earth at which the asteroid will arrive at some exact time. And we arrange that our rockets, coming from one side, arrive at that point in space at precisely the same time. The hope would be that in this way we might actually hit the asteroid and push it off course. As this will be rather like trying to hit a flying bullet with another bullet, you will appreciate that the likelihood of success is not high. But that might be the only shot left in our locker."

"Thank you Dr Chauvel and gentlemen" said the President.

"What I have heard from you this morning is by far the worst news I have ever had in the whole of my presidency. What you describe is a looming catastrophe, not just for the United States but for the whole world. And while it seems that there is some chance we might avert it, that chance is very slim. Nevertheless NASA must immediately get to work on the possible technical solution that you have outlined. Also we must without delay share the information we have with other world governments.

Harry" he said, directing his attention to his Chief of Staff. "See the Secretary of State and get that machinery in motion.

Now given that there is apparently a high likelihood that we will not be able to divert this asteroid we must immediately start considering what we can do to mitigate the consequences of the impact. From what you said earlier it is clear that the consequences depend not only on the size of the asteroid but on precisely where on the Earth's surface it arrives. So what we and the rest of the world need from NASA, as soon as possible, is a calculation of just where the impact will be."

"We now have this asteroid under continuous observation" said the leader of the NASA team. "As soon as we think we have sufficiently accurate data on its trajectory and speed we will carry out that calculation and let you know the conclusion immediately."

A fortnight later the NASA team came together to discuss their latest trajectory observations.

"Clement, something very odd may be happening" said Emmet Riley to the team leader.

"Jane and I have been analysing the trajectory measurements very carefully and, impossible though it sounds, we think the asteroid has very slightly changed direction."

"How could that be?" said Atkinson. "Nothing can disobey Newton's first law - every object will remain at rest or in uniform motion in a straight line unless acted upon by an external force."

"Yes of course" responded Jane Chauvel. "But if our later measurements, which are underway right now, confirm that the asteroid has indeed altered course then it must have been subjected to some kind of external force."

"Indeed" said Atkinson. "All right. We will meet again first thing tomorrow morning by which time you will have the results of your latest measurements."

The following morning the team reconvened. "

"Well?" demanded Atkinson.

"We are now quite certain" responded Riley. "The asteroid has changed direction: only slightly but definitely."

"And furthermore" said Jane Chauvel "our best estimates seem to be telling us that if it continues on its new trajectory the asteroid will miss the Earth, not by much but by a safe margin."

"Well that's very good news" said Atkinson. "We'd better tell the President."

"We can't quite guarantee just yet that the asteroid will miss the Earth" said Riley. "We don't want to give the President false hope. But by, say midafternoon, we will have enough measurements to make a definite prediction. How about we wait till then?"

"Okay" said Atkinson. "Let me know as soon as you are sure and then I will arrange that we immediately meet the President."

By mid afternoon the news was good. The NASA team was ushered into the Oval Office.

"Well gentlemen, and Dr Chauvel. Do you have news for me?"

"We do indeed Mr President. Good news! On the basis of our latest observations we are now confident that the asteroid will miss the Earth: not by a great margin but enough."

"Well thank God for that!" said the President. "Are you quite sure?"

"Yes we are" said Dr Atkinson.

"Well that is indeed good news. Harry" speaking to his Chief of Staff. "As before, tell the Secretary of State and have him communicate this information to other governments around the world."

"Yes Sir!" said Harry.

The NASA team continued to closely observe the asteroid.

"Well? What's the results of our latest measurements?" enquired Dr Atkinson.

"Intriguing, to say the least" said Emmet Riley. "It is travelling at about 3 km/s. It's trajectory will take it about 36,000 km above the Earth's surface, but since that trajectory as it happens is pretty well in line with the Equator, then according to our calculations it is possible that the asteroid may in fact be captured and end up in geosynchronous orbit around the Earth."

And indeed when the asteroid arrived five days later, this is exactly what happened.

Chapter 38

***The Mission Leader** of the Embassy on the Omnian spaceship, which is now only 2 billion kilometres from Earth, specifies to the captain the precise coordinates of its arrival, in particular the requirement to arrive in geosynchronous orbit.*

"Dr Limnos" said the space ship captain, Frin Ebbli. "We are now about 2 billion km from Earth. Do you want to adjust our trajectory again?"

"Yes" replied Limnos. "I will now give you the precise location of our destination. I want you to establish the ship in a geo-synchronous equatorial Earth orbit at an altitude of 35,786 km above the Earth's surface and longitude 77° West, with an orbital speed of 3.07 km/s. This will keep us stationary over one point on the Earth's surface and from that point, with the wide angular range of our instruments we will be able to observe the greater part of the northern and southern hemispheres of the planet at that longitude.

"Why that particular longitude?" asked Ebbli.

"We want to make our presence known, and to begin our negotiations, with the most advanced Earth societies" replied Limnos.

"There are three places on Earth where these are to be found. One is in the continent of Europe where a number of European countries together form the European Union. Another is in the North American continent where we have the United States of America and its northern neighbour, Canada. The third is down in the Southern hemisphere where we have the very large but sparsely populated country of Australia and its much smaller neighbour, New Zealand. We believe it will be simpler if our first interaction is with just one Earth country. The United States is much bigger and more populous than any of the European countries. Canada and Australia are both very large but have much smaller populations and economies than the United States. For these reasons we have chosen the United States as the country with which we shall first make contact. 77° West is the longitude of Washington DC, the capital city of that country. By taking up position there in our geostationary orbit we minimise the distance between our spaceship and the American seat of government, and thus maximise the efficiency of our communications.

Our geostationary orbit at about 36,000 km is of necessity very high. To examine the planet more closely we will be sending out two unmanned probes which will orbit the Earth at about 800 km altitude. These will record everything - surface temperature, topography, ice cover, vegetation distribution, on the land. Over the ocean we will measure wave height, surface temperature, current direction and the productivity of the oceanic ecosystem as measured by distribution and concentration of phytoplankton chlorophyll. To monitor seasonal changes we will continue these observations for a full Earth year. By the time we have finished we will know almost as much about the general character of planet Earth as do the Earth people themselves."

"How soon after arrival will we make our presence known to these Earth people?" asked Ebbli.

"By no means straight away" replied Limnos. "We want to eavesdrop on the Earth population for quite some time, perhaps as much as a year, to familiarise ourselves with Earth culture to a greater extent than was possible from the somewhat random fragments that we intercepted back on Omnos. When we are ready we will then make a direct approach to the American government. We are confident that we will be able to take full control of their telecommunications system at the highest governmental level and that this will give us immediate direct access to the American President and his advisers in what I believe they call the White House."

Chapter 39

After a year in Earth orbit, *the Omnians, their spaceship still presenting the appearance of an asteroid, decide to make their presence known. They begin by communicating with the American President. After initial disbelief the Americans accept that there really is an alien spaceship in orbit around our planet and communicate this to other world governments.*

In the Oval Office the President of the United States was conferring with the Secretary of State and the Deputy Secretary of State. Harry Fiedler, his Chief of Staff was also present. The subject under discussion was the always thorny problem of the relationship with China. Suddenly, without warning the speaker linked to the President's landline phone sprang into life.

"Good morning Mr President."

"What the hell's going on here? I'm not expecting any phone calls" said the President, angry at being interrupted in the middle of an important conference.

"This is not a phone call Mr President. We have temporarily taken control of your communications system because we have an important message for you."

The voice was calm. Male. Authoritative. The accent was English.

"Harry" said the President. "Looks like someone has hacked into our communications. Get Security onto it straight away. We can't have this!"

Harry Fiedler immediately phoned the Head of Presidential Cyber Security and told him what had happened.

"What! That's impossible!"

"That's as may be" said Harry "but the plain fact is it just happened."

"We'll get onto it immediately."

"Now you've got that bit of housekeeping out of the way" said the Voice. "I want you to pay close attention to what I have to say. It is very important. Record it if you wish but the essential message has already been lodged as a file in your computer.

First of all - who are we? We are what you may regard as an embassy to Earth from Omnos - a planet in orbit around the star you refer to as Alpha Centauri. Some years ago we became aware of your existence. We have been observing you with great interest ever since. We finally decided to send an embassy to you to make contact."

Consternation, scepticism and bewilderment were all struggling for control in the President's mind.

"So just where are you?" he said. "I mean, right now.""

"You will no doubt recall" said the Voice "that what seemed to be an asteroid reached the Earth about a year ago and ever since has been in geosynchronous orbit around your planet."

"Yes, of course" replied the President. "For a while we thought it was going to hit us."

"Well" said the Voice. "That apparent asteroid is in fact our spaceship and it is from there that I am speaking to you now. We gave it the appearance of an asteroid to give us plenty of time to observe the Earth, its peoples and societies close up, before we made our presence known."

CHAPTER 39

"But how do I know" said the President "that you are really up there. That this isn't just part of some gigantic hoax."

"We will direct a 100 MHz radio signal to the Goldstone-Apple Valley radio telescope in the Mojave Desert. They have a steerable dish. Get them to use this to identify precisely where that signal is coming from. They will find that it is coming from the apparent asteroid in geosynchronous orbit. That should suffice."

The President turned to his Chief of Staff. "Harry. Get NASA to organise that straight away."

"We will continue this conversation at a later time" said the Voice.

"In the meantime suffice it to say that we, the Omnians, are a humanoid people, not dissimilar to the people of Earth. We come here with entirely peaceful intentions. We are technically more advanced than you are and have much to offer you to help solve the problems that beset your species. In return, there are some things we would like from you. All of this is set out in great detail in the document that we have already lodged in your information system and in the information systems of every significant Earth government. May I suggest to you that under the auspices of your United Nations you organise a conference of all world governments to discuss the implications of our arrival and to put together an appropriate response. We will provide a channel through your Internet system by means of which you can communicate directly with us. And in future we will use that same channel to communicate with you rather than by taking control of the White House internal communication system as we did today.

My name, by the way is Irban Limnos. I am the leader of our Mission to Earth. When you use the communication channel it will generally be me with whom you will be interacting."

In the Oval Office there was a stunned silence. They looked at each other. Finally, the Secretary of State spoke.

"Was that real? Is there really a spaceship in orbit around the Earth containing some kind of humanoid aliens who have come to visit us? Or is this just some ultra sophisticated hack into our system? The Russians? The Chinese? Or some teenage genius in a basement somewhere?" said the president.

"Harry, check with Cyber Security again" said the President. "See if they've turned up anything yet."

Harry Fiedler did as requested and then turned back to the President.

"No. He says it was not any kind of normal hack. It was nothing like anything they've ever seen before."

Another silence."

"Well, hard though it is to believe, maybe there really is an alien spaceship up there in orbit" said the President in baffled tones.

"If the Goldstone radiotelescope finds that there really is a signal coming from the asteroid, then I guess that will confirm it" said the Deputy Secretary of State.

"Indeed. Which being the case we had better find this document which that guy on the loudspeaker tOld us he had lodged in our system and find out what this is all about" said the President.

Chapter 40

Omnians arrival is declared *to the world. Their request to be provided with a variety of samples of human DNA is made known. Their request for an Earth ambassador to accompany them back to Omnos is also made known. A selection committee is set up but a suitable candidate proves hard to find. Knowing Tom's role in the discovery of an Alpha Centauri exoplanet, the Omnians suggest him.*

That there was an alien spaceship in orbit around our planet soon became known to all the nations and peoples of the Earth. The news was greeted to varying extent with amazement, excitement, consternation. The contents of the long Omnos document which had been supplied to governments around the world were closely examined, discussed and debated. It had much to offer: cures for cancer, potent antibiotics, new metallic alloys, fusion power, and a great deal more. The response to the request by the Omnians that in return they would be supplied with the human genetic and cultural material for the establishment of three authentic Earth populations on Omnos, was generally positive although there was some debate about the three specific ethnic/cultural groups that the aliens had chosen.

While every nation within Europe thought it should have been chosen to represent Europeans/Caucasians, there was general agreement, with the exception of some grumbling from England, that Ireland was an appropriate choice. The choice of Mali to represent the peoples of Africa again presented no problem. Asia however proved more problematic. Many people of Indian origin argued that India, rather than Japan, should have been chosen. When they were reminded that, ethnographically, Indians are regarded as brown Caucasians, some took this as an insult, others as a compliment. China, as the largest and most populous East Asian nation thought it should have been chosen, but the Omnians were not to be moved.

Transfer of useful scientific and technical information to Earth had commenced and some of it was already proving valuable. Collection of genetic material from the populations of the three selected countries went ahead. While in each case a special effort was made to collect DNA from people of proven artistic achievement, most collections were made from a random selection of the population at large. DNA was collected also from important crop species, in which the Omnians had expressed a particular interest, and domesticated animals. Seeds also - of crops, tree species, ornamental and other plants - were collected since these should survive the long journey back to Omnos. All these samples were ferried up to the alien spaceship by NASA. DNA sequence analysis of all the samples was immediately commenced by the technical team on board the ship, and the data transmitted to Omnos, where it would arrive in 4.37 years time.

All the interactions between the Omnians and the people of Earth so far had been essentially of a technical nature and has such had been carried out competently and smoothly. But there remained one important matter to be dealt with which was more problematic, and this was the wish, expressed by the aliens, that the peoples of Earth should send an ambassador to go with the spaceship back to Omnos. While of course the Omnians accepted that it was up to Earth to decide who to send, if indeed anyone was to be sent, they did give some indication of the kind of person who in their view would be most useful and acceptable.

They suggested that an ambassador with a scientific background would be best equipped to report back to Earth on the characteristics of the planet, Omnos, and on the physical and the social functioning of Omnian society. But ideally the ambassador should also be someone who can interpret and explain the nature of Earth society - the people, the history, the politics, the culture, in short, a generally cultured person, familiar with literature, music and the visual arts. And in view of the very high regard in which the music of Earth is already held on Omnos, if he or she had reasonable competence on one or more Earth musical instruments, this would be an added bonus. Finally, because of the interest on Omnos in the metaphysical views prevalent amongst the peoples of Earth, it would be desirable, although not essential, for the ambassador to be an adherent of one of the Earth's four major religions.

To find an Earth ambassador with all those qualities, and one moreover prepared to go on what was most likely to be a one-way trip to another planet, was clearly going to be a tall order. When the Omnians' request was made known there was no shortage of volunteers. With the agreement of the United Nations, the American government undertook to put together a multinational committee to examine the candidates. The vast majority, however, were found to be just Science fiction fanatics. Many others were simply mentally disturbed. Rather than relying on volunteers the team launched their own search, primarily among the scientific and also the professional diplomacy professions. A very small number of suitable candidates with the requisite characteristics were identified. While all of these found the prospect very interesting, they were all put off by the one-way nature of the trip.

The person who had been appointed by the United Nations to communicate with the Omnians on the dedicated channel was Barbara McAllister, a distinguished former United States ambassador to China, Germany and Japan. By now she had established an easy relationship with Irban Limnos, the Omnian Head of Mission. She explained to him the difficulty they were having in finding someone to take on the role of Earth Ambassador.

"Not very surprising I suppose. I must say, we did anticipate that there would be difficulty in finding a candidate. However, there is one possibility which has recently occurred to us that you might like to follow up. As you may know, we monitor the science publications of Earth and in a recent issue of the Astrophysical Journal there is a paper announcing the discovery of a planet orbiting around the star you refer to as Alpha Centauri A. As it happens that planet is our planet, Omnos. The lead author of the paper is a Dr Thomas Glennon. I know it is a long shot but since he discovered our planet, perhaps he would like to visit it."

"Hmm. Perhaps he would. As you say, it is a bit of a long shot, but we will follow it up anyway."

Barbara McAllister told the Earth Ambassador selection committee about the Omnian suggestion of Dr Thomas Glennon as a possible candidate. They immediately set to work, first to assess his suitability and then, if he seemed indeed to be an appropriate candidate, to track him down and put the proposition to him. Discreet inquiries were made, mainly in the scientific community, about this Doctor Thomas Glennon and what kind of person he was. They found that he was born in Ireland but had moved with his family to England as a child. He had earned his scientific degrees in Cambridge, had been a postdoctoral fellow in Oxford and then a University lecturer in Wales before moving to the

Institute for Space Science and Remote Sensing in Canberra in Australia. He normally went by the name of Tom Glennon, was highly regarded as a scientist, that he was generally well liked, that he had broad cultural interests, that he was musical - playing more than one instrument, and that he was a religious believer, specifically a Catholic.

When Tom's possible candidacy as the ambassador was discussed in the committee, the response was generally favourable.

"He does seem to tick most of the boxes" said the chairman. There was a dissentient voice, Professor Jacob Schreiber, one of the scientist members of the committee.

"Oh I don't know. Glennon doesn't impress me" he said. His view, however, did not prevail and the committee made the decision to seek out Doctor Glennon and put the prospect of being the ambassador for Earth to another planet, to him.

After the meeting the Committee Chairman had a word with the other scientist member of the committee.

"What's Schreiber got against Dr Glennon?"

"Well, Professor Schreiber is a very clever man."

"Of course. Of course. Nobel prize and all that."

"The thing is - he always likes to feel that he is the brightest guy in the room."

"And so?"

"And usually he is. But its just that if Tom Glennon's around, he is never quite sure."

"Ah.... I see."

Chapter 41

The selection committee *tries to get in touch with Tom but he has disappeared. Tipped into a deep depression by the death of Molly he has left his job and his home in Australia and gone no one knows where. FBI agent Kevin Daly given the job of finding him. Eventually, with difficulty, tracks Tom down in Kilcarra in Connemara. Puts the Ambassador proposal to him. Feeling that without Molly he has no strong wish to remain on Earth, Tom says he will consider it.*

The next step was for the committee to get in touch with Doctor Glennon and put the ambassador proposition to him. The Chairman phoned his number at the Institute but got no response. He then tried Tom's home number and his mobile number, but again no one answered the phone. Email messages also were not responded to. The chairman reported his failures to make contact to the next meeting of the committee.

"I think we'll just have to physically find him and put the proposition to him in person" said one member of the Committee. There was general agreement.

"This committee does not itself have the resources to do that" said the Chairman.

"But I'm sure it could be organised through the American government. I will get in touch with our State Department contact."

CHAPTER 41

The American government was indeed happy to help locate this new candidate for the position of Earth Ambassador. The task was assigned to the Federal Bureau of Investigation. On considering the matter the director of the FBI concluded that one operative should be sufficient for this task. On further consideration he arrived at a decision as to which member of his organisation was best suited to the task. Special Agent Kevin Daly was called to his office.

"Take a seat. I have a special task for you. Now you are no doubt aware that the nations of the world are currently trying to find a suitable candidate to be the Earth Ambassador and return with the aliens to their home planet of Omnos."

"Yes, Director. I am aware of that."

"You may also be aware that none of the suitable candidates they have identified so far are actually prepared to go."

"Yes. I had heard that."

"Well, the Omnians themselves have recently come up with the name of someone who they think might just possibly be prepared to take on the task. He is Doctor Tom Glennon, a scientist currently based in Australia. And I want to stress that his possible candidacy must be kept in the strictest confidence for the moment. But the problem is, the committee responsible for finding a candidate have been unable to get in touch with him. There has been no response by phone or email. So they have decided that the only thing to do is to track him down and put the proposition to him in person. And this is where you come in.

You're Irish aren't you Daly?"

"Er....Yes" said Kevin, wondering about where this question was leading. He was indeed Irish, having been born and bred in Ireland. He had obtained a scholarship to an American university and after graduating had decided to stay.

"Well, so is this Glennon guy. You also being Irish might help in tracking him down."

"I suppose it might" said Kevin.

"Since it was in Australia that Doctor Glennon was last known to be based" said the Director, "that is where you had better start looking. The American government is anxious for results on this one so expense is no object. Do whatever it takes. You will be supplied with a file containing all the information we have on Glennon and I want you to get to work on this straight away. Now is there anything else you wish to know?"

"No. I don't think so" said Kevin.

"Okay. So on your way and good luck!"

Shortly after Kevin arrived back at his office the Glennon file was delivered. He opened it, read through its contents carefully and arrived at a picture of a talented, well-regarded scientist whose career was clearly going well. So why had Glennon disappeared from the radar?

"Well" he thought. "I'd better get cracking."

Kevin arranged for FBI administration to supply him with a government credit card and book him a flight, business class, to Australia. When she got home that evening he told his wife that he was going to be away for an as yet unspecified period on an overseas investigation, but he was not at liberty to tell her what it was about. But he would keep in regular phone and email contact.

"When it's all over I should be able to tell you what I've been up to."

"All right, Kevin my love. I'll look forward to having you back again."

Kevin took the plane from Washington to Los Angeles and then on a Qantas flight to Sydney, from where he continued to Canberra. At Canberra airport he hired a car and booked himself into a hotel. The following day he phoned the Institute for Space Science and Remote Sensing, introduced himself as a representative of the American government and made an appointment to see the Director of the Institute, Professor Mike Hennessy. Having presented his credentials as an FBI agent he explained that he was here to see Professor Tom Glennon but that they had so far been unable to contact him.

"Why does the FBI want to meet Tom Glennon?" asked Hennessy. "He's not in any trouble is he?"

"No indeed. Not at all" replied Daly. "It's just that there is something we believe he can help us with although I am not at liberty yet to tell you what."

"Glad to hear that he is not in any trouble" said Hennessy. "Not that I think he ever would be. The reason you have been unable to contact him is that he has taken himself off somewhere. What happened is that his wife, Molly, suddenly died several months ago – a heart problem I believe. They were a very devoted couple. No children. And Tom took her death very badly. It seems to have tipped him into a very deep depression. He tried to come back to work but was unable to cope. He was even talking of chucking his whole career in, which would be a great pity. On medical advice he is now on extended sick leave and we hope that in this time he will be able to find his way back to normality. He left Canberra but didn't say where he was going."

"Do you think he is still in Australia, or might he have left the country?"

"I just don't know. He is certainly very used to travelling overseas. You could ask the Department of Home Affairs. They control entry to, and departure from, Australia. If he has left the country they would have a record of that."

"Okay. I'll get in touch with them. Thanks for your help."

"No problem. I hope you'll find Tom. We are a bit worried about him."

"I'll let you know straight away if we do."

After leaving the Institute, Kevin went to the American Embassy. They had been forewarned of the purpose of his visit to Australia and he was given an interview with one of the First Secretaries, a Ms Jennifer McFarlane. He brought her up to date with what he had found so far and asked if she could arrange for him to make contact with the Australian Department of Home Affairs. This she agreed to do and made a phone call, on the basis of which Kevin was given an appointment to see a senior member of the Department of Home Affairs, the following day.

At the Home Affairs main building, in Belconnen, one of Canberra's satellite cities, Kevin was ushered into the office of Michael Sharpe, the public servant who had been deputed to help him. He introduced himself and showed his FBI credentials.

"I'm here to try and make contact with one of your scientists - Professor Tom Glennon, who is based here in Canberra at a research Institute on the ANU campus. But he seems to have disappeared from view. He is on extended sick leave, but nobody knows where he has gone. I was wondering if he has actually left the country. I understand that your department would have a record of his departure if he has."

"Yes, I think we can help you there" said Sharpe. "What period of time are we looking at?"

Kevin told him the last date at which Tom had been at the Institute.

"Okay. I will look at all departures from then until yesterday. I will get the computer to scan through to see if anyone called

Tom Glennon, or Thomas Glennon, has left Australia in that time."

The computer search did not take very long.

"No. No Tom, or Thomas, Glennon has departed since the date you gave me."

"In that case I suppose he must be still in the country" said Kevin. "Well, thanks for your help."

"No problem" said Sharpe. "Look. Here is my telephone number" he said, scribbling on a Post-it pad.

"If you think I can help, just get in touch."

"Thanks, I will."

It occurred to Kevin as he left the Department of Home Affairs that it was just possible that Tom Glennon might actually be still at home, but just not answering the phone. He had both of Tom's addresses, the cottage out in the country as well as the one Canberra. First he drove out to the country cottage. He knocked on the front door. There was no response. He then walked around to the back of the house and knocked on the back door. Again no response. Just as one final check, he took a stroll around the property, but there was no one to be seen so he returned to Canberra. He then drove to the Glennon house in Bruce and once again knocked on the front and back doors but no one responded.

He phoned Professor Hennessy at the Institute.

"It looks as if Doctor Glennon has not left the country and I have checked to make sure that he really isn't in one of or other of his houses. Have you any idea where he might have gone?"

"He and his wife sometimes used to drive down to the South coast, a couple of hours away."

"Well, I noticed that his car is still parked in the carport in his house in Bruce, so I suppose he hasn't driven to the coast."

"No. I guess not. The other possibility is that he has flown to some other destination within Australia."

"Yes. I suppose he might" said Kevin.

The thought that Tom Glennon might simply have flown off to some other part of Australia was rather discouraging for Kevin. A nationwide search would require the participation of the police forces of all six Australian states and two territories. This would be a major undertaking which he certainly did not have the authority to request on his own. It would require government to government interaction. He decided to read the Glennon file again, more closely this time, in the hope that it might suggest some alternative course of action. He began by looking at Tom Glennon's origins in the West of Ireland. He saw that Tom had been born on the family farm near the village of Kilcarra in the heart of Connemara.

"Now that's an Irish speaking area" he thought to himself.

"And most of the people there use the original Gaelic forms of their names rather than the Anglicised versions. Now 'Glennon' is surely an Anglicised name - so what is the original version?"

On an Irish surnames website he found that the Gaelic equivalent of 'Glennon' is Mac Leannáin.

"If Tom Glennon is using an Irish passport then the name on the passport is likely to be the same as the name on his birth and baptismal, certificates. Both of those should be accessible. But if I can get through to the church where he was christened, I might get an answer straight away."

In the file he found that Tom has been christened in Saint Cormac's Church in Kilcarra. The village of Kilcarra he knew was in the Diocese of Galway. On the diocesan website there was a list of parishes with information about each one, and here he found the phone number of Saint Cormac Parish in Kilcarra. Because of the time difference across the continents he waited until late that evening before making the phone call. The call was answered by a woman, whom he assumed to be the priest's housekeeper.

"*Cléirtheach Naomh Cormac*" (Saint Cormac Presbytery)

"*Ba mhaith liom labhairt le an Sagart Paróiste, le do thoil*" (I would like to speak with the Parish Priest, please) he said.

" *an tAthair Ó Máille anseo. Is mise an Sagart Paróiste.*" (Father O'Malley here. I am the Parish Priest)

Because his Irish was a little rusty, Kevin chose to continue the conversation in English. He explained that he worked for the United States government and that they were trying to locate a former member of Saint Cormac's Parish because he might be of assistance to them in a matter of some importance.

"These days he normally goes by the name, Tom Glennon. But it is possible that his passport might be in the original Gaelic form of his name, and I was wondering if we could find this in the parish baptismal records."

"Indeed and we might" said Father O'Malley, who was happy to be of assistance.

"Can you tell me the year and date of his birth?"

Kevin provided this information from the file.

"He would most likely have been christened no more than a few days from his birth" said the priest. "The entry should not be hard to find."

A few minutes later - "Yes, I have it here."

"And in exactly what name or names was he christened?" asked Kevin.

"He was christened Tomás Daniel, and the family name was given as Mac Leannáin" said Father O'Malley.

"Thank you very much, Father" said Kevin. "That's exactly what we needed to know."

"Ah sure, not at all" said Father O'Malley. "Only too glad to help."

The following morning, Kevin phoned Michael Sharpe at the Department of Home Affairs.

"Hi. It's Kevin Daly here."

"G'day Kevin. What can I do for you?"

"We have a promising new lead. I noticed in the file that Tom Glennon was born in the far West of Ireland in a region where the Irish language is still spoken. 'Glennon' is actually the Anglicised version of his surname and it occurred to me that the name on his birth certificate, which is the name that he would have used for his passport might be not 'Glennon' but the original Gaelic version. From the parish priest over in Ireland I have found the name that was on Tom Glennon's baptismal certificate and I'm quite sure that this would have been the same as the name on his birth certificate, in which case it is likely to be the name on his passport."

"Aha! Sounds promising. So what is this name?"

"It is – Tomás Daniel Mac Leannáin."

"Oh. That's certainly different from 'Tom Glennon'. Can you spell that for me?"

"I'll do better than that. I have written it out neatly and I will attach it as a photo to a text."

Michael Sharpe looked at the text message which now arrived on his phone.

"Thanks. Yes, that's all I need. I will look for any departures under that name." And then after a few minutes -

"We are in luck! Someone travelling under that name left Australia about six months ago. The destinations listed were London, then Dublin."

"Thanks very much! That's our man for sure" said Kevin. "He must be. In Ireland. So that's where I will head next."

CHAPTER 41

"Okay. Good luck in your search" said Sharpe.

Kevin now booked his own flights to London and Dublin. He thought it most likely that Tom had gone back to the family home in the far West of Ireland. Accordingly, having picked up a hire car at Dublin airport he drove across the country to Galway, where he booked himself into the Harbour Hotel. So as to recover from jetlag before recommencing the search for Tom Glennon he spent the next day strolling around Galway city. The following day after lunch he drove North into Connemara. At the pub in Kilcarra village he asked for, and was given, directions to the Glennon family farm. He stopped at the front gate, and, looking around, saw an elderly man working with lambs in the sheep yard. He guessed that this was Tom's uncle Séamus, the owner of the farm. He walked over and introduced himself.

"Hi. I'm looking for Tom Glennon. Is he by any chance staying here?"

"He is staying here" replied the man, looking closely at Kevin. "In the cottage there. But he is out walking at the moment. Are you a friend of his?"

"No" said Kevin. "We have not actually met. But I have a message for him which is of some importance."

"He said he was going to go to the pub this evening" said Séamus. "So your best bet is to look for him there sometime after dinner."

"I'll do that" said Kevin. "Thanks."

To kill time he drove for a while around the surrounding hilly countryside and then to the sea shore, where he went for a stroll. Finally, having had dinner in a restaurant in Kilcarra, he made his way to the Ó hEógáin pub. Music was being played and there was a sizeable number of customers present. He went over to the bar and spoke to the barman.

"I'm looking for Tom Glennon. Do you know if he's here?"

"He is indeed" said the barman. "Tom's with the musicians. The one playing the fiddle. I take it you don't know him already."

"Well actually, no" said Kevin. "But I have a message for him."

"You may not find him very talkative" said the barman. "He lost his wife recently and it has hit him very badly. He seems to be pretty depressed."

"I'm sorry to hear it" said Kevin. "But I need to talk to him anyway. In the meantime a pint of Guinness please."

"Certainly" said the barman, drawing the pint. "Oh, and one other thing. These days he doesn't want to talk anything but Irish."

Kevin remained at the bar, drinking his Guinness until the music stopped and it seemed that the musicians were taking a prolonged break. He saw that Tom had retired by himself to a small table at the side. Kevin approached and addressed him with the traditional Gaelic greeting.

"*Dia duit*" (God to you)

"*Dia is Muire duit*" (God and Mary to you) replied Tom.

Kevin continued in Irish, occasionally struggling for a word or a phrase as it was some time since he had been fluent.

"May I have a word?" he asked.

"Yes" replied Tom, but not in an inviting manner.

"My name is Kevin Daly. As you can tell I am Irish, but these days I work for the American government. In fact, I am with the FBI."

Kevin displayed his FBI credentials.

"And what, in heaven's name, does the FBI want with me?"

"It's not actually the FBI that want to talk with you. We were simply asked to find you because you had disappeared from the radar. I was given the job. And finally I succeeded."

CHAPTER 41

"So I see. Well if it's not the FBI who want to talk to me, who is it?"

"I'd better give you the background. You are aware of course that for the last 6 months or so there has been an alien spacecraft in orbit around our planet."

"Yes of course" said Tom now showing a flicker of interest.

"You are no doubt also aware that the aliens, who by the way are called 'Omnians', after Omnos, the name of their planet, have asked if the Earth can send an ambassador with them when they return to their home. And that under the auspices of the United Nations a committee was set up to try and find a suitable candidate. A number of good candidates have been found but none of them want to go. But when the Omnians were told this they eventually came up with a suggestion of their own. The person they suggested was you."

"How do these aliens know anything about me?" asked Tom, in some surprise.

"Apparently they read the Earth scientific literature. They noticed your paper, which has just now appeared in print, in which you report finding an Earth-sized planet orbiting Alpha Centauri A. They say that planet is their planet. And since you discovered it, they thought you might have a particular interest in visiting it."

Tom's interest was now thoroughly aroused. To actually get to visit another planet; one actually inhabited by intelligent beings. For a scientist like himself, especially a space scientist, this could be a dream come true.

"But you said a number of suitable candidates had been found already. Why did none of them want to go?"

"Oh, because it will pretty certainly be a one-way trip. The distance is so great and the journey so long that there will be no coming back."

"Coming back?" thought Tom to himself. "Would I care if I don't come back? Without Molly this world is a cold and empty place for me. Maybe a one-way trip to another world is just what I want."

Even as these thoughts tumbled through his mind, he felt himself emerging from his depression and torpor. He made a sudden, impulsive decision.

"You can go back to the USA. Tell the FBI you have completed your mission and tell the United Nations committee that I am interested to hear what they have to say. I'll switch my mobile phone on again so that they can communicate with me directly."

Kevin booked himself the next flight from Shannon airport through to Washington, and immediately made an appointment to see the FBI Director to give him the good news.

"Excellent! Well done, Daly. Write up your report and forward it to me. I'll tell the State Department and they will communicate with the selection committee."

Chapter 42

***Tom goes to Washington** and is interviewed by the Earth Ambassador Selection Committee. He makes a good impression and they conclude that he would indeed be suitable for the post.*

On the Wednesday of the week following Kevin Daly's visit, Tom received a phone call from Washington. The caller, a Mr Sebastian Harrington, introduced himself as the chairman of the Earth Ambassador Selection Committee.

"Doctor Glennon, our committee has been given to understand that you are open to the possibility of being the Earth Ambassador to the planet Omnos. Is this correct?"

"It is. I am indeed open to that possibility."

"In that case, if you are agreeable, our committee would like you to come over to Washington so that we may discuss this further. We will arrange your travel and your accommodation over here and you will receive a generous per diem allowance for as long as is necessary."

I'm happy with that arrangement" said Tom. "I am free to travel at any time so you can send me the flight details as soon as you have finalised them."

Following his decision to break out of his self-imposed exile, Tom had reactivated his emails as well as his mobile phone. On Friday he received an email with his flight information for the following Monday. On Monday he flew from Shannon to Washington, business class, was met at the airport and taken by car to a four star hotel in Washington. He was scheduled to meet the selection committee on Wednesday. They had allowed him the Tuesday to recover from jetlag. On Wednesday morning to present an appropriate ambassadorial image he wore a suit and tie. A car came to collect him and he was taken to the Harry S. Truman building, head office of the State Department, where in a committee room he was introduced to the members of the Earth Ambassador Selection Committee. He was amused to notice that included in their number was his occasional sparring partner, Professor Jacob Schreiber.

The Committee was large, having twelve members: they were seated either side of a long table. The Chairman was at one end and Tom was asked to sit at the other. The Chairman opened the proceedings.

"Fellow committee members. Today we have with us Doctor Tom Glennon. Dr Glennon, as you will recall was suggested to us, as a possible candidate for the role of Earth Ambassador to Omnos, by the Omnians themselves. He has expressed, provisionally at least, a serious willingness to take on that role and we are here today to discuss that possibility with him. To begin the proceedings I would be grateful if each of you in turn could introduce yourself to Doctor Glennon so that he knows to whom he is talking.

One by one the committee members stated their names, country of origin and backgrounds - diplomats, academics including two scientists, and representatives of the arts community.

"To get the ball rolling" said the Chairman. "Perhaps you could tell us what to you is the attraction of taking on the role of Earth Ambassador to this far distant planet."

CHAPTER 42

"I am, as you know, a scientist" responded Tom. "And in particular, I am a planetary scientist. I study other planets. And so to actually visit another planet, to see it up close: to see its geology, its atmosphere, its oceans and above all, its life forms is a prospect of enormous interest. So that is the attraction. But of course I am also well aware that if I go it would not be merely to indulge myself as a scientist. I would be there to represent the people of Earth and to the best of my ability to convey to the Omnians the nature of Earth society, and the history and origins of our civilisations with particular reference to the various forms of our culture."

"That's all very commendable, Doctor Glennon" said one of the committee members, a Scotsman with a sceptical demeanour. "But it's also a very tall order. Is it something you are confident you can manage?"

"I believe so" said Tom. "I have had a lifelong interest in history. As a scientist I have had the good fortune to visit many different countries around the globe and so have had some exposure to different Earth societies. Outside of work I would say that literature and music are my main interests."

"The aliens have expressed an interest" said another committee member "in having an ambassador with a reasonable competence on one or more musical instruments. Do you play music as well as listen to it, Dr Glennon?"

"I do indeed" said Tom. "I have been playing the fiddle, that is to say the violin, in Irish traditional music groups for years. I also play the piano. While I was trained in classical music my performance preference is for jazz, particularly blues piano."

"The aliens have also said that they would like the Ambassador to be a religious believer" said another member. "Are you?"

"I am" said Tom. "I was brought up, and continue to be, a Catholic."

Other questions on various aspects of the mission followed. One member of the committee asked if he thought he was competent to interact scientifically with the Omnicians.

"I believe I am" he said.

Professor Schreiber then spoke up. "There are some matters at the frontier of science about which Doctor Glennon and I are not always in agreement. As to his scientific competence, however, there is no doubt."

"Gee, thanks Jacob" thought Tom.

The last question came from one of the female members of the committee, a woman whose appearance and accent revealed her to be from the Indian subcontinent.

"Doctor Glennon. A number of other suitable candidates for the role of Earth Ambassador have previously been identified. But for every one of them the sticking point was the thought of leaving their family behind and most probably, given the enormous distance, never seeing them again. But in your case this is apparently not an insuperable obstacle. Could you tell us please, why this is so."

"This will be a more difficult question to answer" thought Tom to himself.

"My family consists of two sisters in England, and an uncle and some cousins in the West of Ireland. While I get on well with all of them the fact is that, living as I do in Australia, I see very little of them. We are an Irish family and emigration to distant places, often with little hope of seeing their homeland again was, in previous centuries, very much part of the Irish national consciousness. That I now am considering doing something very similar will not seem so very strange to my family. If my dear wife, Molly, was still alive there would be no question of my taking on this mission. But sadly, very sadly, she died about a year ago. We were not blessed with children. And so my ties to this planet are now much less strong."

Amongst the Committee members Tom's response was met with silence. This was eventually broken by the Chairman.

"Thank you Doctor Glennon. I think that will be all."

Tom rose to his feet, made a small bow in the direction of the Committee, left the room, and was driven back to his hotel.

"Well, ladies and gentlemen. I propose that while all that is still fresh in our minds we discuss Doctor Glennon's candidature now" said the Chairman.

A general discussion ensued.

"Well at least we now know why, unlike the other candidates, Doctor Glennon is prepared to take leave of Earth" said one committee member.

Finally, the Chairman brought discussion to a close.

"Listening to what you all have to say, my clear impression is that there is a consensus that Doctor Glennon would indeed be a suitable person to take on the role of Earth Ambassador. Are we agreed?"

There was a general murmur of assent.

"The United States government has agreed to take on the task of bringing the Earth Ambassadorship into being. They have set up a small team which will interact both with the Omnians and with Doctor Glennon to prepare him for this role. Assuming Doctor Glennon does not decide to pull out the last minute, then our task is done. It remains only for me, on behalf of the United Nations, to thank you for your participation."

Chapter 43

***Tom is offered the post** and accepts. He receives training to prepare him for the journey. At a ceremony with UN Security Council representatives he is appointed as Earth Ambassador to Omnos and provided with his diplomatic credentials. He makes contact with the Omnian Mission Leader, Irban Limnos.*

That evening Tom received an email from the Chairman of the Selection Committee telling him that his candidature had been approved and that he was being offered the post of Earth Ambassador to the planet Omnos. He was asked to confirm his acceptance. Having already made his decision Tom was not about to go back on it and he emailed his acceptance. An appointment was made was for him in the State Department building with a Ms Jane Kovaceski. His arrival at the State Department front desk was phoned through and Ms Kovaceski, a middle aged woman with greying hair came and introduced herself. Back in her office he was introduced to two younger men, Bruce Stevens and Michael Nolan and offered a seat.

"We are the Omnos Ambassadorship implementation team" she said. "It is up to us to do whatever it takes to get you on board the Omnian spaceship and also to organise the cargo, mainly seeds but also some artefacts, which are also being sent from Earth to Omnos. You will need to make your own decisions about what you want to take with you but the Omnians say you can take as much as you want. I suggest you start getting it together now. We will give you a thorough health check before you go. For you to actually get on board their ship we will fly you up on a NASA rocket, but you will have to transfer from our vessel to theirs wearing a space suit, so we have arranged with NASA to give you some space flight experience first. Bruce, who is himself an astronaut, will be your liaison there. You don't have to become a fully trained astronaut. The Omnians assure us that your exposure to weightlessness will be very short. Apparently their living quarters, where you will be spending your time, have a centrifugal gravity equivalent.

You will no doubt want to say goodbye to the various members of your family before you go so you need to think of times and places to carry that out. In addition I assume you will want to put your affairs in order in Australia. We, of course, will pay all your travel expenses. For the time being we are keeping your appointment secret so that you are not hounded by the media.

There is one very important meeting for you to attend. This will be in the United Nations building in New York and this will be with the representatives of the five nations constituting the Security Council together with the Secretary General of the UN. It is at that meeting that you will be officially appointed as the Earth Ambassador and supplied with your diplomatic credentials to present to the Omnian government when you arrive on their planet. A document has been prepared for your benefit outlining what the United Nations consider should be your role as the ambassador of this planet.

There is a smaller separate diplomatic meeting for you also to attend. I have to tell you that because of your life trajectory, the Irish, British and Australian governments each think that you are specially representing them, so we have arranged for you to have meetings with the three ambassadors that those countries have sent to Washington. We will leave it to you to work out a way of making them all feel special. Now there is one very important matter which we must implement without delay. Namely, to put you in contact with the Omnians on their spaceship.

Michael?" she said, turning to Michael Nolan.

On the table in front of him Nolan had a laptop computer. This he now pushed over to Tom.

"This computer is set up for you to talk directly to the leader of the Omnian mission" said Nolan. "His name is Irban Limnos. He will be expecting to hear from you. The password 'Omnos' will connect you directly with their communications system."

"Well Doctor Glennon" said Jane Kovacevski. "We've given you plenty to be thinking about. Our mobile phone numbers and email addresses are on this sheet of paper. Please have no hesitation in getting in touch with us at any time of day. Getting you safely and fully prepared and onto that spaceship is our primary objective. For the rest of the time before you go you will be provided with an office here in the State Department."

There was a pause.

"So. Is that all for the moment?" asked Tom.

"For the moment. Yes."

"Okay" said Tom. "As you say, I have plenty to think about."

He was driven back to his hotel.

Over the next few weeks the preparations for Tom's mission took place. He was taken on numerous parabolic flights in a NASA plane in each of which he experienced 22 seconds of zero gravity. He was given high *g* training on the centrifuge at the NASA Ames Research Centre to prepare him for the for the *g* forces that he was going to experience during rocket acceleration. And finally he was taken as a passenger on the next rocket that went up to the International Space Station. Here, during a brief stay he donned a space suit and was taken outside for a short excursion in space. Tom then returned to Earth together with two members of the ISS crew, splashing down into the ocean off the coast of Florida in a re-entry capsule. All of this Tom found very interesting and as he was physically fit and in good health he was able to cope.

At the meeting with the Security Council representatives in the UN building in New York, the enormous significance of his mission was impressed upon him. He was going to be called upon not only to explain and interpret the peoples of Earth to the Omnians, but also to make a good impression upon them as a representative example of the human population. He assured the Security Council that he was well aware of all this and was confident of his ability to carry out the task before him. Back in Washington he saw the ambassadors of Ireland, Britain and Australia individually and assured each of them while he was going as the Ambassador from Earth, he would make it clear to the people of Omnos that he was in a special sense representing Ireland, Britain or Australia as the case might be. In a short ceremony he was appointed as Earth Ambassador to Omnos and provided with his diplomatic credentials to show to the Omnian government on arrival on that planet.

Although his appointment had not yet been made public, news that Dr Tom Glennon was to be the Earth Ambassador spread amongst the Washington diplomatic community. One morning while he was in his State Department office, Tom received a call from the front desk saying that there was someone here from the Papal Nunciature who would like to see him.

"All right. Send him up" said Tom. He was intrigued. What did the Papal Nunciature, the Vatican Embassy to the United States government, have to say to him?

When the Vatican representative arrived he introduced himself as Father Kevin Quinn SJ, a Jesuit priest currently attached to the Nunciature.

"I understand, Doctor Glennon, that you are a Catholic."

"I am" said Tom.

"I am sorry to appear intrusive" said the priest "but may I enquire if you are a practising Catholic?"

"As it happens, I am" replied Tom. "I don't regard myself as being particularly devout but I do go to mass on Sunday."

"In that case" said Father Quinn "we have a suggestion for you. You will of course have no access to religious services on planet Omnos. But we understand from the Omnian representative on their spaceship that they propose to establish electronic communication between Earth and Omnos. In particular this apparently means that while on that planet you will be able to access the Internet although of course anything you receive will in fact have been created 4.37 years previously, because of the time required for radio signals to traverse the great distance between the planets."

"Yes, of course" said Tom.

"This means" continued the priest "that, let us say once a week, on whatever day you deem to be a Sunday you can access one or other of the TV masses that are put online."

"So I can" said Tom. "I hadn't thought of that."

"Well, our suggestion is" said Father Quinn "that we supply you with a large number of consecrated hosts to take with you so that each Sunday you can not only remotely participate in a mass, but also receive Communion."

CHAPTER 43

"You know" thought Tom to himself "when I'm all alone on that distant planet, with no hope of return, my religion will give me some much-needed support."

"Yes. I think that's a good idea. Let's do it."

"All right. We will" said Father Quinn.

Now that he was officially the Earth Ambassador, Tom decided that the time had come for him to make contact with the Omnians in the spaceship. The morning after he returned from New York he switched on the laptop that the implementation team had provided and entered the password 'Omnos'. The Omnians had already beamed down to Earth a great deal of information about their planet and its inhabitants, so Tom knew that they were a humanoid species whose appearance fitted well within the range of appearances existing within the human race itself. In that respect, Tom was not expecting any great surprise when he made contact.

The computer responded to the password with a set of windows each having a label in English - Science Director, Engineering Director, and others. Tom clicked on the window labelled - Mission Leader. A voice responded - "You have asked to be connected to the Mission Leader. Please wait. He will be with you very shortly."

After a four minute delay the screen cleared and Tom found himself looking directly at the person whom he assumed to be the leader of this alien mission. Clearly male. In appearance predominantly Caucasian with a hint of East Asian character. Of light pigmentation. If it was a human Tom would have assessed him as being middle-aged. The alien subjected Tom to a very intense scrutiny for a few seconds and then his face relaxed.

"If I'm not mistaken, I now have the pleasure of meeting the Earth Ambassador. Good morning, Ambassador."

"Good morning, Mission Leader" responded Tom.

"If we may get a bit of diplomatic protocol out of the way" said the alien. "How would you prefer to be addressed? As Ambassador? Or perhaps as 'Dr Glennon'?"

Tom's natural preference was for informality. He was generally happy to be addressed as 'Tom'. He realised however, that now he was the Earth Ambassador, a certain distance must be maintained.

"'Dr Glennon' will do very well" he said. "And how should I address you?"

"Like you on Earth" replied the Omnician "we generally have two names. A personal name and a family name. My name is Irban Limnos. As it happens, like you I have an academic background and I have what you would call a doctorate. So how about you call me 'Dr Limnos'?"

"All right" said Tom. "I will."

"Good" said Limnos. "Having got that out of the way we can get down to business. We are very much looking forward to having you come on board and accompany us back to Omnos. We have already made it clear to your government, but I reiterate it now for your benefit, that when we get to Omnos, all your living requirements will be met, in as generous a manner as you think fit, by our planetary government. In short, you will want for nothing. And everything will be done to facilitate whatever activities you may wish to pursue.

We will be looking to you to help us understand and interpret Earth society and Earth culture. Our scholars in various disciplines are looking forward to interacting with you. You no doubt, on the other hand, will wish to report back to Earth your observations on our planet and our society. I may say that we hope to continue observing events as they unfold on Earth by monitoring traffic on the airwaves so you will not be cut off from what is happening on your home planet."

"A technical question, if I may" said Tom "about how this two-way communication traffic is to be achieved. Earth and Omnos are 4.37 light years apart. How are you going to overcome the problem of the inevitable attenuation of the signal over this great distance?"

"The signals will be sent by a laser operating at radio frequencies" replied Limnos. "And so attenuation is enormously reduced. And in addition we have repeater stations at intervals of about one light year, along the straight-line trajectory between Earth and Omnos."

Tom was impressed. "Yes. That should do it."

"And now" continued Limnos. "As to the voyage itself. I dare-say you know already but I will confirm it now that because of the great distance to be traversed the voyage takes some years. We have the technology to put all the crew into stasis. This means that for the whole journey you and the rest of us will be in a deep sleep at low temperature and so not only will you be unconscious of the passage of time but you will undergo very little ageing in the process. We will commence our journey just as soon as you come on board our spaceship. NASA will bring you on one of their rockets up to our vessel. I gather that you have already been given some spacesuit experience?"

"I have" said Tom.

"Good" said Limnos. "In your spacesuit you will need to cross a short distance from the NASA rocket to the entrance hatch of our ship. We will have two of our people waiting for you and they will help you across and bring you on board. How do you feel about all of that?"

"I feel fine" said Tom.

"Excellent. So as soon as you have done everything you need to do on Earth, inform NASA and we will get this great adventure started."

"Looking forward to it" said Tom.

And now he was looking forward to it. It was no longer just part of his reaction to the death of Molly. He was beginning to feel genuinely excited about the prospect of heading off into space and visiting another planet.

Chapter 44

***Time for Tom to put** his Earth affairs in order. He goes to Australia, resigns from his post at the Institute, puts his house and farm on the market and directs that the proceeds be sent to his two sisters in England. Pays a last visit to Molly's grave. Flies to England for a sad goodbye to his sisters.*

Tom had two remaining tasks to carry out before he left Earth: to put his affairs in order in Australia and to say goodbye to his family. He flew across the Pacific from Los Angeles to Sydney and then on to Canberra. The first thing to do was resign his post at the Institute for Space Science and Remote Sensing. At the Institute he made an appointment to see his friend, Mick Hennessy, the director.

"Mick, I am here to tell you that I am resigning my post at the Institute."

"I am very sorry to hear that, Tom. Can I ask why?"

"I will tell you why. But I must ask you to keep what I'm about to tell you confidential for at least the next two weeks. You will have heard that the Omnians up there in that spaceship want to take someone from Earth back with them to be the Earth Ambassador to Omnos."

"Yes, I have heard that."

"Well, I am to be that Ambassador."

"What!.... You're going to be the ambassador?"

"Yes I am."

"Tom. Are you sure about this? You know it will pretty certainly be a one-way trip?"

"Yes, I know that. I have thought hard about the implications. But since I lost Molly, my ties to this planet have become much less strong. And, looking at it as a scientist it is an enormously interesting prospect. It will also, of course, be both a great honour and a great responsibility."

"Well. For what it's worth Tom, I think you'll do the job very well. But even so. It's going to be an enormous wrench to leave your own planet and people, knowing that you will never see it or them again. And how confident are you about the Omnians? Are you sure they will treat you well?"

"I've done my homework, Mick. On the basis of all the information they have supplied it is clear to me that they are a civilised people, technically more advanced than us but cultured. I have had a few talks now with their mission leader, who is up in the spaceship, and if he is a typical Omnian then I am favourably impressed."

"Hmm. Well let's hope your impressions are accurate. But it is a risk you're taking.""

"Yes it is. But just remember that I'll be setting foot on a new planet. The first Earth scientist ever to do so."

"That certainly does have its attractions. Well, if you're definitely going then I wish you luck. I hope it all goes well."

"Let's hope so. I am cautiously optimistic. Anyway, Mick, if this project goes ahead, and it looks like it will, then this is the last time I will ever see you. So thanks for offering me the job in the Institute all those years ago. I enjoyed it here and I was able to do some good work. And thanks for your friendship. We've been good mates and I shall think of you sometimes when I am on Omnos."

CHAPTER 44

"Tom, I was glad to have you at the Institute. You were a credit to us. Well" grasping Tom firmly by the hand "I guess this is the last goodbye. We've been good friends and the people here will miss you. And we'll think of you over there on Omnos, especially when we look up at Alpha Centauri in our Southern night sky. Goodbye Tom."

"Goodbye Mick."

And Tom left the Institute and the ANU campus for the last time.

There remained his Canberra house and his farm out in the Yass Shire countryside to dispose of. To achieve this he decided to make use of the solicitor who had handled the property purchases in the first place. Without saying just where he was going, Tom explained that he was leaving Canberra and would not be coming back. He instructed the solicitor to put both properties on the market and when they were sold to transfer the proceeds equally to two bank accounts which Tom, without their knowledge, had set up in the names of his sisters, Aoife and Gráinne.

Tom drove out to his farm for one last look. He strolled around the familiar paddocks where he had enjoyed being a farmer and then went to sit down in the cottage which he had built. He recaptured in memory some of the happy times that he and Molly had spent there.

"Goodbye Gortnakilla" he murmured to himself as he closed the farm gate on leaving.

"I'll never walk your fields again."

Tom's final duty, and a sad one, was to visit Molly's grave. She had been buried in the small bush cemetery near the village of Murrumbateman. Tom had chosen this cemetery because it was not far from their farm and Molly and himself had occasionally visited it in their journeys around the countryside and had liked its bushland character. He stood there looking for while at the granite headstone with its inscription and dates of Molly's birth and death -

Molly Glennon
(Née Ni Chuilleanáin)
Born Ireland ----. Died Australia ----
Dearly loved wife of Tom Glennon

"Oh Molly my love. How I miss you" he thought to himself. "This is the last time I'll visit your grave, my dear. But I'll carry your memory with me always."

As always at Molly's grave, Tom said a short prayer for the repose of her soul. He then drove back to Canberra.

Having discharged his Australian duties, Tom booked a flight to Britain landing first in London and then continuing on to Manchester. He had told his sisters he was coming and arranged for them to come together to have dinner with him at the hotel where he was staying. As they sat down for dinner he told them that when the meal was finished he had something important to tell them.

"All right, Tom. What is it? What do you have to tell us?" asked Aoife, the older of his two sisters.

"Very soon" he said "I am leaving. And I'm afraid you won't see me again. I won't be coming back"

"What!... What do you mean you will be leaving and won't be coming back?" they asked in horrified tones.

Tom told them the whole story. Where he was going and why.

"Oh Tom, Tom. Can't someone else go instead of you?"

"Well, apparently I am the best candidate. And the Omnos people actually asked for me specifically. And you must remember, this is a great honour. An honour for our family not just for me."

"I suppose so" said Gráinne. "But I still wish you wouldn't go."

"Yes, I know. But I have to tell you I've made the decision."

And after many tears, and some reproaches, his sisters eventually realised that his mind was not to be changed and became, with much sadness, reconciled to his leaving. As he finally bade them goodbye there were tears in his eyes also.

▲

Chapter 45

***The day for the departure** of the alien spaceship for their home planet arrives. Tom is flown to Cape Canaveral. Dons his spacesuit. Is farewelled by a group of world leaders headed by the President of the United States. NASA rocket takes him up to the Omnian spaceship in its location in geostationary orbit. Two Omnian astronauts ferry him over to their ship. Meets Omnian Mission Leader. Is put into stasis for the 25-year journey ahead.*

The day for the departure of the alien spaceship to its home planet, Omnos, finally came. Tom had packed a wide range of clothing as he was not certain about what he would be able to obtain on the other planet. Beyond that he did not take very much in the way of belongings. As well as a framed photo of Molly, family photos, letters and other family documents, and his official documents establishing his credentials as Earth Ambassador, he took some favourite books, his fiddle and the flute which Molly used to play, together with his large collection of printed Irish music. His recorded music collection was all on his laptop. He assumed the Omnians would somehow make it possible for him to use it. Included with his luggage was the sealed container from the Vatican nunciature holding the consecrated hosts.

CHAPTER 45

Tom's journey began with a flight to Cape Canaveral from where a NASA rocket was to take him to the point 35,786 km above the Earth, where the alien spaceship was waiting for him in geostationary orbit. He was to be accompanied on the rocket ascent by Bruce Stevens, his NASA liaison, together with one other astronaut, Jim Cardwell, whose responsibility was to pilot the ship. As well as its human passengers, the rocket was carrying a substantial freight container holding the large variety of seeds that Earth was sending to Omnos, together with a number of Earth artefacts in which the Omnicians had expressed an interest, particularly musical instruments.

At the launch site Tom was given a final brief medical checkup and then helped into his spacesuit. Since he was not yet a seasoned astronaut he was given medication to control any motion sickness he might feel in space. Carrying his helmet he proceeded, together with Bruce Stevens and the other astronaut, to the lift which was to raise them up so that they could enter the cabin.

Somewhat to Tom's consternation, waiting for him was a small but very high-powered delegation, there to say goodbye and to give him an official sendoff. Headed by the American President, it included the President of the Russian Federation, the General Secretary of the Chinese Communist Party, the President of the European Commission and - because of Tom's mixed origins - the prime ministers of Ireland, the United Kingdom and Australia.

"Well Doctor Glennon" began the American President. "We are here to express our gratitude to you for taking on this extraordinary and challenging mission of representing the peoples of Earth to the inhabitants of another planet. On the basis of everything we have heard about you from the selection committee and the implementation team we are confident that you are equal to the task, that you are the man for the job."

There was a general murmur of agreement from the other government heads.

"And so we are here to say farewell, and may good fortune go with you."

Each of the other heads of state then, one by one, bade Tom farewell, in English or in their native language, using phrases appropriate to their culture. Last, and as the smallest country represented, came the Taoiseach (Prime Minister) of Ireland. He used the traditional Gaelic form – *"Slán agus beannacht a Thomáis. Go rachadh Dia leat"*

(Farewell and blessings, Tomás. May God go with you)

Momentous occasion though this was, Tom had not been forewarned and had prepared nothing to say to the leaders of the world. He contented himself therefore by saying - "Thank you for your good wishes, ladies and gentlemen. I promise you I will do my very best to be a good representative of humankind to the people of Omnos. And now, as the rocket is about to launch, I must finally say Goodbye."

With a farewell wave, Tom turned, and with his two companions, followed by a chorus of 'Goodbye', 'Adieu', 'Adios', 'Auf wiedersehn', 'zài jiàn', 'Slán' and other valedictory expressions, he entered the lift.

It took several hours of flight for the NASA rocket to rendezvous with the Omnian spaceship in its geostationary orbit, Jim, the pilot, making the delicate final adjustments to position the rocket near to the alien vessel.

"We have to wait a few minutes now" said Bruce. "The Omnians will be making their preparations to bring you across. I am in communication with them" he said, tapping his headphones.

"They will let me know when they are ready."

Ten minutes later Bruce looked over to Tom.

CHAPTER 45

"Okay. Everything is ready now. You and I will put our helmets on, proceed to the airlock and then go outside together. I will keep an eye on you from this end but there should be a couple of Omnians already out there waiting to make sure you get over to their spaceship safely. It shouldn't be difficult." Tom put his helmet on, checked that it was secure and then followed Bruce into the airlock. Bruce closed the hatch behind them and they waited while the air in the airlock was drawn back into the ship.

"So this is it" thought Tom to himself. "When the airlock door opens and we go out into space I will be leaving Earth behind, for good. I could still change my mind, right now. And say I don't want to go. This is my last chance.

Well, Tom Glennon" he said to himself. "What are you going to do?

I'm going to go of course. And I'm looking forward to it."

Bruce pressed the switch to open the airlock door. There was a tethering cable, with a handpiece at one end, looped inside the airlock.

"Okay Tom. We're ready to go now" said Bruce, communicating with Tom through the headphones. "I'll go first but as you follow me hang on to the end of this cable. We don't want you floating off into space. Shortly the Omnians will come and collect you."

Bruce propelled himself out through the airlock door, and very cautiously, Tom followed, holding on to the end of the tethering cable. First he looked down. From this distance, about 36,000 km, he could see the whole beautiful blue planet Earth. He savoured the moment, trying to fix this image in his memory.

He then looked over towards the alien spaceship - a massive, metallic sphere floating in space.

"Wow! It's enormous!"

"It certainly is" said Bruce. "Very impressive."

"But it's quite some distance away."

"Yes. The Omnians didn't want us to come any closer than about 200 metres. They were concerned about the possibility of a collision."

"That makes sense" said Tom.

"Look. I think I see them coming now."

He could now see two spacesuited figures heading their way.

"Yes, they just told me" said Bruce. "After they have delivered you they will come back and collect the freight, including of course your luggage. Well Tom, I reckon this is goodbye. I am the last Earth person you will ever see. And on behalf of everybody let me wish you the very best of luck. We'll be thinking about you."

"Thanks Bruce. Yes, this is goodbye. Let me shake you by the hand." And while hanging on to the tethering cable with his left hand Tom reached across and firmly shook Bruce's hand. Tom now turned towards the oncoming Omnians. One of them waved his hand and Tom waved back. As they got close Tom could see that they were propelled by what he assumed were gas-powered jet packs on their backs. They came to a halt a couple of metres away. Tom then heard a new voice in his headphones.

"Greetings, Dr Glennon. As you may have gathered, we are here to escort you over to our spaceship. May we assume that you are now ready?"

"Yes I am."

"Very good."

They then moved, one to either side of him. Tom turned and gave one last wave to Bruce Stevens. Bruce waved back. With one Omnian firmly grasping his left arm and another his right, Tom found himself rapidly heading towards the alien spaceship, which loomed larger and larger as he got closer. They slowed to a halt in front of what was clearly an open airlock.

CHAPTER 45

"Now Dr Glennon, when you enter the airlock it will automatically close behind you. It will then be refilled with atmosphere. When it is safe to do so, you will be told that you may remove your helmet. The hatch that you can see on the far side will open and you can proceed through this to the interior of our vessel. My companion and I will remain outside as there are further tasks for us to perform."

"All right" said Tom, and pulled himself through into the airlock. He heard the door click firmly shut behind him after which he could faintly hear through his helmet the sound of a stream of air entering the airlock. After a few minutes this ceased and the hatch opposite him suddenly opened. He then heard a voice which he recognised.

"You mean now safely remove your helmet, Dr Glennon. And please proceed through the hatchway."

Tom removed his helmet, pulled himself through the hatchway and found himself in a substantial room-like space from which there extended ahead of him what appeared to be a tubular corridor into the interior of the vessel.

"Welcome, Dr Glennon. At last we meet in person."

Of the two figures in front of him, Tom immediately recognised one. It was Irban Limnos, leader of the alien mission.

"Greetings, Dr Limnos. It is a pleasure to meet you."

"Allow me to introduce my deputy head of Mission, Ilmay Fornos" said Limnos, indicating the person beside him, a tall, mature age woman with short black hair, who was currently inspecting Tom with intense interest. "Greetings...Er..." began Tom, who was uncertain about the proper way to address an Omnian woman. She smiled.

"Since we are speaking in English, how about we use English customs in choosing how to address people. Which being the case, you may address me as – Miss Fornos - since, as it happens, I am an unmarried adult female."

"That's a very helpful suggestion" said Tom "and, adopting it immediately, may I say - Greetings Miss Fornos. I am delighted to meet you as well."

"And I to meet you, Dr Glennon. This is a day we have been looking forward to."

"And now" said Limnos "a few words of explanation about our spaceship. You will already have observed that it is spherical. The spherical outer shell is there to protect us against cosmic rays, which as I am sure you are aware are damaging to biological tissue. Most of the space within the sphere is simply empty. We just don't need that much volume. Our living and work quarters - workshops, offices, laboratories et cetera - are all within a very large annular ring which circulates continuously at about three revolutions per minute and provides us with a centrifugal gravity which is very acceptable, but somewhat less than full Earth or Omnos gravity. To get to the living quarters we will now proceed down the corridor you see ahead of you which will take us to the centre of the ship. There, we will step into the slowly rotating Central node and move out along one of the radial corridors until we reach the annular ring. As we proceed along the radial corridor you will feel a steady increase in the outwardly directed centrifugal gravity. There are ladder rungs in the wall of the radial corridor and by the time you get near the end you will, in effect, find yourself climbing down into the outer annular space."

"I would love to feel some gravity again. I really don't feel at ease floating around like this" said Tom, who was beginning to feel a bit queasy.

"In that case, let's go" said Limnos. With Limnos in front and Ilmay Fornos bringing up the rear they propelled themselves down the corridor to the Central node, entered it, headed along a radial corridor and in no more than a few minutes, Tom found himself climbing down into the annular space. As promised, there was gravity. He divested himself of his spacesuit and looked around. The place where they had emerged from the radial corridor was spacious, brightly lit, furnished with a table and seating - all bolted to the floor. He guessed that this was a communal area extending the full width of the annular ring. At each end of the communal area there was a corridor running along the inner edge of the annular ring along which there were what he assumed were rooms with various functions.

"Let us sit down at this table" said Limnos "and I will bring you up-to-date with what is going to happen in the immediate future."

Tom and the two Omnians took seats at the table.

"We are going to begin our return journey very soon" began Limnos. "I believe the freight from your planet will soon be on board. As you know this includes a very large amount of human genetic material which we propose to use to establish three authentic human populations on our planet. Our molecular genetics team have already begun analysing this and sending the data off to Omnos where it will arrive in 4.37 years time. As soon as it arrives our genetic engineers will begin the task of creating the human populations.

We are also taking seed from your crop plants with us, but to speed things up, the complete genomic sequences of these plants will also be sent off to Omnos and the genetic engineers will explore to what extent the genes from these plants can be inserted into some of our own existing plant species. Unfortunately, it will take about 25 years for you and I and the rest of the crew to arrive on Omnos as the maximum speed of this vessel is only about one sixth of the speed of light."

"*Only* one sixth of the speed of light!" thought Tom to himself. "That's an amazing speed."

"However" continued Limnos "that long delay does mean that by the time we arrive the members of the three human populations will already have reached adulthood and it will be very interesting to see how they have turned out. One of the populations, as I am sure you recall, is of Irish origin, which, given your own origin, will be of particular interest to you.

Now, for us to survive these very long space journeys we all have to go into a state of stasis, or hibernation. On Omnos we mastered the technology for this some time ago and indeed this is what kept myself, Miss Fornos, and all members of the crew alive and in working order for the 25 year journey from our planet to yours. Our journey back to Omnos is about to commence and so we must all go into stasis again, and this of course now includes you. The procedure is fully automated and entirely safe. As you might expect it will involve cooling the body to just above freezing point. Your blood circulation system will be connected to an external system. Your blood will be continuously monitored and its chemical composition adjusted as required, particularly to maintain the oxygen concentration. Your muscles will receive periodic electrical stimulation to keep them working. You will not be aware of any of this as you will be unconscious for the whole time. Also, and fortunately, in stasis we do not age. You will wake up as having the same physical and physiological age as when you went to sleep.

When our spaceship finally arrives at Omnos, it will go into orbit around the planet: not a distant, geostationary orbit such as we presently occupy at Earth, but quite a low altitude one, a thousand kilometres or so, above the planetary surface. Just prior to reaching the end of our journey the automatic stasis system will bring us all back to consciousness again. In short, you will go to sleep above Earth and wake up above Omnos.

CHAPTER 45

When you wake up, you and indeed all of us, will feel somewhat groggy and physically weak. But you will find that with gentle exercise, and normal food intake, you will be fully functioning within a few days. As soon as we arrive at Omnos, although the ship itself will of course remain in orbit, you and I and all of the crew will be taken in shuttles down to the surface. There is no point in hanging around in space once our mission is completed. Our recovery will be quicker down on the planet. You will be taken to special accommodation which will have been prepared for you. It will in fact be the Earth Embassy, where you as Ambassador will take up residence. It will be fully staffed and all your requirements will be met.

So, you get the picture?"

"Yes I do" said Tom.

"Good. Well, I am keen to 'get this show on the road', to borrow one of your phrases, so if you are ready we will prepare you for stasis now. Miss Fornos will take you to a room which has been set aside for you, just down the corridor there. It is fitted with a waste disposal system similar to the one on your International Space Station so please empty your bladder and your bowels as best you can. Then please get out of your clothes and don the standard stasis gown that you will find there - a simple one piece garment such as a patient in one of your hospitals might wear. When you are ready press the button that you will see next to your door. One of our medical staff will come with a gurney to transport you to one of our stasis chambers. Just lie on the gurney and he will give you an intravenous dose of an anaesthetic to send you to sleep. When you are asleep he will take you to the stasis chamber."

"All right" said Tom. "Let's go."

Ilmay Fornos led Tom down one of the corridors, opened a door on the left-hand side opening into a small chamber. It contained a bunk, a waste disposal unit and a small hand basin.

"These are your quarters, Doctor Glennon" said Miss Fornos. "When you wake up from stasis at the end of our journey this is where you will find yourself. How do you feel about going to sleep for 25 years?" she asked, smiling.

"Hmm. Apprehensive" said Tom. "Will I dream?"

"No. We don't dream under stasis. The brain pretty well closes right down. Anyway, I must leave you to get ready. In fact the whole crew is now getting ready for stasis." She left, closing the door behind her.

Tom got undressed, used the waste disposal system as instructed, put on the stasis gown and pressed the button on the wall next to the door. A few minutes later there was a knock on the door. He opened it to find a young man, with a hospital gurney waiting in the corridor.

"Hello, Doctor Glennon. I am one of the nurses on our medical staff and I am here to take you to the stasis chamber. If you get up onto this gurney and lie on your back with your head on the pillow I will administer the anaesthetic to send you to sleep."

Tom did as requested. The nurse swabbed his left arm with alcohol, found a vein and injected the contents of a syringe.

"Relax, Doctor Glennon" he said cheerfully. "In 30 seconds you will be out like a light and then in 25 years you will wake up to find yourself floating in space above my planet."

Tom started counting backwards - 30, 29, 28 - but before he got to zero....

BOOK 6

Chapter 46

***The Omnian spaceship** arrives back at its home planet. Tom is wakened from stasis and he realises that at last he is now at Omnos. The following day he is taken down to Callepta, the Omnian capital city and officially greeted. He meets Finnla Lanos, a member of his liaison committee with the Omnian government.*

Wake up, Doctor Glennon. It is time to wake up. We have arrived."

Tom felt his shoulder being gently shaken. He opened his eyes and saw, looking down at him, a man's face that was faintly familiar. He turned his head and looked around.

"Where on Earth am I?" he said to himself. And then he remembered.

"I'm not on Earth anymore. We must have arrived at Omnos."

"Remember me?" said the man. "I'm the nurse who gave you the anaesthetic to prepare you for stasis."

"Yes. Yes. So you are. I remember now."

"See if you can sit up" said the nurse. "Then swing your legs over the side of the bunk and sit there for a while. You will find that you feel weak and groggy. Then, try standing up."

Tom did as he was told, but when he tried to stand up he nearly collapsed and had to grab hold of the side of the bunk to stay upright.

CHAPTER 46

"Well, you're off to a good start" said the nurse, encouragingly. "It's up to you now to get yourself back in working order over the next couple of days. Try alternating standing and sitting, and when you think you can manage it, go for a short walk out into the corridor and down to the communal area and back. I have provided you with a walking stick which should help if you feel wobbly. There will be a meal prepared for you later, when your appetite comes back. I leave you now. But just press the button if you need any help."

"Okay" said Tom.

"Well" thought Tom "I'd better get cracking."

He reached over, took a firm hold of the walking stick, went out into the corridor and walked slowly and carefully towards the communal space, feeling weak and lightheaded. There were two Omnians seated at the table. He assumed they were members of the crew. They looked at him with great interest.

"Hi" said Tom. "I expect you know who I am."

"Yes indeed" said one of them. "Do you want to sit down?"

"No thank you" said Tom. "Not just yet. What I need is exercise." He continued across the communal space and then down the other corridor, turning around after a while to retrace his steps. He continued this regime for about an hour after which his mind was clearer but he felt in need of a rest. Accordingly, he sat down at the table which by now had been vacated. After some minutes, as he sat there ruminating about what was going to happen next, he heard himself addressed and turned to see the Mission Leader, Irban Limnos, entering from one of the corridors.

"Dr Glennon. Good to see that you are up and about. How are you feeling?"

"Tired, but slowly improving. I am thinking more clearly now."

"Good. If you are wondering why the rest of us seem comparatively lively, it is because we came out of stasis a little while ago. I thought I'd give you a bit of a lie-in."

Tom looked at Limnos in some surprise - a lie-in when I have been asleep for 25 years? He then saw that Limnos was smiling. An alien with a sense of humour – who'd have thought it.

Are you ready for some food?"

"Yes. I think that would help. I am feeling low on energy."

"All right. Now you will, of course, eventually be eating Omnian food, which I assure you is excellent, but just to get you going we did bring some Earth food with us, which our cook is happy to prepare. How does tuna and rice sound?"

"Sounds good."

"Excellent. Just stay seated at the table and the food will be brought to you shortly. Now, while you are waiting, how about I bring you up to date with what happens next. It is currently about midday in our capital city, Callepta, which is where we will be landing tomorrow. We are not going there straight away because I wanted to give you time to at least partially recover from stasis. To help you reset your biological clock I suggest that if you can, you stay awake for about another 10 hours and then lie down to sleep in your room. We can give you pharmacological assistance both to stay awake and then to sleep. In the morning, after you have eaten, you and your luggage, together with myself and my deputy, Ilmay Fornos, will be brought down to the planet surface in one of our shuttle craft. You will then be taken to the Earth Embassy, which has been built especially for this purpose and where you will be living. It already has domestic staff. You will not be expected to begin your ambassadorial role until you feel quite ready. Is this plan acceptable?"

"Yes" said Tom. "Sounds good. I am looking forward to having my feet on solid ground again."

CHAPTER 46

The following morning, after a breakfast of something that seemed very like bread and butter, plus fruit juice, Irban Limnos and Ilmay Fornos led Tom, all three of them now in spacesuits, down one of the radial corridors to the Central Node of the ship. Once again he experienced zero gravity. From the Node they pulled themselves through into a tubular corridor extending at right angles to the plane of the annular ring all the way to the perimeter of the ship. At the end of this corridor there was an open air lock on the other side of which Tom could see the interior of what he assumed was the space shuttle which was to take them down to the planetary surface. As soon as Tom and his companions were securely buckled into their seats, the airlock closed and the shuttle departed. The vessel had no pilot, its movement being controlled by its on-board computer.

The downward journey took about an hour and it was with some relief when Tom felt that the shuttle was at last rolling along on solid ground and slowing to a halt. A door opened in the side. He and his companions removed their seat belts and stepped out from the vessel. Tom looked around him. The sun was shining but he then reminded himself that this was not his Sun but was Alpha Centauri A. The surface on which they were standing look much the same as concrete on Earth. In the near distance he could see buildings, a variety of aeroplanes, two space shuttles and some ground vehicles. In the far distance there were what appeared to be trees. He looked over in a questioning manner to Irban Limnos.

"As you might surmise" said Limnos "this is a spaceport not a commercial airport. Ah. Looks like someone is coming to greet you."

He indicated one of the ground vehicles which was heading in their direction.

"Oh" said Tom. "Advise me please on a small matter of protocol. How do you greet people on this planet?"

"You usually just briefly hold up your right hand like this" said Limnos, bringing his right hand up to a vertical position and holding it there for a few seconds. "And you would normally say the equivalent, in our language, of 'Hi' or 'Hello' or 'Greetings' in your language, as appropriate to the particular person you are greeting. We do not shake hands as you commonly do on Earth."

"Okay" said Tom. "Got it."

The vehicle slowed to a halt and two Omnian males emerged. They both raised their right hands and Tom did likewise. He noticed with interest that there was nothing particularly alien about their dress: simple grey jackets, trousers and white shirts. Not so surprising, he thought. Climate and functionality tend to lead to the same answers.

"Greetings, Earth Ambassador" said one of them, in English.

"My greetings to you" responded Tom.

"My name is Brogni Dona" continued the Omnian. "I am the secretary to the Omnos Planetary Council. I am here to welcome you to our planet. With me is Dr Finnla Lanos, a scientist like yourself. He will shortly take you to your Embassy, and we have appointed him to be the liaison officer between you and the Omnian government. I trust you are agreeable to this?"

"Absolutely" said Tom.

"Good" said Brogni Dona. "Now this may seem a rather low-key welcoming for something so momentous as the arrival of an emissary from another planet. We have in fact a full-scale welcome planned for later. But we thought, given that you have only just emerged from stasis you might not feel up to a major ceremony. And so we propose to wait until you feel ready."

"Thank you for that" said Tom. "You are right. I really don't feel like enduring a major ceremony just now."

"As we expected" said Dona. "You can let us know, through Dr Lanos, when you are ready. Before I go there is just one more thing I wish to say." He turned towards Irban Limnos.

"Dr Limnos, Miss Fornos – to you, to Captain Frin Ebbli and all the crew of the spaceship, on behalf of the Planetary Council I wish to express our gratitude for your successful performance of this great mission. We know very well the great sacrifices you all made in order to be part of it. You may be sure that you will be honoured and rewarded by the Council.

And now" turning to Tom "Ambassador, until we meet again - farewell." He re-entered the vehicle and it sped away towards the distant buildings.

They watched the vehicle disappear and then Finnla Lanos spoke.

"Well, Doctor Glennon. If you are ready we may as well be on our way. Your luggage will be taken separately."

"I'm ready" said Tom. "But first - " he turned to Irban Limnos.

"Doctor Limnos. Now I must say goodbye. Thank you for looking after me on the voyage. Oh, and thank you for that bit of extra sleep you gave me. I'm sure it made all the difference. Once I am installed at the Embassy, perhaps you will pay me a visit."

"I would like that" said Limnos, smiling. "And now, goodbye."

Chapter 47

Tom discusses his *role as Earth Ambassador with Lanos. They proceed to the Embassy. He is introduced to the nine members of the Embassy staff, from First Secretary through to gardener. He showers, gets changed into his new, Omnian, clothes and has his first meal in the Embassy dining room, cooked by the Embassy cook.*

Another vehicle was now drawing close.

"This is for us" said Lanos. After they had entered he spoke a few words, which Tom guessed meant something along the lines of - take us to the Earth Embassy, and the vehicle set off, silently and quickly, passing the buildings and then emerging from the spaceport onto a road.

"It will take a few minutes to get to your Embassy. Your luggage is being brought separately. Now while we are travelling I might as well bring you up-to-date on the people that you will find at your Embassy. There is a cook and an assistant cook who will provide the food, not just for yourself but also for guests if you should choose to hold a dinner. You will have a personal servant who will look after your clothes. There is a security man and a gardener. Supervising the staff, there is what you might call the Embassy manager - unless of course you prefer the word 'butler' - who has the responsibility of making sure that the Embassy runs smoothly. Only the security man will live on the premises - he has his own separate quarters. The rest of the staff come in each day.

Separately from the domestic staff there will be your diplomatic staff. You will have a receptionist at the front desk and also a secretary. At a more senior level we have taken the liberty of appointing a First Secretary to assist you in your ambassadorial role. An Earth person would have been more appropriate than an Omnian, but of course none were available. In the longer run you may of course wish to build up your diplomatic staff. Which being the case I have a suggestion to make. You are aware that here on Omnos we have used genetic engineering to establish three populations which, although born on our planet are genetically almost entirely human. These are now entering into their twenties and are all highly educated young people. You might like to consider sourcing your diplomatic staff from among these populations."

"Yes, I like that suggestion" said Tom. "I am looking forward to meeting my - what shall I call them - fellow Earthlings?"

"'Earthlings' sounds a bit odd. How about just 'Earth people'?" said Lanos.

"Yes. Maybe 'Earth people' would be better. Or perhaps - 'Terrans'"

"Terrans?"

"From the Latin word - *terra* - meaning 'earth'. Latin is an archaic human language, no longer spoken but used to some extent in science, particularly for the naming of biological species."

"Hmm. 'Terrans' could be good" said Lanos. "I'll suggest it to the Planetary Council. Now, on a very practical matter - for your transport around the city you can use one of these ground vehicles, such as the one we are on now. I know - how about we call them 'omnicars'. We will give you what on Earth you would call a 'mobile phone'. With this you can call an omnicar up whenever you want one. All these vehicles in Callepta have now been programmed to respond to commands in English as well as in Omnic. So you just get in and say your destination. You can also of course use the phone to get in touch with me or anyone else you wish to speak to.

Now - a couple of planetary facts to help you understand your environment. Omnos is slightly bigger than Earth so that gravity is correspondingly stronger, but not so much stronger that you should find it a problem. Our day length is also a bit greater - about 25 of your hours, rather than 24 - but you will soon get used to it. Like the Earth the spin axis of the planet is tilted relative to the orbital plane: about 22° compared to your 23.5°. This means that like you we have seasons. Omnos is at a slightly greater distance from our star than the Earth is from the Sun. A consequence is that we have a longer year - 410 days in fact. This city, Callepta, is at a latitude, using your 0 to 90° system, of about 45°, so that it has a cool temperate climate. Our standard week is 10 days, the last two days being in effect the weekend, on which most people don't have to work. By the way, why is your week seven days?"

"Apparently" said Tom "we get that from the Babylonians, an ancient civilisation more than 4000 years ago. They attached great significance to the number seven because of the seven heavenly bodies - the Sun, the Earth and the five visible planets."

"I see" said Lanos. "I suppose that makes a sort of sense. Well anyway, let us finally give a bit of thought to your role as 'Earth Ambassador'. How this works out is of course ultimately up to you but in broad terms the Planetary Council will look to you to help us understand Earth people and Earth culture, not just as it was when you left your planet but also as it continues to develop. We continually monitor the electronic information emanating from your planet. Much of this I assume will be of great interest to you anyway, and you can help us to interpret it. In addition, of course, we can send information back to Earth and you can use this channel to inform your people about our planet, its people and culture. How does that outline sound to you?"

"That sounds good" said Tom. "Those are pretty much the lines along which I was thinking myself."

While listening to Lanos, Tom was also observing the city-scape through which they were travelling. The people in the streets were of similar general appearance to Irban Limnos and the other Omnians he had so far encountered: predominantly Caucasian with a hint of East Asian, but varying in pigmentation, some being much darker than the average. The roads were busy with vehicles, travelling quite rapidly and often passing quite close to theirs. He assumed that they were all on automatic pilot. All the streets were lined with what on Earth he would have called trees. There were buildings of a variety of sizes but none, as far as he could see, higher than about ten stories. All had windows and entrances of normal appearance. Lanos noticed Tom's interest in the passing scene.

"I hope you're not disappointed by the fact that our buildings are not so very different from yours" he said. "Form does generally follow function you know. Perhaps you thought we might live underground, like hobbits."

"You know about hobbits?" said Tom, in some surprise.

"Oh yes. 'The Lord of the Rings' has quite a following on Omnos. It is now more than 50 years since we first discovered your planet and from the very beginning we have taken a great interest in your literature and films as well, of course, your music. It is mainly works in the English language which have captured our attention, to such an extent that a large proportion of our population have made themselves fluent in English. In fact in our schools, students, can opt to learn English, rather than one of the other Omnian languages, as their second language. When you begin to move in our society you will find that most of the people you encounter can speak English very well."

"Well that's going to be quite a help" said Tom.

"Yes it will" said Lanos. "To such an extent that, although you should feel entirely free to try and master Omnian if you are interested, at the same time you really don't need to."

Tom noticed that the buildings were beginning to thin out.

"We have constructed your embassy at the edge of the city, where open countryside begins. We are nearly there. It is at the end of the next turn right, a cul-de-sac."

The vehicle turned down the road on the right hand, and a couple of hundred metres ahead Tom could see a long, single storey white painted building surrounded by a wall. As they drew close and the vehicle came to a halt he could see on the wall next to the entrance, in large letters, the words - Embassy of the Planet Earth. Underneath, in symbols with which he was not familiar, was what he assumed was the same thing in Omnian. In front of and around the embassy there was a well tended garden.

"You know, there is something strangely familiar about this building" said Tom.

"I wondered if you would notice" said Lanos. "The building is in fact a direct copy of the Irish embassy building in Canberra, Australia. We were given access to the original plans. We made this choice partly because of your connection with both Ireland and Australia but also because we like the design. I dare say you have been in the original building."

"Indeed I have. I have attended St Patrick's day celebrations and other events there. I know it well."

CHAPTER 47

"Good. So you will be in familiar surroundings. Now let us go in to your new home. The staff have been alerted to your arrival and will be waiting to meet you. They will introduce themselves to you."

Tom and Lanos got out of the vehicle. The gate in the embassy wall opened automatically as they approached and then, to Tom's alarm he could see a line of nine people side-by-side waiting for his arrival.

"Oh No" he thought. "It looks like I've got to play the part of the Lord of the Manor being greeted by his faithful servants when he returns home."

Lanos and Tom came to a halt a few metres back from the assembled staff. Lanos spoke.

"Members of the Earth Embassy staff, the Ambassador of Planet Earth, Dr Tom Glennon, has now arrived. Please introduce yourselves to him."

A tall man at the left hand end of the row was the first to speak.

"First of all, Mr Ambassador, may I, on behalf of all the staff, warmly welcome you to your embassy."

"Thank you" said Tom.

"I am Mullan Timos, the First Secretary.

"I am Albin Rumac, the embassy manager" a middle aged woman standing next to Timos.

"I am Jephos Ligan, acting as your personal servant" said a young man.

"I am Illo Fomi, your secretary" said a young woman standing next to Ligan. And so the introductions continued down the line, through cook, assistant cook, receptionist, security man and gardener.

"Greetings to you all" said Tom, when the introductions finished. "I am delighted to make your acquaintance."

"Well, Ambassador" said Lanos. " I will leave you with your staff now. The embassy manager will show you around the building. And I will see you again tomorrow morning for further discussion in your office. One further thing - I won't be alone. It has been decided that instead of having just a single Omnian for you to interact with, a small team of three would be better. And the two additional members of the team are people you already know: Irban Limnos and Ilmay Fornos."

"Oh. Good" said Tom. "I look forward to meeting them again."

Lanos then departed in the vehicle in which they had come.

"If you'd like to come with me, Ambassador" said Albin Rumac. "I can show you around your new home."

After the building tour was finished, she asked "and what would you like now?"

"What I would like to do is have a shower then get into some clean clothes, unpack my belongings and then later, at whatever time is here considered appropriate, sit down for an evening meal."

"So be it. I'll take you to your private rooms. Your personal servant will see to your clothes. The evening meal, or 'dinner' as you might prefer to call it will be served in the dining room at 16 hours our time. Since we have a 20 hour a day, rather than a 24 hour day as on your planet, this is approximately equivalent to 7 pm your time. Would that be suitable?"

"Yes, that would be fine."

"Good. In your rooms you will find a timepiece, what you would call a wristwatch, which displays Omnian time."

"Thanks."

In his private suite of rooms Tom found Jephos Ligan, his personal servant, waiting for him.

"Hi" said Tom. "Now tell me please - what would be the most appropriate way for me to address you?"

CHAPTER 47

"Just 'Ligan' will do very well, Ambassador."

"All right. Well Ligan, what I want to do is get out of these clothes have a shower and get into some new clothes."

"Very good sir. I have taken the liberty of laying out for you a set of conventional Omnian clothing. Light grey, excellent quality. They will fit you - we already have your measurements. Would that be suitable?"

"Yes. That will do very well. It has occurred to me that if I go out and about in your city I don't want to be drawing attention to myself by wearing Earth clothing."

"No indeed sir."

When his new Omnian watch displayed 16 hours, Tom went to the embassy dining room where he found the cook, a middle-aged woman, waiting for him.

"Greetings, Ambassador. Now first of all, if I may, there is something I should explain. The complete genetic sequences of your food plants and domestic animals were sent from your planet to ours just before your journey started. This meant that our genetic engineers have had about 20 years to transform our crops and certain of our animals. What we have ended up with may not be precisely identical to the originals on your planet, but we believe the end products are acceptably close. This is why you will find some familiar names on our menus. In good time of course you may well be keen to try our own Omnian foods but perhaps you would prefer to begin with food approximating what you have on Earth."

To Tom, who was conservative in gastronomic matters, and had been in some trepidation about what he might have to eat on Omnos, this was welcome news.

"Yes, that is what I would prefer."

She handed him the printed menu. Tom chose the chicken casserole with mixed vegetables followed by fruit salad. A bread roll with what looked like butter were also provided. The food did not taste precisely the same as its Earth equivalents but he enjoyed it nevertheless. Just after he had finished the cook came into the dining room again, looking slightly anxious.

"May I ask how was your meal, Ambassador?"

"It was good. I think 'acceptably close to its Earth equivalent' would be appropriate."

"Oh, thank you" she said, with a relieved smile.

▲

Chapter 48

Tom has a further discussion *with his Omnian liaison committee. Goes for a walk in the woods adjoining the Embassy, observes the vegetation and wildlife. Asks his embassy manager to take him for a walk in the city.*

The following morning at 8 o'clock, Omnian time, Tom received a message from the embassy receptionist that he had visitors.

"Dr Limnos, Ms Fornos, Dr Lanos - welcome." He took them through to the ambassadorial office.

"Well, Ambassador - how do you like your new quarters?" said Limnos.

"I like them very well. The choice of architecture is particularly appropriate."

"Good. Anyway, the purpose of today's meeting is to fill out some of the details of what we see as your role as Earth Ambassador. First of all let me make it clear that as far as your expenses are concerned, whether for purchases, travel or whatever, you have for all practical purposes unlimited credit. The First Secretary will look after the administrative details. No doubt you will want to travel around our planet, both for your own interest and so that you can give an account of what you observe back to Earth."

"I certainly will" said Tom. "That's something I'm looking forward to."

"Well when you do so" continued Limnos "all your costs, air travel, accommodation and so on will be taken care of. And you can of course take anyone from your ambassadorial staff with you."

"Understood."

"Now as you will be aware, here on Omnos we have taken a great interest in Earth ever since we discovered its existence. And for years now we have been monitoring the flow of information from your planet. We have been following political events and also culture: music and serious literature of course, but also the products of the electronic entertainment industry. Much of this information flow we find difficult to interpret and we would welcome any assistance you may be able to give us."

"I will be happy to do my best" said Tom.

"And a variety of our scholars, university teachers and representatives of learned societies are looking forward to having discussions with you so that we may arrive at a better understanding of the different cultures, civilisations and political systems that have arisen on your planet. "

"All right. I am sure that will be interesting."

"And if it's not too burdensome, we wonder if you could occasionally give public talks, maybe with question and answer sessions. Perhaps particularly to university students."

"I dare say I will be able to manage that."

"Now do you have any particular requests or suggestions for us?"

"Yes I do. I assume that by now you have already downloaded a large part of classical Earth literature in electronic form. I suggest that you use this to create, for your people, a substantial library in the form of printed books. And I would like a smaller version to be created for the Embassy, for the use of myself and my staff. And as new books come out each year on Earth, some of these, selected on the basis of published critical response, should also be printed. As well as literature the library should also include historical and other factual books."

"I like that idea" said Ilmay Fornos. "What do you two think?" turning to her companions.

"Yes. So do I" said Limnos.

"Well, that certainly could be done" said Lanos. "I will put it to the Planetary Council."

After some more general discussion and conversation the meeting ended and Tom's visitors left. Tom sat there for a while thinking about the morning's meeting. He then asked Mullan Timos, the First Secretary, to come to his office.

"Hi. Take a seat. Now first of all, since you and I are going to be working together quite a bit, what is the most appropriate way for me to address you?"

"Well, the most formal way, which you should of course feel free to use, would be to address me, following Earth usage since we are speaking English, as – 'Mr Timos'. However, you can if you wish address me by my first name - 'Mullan'. This is quite common practice on our planet as I believe it is on yours. I of course will always address you as - 'Ambassador'."

"I think I'll go with 'Mullan' if that's all right by you."

"Certainly Ambassador."

"Well Mullan, I don't feel completely recovered from the effects of stasis yet but in a few days time I am sure I will be. An important job I must get out of the way is to present my diplomatic credentials to the Omnos government. As I understand it your week is 10 days and we are now in the middle of a week. Can you please make the arrangements for me to present my credentials to your government early next week."

"Yes. It shall be done."

"To help me get my strength back I would like to go for some quite long walks. Do you have any suggestions as to where I might go?"

"Certainly, Ambassador. As it happens, since the embassy is on the edge of the city, behind it there is extensive parkland, some open, some wooded. There are paths. Another possibility is that you might go into the middle of Callepta and walk around to familiarise yourself with the city. To get to know shops and restaurants. If you do this you might find it helpful to take a member of the embassy staff with you to show you around."

"Those are two excellent suggestions. I will implement both of them, starting with the parkland. I'll take a stroll tomorrow."

The following morning after breakfast, Tom summoned Ligan.

"Ligan. I'm going to go for a walk. It's a sunny day and your sun is quite intense. My people on Earth are particularly pale skinned and we need to avoid UV damage. Do I have a suitable hat to wear as protection?"

"Certainly, Ambassador. If you will accompany me."

Ligan led Tom back to his sleeping quarters and opened one of the wardrobes. There, hanging on hooks was an array of hats.

"As you see there is quite a selection here. You will find that they are all in your size."

"Good. Thank you." Tom selected a light-coloured wide brimmed hat and then set off for his walk in the parkland behind the embassy. The path led first through open ground carpeted with what on Earth Tom would have recognised as grass. He continued on into the woodland. Here there were tall plants, 20 to 50 m high with trunks - 20 to 60 cm in diameter - some with smooth, some with rough surfaces. Given their size he decided that he might as well think of them as trees. They showed a variety of leaf shapes indicating that the woodland contained a variety of species. To support the weight and height of these very large plants he concluded that the trunks must be made of wood, or something with similar structural properties. Flitting here and there among the branches Tom could see small winged animals with what looked like feathers. Birds? That's certainly what they looked like. Brooding, as he walked, on the fact that this planet not only contained a humanoid species very similar to the people of Earth, but apparently also contained animals very similar to birds. He wondered if evolution was sometimes constrained to travel on railway lines rather than ramifying chaotically in all directions.

The next day Tom decided that he would go for his walk in the city rather than in the parkland. As his companion he chose to take Albin Rumac, the embassy manager and so called her to his office.

"Hi. Take a seat. Now first of all, since I am something of a stickler for the proprieties, what is the most appropriate way for me to address you."

"Well Ambassador, since we are speaking English I suggest that we adopt English usage. Since I am, as it happens, a married woman, it would be appropriate for you to address me as Mrs Rumac."

"Thank you" said Tom. "Entirely appropriate. Now, Mrs Rumac, I want to acquaint myself with your city, Callepta. In particular, I wish to take a walk around the streets. It has been suggested to me that when I do so I should take a member of the embassy staff with me to show me around. I wondered if you might be that person."

"I'd be delighted, Ambassador."

"Good. I propose to go after lunch today."

"Certainly, Ambassador. If I may make one suggestion?"

"Go ahead."

"Your appearance is somewhat different from that of the average Omnian. To minimise curious stares I suggest you wear a large hat, pulled down fairly low, to at least partially obscure your features. If anyone does notice you, however, they may well think you are just a visitor from the Irish settlement, rather than someone who has arrived from Earth."

"Thank you for the suggestion Mrs Rumac. I'll do as you say."

After lunch Tom summoned a vehicle.

"I'll leave it to you Mrs Rumac to direct the vehicle."

"Very good, Ambassador. I propose that first of all we take a drive around the city and then we will stop in the city centre, leave the vehicle and take a walk around."

Tom thought Callepta to be a pleasant city. It had a major river running through it with numerous bridges. There were parks and many of the streets were tree-lined. The architecture he judged to be neat, tidy and undramatic: rather, he thought, like the people themselves. The vehicle came to a stop in what appeared to be a busy shopping centre. They got out and started walking along the street. They passed shops, with shop windows, goods displayed, names overhead in Omnian script. Tom had a sudden thought.

"Mrs Rumac, I would quite like to go into one of the shops. Is there anything you wish to buy? Perhaps something for the embassy kitchen?"

"Nothing urgently. But there is a specialist food shop along here which, amongst other things, stocks a wide range of spices. I could, perhaps, purchase some of the more outlandish examples that I don't normally keep in stock at the kitchen."

"All right. Let's do that."

After a few minutes walking they came to the shop in question and Tom handed his credit card to Mrs Rumac. She went up to the counter and began a discussion with the female shop assistant. Tom took a stroll around the shop inspecting, but of course not recognising, the variety of products on the shelves. He could see the women occasionally looking back at him. Eventually, conclusions were reached, the assistant disappeared into what he assumed was an inner store and then reappeared with several small packages which she placed into a bag. Seeing that the deal was done he returned to Mrs Rumac and they went out into the street. He could see that she was smiling.

"So. How did it go? Did you get what you want?"

"Yes, I did. But it was quite funny."

"How so?"

"Well actually, she thought you were my husband. And she said she didn't know we were allowed to marry those Irish people. She sounded a bit envious."

Tom laughed. "But I assume you put her straight."

"Oh yes. But I didn't say who you were. I just said you weren't my husband. I was just showing you round."

"As indeed you were."

Chapter 49

***Tom is taken, in an official** cavalcade, to present his credentials as Earth Ambassador to the President of the Omnian Planetary Council, a female former academic. After a slightly frosty start he eventually succeeds in making a good impression.*

The day came for Tom to present his credentials as Earth Ambassador to the Planetary Council. On the matter of dress he thought he had better consult his personal servant.

"Ligan, today I am to visit the Planetary Council so I should be especially well-dressed. Do I have any garments, perhaps of a more formal character than everyday clothes, which would be suitable for an occasion like this?"

"Indeed you do sir." He showed Tom, hanging up in a wardrobe, a dark coloured suit with a jacket cut visibly longer than an ordinary jacket.

"The material of which this is made is of a particularly high quality and the members of the council will certainly notice that. Also, in accordance with Earth custom, may I suggest that you wear a tie. You have a selection of ties but there is one in particular which might be appropriate. It is in fact the official tie of Saviour college, of which I understand you were a member when you attended university. It was created for you in anticipation of just such an event as this. The pattern was accessible on your Earth Internet."

CHAPTER 49

"Well, not for the first time, I am very impressed with Omnian forethought. Yes, my college tie will do very well."

When Tom was dressed he summoned the Embassy First Secretary, Mullan Timos.

"Well, Mullan I think this is just about time to set off for my appointment. I leave the travel arrangements to you."

"Certainly Ambassador. I will be accompanying you in my capacity as First Secretary and I will carry the documents. The travel arrangements are already taken care of. The government is sending an official vehicle to convey you, and you will in fact have an escort. In days gone by it would have been a military escort but today it will be provided by members of our police force on what you might refer to as motorbikes."

"Well that will be an interesting experience" said Tom. "Now we are bringing three documents which are in fact essentially identical in content. One is the original and another is a copy, of what on Earth is called a letter of credence. They are from the Earth government asking your head of state to give credence to, which is to say to accept, my claim to represent, to speak for, Planet Earth. The original, which is sealed, I present directly to your President. The copy, which is unsealed, I give to your Foreign Minister. The letters are in this satchel" and he handed Timos the leather satchel which had been entrusted to him by the Earth governments.

"Thank you, Ambassador. I believe the official vehicle and escort are just arriving now so if you are ready we will leave."

"I'm ready" said Tom. "Let's go."

Just as they emerged from the Embassy entrance the official vehicle accompanied by eight uniformed and helmeted motorcycle riders, four each side, drew up. The vehicle was larger than the standard vehicles to be seen around the city and had Omnian lettering on the side proclaiming, Tom assumed, what vehicle it was. Its door opened, Tom and Timos entered and they set off.

"The government buildings are on the other side of the city, so we will be going through and beyond the centre" said Timos.

All traffic in the city had been brought to a standstill so their cavalcade traversed the centre without any delays or stops but it aroused curious glances from the people as they passed. They finally arrived at what Tom took to be the government precinct, surrounded with its own parkland.

"That large circular building you see in front of you" said Timos "is what you might call the Legislative Assembly or parliament. It is where the elected representatives from around Omnos come together, to debate and to create legislation. The ten ordinary members of the Planetary Council are elected from among the members of the Assembly but the President of the Council is elected by the people at large. The actual government buildings where the affairs of the planet are administered are those you see on the left."

On the right-hand side of the large Assembly building Tom could see what on Earth he might have characterised as a modest but handsome Georgian mansion, with a three storey centre and single storey wings either side. It appeared to be set in its own gardens.

"And what's that building?" he said, pointing.

"That" said Timos "is the President's residence, and that is where we are going now."

The motorcycle escort drew ahead. The men dismounted their machines and then stood in line, four each side just in front of the building entrance.

"I suppose this must be my 'guard of honour'" thought Tom to himself.

Their vehicle drew to a halt a short distance from the outer end of the guard of honour. Tom and Timos emerged. Checking first that Timos was behind him, Tom drew himself up, doing his best to present the very image of a planetary Ambassador, and walked steadily towards the large door in the entrance of the building. The door opened as he arrived. He continued on through and came to a halt in an open, spacious, wood-panelled area. There was a wide central staircase in front of him rising up to the next floor. At the foot of the staircase on the left-hand side there stood a line of four people, men and women. On the right-hand side there stood a man on his own. All of them looked at Tom with interest. There was something in the stance of the man on the right which told Tom that he was the one in charge. Accordingly, Tom looked straight at him and said, loudly and clearly -

"I am Doctor Tom Glennon, Ambassador-designate of Planet Earth. I am here, with my First Secretary, to present my credentials to the President of Planet Omnos."

He had chosen correctly. The man replied - "Greetings Doctor Glennon. I am Kalligna Elmos, diplomatic Secretary to the President of the Planetary Council. If you will accompany me now I will take you to the President. She is expecting you. The presidential suite is on the next floor. Did you want to use the lift?"

Tom looked back at the man and raised his eyebrows.

"No. Clearly not" said Elmos. He started up the stairs and Tom, accompanied by Timos, followed. At the top of the stairs there was a wide landing with corridors extending on either side. Elmos led them down one of the corridors and stopped outside a broad double door with gold lettering, in Omnian script.

"Here we are."

He knocked on the door, opened both doors wide, stepped into the room and then moved to one side. Tom stepped forward into the room. Before him he saw, seated behind an ornately carved wooden desk a tall, middle-aged woman with iron grey hair. There was a man, also middle-aged, grey haired, standing on her left side. The woman was looking at him closely with what Tom felt to be a somewhat severe expression. Elmos spoke -

"Madam President. I present to you Doctor Tom Glennon, Ambassador-designate of Planet Earth."

Tom bowed deeply and then turned to Timos, who handed him the letters of credence.

"Madam President" said Tom. "May I present to you my letter of credence?"

"You may" she said. Tom stepped forward, and in accordance with standard diplomatic protocol on Earth, holding the sealed letter of credence with both hands, offered it to her. She accepted it.

"And for your Foreign Minister, I have a copy." The President nodded and Tom handed the letter of credence copy to the man on the President's left. Tom then stepped back two paces. The President opened the packet, took out the letter and read it, giving its contents her full attention. She then looked up at Tom.

"My understanding of diplomatic practice on your planet, Doctor Glennon, is that letters of credence are traditionally written in French, the *lingua franca* of diplomacy. This is in English."

"It is, Madam President. We knew you were fluent in English but were not entirely sure that you were equally fluent in French. *Mais néanmoins nous avons ici une letter de créance en Francais.*"

Tom turned to Timos again who handed him the third packet from the satchel. Tom stepped forward and handed it to the President. She opened it, once again read the letter closely and then looked up at Tom.

CHAPTER 49

"The style is somewhat ornate" she said.

"Bien sur, Madame Président. Il est écrit en Francais d'une manière traditionelle diplomatique pour les lettres de créance."

"Hmm. Well it is satisfactory. On behalf of the Planetary Government I accept your credentials as the diplomatic representative of Planet Earth. You are now officially the Earth Ambassador. All levels of government will be informed of this, and announcements will be made in the media."

"Thank you, Madam President" said Tom and bowed again.

"So, Ambassador. You speak French?"

"I do" said Tom.

"Any other languages?"

"Cinnte. Tá Gaeilge agam. Tá mé liofa."

"Which means?"

"It means – 'Indeed. I speak Irish. I am fluent'."

"I see." Tom had the feeling that the President was, somewhat reluctantly, impressed.

"Thank you, Ambassador" she said, with a somewhat dismissive nod. Tom gathered that the proceedings were at an end. He bowed again, turned and exited the room, together with Timos. They were ushered to the building entrance by an attendant. Timos summoned a vehicle and they returned to the embassy.

"How do you think that went, Mullan?" asked Tom.

"On the whole, pretty well" said Timos. "It was fortunate that you thought ahead and had the French language version of the letter of credence ready. And the fact that you are multilingual also made a good impression. She is known to be a somewhat difficult person. She was a Professor of Languages before being elected to the Presidency."

"That comes as no surprise" said Tom.

▲

Lettre de Créance

Secrétaire-Générale, Les Nations Unies
à
Sa Excellence
Annlida HERMOS
Présidente du Conseil Planètaire
De la Planète Omnos

Madame la Présidente

Désireux de maintenir et de developer davantage les bonnes relations qui existent si heureusement entre Les Nations Unies de la Planète Earth et le Gouvernement Planètaire de la Planète Omnos, j'ai décidé d'accréditer auprés de Votre Excellence Monsieur Docteur Thomas GLENNON en qualité d'Ambassadeur Extraordinaire et Plénipotentiaire.

Les qualités, les talents et les mérites de Docteur Thomas GLENNON me sont de sûrs garants du zèle qu'il mettre à s'aquitter de la haute mission qui lui incombe de manière à obtenir la confiance de Votre Excellence et à mériter par là-même mon approbation.

C'est dans cette conviction que je prie Votre Excellence de vouloir bien lui accorder un accueil bienveillant et d'ajouter foi et créance à toutes les communications qu'il lui fera de ma part et au nom des Nations Unies, surtout lorsqu'il exprimera les assurances de ma haute estime et les meilleurs voeux que je forme pour Son bonheur personnel et pour la prosperité de Son planète.

António Serrano
Fait à New York, le 12 Mais 2.....

Chapter 50

The arrival of an ambassador *from planet Earth is now made known to the Omnian population. It arouses great interest. Tom is interviewed on television. Tom travels widely around his new planet. Regularly sends reports back to Earth. Familiarizes himself with Omnian agriculture and their use of genetic engineering to recreate Earth crops and farm animals.*

The announcement that the Omnian government had now finally received an ambassador from planet Earth aroused great public interest on Omnos. It had long been known that one was on the way, but it was only with the official announcement that it was realised that such a person was actually here. Almost immediately the embassy received a request that the ambassador would agree to be interviewed on television. Tom agreed but stipulated that the interview should take place at the Embassy. The event duly took place in Tom's official suite. A team of three interviewers two men, one woman - all well-known Omnian TV journalists - took part. The interview was in English. Because of the great popularity of all media products from Earth, introduced in great quantities to Omnos since the Omnian spaceship had first discovered that planet, fluency in English had become widespread. Tom's physical appearance aroused no surprise in the TV audience. By this time it was already well-known that

CHAPTER 50

Omnians and Earth people were anatomically and physiologically very similar. In particular, people were already familiar with the physical appearance of the members of the three settlements created using Earth genetics.

What the interviewers were interested in was first, Tom himself: his family history, his career, why he had been prepared to leave his own planet forever. Tom gave an account of his life and career but deliberately gave the impression that his decision to leave Earth for Omnos was driven mainly by his curiosity, particularly as a scientist. He said nothing about how significant an element in his decision had been the effect on him of losing his wife, Molly.

Beyond their interest in Tom himself they wanted to know about life and society on Earth. This was not entirely new territory for them since they were all familiar with the products of Earth media but from him they were trying to achieve an understanding of what it was really like to be an Earth person on Earth itself. They wanted to know about Earth social customs, Earth politics, Earth's climate, Earth's history, how the different peoples of Earth regarded each other. Because of what was considered to be its great importance - an actual Earth person in the flesh, on the television - the interview continued, live with no editing, for about two hours, by which time all participants were approaching exhaustion. The last contribution came from the female interviewer.

"Ambassador, you are going to spend the rest of your days with us, on our planet, aren't you."

"Yes I am" said Tom.

"So you will be - what shall we say? Our Man from Earth?"

"I suppose I will."

Now that he was officially the accredited Earth Ambassador, Tom set about structuring and fulfilling his role. A major part of this was to be the conduit for a flow of information, in both directions, between the two planets. The Omnians has already established a communication channel through which the contents of Earth electronic media, transmitted 4.37 years previously, arrived on Omnos. What Tom proposed to do was to monitor this on a regular basis to find out what was happening on his planet - political, social, climatic. To achieve this he needed help. He decided to create a team within his embassy of six genetically Terran people, two from each of the Earth settlements - Irish, Japanese and Malian. The first generation of Terrans was now of an age in which many of them were finishing university and this was amongst these that Tom hoped to find the members of his team. He asked his First Secretary, Timos, to place advertisements, calling for applications for these posts, in whatever media existed in the settlements. There were many enthusiastic applications. He set up a selection committee consisting of himself, Timos and Lanos to interview the applicants and make a choice. The selections were made, one male one female from each settlement and so Tom now had his team.

He called them altogether to explain their duties to them. But the first thing that each of them had to do was to become fully knowledgeable about the history and characteristics of whatever part of planet Earth was their responsibility. To the Japanese Terrans he assigned Asia. Responsibility for the continent of Africa he gave to the Malians and Europe and the Americas to the Irish.

"To educate yourselves for this task you can use the library which at my request has been established which is well supplied with historical and other factual works on the various countries and regions of planet Earth. You should also start sampling the information flow which, through our dedicated channel, is continually being received from Earth. When you are ready you can begin your official duty which is essentially to digest and summarise whatever is happening back on that planet. This I will put together in the form of a report which will be presented on a regular basis from this embassy to the Omnian government."

Just as his team of Terran Omnians had to inform themselves about the Earth, so Tom felt that it was his duty to inform himself about Omnos so that he could report back to the governments who had sent him here in the first place. Accordingly he embarked on a systematic exploration of his new planet. Taking the Embassy First Secretary with him to act as an interpreter, guide and general facilitator he visited all the nations making up the planetary Federation, explored all latitudes from North to South with their associated ecosystems, from tropical jungles around the equator to the frozen Arctic and Antarctic poles. He recorded what he saw with a video camera and made copious notes so that he could report back to Earth. So far as the Omnians themselves were concerned he noted with interest that although physically they were everywhere much the same, skin pigment varied with latitude in much the same way as it does on Earth. Near the Omnian equator the people were as dark skinned as those in equatorial Africa.

Large areas of the planet had been set aside for biodiversity conservation. In all the ecosystems there were life forms similar, but not identical to those of corresponding ecosystems on earth. In the grasslands of the semiarid zones there were vast herds of grazing mammals such as are found on the open plains of Africa. And these were preyed upon by large predatory mammalian species: Omnian lion equivalents. But also in the moister regions there were large herbivorous mammals which were too big and too aggressive to be subject to predation. What struck him most about the wildlife in ecosystems set aside for conservation was the prevalence of large reptiles, some with upright form propelling themselves forward on two large hind legs and stabilised by a large tail behind.

"You do seem to have a lot of reptiles on this planet" he said to Timos.

"Yes we do. Most of them are herbivorous but there are some carnivorous species as well. In most of our ecosystems the top predators are mammalian but there are a few where, because of their better physiological adaptation to extreme climatic conditions, the top predator is a reptile."

"Some of them look like the large reptiles we used to have on Earth, the dinosaurs. Now extinct."

"Dinosaurs are pretty well what they are equivalent to" said Timos.

"Many of our dinosaur species were very large" said Tom 'and some were predatory. One in particular we know from the fossil record. *Tyrannosaurus Rex*. But virtually all our dinosaurs were wiped out when an asteroid hit the Earth 66 million years ago. The only ones to survive were some small feathered dinosaurs which evolved into birds."

"We used to have large dinosaurs, both predatory and herbivorous, on Omnos until a million or so years ago."

"So what happened to them?" asked Tom.

"I am almost ashamed to say - we, or at least our ancestors, killed them."

"What! How did you manage that?"

"Mainly by stealing their eggs, at the first opportunity after they laid them. They were an excellent food source. Also the very young dinosaurs, even of the dangerous predatory species, were an easy target for our hunter gatherer ancestors. Many smaller species have survived and some of the herbivorous forms we have in fact domesticated."

"For what purpose?" asked Tom.

CHAPTER 50

"To provide meat. They are efficient converters of plant matter to animal protein."

"And is the meat good?"

"Yes. If well-prepared, excellent. In fact you will have eaten some already in the Omnian dishes which the embassy cook prepared for you."

"Oh" said Tom, not feeling entirely happy about this revelation.

"Of course we also have domesticated mammalian species, similar to cattle and sheep on Earth both for meat and for milk. You can't get milk from reptiles. I think it's time you visited some farms so that you can see our agriculture at first hand."

On his next exploration expedition Tom decided to follow the First Secretary's advice and familiarise himself with both agriculture and the food production industry on Omnos. In particular he was interested to see the domesticated dinosaurs. He was taken to one grazing property where in addition to animals that looked much like Earth cattle, in a separate field there was a herd of what looked like very large - 2 m long - rather fat, short-legged lizards feeding on the grass sward. On another property, where there were plentiful bushes and small trees, he was shown another herbivorous dinosaur with a long neck. It looked like a small sauropod and was clearly able to graze the foliage of the trees.

Tom knew that the Omnians were highly expert in genetic engineering. He visited one of their plant breeding research stations to see how well they were getting on with their plan to recreate some of the crops of Earth by transferring genes from Earth species into the most similar Omnian plants. He was told that while some species were proving more difficult than others, the project was well advanced and for some crops they believed that success had been achieved. Since the DNA sequences of the crop species had been transmitted to Omnos through space at the time the Omnian spaceship return journey had commenced, the scientists had already had just over 20 years to achieve the transformations. Some Earth crops were already in commercial production and indeed the products were in great demand.

"You see that field over there?" said one of the scientists to Tom.

"Yes" said Tom. "That looks like a field of barley."

"It is" said the scientist. "That's actually a commercial crop of one of your special Earth cultivars of malting barley."

"For beer?"

"Yes. Our brewing scientists are hoping to recreate some of the well-known Earth beers. Transforming the hop plant was more difficult than the barley but we think we've got there now. But of course you are the only person on Omnos who knows what the originals actually taste like."

"Yes. I suppose I am" said Tom, thinking to himself that he would rather like to have a glass of beer right now.

Chapter 51

***Tom becomes well known** and accepted on Omnos. Explores the city, Callepta. Observes that the Omnians have religious buildings. Is given encouragement to have his own. Arranges to have a replica of St Finbarr's Oratory in County Cork recreated in the Embassy grounds.*

After his original major interview Tom made occasional brief appearances on Omnian television, particularly on panel shows where his opinion on particular kinds of music or works of literature from Earth might be sought. The people of Omnos became used to having this Earth man in their midst. After the passage of some time, Tom felt he could risk going into the city without attracting a crowd, not least because Omnians generally were polite. While he did sometimes, out of interest, go into the streets of Callepta by himself, he often thought how much more he would enjoy it if he had someone with him to share the experience. He liked, now and again, to eat out at one or other of the many restaurants in the city, rather than at the Embassy, but he ate alone.

"Oh Molly" he thought. "If only you were with me now."

Here and there, particularly in the older parts of the city he came across quite large, but single storey, buildings of stone construction, often with ornate window design. In every case they had a sign outside with Omnian lettering, but he could see that the lettering, so presumably the message, varied from one building to another. Going past one of them he noticed that the door was open so he looked inside. There were rows of seats from front to back on either side of a central aisle. At the far end there was a dais on which there was a table and at the left-hand side a raised structure which looked rather like a pulpit.

Having seen a number of these buildings now he asked Timos what they were.

"Those are religious buildings" said the First Secretary. "Here on Omnos we have religions, just as you do on Earth - three major ones and numerous minor ones. Those are the buildings, equivalent to your churches, synagogues, mosques, Quaker meeting halls etc, where believers come together for their religious ceremonies.

You are a religious believer aren't you, Ambassador? When, years ago, the Planetary Council were putting together a set of criteria for their hoped-for Earth Ambassador, one of the stipulations was that ideally he or she should be an adherent of one of the major religions on your planet."

"Yes, I'm a religious believer" said Tom. "I am a Christian, in fact specifically a Catholic Christian."

"Well in that case" said Timos. "You should know that in the original plans for this embassy, provision was made for the erection of a building for the religious purposes of whoever the ambassador was. It has not so far been implemented because back at the planning stage it was not known to which religion the ambassador would be attached, or of course what his or her views might be as to the best design of such a facility. But it has been budgeted for, rather generously as a matter of fact. A Christian religious building, as I understand it, would generally be what is called a church or chapel. If you would like to have your own church or chapel in the embassy grounds, perhaps you could give some thought to a possible suitable design. And if you could come up with something that the architects find feasible, then construction could go ahead."

"Gosh, that's an interesting proposal!" said Tom. "It would be a rather small building, so I would call it a chapel rather than a church. I'll tell you what. I will look up some of the old chapels and small churches that were built in the past on Earth, and see if I can find one that would be suitable as part of the embassy. We can then see if the architects think it could be reconstructed here."

In his search for a suitable small church which could be reconstructed in the embassy grounds, Tom decided that he might as well concentrate on Ireland, where there are plenty of such churches. It did not take long before he came across a photograph of one, on the Internet, which immediately took his fancy. It was Saint Finbarr's Oratory in Guagán Barra, County Cork: a very small stone church, on an island in the lake, built in 1901 on the site of an ancient monastery, in a mix of Hiberno-Romanesque and Byzantine styles, with details based on 12th century Irish churches such as Cormac's Chapel on the Rock of Cashel. Inside there was an elegant barrel-vaulted ceiling, a free-standing altar, stained-glass windows, intricate stone carvings, and only four rows of small pews on either side.

When Tom showed him the photo, the architect responsible for the embassy buildings became very excited.

"Do you think we could build a copy of that here?" asked Tom.

"We certainly could! It would be a privilege. I love it!"

On the basis of more detailed information he was able to find on the Internet, the architect drew up a plan for the church. Efficiency was an Omnian characteristic and in no time at all, construction commenced. To Tom's amazement, within the space of a year he had his church, as far as he could tell a faithful replica of Saint Finbarr's Oratory. He decided to call his church, 'Saint Patrick's Chapel'. The building aroused a great deal of interest in Callepta and many Omnians came to visit it, including members of the Planetary Council. Tom often came and sat in the church on his own. He knew that since it had not been consecrated, it was not yet, strictly speaking, a church. As a practising Catholic, out here on this alien planet he felt cut off from his religion, and to sit quietly in this church was something of a comfort. He decided to keep the consecrated hosts that he had been given in the tabernacle on the altar, and their presence alone made the building special.

It was too complicated to line up the seven day weeks still occurring on Earth with the 10 day Omnian week, so he decided to make the last day of the Omnian week his Sunday. And on that day he would go online on Earth Internet that had been transmitted 4.37 years previously, find a live TV mass, and take one of the hosts. Once he had his new church, this was where he would attend his online mass and take communion.

In creating the education systems for the three Terran settlements the Omnians decided that it was important that the children should in each case be exposed to, and given an education in, the dominant religion of their Earth populations of origin. The Japanese children were taught Buddhism. The Malian children were taught Sunni Islam, but specifically a tolerant, non-extreme, version. The Irish children were taught Christianity, from a Catholic viewpoint. In every case it was left to the individual Terrans, as they grew into adulthood, to make their own decisions as to religious belief. The construction of Saint Patrick's Chapel aroused great interest in the Irish Terran population, and it received many visitors from that settlement after its completion.

Chapter 52

***Tom interacts with Omnian** musical, literary and scientific circles. Omnian musical instrument makers have sought to recreate Earth musical instruments so that Earth music, which has become very popular can be authentically played. Tom's advice is sought.*

As part of his role of representing Earth to the people of Omnos, Tom instituted the practice of regularly inviting representatives of particular social, artistic, political and academic Omnian groups to dinner at the Embassy. He found these dinner conversations a valuable source of information about Omnian society and culture. In particular, as a musician, he was intrigued to learn that Earth music in all its forms had become enormously popular on Omnos, indeed somewhat to the detriment of the planet's own music. One of his dinner guests, a professor of music at the University, told him that in order to play Earth music, instrument makers were doing their best to recreate Earth instruments. He asked Tom if he would be prepared to give his opinion on how well they were succeeding. Tom said he would be glad to, and so a meeting was arranged with a variety of instrument makers at a venue in the city.

It was clear to him when he met them that they were all technically highly competent. They explained to him that in every case they had been able to obtain comprehensive information and constructional details, partly from the earth Internet but also from instructions supplied by Earth musical instrument makers as part of the original information package transmitted from Earth to Omnos. They invited him to try the instruments they had assembled there together. Tom was not a brass instrument player so he did not attempt to play any of the trumpets, trombones etc. but he examined them closely and it was clear that they were made to the highest manufacturing standard. He gave it as his opinion that although he could not play those particular instruments himself, it seemed to him, as a scientist with some knowledge of acoustics, that if the brass instruments were made to the precise shape and dimensions of those on Earth, they could not fail to be of similar quality. Being as he was a versatile instrumentalist, he was, however, happy to try out all the wooden instruments.

He began with the violin family: violin, viola, cello. He had brought his own violin with him to the meeting for comparison purposes. The Omnian instruments were all beautifully made. Their sound was pleasant enough but somewhat lacking in intensity. He played his own violin, which he had obtained from an Australian luthier, to the instrument makers. They could hear the difference. He drew their attention to the belly of his instrument, which was made from fine-grained spruce, grown at high altitude in the Italian Dolomites, and told them that they needed to seek out wood with similar acoustic properties in their own forests. His conclusions were much the same when he tried out the plucked string instruments - mandolin, mandola, Bouzouki, guitar: perfectly made, pleasant sounding, but more careful selection of belly wood required.

The Omnian luthiers has also brought a couple of carbon fibre violins along for him to try. He had played such instruments on

Earth and while for his own use he preferred a wooden instrument, he had nevertheless been impressed with the quality of their sound. He was happy to be able to tell the Omnians that their carbon fibre violins sounded just as good as the ones he had played on his own planet.

In the case of the flutes also he was able to give uniformly positive comments. While his preferred version of this instrument was the wooden version, generally referred to as the Irish concert flute, he was also able to play the metal Boehm-fingering flute. Both types had been brought to the meeting for his judgement and he tried them out. He cautioned his listeners that since he was primarily a fiddle player his opinions on the flutes were not those of a professional, but nevertheless he liked the tonal quality of the ones they had brought.

Tom had no experience of playing any of the reed instruments: clarinet, saxophone, oboe, bassoon and others. Once again he inspected the instruments and could see that they were all technically of a high standard. All instrument makers can play the instrument they make and so he asked those who produced reed instruments to play them for him and he promised to give a judgement as to how they sounded. They did as he requested, in each case playing scales and a couple of melodies. He listened carefully and was happy to be able to tell them, with a clear conscience, that they sounded excellent.

It was finally time to look at the the pianos. There were three: an upright, a grand piano and a digital instrument. Tom had brought some classical music with him - some Chopin nocturnes and two Beethoven sonatas and played a few passages from each of them on all three instruments. He also played some blues and boogie remembered from his undergraduate days as a jazz musician. He enjoyed playing all the pianos but felt that the upright and the grand piano lacked the power and the clarity that high quality Earth instruments would have. He shared his judgement with the maker and gave it as his opinion that to achieve the highest quality the soundboards would need to be made from wood as elastic and light as the spruce used for the soundboards on Earth. Once again it would be a question of sourcing the right kinds of wood from the forests of Omnos. The digital piano, on the other hand, he found to be entirely satisfactory. The makers of such pianos on Earth had sent the appropriate sound files, derived by sampling the sounds of real pianos, to Omnos and the piano maker had been able to load them into his instruments. Tom was so pleased with the digital piano that he ordered one for his own use in the embassy.

"These instruments that you have brought in today" said Tom to the assembled makers "are the standard instruments of the Western orchestral heritage. But back on Earth there are also numerous national instruments which are played almost entirely within particular countries or ethnic groups. Do you make any of these?"

"Oh yes" came the response. "Some of us do. Mainly for the benefit of the three Terran settlements. For example, the ngoni lute and jembe drums have been made for the Malians, Shamisen lutes and Shakuhachi flutes for the Japanese, and harps and bodhráns for the Irish."

Tom liked what he was hearing.

"Good" he said. "Good. Well, ladies and gentlemen, instrument makers of Omnos. I've been very pleased and impressed with what I have seen and heard today. I am confident now that Omnian musicians will be able to do justice to the great body of Earth music. Thank you for arranging this meeting." After saying which he returned to the embassy.

Following his successful meeting with the instrument makers, Tom decided that to encourage the Omnian musical world in its ambition to perform Earth music he should start attending performances in his capacity as Earth Ambassador. Omnian musicians were diligent and competent, and had managed to obtain a great deal of information about how these Earth instruments should be played from online lessons to be found on the Internet. He received invitations to recitals by soloists and chamber groups and also by a full-scale orchestra which had been formed in the city. In general, he was pleased with what he heard and was happy to make helpful comments if his opinion was sought.

Because English language literature had become so popular on Omnos, Tom was sometimes called upon to contribute to discussions, often on TV or radio, of particular categories of English language writings. The 19th-century authors – Austen, Dickens, Trollope - were particularly popular and Tom's contribution was mainly to give an account of the social and historical milieu in which they were written. Other popular topics were 19th-century American writers such as Herman Melville, Nathaniel Hawthorne, Mark Twain, or 20th-century writers such as Scott Fitzgerald, Ernest Hemingway and William Faulkner. Irish writing also had its enthusiasts, particularly the plays of Oscar Wilde and George Bernard Shaw or the poetry of WB Yeats and Séamus Heaney. Tom's private nightmare was that one day he would be called upon to explain James Joyce's 'Finnegan's Wake'.

Given his own professional career and inclinations he was always happy to interact with the Omnian scientific community. In particular, he enquired of the physicists whether they has solved the mystery of the. nature of dark matter. They had not. His own contributions to the subject had not gone unnoticed. As to his hypothesis that dark matter consisted of a new, non-particulate form of matter, opinions were divided. As on Earth, the majority opinion was that this could not possibly be the case, but a few were not so sure.

In addition to interacting with the various elements of Omnian society, which as Earth Ambassador he felt he should, Tom had been able, with the help of his Terran team at the embassy, to setup a system of systematically digesting the flow of electronic information coming through space from Earth and presenting it in the form of regular reports to the Omnian Department of Foreign Affairs.

Chapter 53

***In his capacity as the representative** of their planet of genetic origin, Tom visits the three Terran settlements. Gives each of them a gift provided by their countries of origin on Earth. In the Irish settlement Tom is asked to give talks on Irish history, literature, music. At his first talk he notices a young woman wearing a head scarf. She appears again during the other talks. He is intrigued but cannot see her face.*

One duty which, in his capacity as Earth Ambassador he had assigned himself, was to visit the three Terran settlements so that he could report on their progress and general welfare back to their Earth countries of genetic origin. Since the populations were still small, in every case there was just one central town with a few villages nearby. By now the first generation were all in early adulthood. They had completed their education and were, like other Omnians of their age, in employment in farming, horticulture, light industry or manual trades in the town, or in the professions. Many were already married and the babies of the second-generation were beginning to arrive. In each settlement the inhabitants elected the members of a small representative assembly which in turn elected a council to manage the settlements affairs.

The inhabitants of these new settlements were all excited to see him. A real live man from Earth, the planet from which they derived their own ancestry. In every case he was given a welcome in which they wished to display their pride in, and their mastery of, their cultural inheritance. In every case also he found that as settlements they were thriving. They had become part of Omnian economy and society, and were well regarded, and their presence valued, by the people of Omnos in general.

He first visited the Japanese settlement: Nippon Arata – New Japan. This was at a lower latitude - 37° - than Callepta but was in a more mountainous region some distance to the East. This had been a deliberate choice since Japan itself was quite a mountainous country. The welcoming party wore traditional Japanese garments, the female members in kimonos with beautifully embroidered obis (sashes). He was welcomed with short speeches, first in Japanese and then in English. That evening there was a ceremonial banquet for Tom, together with the members of the representative assembly. The banquet consisted of a series of traditional Japanese dishes, following which there was a 30 minute performance of *gagaku* Japanese classical music by an ensemble of 20 musicians playing traditional Japanese instruments.

After the performance Tom gave a short address, in English, complimenting them on their mastery of their cultural heritage, and undertaking to give to the government of Japan, their country of genetic origin, a favourable account of their achievements, in his next report back to the Earth. Finally, he took out from a case he had brought with him, a present from the country of Japan to this far distant group of their people. It was three original Japanese prints: the '25th *Station on the Tokaido*' by Hiroshige, '*The Great Wave off Kanegawa*' by Hokusai and '*Flowers of Edo: Young Woman's Narrative Chanting to the Samisen*' by Utamaro. His audience had of course heard of, and revered, the famous Japanese woodblock prints of the 17th to 19th centuries, and had seen them in reproduction. But to be actually presented with three very fine examples of this art form was far beyond whatever they had expected of this visit from the Earth Ambassador. Their gratitude knew no bounds.

Tom was pleased with how his visit to Nippon Arata had gone. He stayed a few more days, interacting with the people and visiting villages outside the town before flying back to Callepta and his embassy.

His next 'Pastoral' visit, which is how he thought of it, was to the African settlement: Mali Kura – 'New Mali' in the Bambara language. This was centred on latitude 15°, in a tropical region, a long way to the South of the Omnian capital city. While much of the land was semiarid there was a river delta passing through the southern region, where agriculture was carried out. Once again, the site had been deliberately chosen because it provided a physical environment similar to that in the country of genetic origin - Mali.

The members of the welcoming party were for the most part dressed in the *boubou*, the flowing, wide sleeved robe commonly worn in the drier parts of West Africa, and well-suited to the climate. Tom himself had taken the precaution of wearing a light linen suit. He was welcomed this time in French, which in Mali itself is the official government language, although not the first language spoken by most of the people. This suited Tom very well since he was a fluent French speaker, and he responded in the same language. At the ceremonial dinner in the evening there was rice, with sweet potato and spinach, served with a peanut- tomato sauce, together with grilled meat from what Tom understood to be the closest the genetic engineers could get to converting one of the smaller Omnian grazing species into goat. He found it entirely palatable.

The dinner was followed by a musical performance. There were three musicians. The singer, a woman, sat cross-legged on a mat on the ground. She wore a black robe and a headdress consisting of a long black veil extending down her back. A long, triple string of mixed beads extended from the top of the headdress down either side of her face. In each hand she held a dried gourd which she tapped on the ground as a percussive accompaniment to the music. Behind her there were two male musicians, one on either side seated on low stools, each playing a *ngoni*, a plucked four-stringed instrument with a hollowed-out wooden head with goatskin stretched over it. Both men wore a long white *boubou* robe and a simple white *kufi* cap. The woman sang several songs, all in the Bambara language spoken in Mali, and the men accompanied her on their instruments, the songs being interspersed with a few short instrumental passages.

After the recital, Tom gave a short address once again in French, and complimented the musicians. Sincerely, as it happened, since he liked Malian music, and as a musician himself could see that this trio performed at a high professional level. Turning to the young woman, he said "Dites-moi. Dans ton chant, est-ce que je détecte l'influence de Inna Baba Coulibaly?" (A well known and highly regarded mid-20th century traditional Malian singer). "Oui certainement, Monsieur l'Ambassadeur. J'adore sa musique." She responded with a grateful smile. He then revealed that he had a gift from the people of Mali. He opened a music case that he had brought with him and took out a Mali *kora*: a 21 stringed harp-lute of quite complex construction, used for the best Malian traditional music. As he had surmised, the local instrument makers had been able to work out how to make satisfactory examples of the relatively simple *ngoni*, but not the more challenging *kora*. Now they had an actual instrument in front of them which they could copy. The gift was greeted with great excitement by the audience who could immediately see its significance.

Once again, Tom stayed a few more days in the settlement, travelling around the villages and the countryside and interacting with the people, before flying North back to the embassy. Tom had enjoyed his first two visits to Terran settlements, the Japanese and the Malian, but he had a special reason for looking forward to his third visit where he would be amongst his own people.

The Irish settlement was known as Éire Nua (New Ireland). Unlike the other two settlements it was situated quite close to the Omnian capital, in an area centred on 51° latitude just to the North of Callepta. It's town (there was only one town in each settlement) - called Baile Gaelach (Irish Town) - was located in the South of Éire Nua and so was within driving distance of Callepta. Tom noticed with interest that the clothing of the welcoming party, while essentially of modern European character - the men in suits, the women in skirts and embroidered blouses - was made from cloth that looked very like the tweed still woven by hand in Donegal in Ireland and Harris in Scotland. The leader of the party welcomed him in Gaelic and Tom responded in the same language.

The dishes he was served at the ceremonial dinner owed a great deal to the ability of the Omnian genetic engineers. In addition to recreating Earth vegetables, they had also succeeded in transforming certain animal species of Omnos into new animals very similar to agriculturally significant species of Earth: not only cattle, sheep, pigs and poultry, but also fish species suited for aquaculture, such as salmon.

The dinner began with smoked salmon, and also potato soup, as entrees. It continued with boiled bacon and cabbage served together with colcannon (mashed potato with cream, butter, kale and scallions). The next course was Irish stew (lamb, potato, onion). Irish soda bread together with butter was provided throughout the meal. The last course was Apple pie with cream. Tom thoroughly enjoyed the meal although by the time he had finished he knew he had eaten far too much. He resolved to ask the embassy cook to add all these dishes to her repertoire.

As had happened in the other two settlements, the meal was followed by a musical performance. This was provided by an eight-musician ensemble. As an Irish musician himself, Tom took a particular interest in the lineup of instruments. There were two fiddles, two flutes, a tin whistle, a concertina, a bouzouki providing a chordal background and a bodhrán drum marking the rhythm. In addition to jigs, reels and hornpipes from the traditional Irish repertoire, two airs – Páistín Fionn (the Fair Child) and Casadh an tSugáin (the Twisting of the Rope) – were sung, both in Gaelic, one by a man other by a woman. Tom was very happy with what he heard. The musicians were clearly of a high standard and played the music in an authentic manner, and they were visibly very pleased when he congratulated them: to be told by a real Irish musician that they were doing it right was very encouraging.

As he had in the other two settlements, he then revealed that he had brought a gift with him from the people of their country of origin. He put a music case up on the table and then opened it to reveal a full set of uilleann pipes, with chanter, drones and regulators. As he had surmised, the local instrument makers had been unable to make uillean pipes, despite their importance in Irish music, for lack of detailed information on their construction. Now, as with the Malian *kora*, they had access to a high quality example of the instrument, which they could copy. With great excitement, the musicians clustered around to see the set of pipes.

Tom spent more time in Éire Nua than he had in the other settlements. He was very much in demand to talk to musical groups, historical societies and literature enthusiasts. He was interested to find that his surmise about the origin of the material in the clothing of the welcoming party was correct. He found that using wool from genetically recreated sheep a handwoven tweed industry had been set up. Its product was highly valued and sought after by the upmarket end of the Omnian clothing industry.

While giving a talk to one of the music groups he happened to notice a young woman at the rear of the room. What drew his attention was that, unlike the other women present, she was wearing a headscarf which obscured her features. On another occasion when he was having a discussion with a historical Society about the background to the Irish War of Independence, he noticed that what appeared to be the same young woman was again present at the back of the room. And when he was talking to a literary group about 20th-century Irish writers - James Joyce, Samuel Beckett, Flann O'Brien - he saw that she was once again present, although keeping her distance. By this time he was intrigued and thought that he would like to see her face, but the scarf always made that impossible.

Every member of the new populations in the settlements had been provided with information about their family origins and history back on Earth. When Tom talked to the young adults of Éire Nua he would always ask them where in Ireland, genetically speaking, they had come from, and would then tell them something about that part of the country. A few came from Connemara and when they told him their surnames and family history, three of them, to their mutual delight, turned out to be distant cousins of his. He now began to feel that he had something of a family connection with, in addition to his responsibility for, Éire Nua.

The successful creation of his embassy church had given Tom an idea. He continued his pastoral visits to the settlements on a regular basis and took the opportunity to suggest to the representative body in each case that they consider constructing their own appropriate religious buildings - a church for the Irish settlement, a mosque for the Malian settlement and a Buddhist temple for the Japanese settlement. He also suggested that in each case they find a suitable example on Earth, and copy it. His suggestions were greeted with great interest and enthusiasm.

Chapter 54

***At night Tom sometimes** goes outside and looks back at the Sun. He is missing Molly. Realises he must be beware of nostalgia. Back in Callepta he is asked to give a talk on the major religions of Earth. Once again he sees the young woman in the head scarf in the audience. Tries to have a word with her but she has disappeared*

On a clear night Tom would often go outside and look at the stars. Since his vantage point was only 4.37 light years from Earth, a much smaller distance than that of the majority of stars in the sky, the constellations looked much the same as they did from his own planet. The great exception was Alpha Centauri B, the companion star of Alpha Centauri A in the binary star system, Alpha Centauri AB. This was very bright in the night sky, its brightness varying according to at what point of their 79 year orbital period, the two stars happened to be, their distance apart varying from about 11 to 36 Astronomical Units (1 AU being the average distance between the Earth and the Sun, about 150 million km).

Much less bright, but still one of the brightest stars in the sky was the Sun, and Tom often looked back at it. He could not, of course, see the planets but often wondered what was now happening on his own planet, the Earth. In particular, he often thought about Ireland, about Connemara with its cool windy weather and the sheep on the hills. He also thought about Australia and about the happy time he had spent there with Molly.

"I must be careful about thinking these thoughts" he said to himself. "Nostalgia could be a trap."

On one occasion in Callepta, Tom was asked to take part in a public discussion about the religions of Earth, and in particular to compare them with those of Omnos. The three Omnian religions were all different versions of monotheism, each in large part taking their inspiration from the lives and writings of religious figures in the distant past. Tom did his best with the religions of Earth. Christianity, and its predecessor Judaism, presented no problem. He did quite well with Islam but had to admit that he was a bit hazy about Buddhism. Towards the end of the meeting he happened to see, at the back of the room, a young woman with a headscarf, looking much like the young woman he had noticed on previous occasions when he had given talks in Éire Nua.

"So now she's come to hear me in Callepta" he thought to himself. "I really must have a word with her and find out why she is so interested in me."

After the chairman had brought the meeting to a close, Tom set off down the room in the hope of talking with the woman, but she had slipped out the back door before he reached her and he lost his opportunity.

When he arrived for his next pastoral visit to Éire Nua he found that there was a group of brewing technologists who particularly wished to see him. Brewing of Earth-type beers was now well established on Omnos and Éire Nua had its own brewery.

"Ambassador, there is a new Earth beer we have been working on for some time" they told him, "and we are very keen for you to try it and give us your opinion. In particular to see how it compares with the Earth original, which we are pretty sure you will have tasted."

"I'd be glad to" said Tom.

"Now, so as not to give you any visual clue" said the leader of the group. "We wonder if you would mind wearing a blindfold for your first tasting."

"All right" said Tom, who was now intrigued. He sat down at a table with the brewers, put on a blindfold and was then handed a glass of the beer in question. He took a drink, then another drink, and then a long drink and another long drink. He waited a couple of minutes and then drank again.

"Could it be?" he asked himself. "Could it really be? Have they really succeeded in recreating it?" He drank some more, and then some more again, eventually draining the glass.

"Yes, I do believe they have."

"Gentlemen - if I was back on Earth, I would unhesitatingly conclude that I was drinking Guinness. Shall I take my blindfold off now and have a look?"

"Certainly, Ambassador."

Tom took off the blindfold. There on the table before him there was another glass poured, filled with the familiar black liquid and its creamy head of foam.

"Now that's a welcome sight to see on this planet" he said.

"And do you think we've got it right?" said the brewer. "One of the gifts from your planet was a detailed set of instructions from the Guinness Brewing Company of Dublin, together with a sample of their yeast and seeds of the particular malting barley they use. The seeds have been massively multiplied up in a laboratory using tissue culture. They were then planted out to give us a crop and the malt was prepared strictly according to the Guinness company specifications. The company specifically requested that you should try our product out, and stipulated that if you thought it was up to standard, then we could call it 'Guinness'."

"Yes" said Tom. "I believe you've got it right, and it is indeed up to standard. Well done. I wouldn't actually mind having another glass."

There were smiles all round, and they poured him another glass.

"Now this is something I'll be stocking up with at the Embassy" he thought to himself.

Chapter 55

***His Omnian liaison committee** tells him that for his benefit his Australian cottage has been recreated in the nearby countryside. Tom goes out and is delighted with it. Frequently stays, but it reminds him of Molly. Begins to feel depression closing in.*

By the time Tom was into his third year on Omnos he felt that he was fully on top of his role as the Ambassador from Earth. The job was demanding, and kept him occupied during the day, but he no longer spent his spare moments thinking about what he needed to be doing. As part of what he saw as his responsibility to interact with Omnian society, he frequently held dinners at the Embassy with particular groups or individuals, or accepted invitations to dine out. Most evenings however, he dined alone, and increasingly the solitary nature of his life outside of working hours began to weigh upon him. He remembered how he loved being at home together with Molly in the evenings. Even when they weren't actually chatting together they enjoyed a companionable silence.

"It's no use always looking back like that" he said to himself. "The past is the past. I am here on this alien planet now, and always will be."

Tom had regular meetings with his Omnian government liaison committee - Dr Limnos, Ms Fornos and Dr Lanos. On his next meeting they had some news for him.

"Doctor Glennon" said Limnos. "It is the common practice on this planet, as I believe it is also on yours, for an ambassador to have, in addition to living quarters within the Embassy, a separate ambassador's residence. And I can tell you now that we have been having one built for you. And at last it is ready."

This came as a surprise to Tom but then, recalling his time in Canberra, the capital of Australia, he remembered that the foreign ambassadors in that city did indeed invariably have a residence separate from their embassy.

"That's pleasing news" he said. "Tell me more."

"Well" continued Limnos. "We thought that to give you a change from your life here at the edge of the city, we would place your residence in the nearby countryside."

"I like the sound of that" said Tom.

"The house is not large. We thought you would prefer something a bit more user-friendly than an ambassadorial mansion, and so using the kind of terms you might use on Earth, it might be described as a generously proportioned cottage."

"This gets better and better" said Tom.

"Finally" said Limnos. "We hope you will approve of our choice of architect."

Tom was nonplussed. What did he know about Omnian architects.

"Oh. Why? Who is he, or she?"

"You are the architect."

"What! How can that be?"

"Well, Doctor Glennon, when we found that it was indeed you, as we had requested, that was going to be the Ambassador from Earth to Omnos, we asked the relevant Earth governments - Irish, British, Australian - to provide us with as much information about you as they could. One of the things the Australian government told us was that you had designed and built your own cottage in the countryside outside Canberra, and they were able to send us the precise design in the form of the plans which you had submitted to what we believe is called, the Yass Shire Council. Your plan has now been implemented again, exactly as you designed it in the countryside near here. It is on a small rural property which has been set aside for you and the name on the gate is - Gortnakilla, the same as your original farm back in Australia. Your Embassy vehicle will take you there just as soon as you are ready to visit it. You will find it fully furnished and equipped. We assume you will be mainly using it at the weekends. There is a domestic servant who will attend the house to clean and tidy it during the week"

"Gosh" said Tom. "I don't know what to say. You really do think of everything don't you."

"We certainly try to" said Limnos.

"Well all I can say is - thank you very much to the Omnian government for their generosity! This is very exciting! I shall head out to Gortnakilla this weekend."

On the last working day of the week Tom asked his personal servant, Jephos Ligan, to put together overnight clothes in a case and he asked his cook to prepare some precooked meals which he could take with him. On the following morning, on the first day of the two-day Omnian weekend, he entered the Embassy vehicle and instructed it to take him to Gortnakilla. As he expected it was preprogrammed with the route and after about half an hour's driving out into the country, it pulled up outside a farm gate on which there was indeed a notice saying 'Gortnakilla'. The gate opened automatically and the vehicle continued up the driveway coming to a halt outside a single storey brick building which, as far as Tom could see, was an exact replica of the cottage he had built for Molly and himself back in New South Wales.

He went inside. It was pleasantly and comfortably furnished. The bed in the main bedroom was already made. There was milk, butter and eggs in the fridge and the pantry was stocked with a variety of food. The property itself bore some similarity to his and Molly's small farm in Australia, with a pond at the lower end and a wood, composed of course of Omnian tree species, not eucalypts, at the upper. The surrounding countryside with hills and forests provided a pleasant background vista.

"You know, I think I'm going to enjoy staying here" said Tom to himself.

And enjoy it he did. He began to spend most of his weekends at Gortnakilla. He decided to create a garden, similar to the one Molly had established on their Australian farm, and even to grow some vegetables and fruit. But, his weekend idyll led to a problem of its own. The Omnian builders had done such a good job of recreating his cottage that he sometimes found himself momentarily expecting to see Molly within it. This was another reminder of his loss and his solitary situation. Worryingly, sometimes when he woke up in the morning in his rooms at the Embassy he felt himself to be on the edge of depression. He remembered well the two major episodes of depression in his life: in his final undergraduate year at Cambridge and after Molly's death. Knowing how hard it can be to climb out of the pit, he was anxious never to find himself in that situation again. Nevertheless, despite his best efforts he sometimes found that his spirits were lowered and that it was hard to maintain his usual cheerful demeanour with the staff.

Chapter 56

***His Omnian liaison** committee discuss Tom and agree that he has been doing an excellent job as Earth Ambassador. They are however concerned about his recent noticeable lowering of spirits. They conclude that he needs a woman with whom to share his life. In fact a young woman in the Irish settlement has been preparing for this role. At his next committee meeting she is introduced to Tom. But – who is this? How can this be possible?*

Twice a year the Omnian Foreign Minister had a meeting with the three person Earth Embassy liaison committee.

"Our 'Man from Earth' has been with us for some time now. At the end of his third year, how do you think he is getting on?"

"He is getting on very well" said Limnos. He has created an efficient system for digesting the information flow from Earth and distributing it to interested bodies on Omnos. He sends information about Omnos - society, history, culture etc - back to Earth. He has also had a range of our standard textbooks - botany, zoology, wildlife, climate, translated into English and transmitted back to Earth. He interacts on a regular basis with our cultural societies and institutions - literary, musical, historical. Always makes himself available when asked. Clearly he is himself a cultured man. And in particular, he has taken on what he refers to as a 'Pastoral' role in relation to the three Terran settlements. He visits them on a regular basis to see how they are getting on, talks to their representative assemblies and goes out and mixes freely with the populations."

"So" said the Foreign Minister. "Looks like we were lucky in our choice of an ambassador to come from Earth to here."

"Yes, we were" said Lanos. "But just recently we have become a bit worried about him."

"Really. Why so?"

"I have been talking to the embassy staff to gather their impression of him. They get on with him very well. He is always polite and considerate, and is usually cheerful. However, in recent weeks they have noticed that he sometimes seems to be quite down in spirits."

"Do you have any idea why that might be?"

"Well" responded Ms Ilmay Fornos, the female member of the group, "I think he is lonely. And my two colleagues are inclined to agree with me. It's finally getting to him that he is all alone on an alien planet."

"We envisaged that this situation might arise, didn't we?" said the Minister. "He needs a partner. He needs a woman to share his life. We already have a suitable candidate don't we?"

"Yes we do" said Ms Fornos. "A young woman in the Irish settlement. She has been aware since quite early in her life that this role might become available for her if she was prepared to take it on."

"Well, it sounds as if the time might have come. Does she feel ready for it? Does she actually want it? She mustn't be pressured into it if she doesn't."

"Yes, we think she is ready for it. She has been going to a lot of trouble to get to know the Ambassador without, of course, actually meeting him. She knows all his history, his family and professional background. She has seen him in action several times. Whenever he has given a public address or engaged in any kind of public discussion group she has gone to the trouble to attend so that she could have a good look at him and make an assessment of what kind of person he is. When he visits the Irish settlement he always plays his fiddle in Irish music sessions with other musicians. She has heard him play and even sing the occasional song. On the basis of all this she says she is now ready, and indeed would like, to become his partner, always assuming, of course, that he himself is happy with this prospect."

"And we think he will be" contributed Limnos.

"In that case let's bring them together" said the Foreign Minister.

"We propose to do that very soon" said Lanos.

In the meantime, Tom's depression was getting worse. He knew that while for most of his life he managed to remain psychologically on an even keel, that there was lurking in the background a major depressive tendency which could be triggered off. It had happened twice before and now seemed to be happening again, set off by his feelings of isolation and loneliness on this alien planet. He managed to continue his role as Earth Ambassador, but increasingly it took a major effort and he had forebodings about where it all might end up. Nevertheless, his interest quickened when, at his next meeting with the Omnian government liaison committee, Lanos commenced proceedings by saying that they had something new and very important to discuss with him.

"Indeed?" said Tom. "Go ahead. What is it?"

"You are a religious believer I understand, Doctor Glennon? A Christian in fact?"

"Well yes. I am. Not unusually devout. But I am."

"Where on earth is this going?" thought Tom to himself.

"In that case, you are no doubt familiar with verse 18, chapter 2 of Genesis, in the old Testament of your Bible."

"I can't say that I recall exactly that particular verse" said Tom "but perhaps you are about to remind me."

"Indeed I am. The verse begins – 'And the Lord God says: it is not good for man to be alone'."

"Well, I am certainly not about to disagree with that."

"Quite so. Now Ambassador. You have been with us for over three years. You are well settled on our planet. And I can tell you that our government is very happy with the role you have been playing here."

"Thank you. That's good to hear."

"But. You are living alone. For much of the time, yours is, necessarily, a solitary existence."

"Yes. That is certainly true" said Tom, with some feeling.

"I hope you won't think it presumptuous of me" continued Lanos " to say that in our opinion you would benefit from having a partner, a woman - a companion with whom to share your life."

Tom had not been expecting this. He had often wondered, in his lonely state, if it might be possible to find himself a wife on this planet, but did not know how this could be brought about. His interest now quickened.

"I don't think it presumptuous of you at all" he said. "As a matter of fact, I think you're right."

Lanos now handed the proceedings over to the female member of the group, Ms Ilmay Fornos.

"Well Ambassador" she said. "The essential purpose of today's meeting is to tell you that we believe we have found a suitable partner for you."

"What! Already!"

"This may seem very sudden to you" she said "but the reality is that this is a matter which has been in preparation for a long time. There is a young woman, in fact from the Irish community, who we believe would be a suitable companion for you. She knows a great deal about you already. She has had the opportunity of observing you at quite close quarters. She is happy to become your companion.

I hasten to say that she has not been pressured in any way. She was entirely free to accept this possibility or reject it. And of course, you also are entirely free to accept or reject the proposal that she become your companion. However, I have to tell you that we are quietly confident that you will find her very acceptable."

"Are you indeed" thought Tom, his interest now thoroughly aroused.

"Would you like to meet her?" asked Ms Fornos.

"I certainly would!" said Tom.

"Well, actually she is waiting in the next room" said Lanos. "I'll bring her in."

"Gosh! Things are moving rapidly this morning!" thought Tom.

Lanos went into the adjoining anteroom and returned, followed by a young woman. Tom rose to his feet. It was the young woman in the headscarf! She came forward and stood in front of him, and then removed the headscarf. Tom was transfixed. This could not be!

"But...Molly! ... You're Molly!" he exclaimed, in shock and amazement. The room began to turn around him, He became weak at the knees and started to collapse. Alarmed, Limnos and Ms Fornos grasped his arms and lowered him into a chair. In a moment or two he came to his senses but sat there, his heart racing. He saw the young woman looking at him with concern. She then spoke.

"Indeed I am Molly" she said. "I am Molly Ni Chuilleanáin."

The voice. The appearance. The dark hair with its natural curl. Exactly as he remembered his wife when she was young.

"And so you are. So you are" he said, in wonderment.

"How is this possible?" said Tom, looking towards Limnos.

"Well, as you know, all the new populations of the three Terran settlements were created using the DNA information from thousands of individuals on Earth" said Limnos. "Each of those individuals has in effect been recreated here."

"Yes, I understand that" said Tom.

"Once it became likely that you were indeed going to become the Earth Ambassador to Omnos, it occurred to our government that the day would come when you would want your own female companion on our planet."

"You certainly think ahead, don't you."

"We do try to. But the question then arose - how could we find a suitable companion, one we could be sure you would like? Well the obvious answer was to recreate the woman you had been happily married to before. So, to provide us with your late wife's DNA, an Australian government agency was able to obtain hair follicles from a hairbrush in your country cottage. As with all members of the settlement populations some genetic problems were fixed, in this case, heart and predisposition to miscarriage. Otherwise, the young woman you see before you is pretty much the young woman who, many years ago, you married on Earth."

Tom sat there for a minute or so, taking in all the implications of this extraordinary new information. He looked up at Molly. She looked searchingly back at him for several long moments. Her face then broke into a smile. She stepped forward, took him by both hands and drew him to his feet.

"Come along Tom. We have lots to talk about. Let's go home."

www.ingramcontent.com/pod-product-compliance
Lightning Source LLC
Chambersburg PA
CBHW070417170726
48291CB00002B/247

* 9 7 8 1 9 2 3 0 8 7 5 2 1 *